"Theology in a new code."
—Dr. Harvey Cox, Harvard Divinity School and author of *When Jesus Came to Harvard*

"A marvelous book. Jesus' words and actions ring true, with a contemporary feel. You'll be torn between wanting to stop and reflect on each chapter and continuing to read to see whether Jesus will once again have to make the Ultimate Sacrifice."
—B. C. Aronson, author of *Grace* and *Love*

"Reading The Eternal Messiah has rekindled a long term interest in science fiction—a genre with no boundaries, which is brilliantly exploited by the authors as we are drawn into a complex world of intergalactic struggles and intrigue. The fascinating idea that Jesus Christ enters into the mix and has been returning to challenge evolution and to find out if the eternal truth has at last been understood, adds a profound philosophic dimension to the story. And what is the eternal truth? The only way to find out is to read this enthralling book."
—Robert Feather, author of *The Secret Initiation of Jesus at Qumran*

"In The Eternal Messiah: Jesus Of K'Turia, W.R. Pursche and Michael Gabriele dramatize the provocative idea that the appearance of a Messiah is what transforms stagnant, tradition-bound societies into vibrant and humane civilizations. One does not have to be a believer to be intrigued and moved by this well-told story: an excellent work of theological sci-fi."
—Professor Richard E. Rubenstein, author of *Thus Saith the Lord, The Revolutionary Moral Vision of Isaiah and Jeremiah*

"A refreshingly creative re-telling of the mission of Jesus."
—Father Jerry Wooton,. Parochial Vicar,
Holy Trinity Parish, Virginia

"This book captured me and captivated me not only by the brilliance of the authors, but by the Light of their Christ who touched my heart and lifted my soul. Jesus is the Eternal Messiah, no matter where He is. This was a personal spiritual experience."
—Jeff Patnaude, founder, the Golden Apple Center for Inner Excellence and author of *Leading from the Maze: A Personal Pathway to Leadership*.

"A rich, well-written story with compelling characters, taking you on a journey of belief."
—Dallas Hudgens, author of *Season of Gene*

"This new interpretation of the messianic Jesus uses plain talk to illuminate complicated subjects such as faith, sacrifice and the road to salvation. The Eternal Messiah is an imaginative primer for those who want a deeper understanding of the true meaning of the message of Jesus."
—Dr. Judith O'Brien, author of *Way of the Mystic: Seeing through the Ark*

"An amazing tale that pushes one to the boundaries of what is fiction and non-fiction. The Eternal Messiah is an interesting and thought provoking read that is hard to put down."
—Paul Rest, author of *The Lost Gospel of Mary the Mother of Jesus (forthcoming)*

"The Eternal Messiah addresses one of life's ultimate questions. What, after all, is the true meaning of religion? What does G-d really expect of us? Are rules and regulations the essence of religion or is there something more . . . as we journey through life, what will be most helpful is guiding us to "find the way?"

Bill Pursche and Michael Gabriele challenge us to think about people's thoughts about religion, their fears and insecurities, and why religion has such a profound effect on the relationships between people."

—Rabbi Bruce Aft, Adjunct Professor,
Marymount University, VA.

"An illuminating exploration of whether one single being can serve as a catalyst to change the course of history and science. Whether you believe such change comes from the messenger or the message, here is an ambitious story of how a preacher with a message of supreme humanity and sacrifice stirs hearts and passions."

—Sherri Waas Shunfenthal, author of *Sacred Voices: Women of Genesis Speak*; and *Journey into Healing*

The Eternal Messiah:
Jesus of K'Turia

W. R. Pursche
Michael Gabriele

Varzara House

Varzara House
Virginia

Copyright © 2009 by William Pursche and Michael Gabriele.

All rights reserved. No part of this book may be reproduced in any form without permission from the authors, except in the case of brief quotations included in critical articles and reviews. For information contact info@varzara.com.

First Varzara House edition published 2009.

Cover artwork by Michael Gabriele.

Library of Congress catalog number 2008940345.

ISBN: 978-0-9753-7936-3

10 9 8 7 6 5 4 3

for Kim

Authors' note

Any fictional account with a character named Jesus is sure to elicit strong reactions. We are not claiming to speak for Jesus Christ; we have instead tried to imagine how people in another place and time might react to a message of Sacrifice. Though not literally biblical, we believe this message is consistent with not only the Christian ethic, but with that of many other religions. If this exploration leads readers to think more about their concept of God, or serves to get people interested in learning more about the biblical Jesus, all the better.

We wish to acknowledge the help we received from Kim Pursche, Chip Hughes, Alaina Love, Rabbi Bruce Aft, Jeff Patnaude, Susan Lewis, Dallas Hudgens, John Sullivan, Robin Sullivan, Father Jerry Wooton, and Ed Michel. While we are solely responsible for this story, these people all provided invaluable advice and support. Some of them shared with us how the message of Jesus of K'Turia compares to their understanding of the message of the Jesus of the gospels, and all of them helped us understand how those with different religious and spiritual beliefs respond to a universal theme of Sacrifice.

The Eternal Messiah:

Jesus of K'Turia

BOOK I

Chapter 1

He awoke at the insistent buzzing of his cabin intercom. For a moment he lay quiet, dazed from the sleep that had not yet left him. He saw her face . . . just as he did every time he awoke. *His beloved Sooni.* But the space next to him was empty.

He remained still, ignoring the noise that demanded his immediate attention. Unable to shake the memory, he reached over and flipped a switch, cutting the sound.

"Yes?"

"Captain, we have just received a Priority One message from Central Command."

"I'll be right there." Trebor Win was wide awake now. *Priority One?* What could be so important that Central Command would send a Priority One message to a research vessel?

Had the war begun?

Win hurried out of his cabin, his footsteps echoing through the dim and empty corridors. In the lift he caught sight of himself in the slightly reflective wall, the curved surface accentuating his already wide Treb features, lined with worry. He closed his eyes and took a few deep breaths, steadying himself. If they were at war he would need to appear calm and confident to his crew, who were mostly scientists, not soldiers. Though he did not think they would panic, there would be fear nonetheless.

In the brief moments before he reached the bridge he thought about the alerting message and what it might mean. His ship, the *Anatar*, had been part of a small armada, circling the planet Colltaire, currently in the midst of a civil war. Though a research vessel, the *Anatar* was funded by the military, and in times of need was technically under the auspices of the Intergalactic League of Worlds military Central Command. And these were certainly times of need, for the League was being pressured all across the galaxy by the old empires, especially the Lemians.

On the planet below, the unpopular leadership on Colltaire had aligned themselves with the Lemians. A small insurgency had grown increasingly bold, and the League was showing its support to the rebels with the armada. The Lemians had also sent ships, mirroring the League's movements, all but daring the League to start a war.

The League was so weak that it was forced to use quasi-military crafts such as the *Anatar* to make the armadas appear larger. Win didn't think the Lemians were fooled.

The lift slowed to a halt short of Win's destination. The door opened, and Cale, the ship's chief science officer, entered.

"Can't sleep? Or trying to impress your boss?" Cale asked. Cale was one of the few humans aboard the ship, and was always trying to lighten the mood. "By the way, exactly who is the boss these days?"

The door slid shut and the lift continued on. "We received a Priority One from Central Command," replied Win. "So I guess that means they still are."

Cale's levity vanished. "Trouble?"

"I don't know yet. Let's find out." He stepped out into the control center of the ship. All appeared quiet, but Win sensed the nervousness in the room. The tension would have been obvious even if he had not been born with *gheris*, what humans would call a sixth sense. As a Treb, it was just as much a part of him as his sight or hearing. Through *gheris* he was attuned to the aura given off by emotions, especially those from other humanoids. Though this ability came in handy, it tended to make other races nervous. Win never understood why; it wasn't like he could read minds. But as a commander of a ship with many races on board, he had learned to be especially sensitive to what might create unease.

He took a quick look around. The navigation console was

unmanned. No one there was a good sign; it meant that the ship's Executive Officer, the XO, did not think an attack was imminent.

The XO was at the communications console, beckoning to Win. She handed him a small flat disc. Win looked up at her, somewhat surprised. "You haven't seen this yet?"

"No. It had an 'Attention Captain' attached," she replied. She didn't say anything else but Win could sense a question.

"I don't know either," said Win. "I can't imagine why." The XO had saved the encoded message to the disc so that Win would have the option of reading it in private. Though he understood the reason for it, a part of him hated all the military secrecy. He thought briefly of taking the disc somewhere to read but he couldn't imagine what could be on it that he would not end up sharing with his XO anyway. Plus what would his crew think of his trust in them if he ran off and hid to read messages? Still . . .

Win compromised. He bent over the communications console, slipped the disc in a slot, and placed his hand on a translucent plate. There was a slight delay as the decoder read his DNA, then the message came alive in bright iridescent lettering above the unit. The XO, perhaps sensing Win's discomfort, moved off a respectful distance.

Win read the message, scowled, and read it again. He stepped aside and motioned for the XO to read it, then turned to the communications officer. "Send two messages to Central Command. First, verify the last transmission. Use code Delta. Second, request further information regarding this Priority One message. Use code Gamma."

The comm officer repeated back what Win had ordered. He was somewhat puzzled by the seemingly unnecessary complexity of the coding, and was wondering if it meant that a war was upon them, but Win didn't appear worried. On the other hand, the Treb never appeared worried about anything. Of course, the comm officer had never met another Treb, so maybe what he took to be calmness was actually sheer panic.

Nothing in Win's next command to the XO or his tone of voice hinted at what was going on. "Set course for Station Four, normal cruising speed. And prepare for a change in our mission. Then join me in the bridge conference room. You too, Cale. And get I'Char up here."

Win hoped he had not conveyed any nervousness in his command. The war had not, in fact, started for the League.

But it had for the *Anatar*.

Chapter 2

Win, Cale, I'Char and the XO sat in the small conference room just aft of the bridge, where a large window allowed them to monitor the control center. I'Char, the genderless from Illi, sat calm and relaxed, his sharp, hawk-like features not betraying his thoughts. I'Char served as the military adjunct to Win—technically, a military advisor. But Win thought of the Illian as much more; he was as close to a confidant as Win had anywhere in the League. Like Win, I'Char was from a race that few in the League knew much about. This was one of the reasons he felt comfortable with I'Char, who was often perceived as being distant and aloof. Win also knew what it felt like to be alone, far from home, rarely in contact with members of his own race.

Cale, the human, had been pacing the room. When he finally sat down he fidgeted, crossing his legs, knowing that something was about to happen, trying not to appear nervous. He would have seemed on edge just being in I'Char's tranquil wake.

Even the XO, usually quite calm, was ill at ease, so Win decided to dispense with any preliminaries. He punched in the commands that would allow the message to be brought up on the separate consoles around the table.

START.
CARGO FREIGHTER 'HAULER ONE' MISSING. LAST REPORTED POSITION IN SECTOR FOUR, VICINITY OF PLANET K'TURIA SEVEN. BELIEVE 'HAULER ONE' MAY

HAVE EMERGENCY LANDED OR CRASHED, REASONS UNKNOWN.

PROCEED AT ONCE TO SECTOR FOUR STATION, CRUISING SPEED, WHERE SPECIAL REPRESENTATIVE JAIMS GARRICK WILL HAVE YOUR FURTHER ORDERS. REPORT ONLY WHEN 'HAULER ONE' STATUS IS DETERMINED. TAKE NO ADDITIONAL ACTION BEYOND WHAT IS SPECIFIED.
STOP.
PRIORITY ONE. ALPHA.
END.

"Is that it?" asked Cale. "Does that mean Central Command is taking control of the ship?"

"Not very clear, is it?" agreed Win. "We know they can if they want. I requested a confirmation of this message, and also asked for additional information—separately."

"You think the message might be a fake?" asked I'Char. "To lure us away from Colltaire?"

"I don't know." Win explained to Cale and I'Char about the messages he had sent. "If it is a trick, the Lemians—or whomever—will had to have broken three codes. If they could do that it's hard to believe they would chance us finding out they knew our codes just to get a research ship moved somewhere. But I also want to—" He was interrupted by the chirp of an intercom, and out of the corner of his eye he saw the comm officer motion to him from the bridge.

"Captain, we have just received replies to both your messages. Shall I relay them there?"

"Isn't one a Priority One?"

"No. Both are General Status, coded but open."

Win shrugged. It was not a typical Treb gesture, but he had learned to use it. "File them, then. I'll decode from here."

Win brought up the new messages on the monitors. They were even shorter this time. One was simply a confirmation that a Priority One transmission had been received by Central Command.

The second was a very curt refusal of the request for more information.

"Well, it seems unlikely that this is a trap," said Win. "All the coding is fine." He hit the intercom to the bridge again. "Radar-scan . . . Did any other ships leave the armada with us?"

The reply came back almost immediately. "No, Captain. Shall I monitor?"

"Yes, do that," replied Win. He looked around the room. "It appears we are on our own. Comments?"

"Wonder what's in that freighter? It must be something terribly important," said the XO.

"If it were that important, why send us, instead of a military ship? And why at slow cruising speed?" asked Cale.

Win shook his head. "Sending an armored vessel would certainly attract Lemian attention, as would us rushing off. They might even follow. This freighter could very well be important, so important that Central Command does not want to draw attention to it."

"Or maybe it is something that requires our scientific resources?" asked the XO.

"Or it's a way to slowly redeploy the armada without attracting attention, or it has nothing to do with a freighter, or it is a test of the coding system . . . who knows?" said Cale. "Could be just more Central Command cloak and dagger."

"There is also the possibility, slim as it might be," said I'Char, "that the freighter could have been on its way here, to Colltaire. Central Command may want us to retrieve its cargo and bring it back. If this is something they want to keep quiet, we'd appear less suspicious, since we have already been part of the armada."

"Weapons for the insurgents? That would be risky," said the XO. "Would the League ever do such a thing?"

"It's a possibility," replied I'Char. "From a strategic military viewpoint, Central Command must consider that we might never get a Rhean alliance—or how the Rheans would respond if we help the insurgents."

"Or they're hoping the Rheans won't find out," said Win. I'Char had a point. Because of their tenuous situation, the League had appealed to the Rheans, the most powerful race in the galaxy, for a protective alliance. The Rheans were reclusive and mysterious; mighty, yet peaceful, a rare combination. Who knew how they would respond to anything? The League had tried to keep the plea a secret, for fear that the empires would sense the League weakness and launch an all-out attack. It was possibly the worst kept secret in the League.

Win turned his attention back to the discussion. "I agree it is risky, but if we don't get this alliance with the Rheans it is only a matter of time before war breaks out—or the League slowly dissipates. We are stretched too thinly, and the Lemians and the other empires have grown too powerful."

"All the more reason for Central Command to support any insurgency it can," said I'Char. "It has a certain elegance to it. The Lemians are forcing us to over-extend ourselves to protect our members. But if we could make it harder for the other empires to take over systems and retain control, they too would get stretched out."

"You sound as if you approve," said Cale.

"I do not know enough to be sure either way—and do not confuse my assessment of their military strategy with approval of their goals," said I'Char. "If there is something in the discussions with the Rheans that we don't know—such as a prohibition of direct support for a war, then I would agree it is very risky. But even if that is true, it is still a viable military option. Not to mention how we would all feel if we were the people on Colltaire."

There was a brief silence as everyone thought about that. Then the XO said, "We could check the observation buoys in Sector Four. It would tell us where the freighter was coming from—or going to."

"That's a good idea, but I doubt we'd learn anything," said Win. "If Central Command is being that secretive with us, they probably plugged the buoys. Besides, if we could get to them, so could the Lemians."

Cale sounded confused. "What makes you think the Lemians would know of the freighter?"

"I don't know for certain," said Win. "But Central Command must be afraid of something. I know they tend to be paranoid, but we have to assume this freighter is important. And if it could affect the Rhean alliance—for better or worse—then it is critical."

"There's something else about this message that is odd," said I'Char. "'Take no additional action.' They are telling us to find out what happened—but not to do anything about it. Combined with the order for cruising speed, it would seem to rule out that this is any kind of rescue mission."

"That bothered me too," said Win. "Either they don't have enough information yet, or they don't trust even a coded transmission. Which would support the argument there is something in the freighter that Central Command doesn't want anyone to know about." What he didn't say, which bothered him even more, was that this Garrick was coming on board to take over his ship for a military matter. His *research* ship.

"Especially the Lemians," said I'Char. "If there are weapons on the freighter, the Lemians might be trying to do more than just prevent that cargo from reaching its destination. They could have either tried to hijack it, or sabotage it, in order to catch the League in the act of supplying weapons."

"Aren't you giving the Lemians a lot of credit?" asked Cale. "They seem like a bunch of thugs to me."

I'Char stared at him. "Unlike the League, their military tactics are always well connected to the use of politics. It makes for a powerful combination. Just because you do not agree with their goals should not make you underestimate their strength—both militarily and politically."

Cale wasn't upset. "I'd better stick to science. These military and political discussions give me a headache."

Win was thoughtful. He had let the dialogue go on so he could get the benefit of all their thinking. Even Cale's lack of military and political background was sometimes useful, as he often looked at things a little more simplistically—and therefore more clearly.

Time to move on. He turned to Cale. "Let's do something

scientific, then. What data do we have on our destination, the planet K'Turia?"

Cale worked his console. Soon a series of images flashed on their screens. "Atmospheric conditions, size, land masses . . . this isn't very helpful. It looks like the League has been there in the past, probably a survey ship. Rather primitive, although it appears they are aware of other worlds and have had visitors—it is not in the 'no contact' directory. Here's something in the 'Military' heading, a 'Level 3' coding. What does that mean?"

"It means that someone we consider unfriendly has not only been there, but has been actively trying to take control," explained I'Char. He looked at his console. "That coding is not very recent. For all we know the planet could be under total control of the Lemians by now."

"We have to find out what we might run into," said Win. He had almost no experience in military matters, especially covert ones. "I want more up to date information, and a full briefing on K'Turia. Also, get whatever you can about this cargo freighter. Historical routes, types of cargo, crew, anything. And I want everything on this Garrick. Is he with Central Command? Does he have something to do with the freighter? Let's put our time to good use."

The briefing over, everyone except Win got up to leave. He stopped the XO on the way out. "Do a deep space monitor for other crafts on our course," he ordered.

"Do you think someone might be following us?" asked the XO.

"Never hurts to know," replied Win.

Alone, Win looked back over the summary on K'Turia, but it told him nothing new. He had no reason to think that the Lemians would be following him, nor did he even know for sure that the missing freighter had anything to do with Colltaire.

But he also couldn't afford to be wrong. In deep space, his small unarmed ship would stand no chance against an attack. The *Anatar* had to slip away—quietly.

Chapter 3

The Hall of Halven was an awesome sight to behold, sparkling in Colltaire's setting sun. Visitors to the capital of Colltaire found the governmental complex to be the most magnificent structure on the entire planet. The reflective towers seemed to reach up into the clouds, lost now and then in wispy mists, only to reappear at some even more dizzying height. At one time, those who viewed the capitol would have left envious of the glory, the power, and the happiness they believed would be a part of living within those spectacular walls.

But the present inhabitant of that grand dwelling, Krelmar, was far from happy. While he *was* the ruler of Colltaire, his power was less than many imagined, and as for glory . . . there seemed little chance he would attain glory. As he gazed out onto the great square below, he was struck not by what was there but what was *not*—no throngs of adoring subjects, no fanfares of support. In fact, unlike in years past, hardly any visitors even wanted to see the Hall. The few who crossed the broad expanse kept away from the center, furtively stealing along the walls, as if not wanting to be seen or even associated with the Hall and all it stood for.

He knew what the people now thought of him. They hated him. It had not always been this way. He had earned great respect and even outright admiration for how he had handled the deadly drought just a few years earlier. While all the other senators were wringing their hands and making speeches, he was *doing* something about it. He was the one who had thought of looking offworld, of trading

Colltairian mining rights for water, for food, for crops. What good were ores if there was no one alive to mine them?

Only the Lemians had come to his aid. He had approached the League, of course, as well as a few of the empires less despotic than the Lemians, but they were all too slow to respond, or couldn't offer what he needed. And the League—they were almost *too* democratic—it would have taken years to get the kind of approvals that the League insisted upon.

The Lemians, on the other hand, were refreshingly direct and efficient. Almost immediately they had delivered shipments of food, quickly followed by technology which helped stretch the Colltairian resources. The Lemian aid saved the planet, and in their gratitude the senators had elected Krelmar to lead the senate.

The Lemians had set surprisingly few conditions on the deal; in fact, while they casually accepted the mining rights that were offered, Krelmar surmised they were not very interested in ores. Instead, the Lemians insisted only on a rather loosely worded alliance that, to Krelmar, did not really create any constraints nor give the Lemians any control.

Only now was he realizing how wrong he had been.

It had started innocently enough. The Lemians had used military craft and soldiers to deliver the food and supplies. Soon there was a significant military presence on the planet. The implication was unmistakable—the Lemians could take over any time they wanted.

The mutterings of discontent began once it became clear that the most dire of circumstances were at bay—and yet the Lemians seemed here to stay. Groups of protesters had appeared in the very square below, calling for investigations and resignations and the removal of the Lemian presence. As the crowds became larger, the Lemians—in no uncertain terms—let Krelmar know that further aid was dependent upon his taking care of the problem.

Fools! Hadn't he saved them all?

And so he had invoked martial law. This brought on a wave of protests from the senate, and the demonstrations became more violent. Some of the Lemain equipment was destroyed. The first killings came as the Lemians defended their supplies, and this flamed the violence. Krelmar didn't have enough troops to quell the disturbances, so he did the only thing possible—he turned again to the Lemians for help.

Once again, they responded quickly. Sending even more troops to the planet, the Lemians brutally crushed the demonstrators. For a few months there was an uneasy quiet, and then the attacks on the Lemians—and the government soldiers—started anew. A true insurgency had been born.

Krelmar had tried to defuse the tensions by appealing to the Lemians to hold off on sending more troops. But the Lemians had ignored his pleas. Krelmar thought briefly of using Colltairian troops to stop the Lemians but quickly rejected the notion. They would be no match for the Lemians.

So he did what he had done once before—he looked offworld for help. Very carefully, he reached out to the League, knowing that the Lemians would kill him if they found out. Certainly the League would see the need for urgency now—and an opportunity to thwart the Lemians. But to his dismay, he was rebuffed. The League's official statement was that they would not interfere on a planet where the Lemians already were established.

Interfere? Isn't this what the League stood for? To help rid the galaxy of the likes of the Lemians? And the assertion that the League would not try to thwart the Lemians was nonsense.

So he had no choice but to continue dealing with the Lemians, and pray they never found out about his secret communications with the League. The other empires would not get involved, now that the Lemians were already here. No, the League had been his only chance. He redoubled his efforts to thwart the insurgency, using his own troops. He treated the insurgency like any other administrative problem—and dealt with it using his trademark efficiency. He jailed the senators who complained. Captured insurgents were summarily executed. Even simple protesters received long sentences.

Yet, no matter what he did, Krelmar could not completely stamp out the rebellion. The insurgents were surprisingly well organized and supplied. No sooner would he find one group and destroy it when another would spring up.

Krelmar was losing control.

And now he faced an even deadlier threat. Tera-Seil, Highest Councilor of the Lemian Empire, was at this moment en-route to the Hall of Halven. Tera-Seil had never set foot on Colltaire; Krelmar had always been summoned to him. Krelmar did not think it was a social call.

Tera-Seil terrified him. When Krelmar had met with Tera-Seil the first time, he had surrendered an entire planet. This time he might have to surrender his life.

He looked out over what was perhaps the only peaceful city left on Colltaire. Just outside the central square he could see the marketplace, now, in the late afternoon, all but devoid of people. Just beyond the market stood the ancient Fountains of Light, where the aged and sick once bathed, hoping for a miracle that would cure them of their ills. *A miracle,* he thought. *I could use one now.*

His thoughts were interrupted by a melodic chiming. Krelmar took a final look at the quiet city, then went to his writing table. Before pressing the intercom switch, he examined himself in the small mirror he kept there. He looked better than he felt, with his wide jowls and an ashen, hairless face, indicative of a leader who did not have to toil to live. He gave a brief adjustment to his jeweled headband before pressing the button.

"Sire, His Excellency, Lord Tera-Seil of Val is here."

"Show him in," said Krelmar. He hoped the anxiety in his voice did not carry over the intercom.

The chamber secretary ushered in the slight figure of Tera-Seil. It was hard to believe that this small individual was one of the most powerful beings in the galaxy. Krelmar could not help but shiver. He was not one to mistake Tera-Seil's lack of stature for any lack in power. His first impulse was to withdraw, but he forced himself to step forward in greeting.

"Lord Tera-Seil," said Krelmar, forcing a smile. "Welcome to Colltaire."

"Yes, of course." The Lemian spoke smoothly and quietly, with no trace of emotion. If he detected any fear or sarcasm in Krelmar's voice it did not reflect in his countenance. But his eyes were penetrating, the power within them unhidden. Krelmar knew he would need all of his cunning to deal with the Lemian, but he still did not know exactly what to expect, and the unknowing terrorized him.

"You know why I am here, Krelmar." Tera-Seil was wasting no time. He went on, ignoring the dread in Krelmar's face. "Emperor Mala is rather concerned about the current state of affairs on this planet. He was, shall we say, *upset* when he discovered the intensity of your problem. Especially painful were the recent attacks on our supply depots. I—"

"Sire, I assure you—" Something within Krelmar had forced him to speak, interrupting. His voice caught in his throat as Tera-Seil held up a finger.

"The Emperor, of course, does not approve of this violence. It is quite dishonorable to him, as well as embarrassing to the entire Empire. Do you understand?" Tera-Seil asked quietly, but did not wait for a reply. "Good. Now tell me, what is the status of this wretched insurgency?"

Krelmar knew it would be unthinkable to try to hide the truth. Tera-Seil probably knew everything already; he was likely just testing Krelmar to see how he would respond.

So he told the truth. "They are extremely resilient. Every time we beat them in one place, they turn up somewhere else. Recently they changed tactics and began attacking civilian resources, such as the power supplies. What is most difficult to discover is how they are getting supplies."

"Your ineptitude allowed them to steal weapons from your own armory!" Tera-Seil's words cut sharply.

So Tera-Seil even knew about that. No way to hide anything now; all he could hope for was that the Lemian would give him some credit for owning up to his mistakes.

"Yes, my Lord. But since then we have carefully accounted for all that was stolen and matched it to any weapons we have recovered.

The insurgents did not steal enough to explain their current firepower, especially with missiles and explosives. They are using crude weapons to be sure, but—with good success."

Spent, Krelmar stared at the floor and then closed his eyes. He would never appear this feeble to his subordinates, but he could put on no airs before Tera-Seil. An eternity seemed to pass. But when Tera-Seil said nothing and Krelmar looked up at him, the tension in the room had lifted. Tera-Seil was calmly stroking his pointed beard. Somehow Krelmar knew there would be no death today.

"You surprise me yet," said Tera-Seil. "Now I understand how you so rapidly rose to power here. You know when to deceive, and when to capitulate."

Krelmar started to respond, but Tera-Seil waved him off. "Do not worry. Your little deceptions of the past are of no concern to us now. Let us simply consider them, shall we say, overly optimistic reports." Tera-Seil laughed at his own humor.

Krelmar watched him closely. What trick was this? He wondered which deceptions Tera-Seil was referring to. Was it the cover-up of the weapons theft, or could Tera-Seil possibly know of his contact with the League? *That* was something Krelmar could never admit. But Tera-Seil's next words shocked him.

"We know that the League is supplying weapons to the insurgents," said the Lemian.

When Tera-Seil mentioned the League, Krelmar thought he was doomed; it was as if the Lemian had been reading his mind. Krelmar's mind raced. *They didn't know about his appeal to the League . . . or was Tera-Seil trying to trap him?*

"How—how do you know that?" he asked, trying to buy time.

"We know a great deal," said Tera-Seil, cryptically. The words hung in the air, but Krelmar did not take the bait. Tera-Seil continued: "Yes, we know of the smuggling, but we do not know exactly how they are doing it. I was wondering if you had some idea?" He said it smoothly, as if he were asking Krelmar for his opinion on a military matter.

Krelmar sensed the trap. If he offered a theory it would mean he had already thought the League had been supplying the insurgents. On the other hand, if he had no opinion at all it would seem he had not even considered that the insurgents might be getting help, something that was painfully obvious.

He would appear either deceitful or incompetent.

Tera-Seil waited for an answer, and Krelmar could almost sense the Lemian's gloating. This was true power, he thought, the ability to cause fear with words.

"The League has access to a space buoy in quadrant six," Krelmar said. *There, let Tera-Seil chew on that.* Krelmar had given the Lemian a logical answer to his question, but had avoided implying that he was at fault. He almost smiled at his clever response.

If Tera-Seil noticed Krelmar's smugness it was not obvious. "Yes, yes, we are aware of that. We believe that is the only way the supplies are getting into the area."

"Why don't you put a patrol around the buoy?"

Now the contempt was obvious in Tera-Seil's tone. "Fool! Knowing how and where the League is moving the supplies from is only half the battle. If we plug up that hole they will simply create another one. And we do have a good idea of how the supplies are getting to the planet. But how are they getting out to the rebels? That is the question."

Krelmar could not keep the look of dismay from his face. He had avoided one trap only to fall into another one. Did the Lemians suspect him? How could they? If he defended himself now he would certainly sound guilty.

In the back of his mind he realized he should have expected this. If the insurgents were getting supplies from offworld, they were probably getting help from someone on the planet in a position of power. Like Krelmar. But why would he help the insurgents? It would only make him look worse to the Lemians.

But Tera-Seil gave him no hint of what he was thinking. The silence grew. Obviously the Lemian was waiting for some kind of answer.

"I don't know," was all Krelmar could muster. He knew it was a weak response, but for him it was the truth, an admission of total failure. Krelmar felt drained of all energy and feeling, he could no longer think clearly.

The Lemian walked to the window. The reflected sun shone off his bald, polished head. With his back to Krelmar he spoke, again without any recognizable emotion. "Krelmar, your current failings do not keep us from remembering your worth to the Empire. After all, you did manipulate things so that we have been invited here, in a way that even the League cannot argue with. So we feel you can be helpful in the future."

Krelmar breathed a sigh of relief. But the Lemian was not done.

"However, it is clear that the situation will not improve in the immediate future. You have tied up too many of our resources here, and we cannot let the situation worsen. Therefore, you will have to leave Colltaire."

Krelmar was speechless. *Leave Colltaire?*

Still without facing Krelmar, the Lemian continued. "In Sector Four there is a small planetary system called K'Turia. We have gained control of all the worthwhile planets in that part of the sector except for K'Turia VII. On that planet we have already established a small presence, posing as traders. You will go to K'Turia and function as our representative. Your purpose will be to convince the K'Turian leaders of their desire to join with us—something you seem to have a knack for. The people there are not at all technologically advanced, so you will not be faced with any resistance that cannot be handled. But you must do with less than you have here—we simply will not commit as many troops. You must instead rely on your powers of persuasion to get the K'Turians to invite us in."

"Why—why do you want me to do this?"

Now Tera-Seil turned to face him, and the threat in his voice was obvious this time. "You should not question such generosity."

Krelmar sagged, all sense of spirit gone. *Better to die here than be exiled to some primitive backwater planet.* Would he ever see beautiful Colltaire again? How foolish he had been to think that he could barter with the Lemians. He would not die, but his fate might be worse than death. And who was to say what they would do with him even if he succeeded?

Tera-Seil went on: "Despite its Class Three rating, K'Turia is important to us. It is important to you as well." The Lemian turned a harsh gaze on Krelmar. "This is not a second chance—the Empire does not give second chances. This is merely a redirecting of, shall we say, one of our assets."

An asset, thought Krelmar. *They want to use me like a tool.* He was certain what would happen if he failed this time. But no matter what the Lemian said, it was another chance. How hard could this be? He had risen to lead a Class I planet. If the Lemians wanted control, he'd get it.

He'd make it back to Colltaire yet. He'd take care of this K'Turian situation like he had any other problem—quickly and efficiently.

Chapter 4

"You let him off too easily," said the Lemian commander.

"He has not been let off at all," replied Tera-Seil. He had returned to the military cruiser circling Colltaire. Normally Tera-Seil would not have shared the details of his activities with anyone other than the Emperor, but this was no ordinary soldier, it was Rahn-Sess, Supreme Military Commander of the Lemian Empire. Rahn-Sess had taken Tera-Seil on his own ship for the visit to Colltaire, since the commander wanted a first hand look at the League armada. He had not been impressed.

As for Tera-Seil, he fully realized it was no longer possible—if it had ever been in history—to separate politics from military operations, or at least the threat of military might. But just because he needed Rahn-Sess and the military to further his aims—*the Empire's aims*—it did not mean the military knew how to handle every situation. Fortunately, Rahn-Sess, though one to prefer the most direct action, was no fool. Tera-Seil would not have to stroke his ego.

"Krelmar has either outlived his usefulness, or he is a spy," said Rahn-Sess. "Either way he should die."

"On Colltaire, he is no longer useful, in that you are correct, Commander. That does not mean he has no value." And then he added, "And you should hope that if one day you are no longer useful to the Empire, you will have a fate other than immediate death."

Ever the soldier, the words rolled off Rahn-Sess. "If I am no longer useful, then I do not deserve to live."

"Ahh, Commander, the question is, who decides whether you are useful? Certainly the Emperor, but would you have him decide the usefulness of every being in the Empire? He has more important matters to concern himself with than even the usefulness of his Supreme Commander—or his Councilors. But enough of this. As for Krelmar, if he is a spy, we will know soon enough. If he has been the conduit for the League, removing him from the planet will cut off the flow of weapons. You must carefully monitor the insurgent activities to determine whether they appear to be running out of supplies. If they are, we will know that Krelmar was helping them."

"Then what?" asked Rahn-Sess.

"We will step up our attacks on the insurgents. They will be forced to find another source of supply. They will be hard pressed to find one, since we no longer allow anyone on the planet. So we will provide the conduit for them."

"What do you mean? We will help the insurgents?"

Tera-Seil smiled. "Of course. They need a conduit to get arms from the League, and we need proof that the League is supplying the insurgents."

"But why? Why would we help them?"

"Because my friend, although we suspect that the League is supplying the insurgents, as of now we have no proof. Yes, if Krelmar is the conduit we could convince him to tell us, but who would believe him if he confessed under duress? No, we must have real proof. And so the insurgents will get their go-between. We will let the shipments resume, and then we will have proof."

"But why is this so important? We already know the insurgents are getting support from somewhere offworld, mostly likely from the League. Allowing the insurgents to continue getting arms only serves to delay us."

Tera-Seil looked at him coolly. "Such would be a small price to pay. There is more at stake here than Colltaire." *Much more,* thought Tera-Seil. He knew that the League was very weak—so weak they might do something either very smart, or very foolish. Or both. The foolish thing would be to launch an attack against the Lemians. Such an attack would be beaten back, but it would be messy and wasteful, and Tera-Seil hated waste.

The smart thing would be for the League to do exactly what Krelmar had done when he had been at his weakest—to get help. But who would the League approach? Certainly not one of the other Empires; it would be a sign of League weakness, and would virtually invite an attack on the League. That left very few options. Only one, in fact.

The Rheans.

Tera-Seil said nothing of this to Rahn-Sess. The Commander would have laughed at him. What would the League have to offer the Rheans, the most powerful beings in the galaxy? Beings so powerful that even the wars between the Empires and the League were insignificant to them.

But it would be the smart thing to do. It was what Tera-Seil would do. *That* was something Tera-Seil would not even admit to the Emperor, who so hated the League that even with his cunning he would be blinded to this strategy. But Tera-Seil was a realist.

An alliance between the League and the Rheans would doom the Empires. Without the ability to wrest control of planets protected by the League, the Empires would turn on each other.

And die.

So while he had no evidence whatsoever that the League had approached the Rheans, he had to be ready for just such a strategy.

And he knew of one sure way to destroy any possibility of a Rhean-League alliance, and that was to catch the League in the act of supplying the insurgents. While he did not think the Rheans cared a bit about the insurgents on Colltaire, one thing they did care about was the rule of law. The Rheans would not look kindly on the League if they were helping overthrow a duly elected government. Tera-Seil actually appreciated the irony of it. The Lemians could take over the planet by force, and the Rheans would not care. But if the League was caught helping the insurgents, the Rheans would certainly refuse to ally with the League.

This is what makes politics so much fun, he thought.

Rahn-Sess said, "I'll leave the politics to you. I prefer a simple war."

"You may have that yet," said Tera-Seil. "I am sending Krelmar to K'Turia VII, a rather nothing of a planet. It is, however, the last planet in the sector that we do not have complete control of. Krelmar shall once again convince the populace to join us, just as he did here on Colltaire. And we will carefully monitor him to see if he makes any attempt to contact the League. We shall be in a much better position to track his communications from a planet where he does not have a lifetime of contacts to rely on."

"And if he is not the go-between? Then all this would have been a waste."

"Not at all. If he fails, we are no worse off there than we are now. And if he is successful on K'Turia, we will have kept another entire system out of the League."

"What if the League supports an insurgency on K'Turia as well?"

"In fact, that is an even more desirable outcome. They are already overextended with their useless armadas and patrols. For all their talk of democracy, the League are political amateurs. The fools will be battling amongst themselves, trying to decide what is worse, the loss of Colltaire or the loss of the last planet in an entire sector. A difficult choice, because it has no answer. So we will win in both places. Patrolling ships cannot take the place of a more, shall we say, personal contact."

What he did not tell Rahn-Sess was his other reason for sending Krelmar to K'Turia. Tera-Seil needed control over that sector more than he admitted to the commander. For he had received word that the League had lost a freighter in the vicinity of K'Turia—a freighter en route to Colltaire. If the freighter contained weapons, it would be the proof he would need in case his worst fears were realized—that the League was going to ally with the Rheans.

But before the Rheans would accept his proof, he would have to know how the League had been moving the weapons. If Krelmar had been the contact, surely the League would contact Krelmar on K'Turia. Tera-Seil already had a spy in place on the planet, someone

Krelmar would not suspect. Even more important, it would not serve his purpose if the freighter was discovered on a planet already controlled by the Lemians—the League would simply claim that any weapons on the freighter had been planted there. This was why he was sending Krelmar, instead of a true Lemian, to K'Turia.

All of this he could have told Rahn-Sess, but he did not. Not because he wished to keep the freighter a secret—sooner or later Rahn-Sess would have to know about it. Rather it was because Tera-Seil *knew* that the freighter would be found carrying smuggled League weapons.

This was his plan within a plan. Even the Emperor did not know of his plot. The Emperor would not fear a Rhean alliance, because he could not imagine one unfolding. Yet Tera-Seil was convinced that this was the greatest threat to the Empire, a threat that he alone might recognize. To save the Empire, he would thwart the potential alliance by finding the weapons in this freighter.

Even if he had to put the weapons there himself.

But he had to find the freighter before the League did.

"What if the League attempts a personal contact of their own on K'Turia?" asked Rahn-Sess.

Tera-Seil looked up at the commander. "You surprise me yet, Rahn-Sess. That is a very—*political*—observation. They may try, but remember how slowly the League moves. Their methods of persuasion are much more time consuming than ours." *And nothing would be better for my plan than if the League tries to intervene on K'Turia.* If the missing freighter was discovered there, it would look like the League was trying to cover up the evidence.

Plans within plans within plans.

"And what if Krelmar turns out to be the League spy?"

Tera-Seil smiled coldly. "Then, Commander, you will have your wish. Krelmar will die."

Chapter 5

"Any change?" Win looked over the radar officer's shoulder at the deep space scanner.

"No, sir. She's matched course and speed all the way."

As Win had half expected, a Lemian ship had broken away from Colltairian orbit to follow the *Anatar*. Nothing altogether menacing, but potentially problematic if the League wanted to keep the mission a secret. They were just about out of the Colltaire system. Would the Lemians follow them beyond the station rendezvous?

The blip on the screen that represented the Lemian ship suddenly disappeared, as if in answer to his question. Perhaps the Lemians thought the departure of the *Anatar* was a ruse to lure them away from Colltaire—a possibility that Win found somewhat amusing.

Free from the shadow, he ordered a slight change in course which would allow the ship to intercept the recording buoy in Sector Four. The buoy might not have much information, but anything was better than what they knew now.

On the voyage to Sector Four station the crew had resumed the normal deep space research activities that had been interrupted by the assignment to the Colltaire armada. But it was impossible to keep a secret on a ship, and Win knew that everyone was distracted by what was obviously yet another military mission.

Win also found it hard to concentrate on his own scientific duties, but for a different reason. He had been in a virtual mental slumber, growing more and more disinterested in his work. Though for years he had dutifully carried out his tasks, he was more or less going through the motions. Now he barely reacted to findings that would have thrilled any other scientist.

He had joined the League primarily as a means of escape; to get away from his home world, a way for him to get so involved in other matters that he would forget his beloved Sooni, his Treb mate. Her untimely death had torn something from him, as if she had been the living embodiment of his drive, his interest not only in her, but in his work, and everything around him.

Sooni. I miss you so very much...

When he had met her, many years ago, she had already attained *ana*, the higher purpose sought by all Trebs. Those of his race could reach this higher state of being only after a long period of introspection and self study. Many never did achieve this level of awareness, striving all their long lives—twice that of most humanoids—in a constant search for enlightenment. *Ana* was a lifelong desire and a Treb duty, but one they all happily embraced.

Ages of scientific breeding had resulted in a minute death rate; Trebs were forced to carefully manage births so as not to overpopulate the planet. Only those who had reached *ana*, and who had found a true loving mate, would even consider offspring. And even then, they needed to possess the genes that were considered appropriate for reproduction. Few passed all of these tests.

Though Win had not yet achieved *ana*, and might never, Sooni had so loved him that she had been willing to wait. They felt blessed after passing the necessary medical examinations, which granted them the right to have children once Win achieved *ana*.

In the meantime, Sooni had pursued her worldly path, that of science. Sooni had said she was conceiving ideas while awaiting her chance to conceive life.

But this passion had killed her. A rare accident in the laboratory, as she endeavored to bring learning to her people. In that instant, Win had not only lost Sooni, but he lost all desire for *ana*, his very spiritual essence extinguished. He became numb, unable to regain his emotional balance, a feeling made worse by being surrounded by an entire race seeking to attain higher purpose. Unbearable.

And so he had left his planet. For a while he wandered aimlessly, so utterly uncharacteristic of any Treb. He did not know what to do. Because he had been born into a culture where everyone made their own decisions on what they would do in life, he realized it would be difficult to take orders, which limited his options.

So he had become a scientist. Analytical, emotionless.

Numb.

Only much later did he join the League, where he was able to toil in relative obscurity, far from his home and his people. Still not good at taking orders, he was fortunately left to his research projects. He knew that joining the League would never cure him, but it would at least fill his life with other responsibilities. And he had performed his work faithfully. Yet he was finding it harder and harder to make decisions; he weighed everything almost to the point of paralysis. He struggled to capture the desire for scientific discovery. He could just as well have been doing something else, anywhere.

For a Treb, having no desire was akin to death. He was as far from *ana* as could be imagined.

But now, for the first time since he had left home, he felt a stirring, as if something in this mission would be especially important, not only to the League, but to himself.

* * *

When they reached the recording buoy, Win reconvened the officers in the conference room. They waited while the XO scanned the buoy records. Her brow wrinkled as she said, "This is interesting."

"Nothing there, right?" asked Cale.

"No, in fact just the opposite. The buoy reports that a cargo ship *Hauler One*—and now we have the ship's id code—did pass through the sector. All the normal information is here—speed, direction, everything."

"Where was it heading?" asked Win.

"Its straight line flight pattern would have taken it to a service depot in Sector Two—not far from Colltaire, if that is what you are thinking—but not close enough to conclude anything. Naturally, it could have changed course once there and landed on Colltaire anyway—this buoy just logs the flight path as the ship passes by this point. Its range is quite limited."

"And from the other direction?" asked Win. "Can you extrapolate as to where it came from?"

The XO brought up a star chart for them all to see. She didn't have to say anything—it was pretty obvious that the freighter had not started its journey within the range of the space buoy monitors. It could have come from anywhere.

"So we are back where we started from," said Cale.

"What do we know about that service depot?" asked Win.

I'Char's quick response told Win that the Illian had anticipated the request, reminding him of the value of having the military representative on board.

"It's a large unmanned depot," said I'Char. "Plenty of room to store parts, food—weapons."

"So the *Hauler One* could have been en route to drop off something at the depot for later pickup and transfer to Colltaire, perhaps by smaller scout ships."

"Yes," said I'Char. "A freighter would certainly attract attention if it landed on Colltaire. I would suspect the Lemians would have patrols all around that depot. The freighter could dock there, and hide cargo, but it would be difficult to get it to the planet. Unless the League had help from someone on Colltaire."

"How could they do that?" asked Cale. "You just said the Lemians would be watching the depot."

"Those depots get a lot of traffic," said the XO. "We've docked at them before."

"Yes, and we know that the Colltairians do some trading. They might have some ships going there," said Win.

"Without the Lemians knowing?" asked Cale. "That doesn't sound likely."

"You are thinking too literally," said I'Char. "Just because they know ships might be going there from Colltaire doesn't mean that they know what is on the ships."

"Perhaps someone in power—or at least someone who the Lemians trust—is helping smuggle in supplies."

"The Lemians trust no one," said I'Char. "But it wouldn't have to be someone they trust, just someone who has access to the depot. But let's not get ahead of ourselves. The *Hauler One* might have nothing at all to do with Colltaire."

"What about Garrick?" asked Win.

"Surprisingly, nothing," said I'Char. "Not a single record in our database, or in the central register."

"That's impossible," said the XO. "There must be *something*."

"Similar names came up, but none associated with Central Command. All the records on him must have been wiped clean—no easy task. Either he is a covert agent, or he's very high up in Central Command."

Win shook his head. "Too many unknowns." He turned to Cale. "What have you learned about K'Turia?"

"Actually, I've found someone on board who can help us on that. Her name is Kalinda Prentiss. She just came aboard during our last stopover at Sector Two station. I hadn't had a chance to review her background, otherwise I might have thought of this earlier. She's a First Class Interplanetary Research Specialist, and is one of the League's leading experts on early cultures like the one on K'Turia. She's preparing a briefing for us."

"First Class you say?" said Win. "First Class Specialists usually have their own staffs, or their own ships. What is she doing assigned to us?"

"Her service history is a bit sparse on that," replied Cale. "But from what I gather, I believe we are somewhat of a demotion for her."

"This'll be interesting," said Win.

"Wait til you meet her," said Cale. "Interesting is not the half of it."

* * *

They had barely docked at Section Four station when Jaims Garrick stepped aboard the *Anatar*. Win met him at the portal. Garrick was tall, even by human standards. Middle aged, and very fit. He wore no uniform or any other indication of his position.

The League representative wasted no time with small talk. "As per the orders you have received, I am here to join the mission to K'Turia."

"Are you formally taking control of the ship?" Win tried to keep any emotion out of his voice.

Garrick eyed him narrowly. "Are you trying to avoid responsibility for the mission?"

"No," said Win. "I just want to know—and my crew will need to know—who is in charge."

"I see. Let's keep things as they are—for now. As I am sure you are aware, Central Command can order you to cede command. If things go smoothly—meaning if you and your crew carry out the mission as ordered—we won't need to formally transfer command."

What did that mean? thought Win. Garrick was implying that he could take over, but he had carefully avoided saying he actually had the authority.

Was it Garrick who was trying to avoid responsibility, in case something went wrong?

He'd have to watch this Garrick. *What was he hiding?*

* * *

In the conference room, Win and his officers learned nothing new about Garrick; he did not even tell them what branch of Central Command he represented. When Prentiss was introduced to Garrick his eyes narrowed, and Win noticed a flash of recognition—and annoyance.

Meeting Prentiss for the first time, Win was struck by her demeanor. She was not in awe of anyone in the room—her attitude was not exactly disdainful, she simply appeared not to care who they were. Almost haughty; not at all like the other First Class

Interplanetary Specialists he had met. *She must be very good to have overcome such an aloof attitude.*

Everything about her screamed 'scientist,' her close cropped hair, her lack of jewelry, her calloused hands. Even her voice was clipped, as if she were carefully cutting off any trace of emotion.

"K'Turia is a Class Three planet, sparsely inhabited, all humanoid bipeds, well dispersed. The level of development and culture is reasonably uniform on the entire planet, falling into the Late Pre-Advanced Stage on the League Developmental Continuum. This means that as a whole the inhabitants are aware that they are not alone in the universe, and they are also aware they have been visited by offworlders. The use of tools is well established, but technology is primitive by our standards; no high speed communications, no motorized transport, no computing."

Prentiss stopped and glared at Garrick, who didn't seem to be paying attention. Only when he looked up in the silence did she continue.

"The climate varies widely even within the same land masses. As such, the people have a range of physical characteristics—skin color, body mass, hair thickness, and other features. These differences are accentuated by geography—K'Turians from one part of the planet will look quite different from those elsewhere. Such physical differences may create an easier acceptance of offworlders than might be expected of such a technologically primitive people, because they are already accustomed to seeing beings that look dissimilar. However we do not know how the K'Turians actually react to offworlders.

"Religion is central to the culture and is intermixed with the societal leadership, which is likely set within a strict caste system. This must be kept firmly in mind—" she looked directly at Garrick again "—in order to understand these people. They will be guided more by the rules of their religions than by what we might consider social rules. In other words, one could make all the right societal and interpersonal overtures and still run afoul of some religious edict."

Prentiss turned to her console and brought up a picture of the entire planet, then flashed through a series of shots, each one providing greater detail. The photos gave way to an infrared image, followed by others showing radiation output and other emissions. Even without Prentiss's introduction it would have been clear that the planet was not technologically advanced.

The next image was detailed enough to show land demarcations and some larger structures. Prentiss continued, "As you can see, most of the arable land is farmed. Like most planets at this developmental stage, there are very few big cities due to the lack of large scale transportation for foodstuffs. We do not even know if there is a uniform currency exchange that would permit cross geographic transactions. Bartering is probably the primary means of exchange. Though we do not have direct evidence, it is likely that the population is very regionalized, with local city states or other forms of control—or none at all in some areas.

"There is, however, one larger city." She clicked through another series of zooms, this one ending in an image that was taken from ground level, showing a marketplace of some kind. A wide dirt roadway, crowded with people, was lined with shops and vendors. "This is Merculon. It is located in a valley, at the base of a mountain chain. Though in a relatively arid part of the planet, the mountains provide a source of water, allowing for controlled irrigation, which has probably led to the growth of the city." Between Merculon and the mountains the photos showed a series of hills, but in the other direction only farmland, and beyond that, what looked like desert.

I'Char glanced over at Win, but Win shook his head. He could see the same thing—if they had to approach Merculon, there were not many ways in, but they could discuss that later. He didn't want to start interrupting the briefing with questions just yet.

Garrick, however, had no such compunction. "If anyone on the planet knows something about where the freighter is, Merculon is the place to start."

Prentiss's stoic demeanor immediately dropped away, and with clear emotion she said, "Direct contact with these people could be disastrous to their culture. We do not even know to what degree they have dealt with offworlders. We could initiate a devastating cultural shock that would affect them for generations. We should not—I repeat *not*—take this risk."

Garrick looked over at Win and rolled his eyes, but when he turned back to Prentiss he merely said, "The Lemians are already there, so the damage has been done."

So Garrick has more information than we do, thought Win.

But Prentiss was still focused on the direct contact. "The information we have is only that someone has been there. We don't know how deep the contact was, or whether the populace as a whole was even aware of it."

"Your information is incomplete," said Garrick, dismissively. "The Lemians are not only there, they have been there for a while. Whether or not the populace knows that the Lemians are offworlders doesn't matter. What matters is that they are there. If they manage to take control of K'Turia we will lose another system."

"Perhaps if the League had shared this information with us we might have prepared a better briefing," said Prentiss, hotly.

"You speak of the League as if it were another entity," said Garrick. "Remember who you work for."

Cale looked over at Win as if to say, "I told you so." But Win felt he was learning a lot from the interplay. *So there was more to this than the freighter. The League was worried about losing K'Turia to the Lemians.* He decided to let the discussion continue a bit longer to see what information Prentiss could goad from Garrick.

"I don't work for you," replied Prentiss. "I report directly to the Research Council. My job is to represent these people and make sure the League understands them before barging in and harming their culture."

This time the disrespect was clear in Garrick's voice. "That's a charming way of describing your role. But you don't *represent* anyone. The League can offer these people much more than the Lemians, who only want control—and who have no concern at all over cultural destruction. We know the Lemians are on the planet; I doubt very much *they* are worried about whether the K'Turian culture is harmed."

Prentiss glared at him, and started to respond, but Garrick cut her off. "As for who you work for, this ship is now under the control of Central Command. Isn't that right, Captain?" He turned to Win, a slight smile on his face.

Win avoided the trap. "Yes, Mr. Garrick, it is. But I am responsible for, and in charge of, my personnel, until I receive orders to the contrary."

"I'm willing to accept that for the time being," said Garrick. "Just see to it that your people stay in line."

Win ignored the insinuation. "Very well. So that means Specialist Prentiss is under my command for this mission." If Garrick was going to claim a greater authority, now would be the time he would do it.

But Garrick simply said, "Exactly. And the mission is to find that freighter."

He's no simple bureaucrat, thought Win. *He handled that rather well.*

"Perhaps now is the time for you to add what you know," said Win, "since it appears you have more—recent—information."

Garrick shrugged. "Not much more to tell. The Lemians are trying to control this system, just like everywhere else. They already have a presence on two of the five other inhabited planets in this system. League rules say that if the majority of planets are under outside control, then the entire system is off limits to the League."

"You don't sound as if you approve of the League rules."

"Whether I approve or not doesn't matter, that's the way it is," said Garrick.

"It wouldn't be the first time the League bent their own rules," said Prentiss.

Garrick ignored her. "The point is that the Lemians know our rules just as well as we do. While this isn't the most important system in the sector for them, it would be another one on their side. And the other planets in the system do have some economic value."

"How often are the Lemians there?" asked I'Char. "Do they have permanent bases, patrols?"

"There is nothing much to patrol," said Garrick. "It's just dusty farmland and a bunch of peasant shacks. But we do think they have been bringing in some goods from offworld, probably using some flashy technology to try to gain quick influence over the people."

"But you still aren't sure if the K'Turian's realize that the Lemians are from offworld," said Prentiss. "For all you know, the Lemians have passed themselves off as some nomadic tribe from the other side of the planet."

She doesn't give up, thought Win. Though he recognized her stubbornness could be a problem, he found himself liking her.

"They wouldn't go to all that trouble," said Garrick. "In one way the Lemian presence helps us." He mocked Prentiss's tone. "We don't have to worry about *cultural destruction.* The Lemians have already done it."

Prentiss turned to Win, exasperated and clearly angry. "Captain, we cannot know that for sure. Direct contact with a primitive culture is always risky. We cannot take the chance. Just seeing us or any of our technology could affect their entire development."

"It may not come to that," said Win. "When we get close enough we may be able to find the freighter with our sensors. If it is not in a populated area, we might be able to get in and out without being seen."

"I doubt that will be possible," said Garrick. "We—had mechanisms in place to track the freighter. Even in an emergency like a propulsion failure it would have had plenty of time to broadcast its problem and let us know where it was. But we have no information that it ditched somewhere."

"You suspect sabotage?" asked I'Char. "And that the freighter is being hidden by the Lemians?"

"It is a possibility we have to consider," said Garrick.

"Maybe this is the time to tell us why this freighter is so damned important," said Cale. "What exactly is it carrying?"

"Knowing what it carries is not critical to the mission," said Garrick. "All you need to know is that it is important to the League."

Cale seemed ready to respond but Win cut him off. This wasn't the time to argue politics. "What about the Lemians? Certainly the League would not want them to know we are there. That would be an argument for our keeping a low profile."

"We don't care what the Lemians think," said Garrick. "It isn't their planet yet. But you are correct, better to stay out of sight of the Lemians. Our presence might cause them to do something drastic."

"Like what?" asked the XO. "We aren't exactly a battlecruiser."

"Nothing like that," said Garrick. "I mean they might do something about the freighter."

"So the Lemians know about the freighter?" asked I'Char.

Garrick looked at him. "Let's hope not. Otherwise we are too late."

Chapter 6

The Rhean once known as Prome activated the neural net which would connect its sentient protoplasm to that of Rhean Ceme, millions of miles away. After the slightest of hesitations the link was established; both Rheans becoming aware of the other's sensations along the tendrils of their exoskeleton. For some time they did nothing, reveling in the expansion of their own senses. There was no hurry, for they were Rheans, the most powerful race in the galaxy. For the Rheans, time was an illusion, as was the physical universe, an illusion to be played in.

This neural connection was their racial secret. It is what set them apart from virtually all others in the universe, this ability to connect over vast distances. The Rhean power came not from weapons, or strategy, as most others believed, but from this combination of their sensations, memories, and intellect, bringing together millions of their race into one gigantic sensory power, with almost instantaneous communications ability. Able to react with astounding speed to new technologies, the Rheans could copy and develop the best of what the galaxy had to offer faster than anyone. In ages past it had given them a supreme edge in war, allowing for rapid changes to strategies and military plans.

After a time there were fewer battles; their power becoming recognized by all. Planetary systems which offered them conflict were casually immobilized. Later, the Rheans became a race of peace. Not interested in material things or power for its own sake, the Rheans sought only to advance their own development, seeking a racial nirvana that they were uniquely equipped to achieve. They left the galaxy alone, and thus, though powerful, were a threat to no one. Once the empires understood this, and discovered that the Rheans would not interfere, they continued their galactic plunder. The Rheans saw all this, instantly, knowing of far off empire victories even before the emperors did. And for the longest time, the Rheans did not care.

Until now.

"The confluence of forces shows a path that could lead to a tidal shift in the galaxy," sensed Prome. "The empires, should they join together, will defeat the League. Combined, they could become a threat to our development."

"That is but one path, and the nexus of possibilities indicates many other outcomes," responded Ceme. "Even if that future were to occur, it is unlikely that the empires, even if they come together against the League, will stay in union. Nor is it certain that they would then turn against us."

Prome shifted color into the yellow band, a sign of congenial disagreement. "Most of the empires can only survive by expanding, constantly growing through conquest. We have seen ages of this, across the galaxy, in almost every race."

"Except us," sensed Ceme, across the great distance.

"Yes, but we are different," sensed Prome, and for a moment both luxuriated in the bliss of their uniqueness.

"Yet you still wish us to become involved with these lesser beings," hummed Ceme.

"You have seen the nexus. Though the possibilities are low, the risk is real."

"Should it come to that, we would win such a war," chimed Ceme.

"Of that the nexus is much clearer. There seems little doubt of the outcome."

"So why proceed?" queried Ceme. "Certainly even the empires can see this, even though they do not have our skills."

"For many reasons," sensed Prome. "They may see the outcome, but be compelled to attack us, for fear of losing power over what they have, or simply because it is their nature. They would not be the first to engage us out of sheer arrogance. But mostly because it would be such a waste."

"Of life?" Ceme seemed intrigued.

"Of time. Ours. Would you rather revel in the immersion of our joint knowledge, advancing toward our supreme goal, or use even an iota of that time to fight a useless war?"

Once again they paused, caught up in the very immersion.

"You would give the League protection?" asked Ceme. "If so, others would ask for it as well. What makes the League different? Their goals are unlike ours. They wish power, but do not wish to be left alone. In many ways they are like the empires, seeking to ever expand."

"That is true for them as a whole, but there are those within their races who show great promise. The true awakening of even one in such a primitive race would be a profound development, one that even we might learn from."

"Would one so developed ever become a threat?"

"Not to us. The very essence of that development would preclude it."

"Unless they change," cautioned Ceme.

"Perhaps. But not all powers must be a threat. There are many powers in the universe. One is of far greater enormity than even we are, than we perhaps can be. Yet we all feel that it will never be a threat to us."

"But it will to others," agreed Ceme.

"Yes," responded Prome. "The empires will feel threatened, should they ever accept the reality of that power. As will any other beings that live in fear."

"Is a power unknown a power nonetheless?" mused Ceme.

"It is," replied Prome. "Many fear that which is unknown, and this is especially true for those who live by conquest. See how many act toward us. They fear not only the power they know we possess, but the power they imagine we possess. If their eyes are opened to an even greater power than ours, they may fight it before they realize its extent."

"You like them, don't you?" hummed Ceme. He meant the League now, and of course Prome understood. "I am surprised. I did not think they would be of import."

"I think only of us, and our path," sensed Prome. "If any other beings with such potential were established in the nexus, I would do the same."

"Yes, but these beings of the League, are they worthy?" asked Ceme.

"That the nexus cannot tell us," admitted Prome.

"So what do you propose?" Ceme already knew the answer, but the flow of communication was comforting in its familiarity.

"The test, of course," sensed Prome. "It has already begun."

Chapter 7

Win sat alone in his cabin, his mind filled with thoughts of Sooni. She was always there, and only the tension and immediacy of the mission had kept him from being dangerously distracted by the memories.

He was so numb he could not even be angry at himself for his inability to focus. Now, left to his thoughts, he had only one escape.

He took three long breaths and made the subtle shifts in his metabolism as he prepared to enter *nore,* the Treb state of heightened awareness. The change came quickly here, where the environment was totally under his control.

His breathing deepened, the blood flow to his brain increased, his nerve endings became more sensitive. *Nore* allowed awareness to shift between the outer and inner senses. He would not need external sensitivity now; what he required instead was *control,* so he could focus. He needed to expand his mental capacity and see patterns in complexity.

After the briefing he had carefully reviewed the information he'd been given from his officers. They had covered the tactical elements of the mission and felt they were as ready as they could be. And though she clearly disapproved of the mission, even Prentiss was at work fabricating the clothing and other essentials they would need.

But Win still felt unprepared—and uncertain. His unease, he knew, came mostly because he did not understand—or more accurately, had not been told of—the real reason for the mission. It was anathema to him to not understand a major effort before beginning it—especially one that, Garrick's dismissals notwithstanding, would be dangerous.

Now he needed more clarity, and he feared that in his numbed mental state he would put them all in danger by not being able to make the right decisions—or make any decisions at all. But where could he start? There was no more data to be retrieved from the ship's storehouse of information, nor was he likely to get anything from Central Command.

Spontaneously, Win sank deeper into his *nore,* letting all the facts swirl around him. This was not a linear exercise; he would not attempt to create arguments and use logic. That was a job for his ordinary, scientific mind. *Nore* offered something different; he would call upon the same facts, but now they would flow into patterns, patterns that would take shape, combining and recombining, remembered and ready to be analyzed by his logical brain when he emerged from his trance.

He never knew how long the process would last. His heightened external senses told him how much time was passing; *nore* was not a sleep state.

Still, he was surprised how quickly it ended. What had seemed to be a confusing array of multiple unknowns had quickly congealed into an unexpectedly limited number of patterns.

It was time to confront Garrick.

* * *

Win found the League representative at one of the ship's library stations, intently staring at a screen. He took a moment to study the man, in a way he had not been able to in the briefing room. Garrick was hard to define. He was human, but not Earth-born—his features were too angular. He had some of the same bearing as I'Char, a kind of efficiency of movement. But that was as far as the similarity went; Garrick's other mannerisms were almost casual, as if he did not care how he did things. I'Char could seem effortless, but no one would ever call him casual.

Win sensed exactly when Garrick realized he was not alone, and he half expected Garrick to snap off the display and hide it, but to his surprise the human moved aside to show Win what he had been looking at.

On the viewer was another series of photos of the area around the large K'Turian city, Merculon. "Before you ask, I wasn't holding these back," said Garrick, dryly. "Prentiss had them." He changed the screen so that a number of the pictures were displayed together, and indicated them one by one as he spoke. "Here, and here, behind these hills. We could hide a shuttle there, and then enter the city from the end of the valley." The pictures changed again. "It's a long walk, but it would reduce the chance of being seen by the Lemians."

Win followed the route that Garrick was proposing. It might work. But he was less interested in that now—he'd leave their tactical approach up to I'Char. Instead, he was focusing on Garrick. What was Garrick not telling him by choosing to tell him this?

"I thought you said that we don't care if the Lemians know we are there?" Win purposely misquoted what he remembered Garrick saying at the briefing.

If Garrick noticed the misrepresentation he did not seem offended. "I said that we didn't care what they think, not that we should jump in their faces. Once they know we are on the planet it certainly limits our options, and cannot be undone. Better to go in quietly and see what we can find out that way."

"What else do you know about the Lemians on K'Turia?"

"Nothing more than I told you. They are there, have been there a while, and would very much like to have that planet. That is all we know."

I doubt that, thought Win. But instead he said, "I assume you have a lot more experience dealing with the Lemians than I do. What do you think they are doing on K'Turia now?" He had no trouble keeping any sarcasm out of his voice; verbal irony was not typical for a Treb.

"They aren't very subtle," said Garrick. "But that doesn't mean they always go in with force. Though they love to fight, they're not stupid—fighting takes resources. So they try the easy way first. They'll try to buy their way in, not with exotic items, but with food, more efficient ways of farming, tools, things the K'Turians will appreciate."

"Not all that different from what we might do," said Win.

Garrick smiled, but he didn't appear amused. "Few in Central Command would state it that clearly, but you are right; we'd do the same thing. But the entire process to get there would be different."

"We'd take longer, you mean."

"Yes, but that is only part of it. It is the alternatives that set us apart—the alternatives to the locals if they don't want what is offered, or refuse the other half of the bargain."

"Meaning the acceptance of some kind of representation," said Win.

"Control. The Lemians don't represent, they *control*. The League represents."

"Representation, control, it just depends on who is describing it," said Win. "To the K'Turians there may seem very little difference."

"A politician you'll never be," said Garrick. "Don't forget the alternatives. If the locals don't want the League, we leave. If they don't want the Lemians—the Lemians will take control anyway. If the easy way doesn't work, there is always the military approach."

Win was a bit surprised by Garrick's attitude. In the briefing he had been arrogant, and especially disdainful of Prentiss. Here he seemed to be trying his best to be polite. In any event, Win was stuck with Garrick, so he might as well make the best of it.

"And this is why I need your help," said Win, trying to sound congenial. "What is your estimation of the size of the Lemian presence on K'Turia? Will they already have the military in place? These are the things I must know if I am going to send my people into danger."

"You still think I'm keeping something from you," said Garrick.

"As a matter of fact, yes," said Win.

"Don't take it personally. You have what you need to know." Garrick's eyes darted away briefly. "As for your question, remember that all Lemian presence is military in nature. Don't ever forget that. So yes, the military will be there. What we do not know is how far along things are. The Lemians don't have a lot of patience. But they probably also do not want to commit a lot of effort to a backwater like K'Turia."

"I thought you said they wanted the system?"

"They do, but they want a hundred others as well. The fate of their empire won't be decided on K'Turia. But they don't like to lose, or back down. It will not take much force to overcome these primitive people. I don't want to be down there when they decide to roll up the city. We might not have much time."

Win wondered how far he could push Garrick. If Garrick thought Win was not being cooperative, he might formally take charge, leaving Win with no way to protect his crew. Still, he needed more information. "Which brings us back to the freighter. It would be much faster to search for it with low level orbits and multiple sensor drones. There are no other Lemian ships in this sector now. We could get in and out without putting anyone in danger."

Garrick shook his head. "You are assuming the freighter is just sitting there, waiting to be found. If the freighter was transmitting a distress beacon, or even emitting a large amount of energy, we'd know it already. And so would the Lemians. No, we have to go in on foot."

Win didn't need any special sense to know that Garrick was hiding something. One didn't search on foot for a lost ship. He decided to try a different approach. "You realize this is a scientific crew. As such, they are used to operating under completely different circumstances. This entire air of—secrecy—is uncomfortable for them, and for me. Unless we know more about this freighter, and why it is so important, it might compromise our chances of finding it."

"I would have thought you had enough control over your people to deal with that," said Garrick.

"They'll do what they have to," said Win. "That is not the point. But you have already invited our distrust by refusing to tell us all we want to know. Why create such a hostile environment? Things will work better if everyone understands the priorities."

"The priority is quite clear," said Garrick. "Find the freighter. Period."

"What about the freighter's crew?" asked Win. "I'm surprised you haven't mentioned them."

"Don't take me so literally," said Garrick. "Obviously we are looking for the crew. But since we've received no communication from them we assume they are dead. Otherwise we would have come here a lot quicker."

I wonder about that, thought Win. He was as loyal to the League as anyone, but he wasn't sure he would want to rely on Central Command to rescue him and his crew if his ship went down—unless they felt it was of military importance.

He shifted back to tactics. "With the Lemians already on K'Turia, I would have thought this would be a military mission. Why did we get this job?"

Garrick looked away. "There was no one else close enough that could be spared. Plus we didn't want to draw too much attention to it. A small team, that's all we needed. And don't sell yourself short, your crew probably has more experience dealing with locals than most military crews."

Win sensed unease in Garrick's tone, and how the human had tried to avoid the question with flattery. *I don't believe him.* But maybe Garrick had spoken a partial truth—the part about not wanting to draw attention to the mission.

Which meant the freighter was very important, and getting to it more dangerous than Garrick was admitting.

Arguing now would get him nowhere, so Win said, "Yes, you're probably right, we do have experience dealing with indigenous populations. And if we are going to keep a low profile, we must understand how to blend in. If we do not we might as well drop the shuttle in the city square. That's why I want Prentiss to be part of the contact team. She is an expert in direct contacts. Unless you are?"

Garrick bristled. "I'm not. But taking her is not a good idea at all.

This is a military mission. Take I'Char, he seems competent. By the way, is—do you call I'Char a 'he' or a 'she'?"

Win had already decided that I'Char would be part of the contact team, and was amused at Garrick's characterization of the Illian as *competent*. Basic competence for an Illian was lightspeed ahead of most beings, and I'Char was no ordinary Illian. Garrick should have known this. Or did he just not care about anyone else? Just who was he, anyway?

"You can refer to I'Char either way. As for Prentiss, military mission or not, we need her expertise. Having her with us will be far better than leaving her behind."

Garrick seemed to be making up his mind about something. Finally he said, "What do you know about her?"

"She's a First Class Interplanetary Research Specialist. You should know that is a pretty rare breed. You don't get to be one unless you are extraordinarily talented and knowledgeable."

"Really? If she's so good, what's she doing on your ship?"

Someone else might have been offended, but Win, being both a scientist and a Treb, was not. It was a logical question. "I don't know. Her file implied some kind of demotion."

"It *was* a demotion," said Garrick, leaning back in his chair and lacing his hands behind his head. "Let me tell you about First Class Specialist Prentiss. She does, indeed, have a lot of expertise, and a lot of experience with direct contacts. She'd prefer you to believe that all direct contacts should be avoided, but in fact she loves them. She spent the better part of her early career in contacts."

"Maybe it isn't that she does not want contacts, she just doesn't like how they have been conducted," said Win.

"That wasn't the problem. She didn't get demoted for nothing. Let me ask you—when was the last time you heard of the Research Council demoting someone, especially a First Class?"

Win caught himself. He had assumed that Central Command had played a role in her demotion. A mistake in logic, a bad assumption. Had the loss of Sooni so dulled his mind that he had lost his ability to think clearly?

"I don't know of any, but that doesn't mean it hasn't happened."

"It's beyond rare," said Garrick. "The Research Council is a bunch of self important egotists. Even if someone they put in a high position turns out to be incompetent, they never do anything about it, otherwise it will reflect on their own mistake of promoting the person in the first place."

Though Win didn't share Garrick's obvious disdain of the Research Council, Garrick had a point. Something was wrong with the Prentiss story.

"There must be something else," argued Win. "She could not have made it to First Class if she were incompetent."

"Probably not," said Garrick. "But that isn't the point. I never said she was incompetent, just that it was extremely rare for the Research Council to demote anyone. No, Prentiss's problem is not about competence. Her problem is that she started believing too many of her own theories."

"What does this have to do with the mission?"

"Because you are expecting her to give you guidance on primitive cultures, and that is where she went haywire," said Garrick. "She started seeing all these similarities in the cultures she was studying—similarities to Earth, of all places. She wasn't even born on Earth, although she knows the history. She became almost fanatic trying to make the case that the development of all these cultures—spread all over the galaxy, with no means of association with one another—had similarities to the development of culture on Earth. Everywhere she looked, no matter how different and far away the culture, beings that weren't even biped—all she saw were parallels to the evolution of culture on Earth. She saw herself, first, as the conduit of this knowledge to the League, and then when they ignored her, as the protector of the local cultures, doing whatever she could to keep the League from affecting the cultural progression. In her mind, *any* kind of contact was detrimental. With her high-level position, she was very visible. It became embarrassing, even for the Research Council, because she was seeing these parallels and similarities in every shadow. So they demoted her—and plopped her in your lap."

"What kind of similarities? What kind of theory would cause the League such a problem?"

"It's not the problem to the League you should be concerned about," said Garrick. "Just the problem for the mission. You want an objective expert on the local culture? The local culture of the K'Turians, dominated by religion? You aren't going to get it from Prentiss. For those were the parallels she was seeing—*religious* ones. Her unifying theory of the universe is that every sentient culture echoes the religious development of Earth. She's a scientific nut. She's more likely to doom the mission than help it."

* * *

In the Materials Fabrication center, Prentiss wiped her sketch of the K'Turian clothing off the design screen for the third time. *No, no, no!* She forced herself to take a deep breath. It wasn't the image she was reacting to, it was the idea of the direct contact as part of a military mission. Every time she got the sketch right, she knew it brought her one step closer to colluding in the plan to land on the planet, to risk altering the culture of the people.

A sin. That's how she thought of it.

She hadn't always felt this way ... Her thoughts wandered back to the day she had made her presentation, entitled "A Catalyst for Cultural Transformation," to the most senior members of the Research Council. On Earth, of all places, where they had summoned her to explain—*to defend*—her theory.

"Let me see if I understand this, Specialist Prentiss," one of the members had said. "You are saying that cultural transformations can only come about by way of religion?"

Prentiss had tried to remain calm. She had already explained this, time and time again, in her writings, and in this meeting. "Not exactly. I am limiting my conclusions at this time only to societies that are under a repressive set of religious rules. Many such societies have stagnated because these rules do not allow for the personal freedoms that lead to self expression, to free thinking, to intellectual breakthroughs. I am making no claims for non religious cultures."

"But what, precisely, unblocks this cultural stagnation? You refer to," the council member gestured at Prentiss's presentation, "a *catalyst*, who frees the people. This is shorthand for a god, is it not?"

She wanted to scream as she watched the smirks flicker around the table. That wasn't what she had written, and they knew it. The entire idea of intellectual advancement having anything at all to do with religion was something the council could not—or would not—even consider. At that moment she realized the entire meeting was a charade. They weren't there to understand; they only wanted to be able to say that they had "considered all the evidence."

Shortly after the meeting she had been demoted. They hadn't taken away her title, which would have been embarrassing to the Research Council, the same council that had chosen her to be one of the few First Class level scientists. Instead, her ship and her crew had been "reassigned"—without her.

She was humiliated.

Prentiss had been given a choice between a dead-end research position on Earth—under the watchful eye of the council, she presumed—or stationing aboard another research vessel. It had not been a difficult decision for her, but the ignominy of it did not hit her until she had arrived on the *Anatar*. This aging, tiny craft, filled with pedestrian technicians that barely qualified as scientists. Geologists, chemists, astronomers. Not a cultural specialist in the entire crew. No one who dealt in *people*.

The *Anatar* was scientific purgatory.

After the demotion, she had vowed—partially out of spite she now realized, but this didn't change her mind—never to do *anything* that would ever draw attention to herself, or risk the ridicule and attacks of her peers or the council. She would reformulate her data, redraft her arguments, and find new evidence. She knew she was right; she simply had to find a way to convince everyone.

Yet here she was, preparing for a direct contact on a religiously governed world. Precisely the high visibility type of situation she had vowed to avoid. Normally a direct contact would have excited her, if she had her own crew of highly trained experts, sensitive to the culture they were about to study. Such a contact would have been carefully planned, and would have been designed to completely eliminate the risk of cultural contamination.

But that was not the case on K'Turia. They were rushing in to carry out some kind of covert military mission, and the local culture be damned. No telling what this group of clods would do.

Yet she was torn. Someone had to help mitigate the damage, and there was no one better able to do that than herself. At the least, she would try to convince Win to keep the direct contact as far from the people as possible, and to not bring in any technology at all—no weapons, no recorders, no communication devices. Just a glimpse of some advanced technology might give rise to wild cults of mysticism and magic. She had seen it happen.

She began another sketch. If they had to go to the planet, she wanted them to at least blend in.

* * *

"I don't like the way Central Command is handling this situation," said Win, as he offered I'Char a drink in his cabin. As usual, the Illian refused. "It's dangerous for us to be kept in the dark."

"What's best for us might not be best for Central Command—from their point of view," said I'Char.

"Meaning we are all expendable?"

"Exactly."

How could I'Char speak so calmly about a mission that might end in their deaths? Though he did not like the answer, Win was comforted by I'Char's honesty and directness. He sighed. "I know. What I really want to talk to you about is Prentiss."

"Yes. I thought you might."

"Garrick doesn't want her to be part of the direct contact team. He thinks she'll be a liability."

"On what grounds?"

"He doesn't trust her. Supposedly she has an obsessive fascination with religion, and we are about to make contact with a society that is very religious. Garrick thinks she'll be distracted."

Win got up and walked to his cabin window, looking out into the expanse of space, thinking of his own distractions. "I need her," he went on. "I need her expertise, her experience in direct contact. But if Garrick is right, if she becomes more interested in studying the culture—"

"She could draw attention to us."

"Precisely. So, from a tactical point of view, do I bring her?"

"Let me pose a question," said I'Char. "If Central Command had shared with you everything they knew about K'Turia, the people there, how they might view us—in short, all the usual information about a mission, would you be thinking of taking Prentiss?"

"Probably not." Win considered, then realized that I'Char had posed the question to teach Win something. "I see. They didn't share the information. It means they have left us on our own. Deniability?"

"Yes. For us, less knowledge is rarely better than more. I'd take her—as I can tell you want to. This isn't why you wanted to talk about the human. Something else is bothering you."

"Really?" Win was intrigued.

"You're wondering if you are only taking her to annoy Garrick, and to demonstrate your own authority."

Win smiled. "Perceptive. You'd make a good Treb."

"Not everyone would take that as a compliment," said I'Char.

"Just an observation. But what if Prentiss *does* get in the way?"

"I'll deal with it," said I'Char simply.

* * *

After I'Char left, Win went into *nore* again. This time he emerged even faster than before. The complex situation had resolved into only two possibilities, as diametrically opposite in implication as any he could imagine.

The first was that the mission was, essentially, as Garrick explained it: a search for a missing freighter on a planet that happened to have Lemians on it. Not that Garrick wasn't holding anything back, or that Central Command didn't have secret reasons for wanting the freighter, but the entire mission was separate from anything else going on in the galaxy.

The other possibility was far more disturbing, that the *Hauler One* had in fact been smuggling weapons to the insurgents on Colltaire, and that there was something in the terms of the Rhean alliance that prohibited such military action. The search was about the *cargo*, not the freighter. The League had to find the freighter before the Lemians did, without drawing attention to their search. Thus the urgency but no military vessel, a direct contact but one without the use of sensory technology.

But why would the League care if the Lemians found a cargo of weapons on a League ship? The League moved weapons around all the time.

It could only mean one thing. The League was afraid that the Lemians would understand the implications of finding those weapons on that particular freighter. It meant the Lemians knew—or the League thought they did—that the League had appealed to the Rheans. An appeal the League would only make out of desperation, a recognition that their days were truly numbered.

The mission would be a risk not only for his crew, but perhaps for the entire League. Failure might lead to galactic war—a war the League would certainly lose.

Even his numbness could not keep Win from shuddering at this thought.

Chapter 8

"Right this way, Sire." The Lemian soldier gestured down a long corridor. Dim light reflected off the gray walls. To Krelmar, all military buildings looked alike. He was thankful for the guide; he would have been lost in the maze of the offworld prefab building. The Lemians obviously did not want to suffer the ignominy of living in K'Turian buildings, which seemed to Krelmar from his brief view of the city to be nothing more than stone hovels—large enough, but hovels nonetheless, compared to the architecture on Colltaire. Or were the Lemians just trying to be sensitive to the locals, by not commandeering their buildings? Krelmar doubted it.

They came to an intersection of hallways, both the corridors exactly the same, unadorned and precise. *Soldiers!* he thought. *No imagination...*

The aide turned left and ushered Krelmar through a door marked "Commander."

From behind a simple, bare table a stern faced Lemian rose in greeting. "Lord Krelmar. Welcome to K'Turia. I am Commander Neel." Neel had the slight build and ruddy skin typical of Lemians. His uniform was impeccable. And like all the Lemians Krelmar had met, he had that haughty bearing of supremacy and undisguised strength. A brief image of Tera-Seil flashed into Krelmar's mind, the same cold, impersonal attitude.

"Thank you, Commander Neel." Krelmar kept his tone even, not letting any of his unhappiness show. He might not have been able to hide his emotions from Tera-Seil, but Neel was just a commander, not a High Councilor. Still, Neel was the highest authority on the planet—*was* the highest authority, until Krelmar arrived—and Krelmar would need Neel if he hoped to accomplish his mission.

Yet it would not do to appear weak. Krelmar was, after all, in charge. He motioned for Neel to sit, then eased his corpulent frame into one of the uncomfortable chairs in front of the table. He would have insisted on Neel's chair but he noticed it was exactly the same. "Tell me about our situation," he ordered.

Neel managed to appear at attention even while seated. "It has been mostly uneventful. This city has the largest population base on the planet. We have only a very small garrison, so we have concentrated our forces here. When we first arrived we posed as traders, bringing goods. But it was soon evident that the locals were not interested in our goods or where we came from. There has been no opposition to our presence; the society is very structured and orderly. Peaceful."

"How is this order maintained? Is there a local government?" asked Krelmar.

"There isn't one, or much of one. The people are very religious. Authority is held by the religious leaders, priests who sit atop a caste system—separate from it, actually. The priests have a lot more than the rest of the people, better homes, better clothing, better food." Neel spoke as if he disapproved of the religion, but approved of the authority. "Within their caste, which they call "the Order," the builders and craftspeople have the highest position, probably because of the difficulty of making anything on this infertile rock of a planet. Beneath them are the caretakers, and the rest of the villagers, like the old and the infirm. Then come the farmers. At the very bottom of the Order are the traders—they seem to be held in very low regard, because they don't actually make anything of value. It's another reason we stopped pretending to be traders. Each group in the Order is supported by the ones below it. The system, combined with the religious rules, seems effective at maintaining order."

"You say the priests are in charge? What has been their reaction to you and your troops?"

"As soon as they realized we were not going to challenge their religion, they ignored us. They seem not to care what we do as long as we do not run afoul of their religious rituals. I have yet to understand this religious nonsense, but for the most part it seems to require a lot of praying. They have a host of strict rules, only one of which concerns us—they don't want us in their temples."

"Is it possible they are hiding something?"

"They don't want us there, but I did not say we did not look." Neel said this without any emotion in his voice.

Krelmar understood the meaning in the Lemian's words: Neel was making it clear he was efficient and was not afraid of the locals. Krelmar nodded for Neel to continue.

"The temples are stone buildings, nothing more. The rules have to do with non-believers desecrating their religious sanctuaries. The doorways are wide open, we can look right in while they are praying, they don't care about that. They just don't want us inside."

"So a host of Lemian soldiers shows up on their planet, and they don't care?" Krelmar was unconvinced. It was not the kind of acceptance he would have expected anywhere.

"I know it is surprising," agreed Neel. "But from their point of view, no authority has been challenged, and we have kept a low profile. And since one has to be born into their religion to be part of it, we cannot be converted. So for the most part, they don't mind that we are here."

Krelmar noticed the equivocation. "For the most part?"

"They have their own subversives, just like every other culture. People who rebel against any authority. A few extremists within the religion. Some of them tried to stir up a little trouble, demanding that we leave. It didn't take hold, so we ignored it. They've also been suffering from a very long drought; crop yields are way down, and that has caused some discontent. The younger farmers want to do something else with their lives, but of course they cannot because of the Order."

Krelmar thought for a while. He didn't disagree with the Lemian's tactics. If the locals were not interfering, why push them? He was pleasantly surprised by the commander's restraint. But one thing bothered him.

"So we are not really in control, are we?" he asked.

"There really is nothing *to* control," said Neel. "They have no military, just a few sanctuary guards, armed with laughable swords. From what we can tell they've never had an armed conflict. They have no widespread communication network, in fact no mass communication at all. No technology, no important raw materials. We could imprison the religious leaders, but what would that accomplish? Then we would have to rule the planet, and perhaps deal with a rebellion, and we have very few troops here."

"So how will we get them to join us? As you know, we need this planet." *I* need this planet, Krelmar thought, otherwise I'll never get out of here.

Neel looked directly at him, still no emotion in his voice. "That is what I understand your role to be, Sire. I am, after all, only a soldier."

* * *

Krelmar sunk into the uncomfortable bed, nothing more than a thin mattress across some boards. Not even on K'Turia one day, he was already exhausted. After his meeting with Neel he had been shown to his 'accommodations,' one of the common sleeping rooms in the Lemian prefab. *This will not do,* he thought. *I am not going to live in a Lemian shed.*

He had already changed his mind about how to deal with the K'Turians. At first, Neel's strategy appeared sound. But with no government, it could take a long time to convince the locals it was in their best interest to join with the Lemians. Though Neel thought the Lemians had little to offer the religious leaders, Krelmar wanted to meet with them himself. Surely they wanted *something.*

Restless, he got up and looked out the window. Even the view was dreary. An unpaved street led away from the prefab toward the center of the city. All the buildings were similar, drab, nothing more than mortared stone. The people he saw were dressed in robes, wearing more clothing than he would have expected given the arid conditions.

From his vantage point he noticed a few taller buildings, but even these were barely a few stories. One had a rounded dome which shone in the sunlight, the only adorned architecture in view. Besides it, a few larger buildings, which even from this distance looked to be more carefully maintained. *There*. Those must be the living quarters of the wealthier residents. They must be more comfortable than this.

He looked around the bare room, clearly built for a soldier. *I'm going to be ruler of this planet, whether these people like it or not. Otherwise I'll never get back to Colltaire. And a ruler can't live in a barracks.*

More relaxed now, with a course of action clear in his head, he collapsed back into the bed and immediately fell asleep.

Chapter 9

The shuttle was flying low, running the valleys and staying behind as many hills as possible. I'Char was piloting the shuttle, the smallest transport vehicle available which would hold four. I'Char had narrowed the possible landing sites to two, and they were now quickly approaching the first chosen area. Win was watching for any sign of Lemian foot patrols or low copters. Prentiss, crammed into the back of the shuttle, was still upset about the direct contact and had said nothing on the entire trip. Garrick, not happy about having Prentiss along, was at least helping Win watch for Lemians.

The shuttle cleared a low hill, and immediately slammed to a halt, reversing course, jerking everyone back in their seats. Win had been looking out the side window and was surprised, saying, "What?"

I'Char was intent on banking the shuttle even lower than before, barely off the ground. Only when the craft had left the valley and cut behind a tall hill did the Illian calmly say, "There was a ground patrol on the access route to the landing site."

"Were we spotted?" asked Win.

"Not likely. They were on the far side of the valley, heading the other way. But we would have had to fly right over them."

"Lemians?" asked Garrick.

Prentiss finally spoke up. "Probably. The K'Turians have nothing to patrol, and they don't have a military."

"That we know of," corrected Garrick. "How did you know it was some kind of patrol?"

"Six on foot, wedge formation," replied I'Char.

"Typical Lemian tactics," said Garrick. "You're right, Lemians." And then, in a slightly different tone, he added, "Good eyes."

"Is there another way to the site?" asked Win. He had briefly reviewed and approved the landing sites, but this was I'Char's area of expertise.

"There is one, but if the patrol stays in the area they would surely spot us. Better to try the other site; we can always come back here if that one is no good."

Win nodded, but I'Char was already maneuvering the shuttle along the hill and away. From his briefing Win remembered that the second landing site was more remote, easier to hide in but a much longer walk into the city.

Soon they were in a more hilly area, the late day shadows already creeping into the slopes. Ahead the knolls rose up into a prominent tor, not exactly a mountain, but an extended ridge of some height. The shuttle ran along it and then skirted around to the back side, away from the city. On the other side of the ridge the land changed to a desert, bleak and empty.

"Better here," said Win.

"Unless someone enters this valley from the other side," said Garrick. "If they do they will see the shuttle."

Win craned his head to look at the valley. "Doesn't seem to be much here. Anyone heading toward the city would most likely go through the valley we just left."

"Or via the road, on the other side," said Prentiss. "Just because the K'Turians aren't technologically advanced doesn't mean they are stupid. They'll travel on the roads." Her voice was emotionless but the disapproval was clear.

Win ignored her insinuation. "Very well. This is it then."

I'Char ran the shuttle along the wall, looking for the best hiding place, finally setting down behind a rocky outcropping. The landing was so gentle they barely felt it.

"Not bad," said Garrick.

"Flattery won't work on him, Mr. Garrick," said Win, as he pushed open the shuttle door. Immediately his *gheris* lurched, a massive sensory overload of—what? He slumped back in the seat, the door snapping shut.

"Are you all right?" asked I'Char.

Win closed his eyes, breathing deeply. "Yes, just . . . never mind." He sensed no danger, just a staggering intensity of emotion. It reminded him of how he had felt back home, standing next to Sooni. What could have caused it? He looked through the window. Nothing but sand and rock.

Win cautiously opened the door, bracing himself. The sensation was still there, but he was ready for it now. What he wasn't quite ready for was the heat, which hit him like a furnace.

One by one they emerged from the small craft. They had already donned the garments that Prentiss had designed: loose fitting, hooded robes, tied at the waist, and open-laced sandals.

Before leaving the *Anatar* they had done what they could to alter their appearances. Prentiss had found some detailed information about K'Turian facial features, including some grainy photos, from the earlier contact. She had combined this with her knowledge of the planet's environment and probable lack of advanced medical care. For Win, this meant that instead of trying to hide the vertical creases on his high Treb forehead, the ship doctors did some minor cosmetic surgery that actually enhanced the lines, but made them look more like scars. I'Char had the ability to control his muscles in such a way that his entire facial structure changed. This was not something the Illian often did while on board; the shift tended to distress some members of the crew. Garrick's skin was already dark. Some simple chemicals had grown out his facial hair to hide his human features as much as possible. Prentiss had dyed her light colored hair and had her skin darkened. How much of a problem her human features would be was still a question; even her deep hood could not completely hide all of her face.

"If we're lucky, the people in Merculon won't get a good look at us, and if they do, perhaps they will think we are from somewhere else on the planet," Prentiss had explained to Win. "At least, I hope so. Otherwise, we might be a real shock to them."

The final preparation had been for the local language. They had tracked down the detailed logs from the earlier League survey visits, and had used the bio-algorithm system to spin out the language. It had been encapsulated into a memorygram and they had each undergone the immersion procedure. Limited technology, but efficient. Though many words were missing, they would have no problem communicating.

Prentiss had insisted that they not take instruments of any kind; nothing that would hint of an advanced technology. That meant they would have no way to communicate with the *Anatar*. Garrick had argued for weapons, but Win agreed with Prentiss. If discovered, a weapon would surely attract attention from the locals—perhaps enough attention to alert the Lemians.

The one thing they did take was a supply of food and water. Neither would last long, but they did not know what they could offer in barter, and they had no samples of the local currency. When Prentiss had brought this up, as yet another reason not to do a direct contact, I'Char had said, "We'll steal some." Prentiss stared at him, but Garrick had simply nodded.

I'Char was the last one out, and he secured the shuttle door. A slight breeze, not enough to dispel the heat, swirled the sand about their feet.

Garrick was in a hurry. "Let's get going. Which way?" He spoke to I'Char, apparently having come to the conclusion that the Illian's opinion was the most valuable.

Win was not upset. He was in charge, and he had some direct contact skills, but he would defer to I'Char on this. It also meant he didn't have to make a decision. Mediating between Garrick and Prentiss was already beginning to tire him.

"We have to go back around the tor," said I'Char. "From there we can cut directly across the valley, which will be faster than going through the hills."

"What do we do then?" asked Prentiss.

"Look for the road, of course," said I'Char. "We're not stupid either."

* * *

The setting sun brought no relief from the heat. They had been walking for quite some time but had not come upon any life on the planet—no animals, no people, nothing. The loose sand slowed them considerably, and their feet ached from the coarseness of the terrain and the uncomfortable sandals.

As they got closer to the city there was a brief discussion about how to make the final approach. Win wanted to stay out of sight as long as possible, at least until they understood more about what they were getting into. But Garrick insisted on the fastest route, the main road. Prentiss had pointed out that it would look suspicious to both the K'Turians and the Lemians if they traveled on anything but the road. This put her in agreement with Garrick, which neither one of them seemed to enjoy.

They finally saw the road as they emerged from the far end of the narrow valley. It wasn't much. Just a break in the sand, here and there a cairn, probably to guide travelers in a sandstorm. When they reached the road they discovered it was not paved, but was sufficiently hard packed, like clay.

"From now on, only speak in K'Turian," said I'Char. "If anyone spots a Lemian patrol, just keep walking, but don't ignore them—that would be more suspicious. Just nod, pay them marginal deference, and keep going." They had discussed all of this; he was just reminding them.

"Emphasis on the marginal," said Garrick.

"You want to get this done quickly," said Win, "then stay low profile and do as the K'Turians do."

Garrick grunted and increased his pace. The others followed suit. Ahead the road seemed to run directly into a hill, but as they approached it became clear that the road gradually wound its way up and around. As they began to climb they got their first surprise: here the road was paved with an artificial substance.

"Unicast," said Win, stooping to examine the pavement, unconsciously shifting into scientist mode. "Reasonably well laid.

Surely the K'Turians don't have this technology."

"I doubt they do," said Prentiss. "This must come from offworld."

Win looked ahead, following the neat, unbroken road. "This is a good deal of work. What would the K'Turians have to offer in exchange to get all this done, even from some offworld traders?"

"The Lemians," said Garrick. "The Lemians gave it to them."

"Is that something you know for sure?" asked Win. Meaning, *something else you haven't told us?*

"No, just an educated guess," said Garrick. "They are trying to buy their way in." He turned to Prentiss. "See? You don't have to worry about us contaminating the culture. It's already been done."

Prentiss eyed him coldly. "A few roads won't change a culture," she said. "We already know they have had offworld visitors. The road could have been built by anyone. Them knowing about offworlders doesn't mean that our presence won't have a dangerous effect on their culture."

Win cut her off. "Let's not have this debate now. What I need to know is: does this affect our contact strategy?"

"It might make it easier," said I'Char. "If the locals are comfortable with offworlders, we could pose as traders."

"We can't presume anything," argued Prentiss. "Our priority should still be to blend in as much as possible."

"Our priority is to find the freighter," said Garrick, sharply. Without waiting for an answer he started on up the road.

The others fell in behind, Win stopping occasionally to examine the roadwork and the extensive drainage. He could not tell how recently the construction had been completed. If the Lemians were providing this expertise, it would be something that the K'Turians might well appreciate, he thought. Might the K'Turians have already accepted Lemian control? If so, the K'Turians might report anything suspicious—like the appearance of strangers—to the Lemians.

Soon they reached the highest point on the road, which was well below the apex of the hill. The roadway turned a corner, the unicast construction forming a neat, gradual turn. When they rounded the bend they caught sight of the city, still a ways off in the distance.

Below them, the road wound its way down into the entrance valley, and then ran straight as an arrow into the center of Merculon. The tall ridge they had hidden the shuttle behind ran along to their left, forming one side of the valley. The other side was open, just a hint of mountains far off in the distance. Between them and the city lay a vast farmland, the first green they had seen on the planet.

"Look at the taller building in the middle," said Garrick. "Looks to be precast metal. Probably more Lemian interferences."

Prentiss shook her head. "I believe it is a temple," she said. "They would adorn the temple with something of value, a local ore probably." She seemed pleased to have found something else to disagree on with Garrick.

"We'll see," said Garrick. "But if that isn't prefab, I'm sure something else will be. I can't imagine that the Lemians are living in stone huts."

Win had tuned them out. They were arguing about nothing, a foolishness he was growing weary of. He concentrated his attention on the road that led into the city, lined with small buildings which appeared to be houses. He could not tell specifically where the city proper began and the outskirts ended, but there was a gradual thinning out of the buildings on this end of the valley. They had still not seen any people. The houses appeared deserted.

"No one around?" mused Win.

"Most of the people will be working in the fields." Prentiss pointed off toward the farmland, "Or they will be in the city during the day. Remember that this is an agrarian and trading culture. If they are not working the fields, they are preparing foodstuffs or are in the marketplaces. The craftspeople will also be in the city."

"The day is almost over," said I'Char. "Which means that soon people will be returning to these homes. If we go into the city now we'll be going against the flow. It might make us more noticeable."

"We can't wait here and waste any time," said Garrick. "Let's get a move on."

Win was torn. He wasn't accustomed to making these snap decisions, especially when he had little data, and where his primary sources of advice had personal feelings that might be affecting their judgment. He wanted to get this over with as soon as possible, but he also wanted to avoid unnecessary risks. He hesitated, hoping he would see something below that would help him decide. But nothing moved. The road remained empty all the way to the city. He looked up at the sky; not yet dark, but the sun would be behind the ridge soon. He had no reason to doubt I'Char's assessment that the road would soon be filled with people, all heading toward them.

"What about the Lemians?" he asked. "They more likely to be coming this way too?"

"I doubt it," said Garrick. "They aren't going to follow the locals home."

"I agree," said I'Char. "The Lemians will stay in the city if they are in their typical policing mode."

Win still couldn't decide. "Prentiss?"

"I don't think we should go in at all," she said sullenly.

"You've made that clear. But we have to get this done, whether you like it or not." Win was getting annoyed at her. "So you might as well help to minimize the risks to us—and to the locals."

Reluctantly, she said, "The locals will see us soon enough. Let's go down to the valley. If a host of people head out of the city all at once and we look out of place we can always turn around. On the other hand, if we see anyone else heading in, we might have a chance to blend in with them. There will always be some people in the city, for food and entertainment, and perhaps evening prayers."

"Let's go on then," said Win. He led the way down the road, and soon they reached the valley floor. Here the road was still paved, and it looked to be all the way into the city. In moments they passed the very first of the huts, crudely made of stacked stone. A small livestock pen bordered one side of the house. It was empty.

"Probably the home of a farmer or laborer," explained Prentiss. "The poorest people will be farthest from the city. It's unlikely anyone will be in any of these homes until dark."

"Don't count on it," said I'Char. "We're being watched. From the window of the next house. Keep moving, don't stop and stare."

As Win glanced at the building he at first saw nothing, but then made out a slight movement behind a window. An old man? Win marveled at I'Char's powers of observation; surely he would have never picked out the silhouette in the dimness.

They continued on, passing the hut, Win feeling the eyes on them, his *gheris* prickling. *I must be getting jumpy,* he thought. *Just an old man...*

"Probably an invalid," whispered Prentiss. "Or a pauper, too old to work. This indicates—"

She was interrupted by the sound of footsteps behind them, coming quickly. Almost as one they whirled around, coming face to face with the old man, who stopped suddenly, his eyes widening as the four turned on him. For a moment no one spoke, and the man studied them one by one. His face was withered and thin, gaunt and dark from years in the sun. A tattered cloak scarcely covered his bony body, the hood thrown back, showing his bald head. A scraggly beard grizzled out from his chin.

Win was trying to decide whether or not to speak. The old man saved him, breaking the silence.

"You are strangers!" challenged the K'Turian. He stared straight into Win's eyes, his fingers twitching. He seemed either deranged, or he had seen through their disguises. Or both.

Win looked at Prentiss for help.

"Yes, we are strangers, travelers!" she responded quickly.

The old man looked them up and down, as if searching for clues. He gave only a cursory glance at I'Char, but stared for a long time at the others. "You are pilgrims then!" he said finally.

Prentiss tried to buy some time. "This is our first visit here, to this part of the world," she said.

The old man was not appeased. "Pilgrims!" he repeated. His voice dropped to a whisper. "You are here to see *him*." He seemed to grow nervous, looking over their shoulders toward the city. "They will find you. You must come with me!" He turned away and started to move back toward his house. "I will hide you, for a little while. That is all I can do. But you must hurry!" he said over his shoulder.

"Wait!" called Win. "Why must we hide? *Who* will find us?"

The old man stopped, but before he could reply Garrick cut in. "Are you going to waste time here with this old fool, or are we going into the city before the horde starts this way?"

The old man ignored Garrick. "The Pertise! If you are not one of the Lemians, or the Pertise, then—"

"The Lemians?" interrupted Win, his worst fears realized.

"The Pertise?" asked Prentiss. Win glanced at her, annoyed; they needed to find out about the threat from the Lemians.

The man was almost babbling now, and he ran back to grab Win's arm. "You must hurry! You are not Lemians, and so the Pertise will think you are pilgrims!"

"Pilgrims?" asked Win. Was the old man telling them they needed to fear someone other than the Lemians? "Who are the pilgrims coming to see?"

"Why Jesus, of course!"

Prentiss gasped, "Jesus? You mean Jesus *Christ?*"

The old man appeared confused. "Who?" He began to mumble, rapidly, as if in prayer, while pulling on Win's arm, trying to drag him away. Then he let go and ran off, calling out, "You must hide! Hurry!"

Prentiss started after him, but Garrick grabbed her arm. "You are *not* going to follow that idiot." It sounded like an order.

Prentiss shook him off. "You don't understand," she said, as if Garrick were the idiot. Excitedly, she turned to Win. "They should never even have *heard* of Jesus Christ here! We have to find out what this means!" Without waiting for a response she ran after the old man.

Win did not argue. They had to learn more about what dangers they might be facing. And though he didn't know as much about primitive cultures as Prentiss, her excitement was contagious.

Jesus Christ?

Chapter 10

Krelmar had demanded that his office and quarters be located in the best K'Turian building available, rather than the Lemian base. Although the locals would certainly associate him with the Lemians, he wanted to do whatever he could to quickly gain their trust—or at least avoid their hatred. Besides, the camp was too uncomfortable.

It had taken some doing. Being primarily an agrarian society, there were almost no facilities to rent other than market stalls and storage areas. Tsaph, the local aide who Commander Neel had assigned to Krelmar, had finally found a solution. Tsaph offered the use of a large house that had belonged to some recently deceased relatives, in exchange for some offworld products to be sold in the family market.

Tsaph had already become indispensable to Krelmar. The K'Turian had completed all the work necessary to establish Krelmar's office and had done much to improve the comfort of his residence on the second story as well. Neel had explained that Tsaph was of the trader caste. The traders, at the lower end of the Order, were the only ones willing to deal openly with the Lemians. Tsaph was the primary liaison for goods coming into the city and had been one of the first to barter with the Lemians.

Once established in his new quarters, Krelmar's first order of business had been to summon Commander Neel. The Lemian arrived promptly, his uniform crisp and neat.

"I want to meet with the local leaders today," said Krelmar.

Neel hesitated. "Today would be—difficult—Sire."

"Difficult? Aren't they here in the city?"

"Yes. In fact, they are all together, Sire. But today is their weekly holy day. They are in their temple right now."

"Excellent! I'll simply go see them there."

Neel started to respond but Krelmar held up his hand. "Yes, yes, I remember now. They don't want us in their temple, right?"

Neel appeared relieved, but Krelmar went on: "This will have to change at some point. When the planet comes fully under Lemian domain, you certainly must not let the locals dictate the rules on where you can and cannot go."

If Neel noticed Krelmar's use of the word "you" he did not mention it. "It seems a small price to pay for the time being. As I said before, there is little they could hide in the temple. Of course we could force our way in, if that is your order."

This Neel is no fool, thought Krelmar. He'd send the troops into the temple, but only if Krelmar insisted, so if it riled the locals it would be Krelmar's fault.

"No, no, that won't be necessary. Tomorrow then? Can we see them tomorrow?" Krelmar asked, not bothering to hide his sarcasm.

"As you wish, Sire. In fact, I think they very much look forward to meeting you."

"And why is that? I thought you said they were not particularly interested in us, or what we had to offer."

"I believe they are more interested than they let on. And most likely, they have no idea of what we could offer. We have made no significant overtures to them as of yet, other than providing some basic goods and paving the main road as a goodwill gesture. I have no orders—or authority—to negotiate on behalf of the Empire. My orders were only to establish a forward base, keep it secure, avoid initial hostilities, and wait for you."

Wait for me? thought Krelmar. That wasn't possible—unless Tera-Seil had planned on sending him to K'Turia for a long time. Krelmar decided to let this pass for now; there was no sense in telling Commander Neel more than he needed to know, for the man certainly would be reporting back to his Lemian superiors.

But Krelmar would certainly remember this little slip.

In his smoothest voice he changed the subject. "From what you have seen, what will convince the people to join us, short of using force?"

"It is hard for me to tell, Sire. The reaction to our offerings, such as our paving of the road, was quite mixed. The traders and farmers seemed to appreciate it, for it makes their lives easier. The religious leaders have said nothing, not even acknowledging the work. I will tell you that few people here seem to need or want any," Neel groped for the right word, "*material* things. They own very little. There is some special coinage, but it is used only for specific religious transactions. There is no desired ore, the people do not wear jewelry, and there is nothing hoarded for value."

Krelmar found this hard to believe. "Certainly there must be something they covet."

"They do, Sire, but those items seem to be religious in nature and are not used to measure wealth."

"What about taxes? There must be taxes, how are they paid?"

"Yes, they do understand taxation. They actually have a very complex tax system, all managed by the priests. The taxes are paid in goods, and flow up through the castes; the priests keep what is left."

"But they trade for goods, yes? Wouldn't they want to trade for some offworld things?"

"There is some trading. But mostly out of necessity, like for food. Those who trade to make a profit are held in low regard. And the religious leaders—the Pertise—shun the offworld products we have brought, which dampens how the people look upon anything not made here."

"These leaders—the Pertise? They seem to control everything," said Krelmar.

"They do. They set the rules upon which the people conduct their entire lives, how and what they eat, where and when they pray, how they interact with each other. There are strict rules, for instance, in how men and women act, and even how they communicate with each other."

Krelmar was thinking ahead. "This control they wield, it could be a benefit to us."

"What do you mean, Sire?"

Krelmar smiled, seeing how he might use his political skills. "Think about it. You understand the idea of control, of how the few decide for the many. We need not convince—or control—the entire population. Just the religious leaders. Get them to go along, and the whole planet is ours." *And I can go home.*

"Yes, Sire, although . . ."

"Although what?"

"The religious leaders may be rather difficult to convince by just offering them offworld goods."

"You surprise me, Neel. It seems you would prefer negotiation to force. Not what I would have expected of a military man."

Neel sat up straighter. "Do not misunderstand me, Lord Krelmar. I am willing—and able—to do whatever is necessary. But these people are very independent, and we have very few troops. If there is a general uprising we will have to use extreme force. Once we do that, it cannot be undone. The chance for negotiation would be lost."

Krelmar apprised the Lemian. "You missed your calling, Neel. You should have been a politician."

Neel eyed him suspiciously, perhaps trying to see if Krelmar had been serious—or had been insulting him. Krelmar decided to let the Lemian wonder. He changed the subject again. "You said that the Pertise might actually want to see me. Much as I'd like to think they desire to join the Empire, it makes me suspicious."

"I agree, Sire. They usually go out of their way to avoid us."

"Can you think of any other reason they would want to meet with me?"

Neel hesitated. "I am a soldier, not an expert in politics, Sire." A slight smile crossed his lips. "I do have one idea. I think they may be attempting to use us to help them solve a—dilemma—that they are facing. If you recall I reported there were some problems with local subversives. It seems one of them in particular is causing trouble. He is trying to stir up the people against the religious leaders."

"Why should they care?" asked Krelmar. "If they are as powerful as you say, why not deal with this insubordinate themselves?"

"Because he appears to be growing in popularity. The Pertise may have missed their chance—he may already be too powerful. From what I understand, the priests have only two options in their laws to solve this problem—banishment or death. Neither would be popular with this man's followers, and may even lead to some kind of revolt."

"So these religious leaders are not so different after all," said Krelmar. "Just looking out for their own power."

"Perhaps," said Neel. "The Pertise may openly ask for help in controlling this threat, or they may try to manipulate us into doing something which causes the locals to blame us. The Pertise think we are rather dimwitted. I do not trust them."

And I doubt they trust us either, thought Krelmar. Still, this gave him an idea. Maybe he could offer a trade. He'd take care of their problem, if they would take care of his. After all, he didn't care if the people hated the Lemians. He'd be long gone anyway.

Chapter 11

The old man beckoned them in. After the briefest of hesitations Win started forward, but I'Char blocked him. Without taking his eye off the hut the Illian said, "Me first," and he pushed past the old man. The others waited tensely until I'Char reappeared at the door and said, "It's clear."

They quickly filed in, squeezing past the old man, who continued his furtive looks toward the city. When they were all inside the man latched the flimsy door and closed the shutter on the window facing the road.

The hut was dark, lit only by a small lantern on a simple table. The room was bare except for the table and a bench, two chairs, a small stove, and some cooking utensils. Along the back wall were two open doors leading to other rooms. I'Char stood in one of the doorways. "No rear door, but we can get out through a back window if we have to. One room is a sleeping quarters, the other a storeroom. That's it." I'Char disappeared into the sleeping room and they could hear what sounded like a window shutter being opened.

The old man was leaning with his back against the door, as if his frail frame could provide another layer of protection. "You will be safe here—for a while."

"You said we should hide from someone?" asked Win, carefully. "The Pertise?"

"They do not like strangers . . . You must be very careful—they will punish you!" The man began to babble again, talking rapidly, launching into some mysterious litany they could not follow.

His fingers continued their agitated twitching.

Win tried not to get exasperated. *Think of it as a scientific problem,* he thought. *First, gather information...*

He tried another approach. "How did you know we were strangers?"

The old man's fingers stopped their frantic movements. "You came from across the mountain, from Valdar. I saw you." He pointed in the direction of the hill they had climbed.

"Valdar?" asked Garrick.

Prentiss answered his question. "Another city, on the other side of the ridge, then a few days walk across the desert."

"What's wrong with coming from Valdar?" asked Win.

"The Valdenese do not come here anymore. The Pertise do not allow it. They drive them out, or worse." At the mention of the Pertise the man became agitated once again.

Take it slow, thought Win. "Why do the Pertise drive the people from Valdar away?" he asked.

"Because they are believers. Truthseekers! They believe in him!"

Before Win could respond, Prentiss said, "Believers? Believers in Jesus Christ?"

Once again the old man appeared confused. "What is 'Christ?' I speak of Jesus." His eyes sharpened. "Are you followers of Jesus? Then you must not let them find you!" The K'Turian shook his head passionately. "I can hide you for the night." He leaned back against the door and closed his eyes. "Then you must leave..."

Win turned to Prentiss and said quietly, "We need to do this one step at a time, Research Specialist Prentiss. I understand your desire to study this—*situation*. But first we must find out about any threat to us. Do I make myself clear?"

Prentiss stared at him and nodded curtly. "But then we have to explore this further. It is—"

Win cut her off. "Agreed. But only when I say." He turned back to the old man. "What is your name?"

The man opened one eye, quizzically, as if looking for a trap in the question. Finally he said, "I am Symes."

"Symes," said Win, "we *are* strangers. Please tell me why you think we are in danger."

"You are from Valdar," said Symes, cautiously. "You must know."

Garrick cut in. "Win, the man is senile. Let's get out of here. We've got work to do."

Win stepped in front of Garrick, angry now. He whispered, "There is something going on here, Mr. Garrick. I'm not walking us into danger. If he was able to figure out we were strangers, so will others. And apparently, strangers are not welcome here."

In too loud a voice Garrick snapped, "Pure luck on his part. He saw us walking from the direction of Valdar—you heard him."

"So you did come from Valdar!" exclaimed Symes. "Just like I said!" But it was less an accusation, and more like a child confirming a discovery.

Win turned back to the K'Turian. "We are not from Valdar," he said quietly. "We are from—another place."

"Then you are offworlders!" said Symes, smiling broadly, once again appearing to revel in his own powers of deduction. But then his voice turned dark. "You must still hide. The Pertise do not like offworlders either!" He lowered his voice. "Especially the Lemians."

That is interesting, thought Win. "Why don't the Pertise like the Lemians?"

The old man looked at him suspiciously again. "Are you sure you are not Lemians?"

"We can assure you, we are certainly not Lemians," said Garrick, dryly.

Win glanced over at Garrick, but the curt denial seemed to actually calm the old man. "The Pertise do not like the Lemians because they are not of us, and do not follow our Ways," explained Symes. "And the Pertise do not like the Valdenese because they are believers. So the Pertise will not like you if you are from either Valdar or offworld!" He smiled, pleased with his logic.

This man is not as senile as he appears, thought Win. *And he doesn't seem to be surprised by offworlders. That might help . . .*

"What if we are not from Valdar or offworld?" asked I'Char, who had reappeared in the doorway to the back room. "Will we be in danger if we go into the city?"

"That depends," said Symes, scratching at the gristle on his chin. "On whether you are believers!" He lowered his voice, as if asking to share a secret. "Are you?"

"Not yet, anyway," mumbled Garrick. Win cast him a stern look, but the old man appeared not to have heard.

Prentiss caught Win's eye. "I think it is time we understand more about the believers. If we might be in danger—"

Win raised his hand, cutting her off. He knew she was simply trying to find another way to question the old man about Jesus, yet he could not see any way of avoiding it. And the scientist in him was intrigued. He nodded.

Prentiss took a step toward the old man and touched his shoulder. Very softly, she said, "We do not know enough to be believers. Can you tell us more, about—about what they believe?"

The old man smiled, apparently relishing the role of teacher. "They believe in Jesus, and his message."

Win thought he would go on, but Symes seemed to think that was explanation enough. Win asked, "And this is what puts people in danger?"

"Yes, yes!" said the old man. "The Pertise hate the believers, and they hate Jesus. If they ever catch him . . ." Symes's voice trailed off, as if the thought was too much to even consider.

"What do the Pertise do to the believers?" asked Prentiss. Her voice was patient, quiet. "Do they hurt them?"

Win was amazed at the transformation in her. Her icy, scientific manner had softened to one of concern, but he could also sense an excitement in her, as if she had discovered a new specimen to analyze.

The old man looked away. "Sometimes," he said.

Prentiss leaned closer, but her entire demeanor was one of empathy, not threat. "Did they hurt you?"

Symes' ducked his head and his hand went to his back, as if

reaching for a injury. "Yes," he said quietly. "They hurt. They call themselves righteous, but they hurt."

"Did they think you were a believer?" she asked.

Smart, thought Win. She had not asked him directly if he was one of the believers, which would have forced Symes into a corner. *So this is how she got to be a First Class Specialist . . .*

The old man looked directly into her eyes. "I am!" he said fiercely. "I am a believer!" For a moment he seemed defiant, but then he cowered, searching all of their faces. "You won't tell, will you? If the Pertise find out . . . Please don't tell!"

Prentiss tenderly put her arm around the man, soothing him. "We won't tell them, I promise. But we are strangers, and do not know anything about all this. We would like to learn more, and we need your help." She led him to a chair.

"Help?" Symes's voice was calmer.

Win picked up on what Prentiss was trying to do. "Yes, help. We don't want to upset the Pertise. Can you tell us how we can be safe?"

The old man straightened up, the growing importance of the position that Win was bestowing on him having an effect. "Yes, I will help you. I can hide you, that way you will be safe."

"We need to go into the city," said Garrick.

Symes shook his head. "No, not now. Now is not the time. You must stay here for the night."

"This is getting us nowhere," said Garrick.

"Do many strangers come to Merculon, besides the Lemians?" asked Win, ignoring Garrick.

"Not any more," Symes replied sadly. "At one time, many came, from Valdar and other places, even offworld. But the Pertise banished the strangers, and punished the believers."

"But what of those who visit who are not believers?" asked Win.

"Who would come to Merculon unless they wanted to hear Jesus?" asked Symes, surprised. "The Pertise will think you are believers, they will punish you too!"

Win sensed an opening. "But if people do not display their belief openly? Are they safe then?"

"Yes, but this is not the way of Jesus. He teaches everyone that they should proclaim their belief. But many are still afraid to do this, because the Pertise are watching. They keep believers from entering the temple! Yet many do believe, but only in secret, because they do not wish to lose the Way." Symes took a deep breath, as if this long flow of thought had taken a toll on him. Again he reached around to his back.

"We will do nothing to get you in trouble," said Prentiss. "If staying here is dangerous to you we will leave."

"Might be hard now, given his suspicions," said I'Char, quietly. Prentiss spun on the Illian. "What are you suggesting?"

"Nothing—yet," said I'Char calmly, not flinching from her gaze.

Prentiss looked back at Symes and said, "We will not let anyone harm you, nor harm you ourselves." She looked over at Win, defiant, her gaze challenging him to rebuke her.

The woman was confounding. Now I understand why she was demoted, thought Win. But he would deal with her later. Right now they could not afford a confrontation that would upset the old man, and they needed more information from him. "Tell us more about the Pertise," he said.

Symes glanced up at Prentiss, as if looking to her for approval before answering the question. It appeared he had accepted her promise of safety. Only after she nodded did he say, "The Pertise are the most chosen of the priests; they are the guardians of the Way. They tell us how to live the Way, so that we may reach Paradise."

"What is the Way?" asked Prentiss.

"It is how we live, how we act, who we are," said Symes, as if reciting a childhood litany. "Each is born to their own position in the Order: the builders, the craftspeople, the caretakers, the villagers, the farmers, the traders. We must all pay a Sacrifice—the traders to the farmers, the farmers to the villagers—all the way up the Order to the priests of the Temple. The priests keep all that is left over, on behalf of the people, until it is needed in Paradise. Being satisfied with our positions keeps us at peace. We must follow the rules of the Way exactly, so that we may reach Paradise." As the old man said this his eyes glowed, and his voice softened, as if just the mention of Paradise brought him happiness.

"Paradise," said Prentiss, gently. "It sounds beautiful. Have many found it?"

"I don't know. I don't think so," said Symes, sadly. "The priests say it is very difficult, and that we will have no chance if we stray from the Way. And that any who do not follow the Way will be damned, and lost, and will never find Paradise."

"And what does Jesus teach?" asked Prentiss.

Symes's tone changed, no longer reciting from memory. His voice was stronger, more passionate. " Jesus tells us the Pertise should not keep our Sacrifices, and that they have no right to threaten us or punish us. He says all of us can find Paradise, but to do so we must give up many of our old beliefs. We have to do more than just blindly follow the rules of the Way."

Prentiss whispered, almost in awe, "The catalyst!"

Garrick spun on Win. "I told you it was a mistake to bring her!" Garrick strode forward and grabbed Prentiss by the arm, forcing her to face him. "I will not say this again. Our mission is to find the freighter. We are not going to get sidetracked by your crazy theories!"

Prentiss shook her arm free. "And I will say not say *this* again. *I don't work for you!*"

She looked over at Win, her face a mix of defiance and pleading.

"Mr. Garrick—both of you. Stop it." Win turned back to Symes, softening his tone. "I am confused," he said, trying to appeal to the man's helpfulness. "Are the Pertise in charge, or have the Lemians taken over the government?"

Symes frowned. "Government?" He pronounced the word as if he had never heard it.

"The representatives of the people here," explained Win. "The ones who make the decisions, enforce the laws."

"I do not understand what you say," said Symes. He did not appear suspicious, only puzzled. "All our laws revolve around the Way, as taught to us by the Pertise. We live our lives based on the Way. The Lemians have nothing to do with the Way."

"And so the Pertise have great power?" asked Win.

"Yes," replied Symes. "They enforce the Way."

"And so the believers are—trapped," said Prentiss. "They have been taught to follow the Way, yet they are drawn to the message of Jesus: that the way to Paradise should not be based on a fear of punishment."

"Yes!" said Symes, his eyes widening. "You understand!"

"But the Pertise cannot punish all the believers, can they?" asked Win.

"It is too late now, there are too many of them," said Symes. He reached up to pull Prentiss close to him, as if sharing a secret. "And there are other reasons!" he whispered loudly.

Prentiss leaned close. "What reasons?"

The old man continued in his whispered tone, although they could all hear him clearly. "Because some of the Pertise are believers too! And—," he looked around the room and lowered his voice even more, "because they are afraid of Jesus! Some say he has worked miracles. This makes them afraid."

Garrick let out a grunt. "Come on, Win," he said, the exasperation clear in his voice. "It's obvious what is going on here. Some local lowlife is angry because he was born on the bottom end of the ladder, and he is using this as a way of getting some power. Or some crank from offworld is leading these people on by pretending that he is Jesus Christ."

Symes leapt up and cried, "No, that is not true! Jesus is not an offworlder—he is from Valdar!"

"How do you know that?" asked Garrick, harshly.

"I—I—I've heard people talk. It is no secret," said Symes, his voice defiant.

"Do you know it for sure?" Garrick persisted. "The Lemians are from offworld. You think we might be from offworld. Why not this Jesus?"

"No, he is one of us! He is . . ." said Symes. But he seemed confused again.

"You see?" said Garrick. "This is not a problem for us. We just need to avoid being taken as believers, or whatever, and stay out of this grand charade. Let's get going."

Prentiss said, "I agree. We should go." When Win looked at her in surprise, she explained, "We need to find out more about *this* Jesus."

"We have something else to look for," said Garrick. "And that something is not a charlatan."

Win looked back and forth between Prentiss and Garrick, both of them defiantly staring at him. Reluctantly, he felt himself agreeing with Garrick. Almost apologetically, he said to Prentiss, "While this—," he struggled to come up with the right word, "—*situation* is very interesting, we have something we must do." He turned to Symes. "If we go into the city now, will we be recognized as strangers, and be in danger?"

"Yes!" said Symes. "That is why you must hide here!"

"But what if we do not say we are believers?" asked Win. "Surely other strangers have come who are not believers. Like the Lemians. It will be dark soon. Perhaps no one will notice us."

"You do not understand," said Symes. "No one goes into the city at night!"

Win suddenly realized that the man had never said they could never go into the city; they were forgetting his simple thought patterns. "Do you think we could safely go into the city tomorrow?"

Symes looked at each of them, especially Prentiss. "You must wear your hoods," he said. "And tomorrow will be good, for the city will be very crowded. You should not be noticed." He pointed a bony finger at Garrick. "There will be crowds tomorrow. You'll see."

"Why will it be very crowded tomorrow?" asked Prentiss.

"Because Jesus will be preaching, in the arena! He has never done this before. Never! Many will come, to hear him!"

"Or to see what happens to him," said I'Char.

But Symes appeared not to have heard. "Yes, you can go tomorrow. Then you can hear him too—and you will believe!" And with that he broke into a huge smile, radiant, and he reached out for Prentiss's hand. "Yes, you will believe!"

Chapter 12

"I don't like it," said Garrick. "While we are sitting here a whole regiment of Lemians could be sneaking up on us. This could be some kind of trap."

Early evening, and they were still in the hut. The old man, much calmer after confiding in them, had offered up some bitter wine and then had quickly fallen asleep in one of the chairs. Now the *Anatar* crew sat around the small table, talking in whispers.

"A trap? That's nonsense," said Prentiss. "You think they sent an old man to weave an intricate story to trap us? About someone named Jesus, of all things! If they knew we were here, they would have just rounded us up. What you can't seem to get through your head is that the people on this planet should never have heard of Jesus Christ. This is something we have to investigate! It could have profound implications for our understanding of the religious impact on primitive cultural development."

Garrick said coldly, "You don't know that he was talking about Jesus Christ. He didn't even recognize the word 'Christ.' And don't pretend that we don't know of your infatuation with this universal religious theory."

Prentiss hesitated. "I'll admit that this is an area of interest for me. But even if it were not this would be something to look into. Captain Win, certainly you must realize we have an opportunity here that might never come along again."

"I'm growing weary of you and your obsessions, Prentiss," Garrick responded, dismissively. "You can look into it after we find the freighter, for all I care. But not now. Or have you forgotten why we are here? Win?"

Win looked at Prentiss. She was obviously trying to appeal to his scientific curiosity, and was perhaps even attempting to manipulate him. Part of him *was* interested. And his *gheris*—still vibrating. *Something* was going on here.

Still . . .

"We *will* look for the freighter," said Win, "although if we knew why it was so important it would help us understand why we should focus on that exclusively." He waited, but when Garrick didn't take the bait he continued, "But Symes's story makes me uneasy."

Win turned to Prentiss. "Do you really think he is talking about someone named Jesus Christ? Garrick has a point. Symes just said 'Jesus.' It could be a common name on K'Turia, or some bad translation in our language algorithm. Or an imposter. Are you sure they should know nothing of Jesus Christ here?"

"I can't see how," she replied, shifting once more into her formal scientific demeanor. "I saw no mention of him in our research of the planet."

"Perhaps by way of literature, or an offworlder's written history?"

"Possible, but who would have brought it? Certainly not the Lemians."

"I can't believe this conversation!" exploded Garrick. "I'm not from Earth, and I know of Jesus Christ. You're not even human and you know him as well, Win." He turned to I'Char, who nodded. "See?" said Garrick. "Everyone in the League knows who he is. Someone found out about the story and is having a little fun with the locals. They could have got a Bible from anywhere, some trading or colonizing vessel a long time ago. Maybe someone from the prior League contact left one behind."

"That's unlikely," said Prentiss. "Who would have translated it? And if it did happen that way, certainly everyone would know that the origin of the story was from a book. Symes didn't mention a book."

"The book might be in Valdar," said Garrick. "Or it could have disappeared. None of it matters. We've got to find the freighter. Once that is done—and we need everyone here working together on that—you can come back anytime and analyze to your heart's content. These people aren't going anywhere." He added, "Of course, the Lemians might object, but maybe you can just explain to them how *important* it is."

Prentiss stared at him. "I just might," she said. "They probably have more interest in science than you do."

"I'd be careful if I were you," warned Garrick. "Not only is that treasonous, but you might find the Lemians unlikely to believe your story, and think instead that you are some kind of spy."

"Enough of this," said Win. "Let's focus on the job at hand. This entire situation may be a blessing in disguise. If we are in any danger—from these Pertise or the Lemians—Symes can help hide us. He can also supply us with valuable information about the city."

"If he's telling the truth," said Garrick.

Win glanced over at Symes, who was snoring quietly. "I admit his faculties might be impaired. But clearly he is afraid of something. And why would he lie? We will certainly find that freighter faster with some local help. He's already proven his worth by telling us we'd be marked as outsiders if we went into the city at night."

"It's getting late," said Garrick. "We could sneak in when there is no one on the road."

"And accomplish what at night?" asked Win. "Darkness has its advantages, I agree. But if we are the only ones moving around, we might draw attention to ourselves, if not from the locals, then from the Lemians. Unless you think the Lemians have the freighter and have brought it to the city?"

"Anything is possible," said Garrick, his eyes darting away. "The first thing we need to find out is if the Lemians know about the freighter. And the place to start is the Lemian base."

"You didn't say anything about sneaking around the Lemian base," said Prentiss, hotly.

Garrick turned cold eyes on her. "What did you think this was going to be, a picnic?"

"This is why everyone hates Central Command," said Prentiss, the anger clear in her voice. "All this playing soldier. We'd have a better chance of moving around unmolested if we just walked up to the Lemians and explained to them that we are a scientific crew—which we are, except for you!—and we've come to research Jesus."

Garrick shook his head. "I can't believe you are such a fool. You keep forgetting the Lemians are our enemies."

"*Your* enemies, maybe," said Prentiss. "I'm a scientist."

"The Lemians don't care about science unless it will help them," said Garrick. "You think they would fund a Research Council? And don't forget you are human. Even though we are not at war—yet—to them, you will *always* be the enemy. You can heap as much scorn as you want on Central Command, but they are the ones who keep you alive." He turned to Win. "I told you not to bring her."

"I make the decisions about my crew," replied Win, holding Garrick's eye.

After a long moment Garrick said, "Look, this is getting us nowhere. You have to agree that approaching the Lemians is crazy. And there are things we can find out at night that we can't during the day."

Win turned to his military advisor. "I'Char?"

"The freighter is big enough that there will be few places where it can be hidden," said I'Char. "We'll be able to spot any such building easier during the day than at night. If we are going to break into a building, we need to know the best routes in—and out. I've studied all the ground photos from the records, and the long distance scans from the ship, but none of this tells us what the Lemians have in the way of patrols and what they may have done in terms of creating a perimeter. My advice would be to go in during the day and lose ourselves in the crowd, so we can gather as much information as possible—and then return tomorrow night if we have to."

Win nodded. As usual, I'Char made sense. "Would the Lemians buy a story that we are here to do research?"

"We'd have to make that decision now, and it is very risky. If we go in under any other guise, the Lemians will never believe us if we tell them later that we are scientists. They'd want to know why we were sneaking around and didn't come to them directly—or more logically, make some kind of request through the Research Council. It's rare, but it has been done before."

Prentiss nodded. Before she could say anything I'Char continued, "But I agree with Mr. Garrick. The Lemians are our enemy—and should not be taken lightly. We should assume that if they find us, they will certainly think we are spies, or part of some advance military team. Just because you may think like a scientist, do not assume they will. They are in general militaristic—and certainly whomever they have on this planet will be."

"And while we sit here they could find us—or find the freighter," said Garrick. "Time is of the essence."

"It will all be wasted if we get picked up by the Lemians," said I'Char. "We don't know their position here, and how much authority they assert. Certainly their base will be off limits to the locals. If we get caught there at night, it will be hard to explain."

"We could pretend we are pilgrims from Valdar," said Garrick sarcastically, "and we are lost."

"Actually, posing as pilgrims is an excellent idea," said I'Char. "It would explain a lot about our lack of knowledge, and perhaps even explain our physical differences. Symes spotted us right away, but there seems to be an awareness of pilgrims who are strangers."

Win turned to Garrick. "You said the Lemians might not know about the freighter," he said. "And we didn't exactly rush to get here. I agree we want to get this over with, but one more day shouldn't make a difference."

Garrick shook his head. "We can't be certain what the Lemians know. They could stumble upon the freighter anytime—or upon us. We saw their patrols earlier. We can't just sit around and place our lives in the hands of this crazy old man." He indicated Symes, still fast asleep, sprawled half out of his chair. Garrick paused. "I'll agree to stay this one night, on the condition that we go in at first light. And we have to post a guard."

"I agree," said I'Char. "At the least we'll get a sense if their normal perimeter patrol comes out this way, and when."

"Good to see that someone in your group understands survival tactics," said Garrick. "I'll take the first watch." Without waiting for an answer he got up and tramped to the door. Lifting the flimsy latch, he peeked out and then silently slid into the gloom.

After a moment Prentiss let out a held breath. "I hate that man."

Chapter 13

Evening prayers had ended, and the junior priests had completed the final rituals. Now the only sound was the swish of the acolytes' brooms as they cleared the cavernous temple.

Tonight they swept more urgently, making sure not to miss a speck of dust. For the high priest himself, Methurgem, was still there. The acolytes were careful not to sweep any dirt onto his fine robes.

Not accustomed to being watched by Methurgem as they performed this lowly chore, the acolytes did not quite know how to act. Was he there to see how well they worked? No one wanted to be the first to leave.

A side door opened. Amora, the eldest of the Pertise, and just below Methurgem in rank, strode into the temple. After a moment he clapped his hands once, the sound echoing throughout the stone chamber. "Enough!" The acolytes quickly filed out of the room, bowing as they passed Amora.

Amora reached out and stopped the last acolyte, a young woman. She kept her head low as the priest closed the door.

"Come," said Amora. She followed him to the front of the temple, where Methurgem sat in the High Priest's ornate chair.

"Sahme, your report," said Amora.

The nervous acolyte kept her eyes lowered. "As you have ordered, I have been listening for any mention of the heretic, Jesus. Each morning after prayer I have removed my Temple garments and exchanged them for the clothing of a caretaker, and have gone to the market."

"Yes, yes," said Amora. "We are aware of that. What have you learned?"

Sahme hesitated. "There is much talk of Jesus in the market."

"Come child," said Amora, softening his tone. "Do not be afraid. Tell us what you have heard."

"It is hard for me to repeat it," said the acolyte, her voice quavering. "It feels—wrong."

"We will decide what is right or wrong," said Amora. "You will not be responsible for uttering the words you report."

Sahme drew in a deep breath. "The farmers are very unhappy. The drought—they wonder why they have to go to the fields every day, when there are so few crops."

"What does this have to do with Jesus?" prodded Amora.

"The farmers say that Jesus is telling them they don't have to stay farmers, that they can do something else. When I first heard this, I could not believe it, and could not imagine the farmers would even consider such a notion. That they did not have to be bound by the Order. But many now repeat it."

"Indeed," said Amora, looking up at Methurgem. The High Priest said nothing, but motioned for the acolyte to continue.

"Now, I have not heard Jesus say these things directly—it is just what is said in the marketplace. And mostly in whispers, although a few of the farmers have become bolder in their speech."

"What have you heard Jesus say, with your own ears?"

"I have not seen or heard Jesus again, not since the one time I already reported to you. He has been in the city, preaching, but I did not want to be recognized—"

"Yes, we know," said Amora. "Tell us, have you heard where Jesus and his followers go when they are not in the city?"

The acolyte shook her head. "No. His closest followers—the ones they call the disciples—have mostly left their homes in the city, after they were—punished. I—I can try to find out, but someone might recognize me if I ask too many questions."

"Perhaps later," said Amora. "What else are the people saying? Are more beginning to follow him?"

"It is hard to tell," responded Sahme. "Many are afraid to speak openly. I would say they are—*interested* in what he has to say, more than being followers. There is a rumor that he will speak tomorrow—at the amphitheater."

Amora looked up sharply. "The amphitheater? Are you sure?"

"It's just a rumor—but everyone is talking about it. Everyone."

Methurgem had heard enough. "Leave us," he ordered.

The acolyte bowed low and scurried out the side door, leaving the two priests alone.

"We have let this go on long enough," said Methurgem.

"But what can we do?" said Amora. "No one from the Temple has witnessed Jesus break a Law—or even heard him tell others to do so. Rumors, nothing more than whispers and rumors! If we act now, we are likely to cause even more problems. We need proof."

Methurgem sighed. "Yes. It appears the memory of the punishment of his followers is no longer enough. And now I fear there are too many to try that again." He stroked his beard, thinking. "It is time to take a different approach. Send some priests to the amphitheater tomorrow, so they can hear what he has to say."

"In disguise?"

"No. In their robes. Let us see what this Jesus will say in front of the keepers of the Law. Nothing, I expect. It is one thing to tell a few stories to some impressionable young farmers—it is quite another to speak against the Order and the Laws when there are priests to bear witness."

"I will see to it," said Amora. After a pause he continued, "There is another matter."

"Yes?"

"The Lemians. They have a new leader here. He wants to meet us."

Methurgem sighed again. "Very well. Let's see what the heathen wants."

Chapter 14

"I don't think much of him either," admitted Win, after Garrick had walked out of the hut. "But he's here, and we have to make the best of the situation."

"He clearly knows more than he is telling us," said I'Char. "And what he keeps from us may put us in even greater danger."

"I agree. I've tried to find out what he knows. He gives out information only when it is needed, instead of trusting us with the entire story."

"It's a very military attitude," said I'Char. "Which has its advantages at times. Right now is probably not one of them."

"It's something about the freighter," said Win. Before leaving the ship he had told I'Char about his fear, that the freighter cargo might be a threat to the Rhean alliance. Win glanced over at Prentiss, trying to decide how much he should tell her of their suspicions about why the freighter was so important.

But Prentiss was thinking about something else. "No matter how vital Central Command thinks that the freighter is, it pales in comparison to what we have stumbled upon." She laughed, but without humor. "For once I can thank the military for something, otherwise I wouldn't be here. Certainly you can see what that neanderthal of a spy—or whatever he is—can't. We have a chance to witness something amazing, the precise turning point of an entire culture."

"Why do you believe that?" asked Win.

"Because I've seen it before. Cultures at this stage in their development are at a critical point, a teetering, you might say. Do they stay in one place, technologically and culturally stagnant, or do they move ahead? I believe the ones that do progress need some kind of shock, a catalyst if you will. This catalyst is often religious in nature—almost always, in fact. It leads to a transformation, one that moves the people either into an organized society, or, in a place like K'Turia where an organized society already exists, the transformation jars them out of the stagnant ceremonial rules which limit their development."

"It is an interesting theory," said Win. He paused, trying to decide how best to ask the next question, aware that she would be sensitive on this topic. Finally he tried, "I understand your theory is a little controversial."

He saw the anger in her eye, but when she spoke it was with her usual detachment, as if she were still passionate about the topic but had become hardened to the attacks on her ideas. "I don't know what you have been told," she said, glancing at the door where Garrick had gone. "But you probably realize that this is an idea which scares a lot of scientists. They have long resisted any connection between religion and science. Some go so far as to say that religion is the absence of science, and science is the absence of religion."

"And you?" Win prodded.

"*My* religious beliefs are not the issue," she said. "I am explaining cultural development in a *scientific* way. Just because it has an element of religion does not mean it is not scientific."

Win noticed how she had carefully avoided linking science and religion, the very separation she was claiming that her critics were unfairly demanding.

Still, he was intrigued. Surprisingly so, given how disinterested he had been in anything. "Okay, Specialist Prentiss, we have some time. Consider me an open minded audience. Tell me your theory—and how you think it might help us understand how to proceed here on K'Turia."

She looked at him suspiciously, but when she saw he was genuinely interested she began, "Consider the realm of populated planets. Have you ever wondered about their stage of development, or more specifically, why some progress and others do not, and why the ones that progress do so at the rate that they do?"

Win searched his mind for what he knew about cultural development. "I am aware this has been studied in depth. The development cycle is fairly well understood and is similar on many different worlds. It has to do with variables such as natural resources, proximity of population areas, predators, and the environment."

"Yes, yes," said Prentiss, impatiently. "But why? Even with similarities in the variables you have described, some cultures never get past what we think of as technologically primitive. What is it that results in some moving ahead, and some staying stagnant?"

"You believe it is religion?" asked I'Char.

"No, not religion per se. It is much more specific than that. Almost all populated worlds have something we can categorize as religion. That is the one universal in the universe. But what is it that differentiates these religions? What is it that actually transforms the very culture? I'll tell you. It is not only the religion, the belief in some kind of external power, but the *presence* of that power in the culture. In other words, the people need not only believe in some kind of deity or power, but that power must appear to them, not as a dream or an oracle or be represented by a statue, but actually appear in a physical form they can all see."

"You mean they have to see a god?" asked Win.

"They have to see what they accept as a god," she said. "Or at least what they view as a messiah, someone who will show them how to reach whatever their religion holds out as its goal—its heaven, so to speak. What Symes called Paradise. This messiah is the transformational catalyst. After the messiah appears, the entire culture changes from one of religious rules, which serve to shackle development, to one of freedom and self expression. It is this change which leads to the creation of new ideas, of ideas that will free the culture from ritualized ceremonialism and dogma. The pace of technological development accelerates. In fact, without such a messiah, I believe that no cultures exist with what we think of as advanced technology—though I do not yet have enough evidence to support this."

Now Win understood why her theory was so controversial. "So

you are saying that God must exist—and actually appear—for cultures to evolve?"

Prentiss shook her head. "No. My theory doesn't actually require that a god must exist."

Win thought he was following her, but now he was confused. "But you just said they have to see their god. Even leaving that aside, how can this be universal? How can this process be the same on multiple worlds if there is no common entity?"

"There need not be a common entity, just a common *consciousness* of that entity," she explained. "Certainly there is irrefutable evidence of shared consciousness—that of twins, for example. But many other cases have been proven, on many worlds, of a population sharing the feelings and even thoughts of a common consciousness. So what transpires on one planet can easily transpire elsewhere—or what is believed and felt on one planet can be believed and felt elsewhere."

"I thought such shared consciousness was only evidenced over a much shorter distance," said Win. "Twins, sure, you also have the genetic link. And certain populations have such a capability, but only in close proximity." He was thinking of the Treb *gheris*, his own ability to sense the emotions of others. "You are talking about great distances here."

Prentiss got up, animated now. "The consciousness doesn't travel, it simply *is*," she said. "Just like the natural laws. It means that any idea or concept—including that of Jesus Christ—can exist simultaneously as a *possibility* everywhere in the universe. The messiah could appear, or not, depending on the conditions."

"I think I understand your argument, but it is unnecessarily complex."

Prentiss sighed. "Explain."

Win could see that she had heard all this before, but he pushed ahead anyway. "First, if there is a universal consciousness, why of all things that are—shared—across cultures should this transformational element of the appearance of a deity be one of them? It seems like a very indirect path from that to technology. Why is a specific technology not shared instead?"

Prentiss was not deterred. "Who said it might not be—on some worlds? Your example doesn't preclude the idea of a religiously inspired transformation. Perhaps a religious transformation only happens when a culture is ready for the technology."

"Some kind of test?" said Win. "But by whom? We are back full circle. Such a universal consciousness is what many would argue is God. Now you have left the realm of science again."

"And who are we to say that is incorrect?" said Prentiss, her face now flushed with emotion. "This is exactly my point of the limitations of those who refuse to accept this idea, who start with the premise that science and religion are incompatible. Let's say it *is* God, this universal consciousness. Or that the universal consciousness is God's consciousness. Why is that so hard for everyone to accept? I've simply used a scientific method to show this as a possibility."

"It's elegant, but still too complex," said Win. "There are much simpler explanations, at least on this planet. First, Garrick may be correct. An offworlder, someone who knows the Jesus Christ story, is playing the role, taking advantage of the inherent importance of religion here, using it as a way to move up the caste hierarchy. From what Symes has said about the religious rules, it would be a logical fit, overlaying Jesus Christ on this culture. The miracles this person has supposedly performed could simply be the use of some outside technology." He saw Prentiss about to object but he put up his hand. "And there is another easy explanation. A K'Turian has simply learned of the story of Jesus Christ, from some offworlder visit, or more likely, from some copy of the Bible. Just because the League or the Lemians didn't bring it does not mean it did not get here. Copies of it are on my home planet, which is a very long way from Earth."

"Just because an idea is complicated doesn't mean it is wrong," said Prentiss. "But while your simple explanations might work for K'Turia, they don't fit what I have seen on other planets. First, I have seen cultures where we know for a fact that no written history from the outside has contaminated the culture. Yet in every case the message brought by the messiah has been the same—that the ritualized rules that have been handed down, and enforced by the religious leaders through fear, are wrong. That there is a truth to be discovered, a truth that is being hidden by the rules. The message requires a new way of living, and it serves as an assault on the powers that be."

Her voice rose in excitement. "You have to understand, while I have seen this phenomena before, this is the first time I have heard the name Jesus. Usually the catalyst is someone with the same characteristics, and a similar message, but with a different name—yes, yes, I know, that could still be the result of a Bible, or a poor language translation. But all of them were real people — and viewed as messiahs—not just as concepts."

She paused, as if deciding to continue. "And, if you are demanding a much simpler explanation, there is one, but one that my scientific colleagues are totally unwilling to even consider."

Win asked, "What is that?"

"Simply that this *is* Jesus Christ," she said quietly. "The real one."

Chapter 15

The rain pelted his face so hard it bled. Still he went on, his purpose as unrelenting as the rain. Nothing short of death would stop him now, as he made the pilgrimage to Braay, the site of the Great Meet.

Win was not alone. Thousands of others were on the move, from all over the planet Treb, making the arduous trek to Braay.

This was Win's second pilgrimage. The first one, years before, had left him both elated and exhausted, one step closer to *ana*, to be sure, but also a clear sign of how much he still had to learn, how much further he had to go to reach the heightened state of awareness of his ultimate purpose.

This time, he had prepared even harder, and now, so immersed in the path to his spiritual goal, he would not even feel the pain from the elements. Or more precisely, he could, but his goal was so important he pushed aside the pain.

By the time he arrived at Braay, many were already there, and he added his consciousness to the throng, his *gheris* vibrating with the mass of spiritual energy. Thus supported, he turned his focus in, in, using all of his sensory energy to undertake the search into his inner core, to answer the most fundamental of questions: *Why was he alive?*

Here, deep in the ocean of his inner being, he was still connected to the other Trebs; they were as ripples on the surface far above him. Present, but no hindrance to him as he dove deeper into his inner self.

Days passed. But no matter how deep he went, there were always others before him, deeper, more focused, more attuned to themselves.

At a depth he had never believed possible, with nothing but a great abyss still before him, it became painfully clear that this was not to be his time—he would not reach *ana* in this Great Meet.

With the realization came a wave of sadness, the final proof of how far he still had to go. For no one near *ana* would have felt any such emotion as disappointment.

Just as he was about to give up hope, there was a flash, a spark of bright light, seizing his attention. The light streaked down into the abyss, like an arrow drawing him to a place in the deepest part of his core, passing through him and emerging into an expanse, an endless universe of space and possibilities.

In this space, which he somehow knew was the *gheris* of those who had reached *ana*, he could still see the light. Like a beacon it called him, promising truth, and as he reached for it with his *gheris*, he felt someone at the same time reaching toward him, calling to him not from the light, but from where the light had led him.

"Do not be disheartened." He heard, or rather felt, the essence of the words. "You have come so far."

"I know," he replied. "It is just such a great distance to go."

The voice came again, this time bringing a great joy, the very air around him humming in warmth. "And far beyond that."

"How long will it take?" He could not help but wondering.

"It does not matter. I am Sooni, and I will wait for you . . ."

* * *

Win awoke to a light touch. The room was dark, but this was not the darkness of the Great Meet. That was a memory, a time long ago, but a time he could never forget.

A figure hunched over him, but his *gheris* told him it was not a threat. I'Char.

"Garrick is gone."

Win sat up, forcing the memory away. He saw Prentiss on one of the chairs, still asleep.

"What happened?" he asked.

"When I went out to take the second watch he wasn't outside, or anywhere nearby."

Win didn't bother to ask I'Char how well he had searched. If I'Char could not find Garrick, he was gone. "The fool must have gone into the city. We'll have to go look for him."

"I'd advise against it," said I'Char. "Not all of us anyway. We'd probably attract even more attention than he would alone."

Win sighed. "You're right. Even if we find him, I doubt he'd come back here willingly. Damn that man." Win thought for a moment. "Better stick to the original plan. Go into the city in the morning, learn our way around. We can look for him then."

"I could go now—alone."

Win considered. He trusted the Illian's skills completely. If anyone could make his way through an unfamiliar city at night, I'Char could. But he shook his head. "Same thing. What would you do if you found him?"

"I could bring him back."

Win didn't doubt it. "Quietly?"

I'Char did not hesitate. "Perhaps. But I can't be certain."

That settled it for Win. "It's not worth the risk. At least not yet. I hope that Garrick is good at sneaking around."

I'Char nodded. "I'll be outside." He slipped quietly out the door.

Win looked at Prentiss, uncomfortably twisted in the chair. There was no point in waking her. He could hear Symes snoring in the other room.

He lay back down on the bench, frustrated that he could do nothing, knowing their problems had just gotten a lot worse.

* * *

Dim lights shone in some of the huts along the road, and ahead Garrick could make out the glow of torchlight in the city. Though dark, he had no trouble following the newly cast road. He found it mildly amusing that his way had been made easier because of the Lemian technology.

Now and again he turned back to see if he'd been followed. He didn't think they would come after him tonight. Win wasn't a risk taker—and I'Char would know it was not a good idea. I'Char. He'd have to be careful about that one. I'Char was a true warrior. Garrick knew more about Illians than he had let on. An Illian who had become a warrior was a rare thing indeed. He doubted even Win knew how powerful I'Char was.

Win frustrated him. Central Command had reviewed Win's history, and they had concluded he could be trusted. What they had not planned on was Win's cautiousness and indecisiveness. Perhaps it was because they had kept a lot from him. But they had to. They couldn't afford any leaks about the freighter . . .

He felt he had pushed Win as far as he could. The Treb would only move so fast with what he knew, and now that the fanatical woman Prentiss was along, they risked getting sidetracked on one of her crazy religious quests. So he would have to speed things along, and the best way was to do it alone; he had always known it might come to this at some point anyway. With luck, he could find out what he needed to know and get back to the hut before they even knew he was gone.

The road was deserted. As he approached the city, the road entered through a gate in a stone wall, a high arch marking the entrance. He did not enter the city, but instead turned left, making his way along the wall. There, deep in the shadows, and well away from the road, he stopped to listen. He heard only the sounds of some animals, probably penned behind one of the sheds he had passed.

From under his robe he took out a small case. He opened the cover, shielding the luminescent glow with his hand. A map appeared on a dim green screen. He deftly ran his hand over the controls and the map changed. He looked up to get his bearings, and then continued on along the wall, holding the tracking unit before him.

After a few hundred paces he turned a slight corner and stopped again. Ahead of him, just outside the city, he could see the Lemian camp, the buildings clearly outlined in the dark by harsh lights. He worked the controls again. The map realigned to his new position. It did not show the actual camp, since it had been made from the photos taken before the Lemians had arrived. But it gave him a good approximation of where he was and what direction he should take.

The unit had another function. He clicked a button and the screen changed again, and now it was set to register the signature from the missing freighter. But he could get no reading. Either the freighter was not here, or he was not close enough. The unit only had a range of a few thousand paces. Anything more powerful would have been picked up by the Lemian sensors; this was risky enough.

He hadn't told Win about bringing this device. If they got caught with it, the Lemians would think they were spies—which, of course, was true.

But he *had* to find the freighter. He was one of only a few people in the entire universe who knew what it carried.

If the Lemians found it first, the very future of the League would be at stake.

With luck he could circle the entire camp undetected. If the freighter was there—and the transponder was working—he'd be able to find it. Then all he had to do was—

He heard a sound behind him and spun around. Voices, along the wall, from the direction of the city. He recognized the language immediately. Lemian.

Quietly he made his way along the wall, away from the voices. But he had barely moved when he heard footsteps ahead of him, somewhere in the shadowy gloom cast by the wall.

Coming toward him.

Trapped. Lemians behind him, and more ahead. The entire Lemian camp lay between him and the valley; there would be no escape that way. He looked up at the wall. Not high, but too smooth to climb.

The voices came closer. *Sentry patrols. Didn't expect them here, along the wall . . .*

He frantically pushed buttons on the box, working from memory, then closed the case. He looked around a last time, seeking a way out.

The footsteps were almost upon him. Not much time.

He stepped away from the wall and threw the tracking device over, hearing a gentle thud when it landed on the other side. It would self destruct immediately, leaving nothing but ash.

He fought the urge to run, knowing it would be suspicious.

Speed couldn't save him now, only guile.

Chapter 16

Krelmar looked over the group assembled in his new office, formerly some kind of dining area. *So these were the religious leaders. The Pertise. Not too impressive.* Their robes were much finer than what he had seen on other locals, but otherwise they looked the same, although perhaps a bit more haughty. Krelmar had ordered his K'Turian aide, Tsaph, to inform the Pertise about the meeting, and though the priests were supposedly an independent group, they had all come running. Odd, though he could not set foot in their temple, they had no compunction about coming to his residence.

Krelmar had asked Tsaph to stay, but the K'Turian had advised against it, explaining that the Pertise would be less open in his presence. Krelmar also found that odd; if the Pertise were so powerful, why would they care what Tsaph might overhear? Perhaps they simply did not want to be in the same room with someone of the lowest caste. Either way, he took Tsaph's advice, since the trader understood the local customs.

Krelmar did, however, have Neel present. A little show of force, or the hint of it, would remind the locals of his power.

As the three priests sat he welcomed them. "Gentlemen, thank you for coming. I am Krelmar."

The tallest priest responded, "I am Methurgem, leader of the Pertise." He indicated the other priests. "And this is Amora, and Cemb." They each nodded in turn.

Krelmar waited, expecting they would welcome him in some way, or ask what his role was, but they said nothing. So he continued, "I find your city delightful. I look forward to working with you."

Still they said nothing, and in the silence, Krelmar examined each of them. Methurgem had gray hair and sharp eyes, and an air of self-importance. His dark robe was the most ornate, with delicate and colorful embroidery. Amora had bony features and was slight of build, even smaller than the other locals. He too had gray hair. The third priest, Cemb, was clearly younger than the others, and he had the simplest robe, though it was still finely made.

Krelmar tried again. "As you may know, I am the new representative of the Lemian Empire. I am of the hope we can discuss matters that will be mutually beneficial."

"Our ways are simple," replied Methurgem. "Our only interests are our religious ways of life, which have endured for centuries. I would not expect we would have much in common."

Krelmar tried to judge the priest's tone. It appeared to be disinterest, as if he thought the Lemians were simply not important to him. "Perhaps we will surprise you," said Krelmar. "We might be able to offer things which will make your lives easier."

Methurgem shook his head. "We do not seek easier lives. Subsistence and sacrifice are part of our Way."

Krelmar could not tell if the K'Turian was teasing him. But Methurgem appeared deadly serious. "Still, there would be mutual benefit from a relationship with the Lemian Empire."

"We have little of value," said Methurgem. "We do not understand why you are here."

"Your planet, in and of itself, has a value, to others if not to you," said Krelmar.

Again Methurgem shook his head. "What happens offworld does not concern us. Our Way is for our people, not for others."

Could this be real? thought Krelmar. Certainly these people wanted *something*. He glanced over at the Lemian commander, who remained stoic.

Krelmar changed tactics. "We can offer you more than offworld goods," he said.

Methurgem eyed him narrowly. "Such as?"

"Knowledge, for example. We could show you how to increase your crop yields."

Cemb spoke up. "Could you help us avoid the droughts?"

Methurgem glanced sharply at the younger priest, who withered under his gaze. Krelmar noticed the silent rebuke but ignored it, instead saying smoothly, "Of course. We have farming technology that will help you develop crops which require less water. And we can also help you safely store food for emergencies."

"We've survived droughts before, and we will again," said Methurgem.

"We can also help in other areas, such as matters of security," said Krelmar.

"We have no need to be protected from anyone offworld," replied Methurgem. "There is nothing here that would interest offworlders."

Now that was an interesting comment, thought Krelmar. How careful Methurgem had been to say they did not need protection from anything *offworld.* Was this a slip of the tongue, or a hint?

Cautiously, he probed. "Just because you do not value a thing, others may, or may seek to disrupt your way of life. The Lemian Empire could help shield you from that disruption."

Now it was Methurgem who changed the subject. "You speak of the Lemian Empire as if they were separate from you. Are you not one in the same?"

"I am a representative of the Lemian Empire, though I am not myself a Lemian," said Krelmar. "Like many others, my people have chosen to align themselves with the Lemians for mutual benefit." While this was not quite true, he knew the K'Turians would have no way of knowing otherwise. "I come to offer you the same kind of assistance—and protection—that my planet Colltaire now benefits from. At first, we too saw little need for outside help, but now are very happy with our association with the Lemian Empire." This of course was an outright lie, but one that would be hard for the K'Turians to refute.

Cemb spoke again. "This security, would it be limited to protection from offworlders?"

Again Methurgem gave the young priest a sharp look, but surprisingly Cemb went on. "Would you also help with local security, from—bandits, or others who disturb the peace?"

This is very interesting, thought Krelmar. The other priests were totally deferential to Methurgem. Yet even after being rebuked, the youngest one brings this up. Was all of this being carefully staged, so that Methurgem would not be the one to have to make such a request?

Krelmar glanced at Neel, who sat expressionless. When he looked back at the priests, he carefully directed his response to Cemb, leaving Methurgem a way out. "Certainly. We abhor any disturbances which jeopardize a peaceful way of life. Even the best of societies have some who do not accept the rule of law."

"We have our own ways of dealing with lawbreakers," said Amora. "We cast them from the Temple. You would not understand, but here that is a terrible fate. Without the Temple, these people cannot find the Way. Few dare this punishment."

"Ahh," said Krelmar, sensing an opening. "But what of those who are not deterred?"

"There are very few such people," said Amora.

"It takes but a few, or perhaps even one," said Krelmar. "Great insurgencies have been born from the mouth of a single man. Disruption of the peace is a problem common to many societies—and one that would certainly affect how your law-abiding residents live."

"And how they are able to satisfy the demands of the Way," said Cemb.

"Exactly!" exclaimed Krelmar. "You see, no matter our differences, there are some challenges all societies must face. On many worlds, security is necessary for prosperity and trade. Here you must have security so that your religion can be correctly practiced."

Amora eyed him narrowly. "We have our own Temple guards. They have been more than enough for ages. There is little crime here. The presence of—foreign—authority would only confuse the people. Our rule of law, and the Order we live in, is what maintains our peace."

And brings you great wealth, thought Krelmar, *as you bleed the castes below you.* Smoothly, he said, "I see. I admit, I am quite ignorant of your local customs and religious rules. Of course I am very willing to learn. But I ask you: could we not help in a way that would be consistent with your laws? I understand you do not have a government. How, may I ask, do you deal with those who do not accept your religious laws? For a punishment to be effective, there must be a fear of the consequence. Without such fear, there is no control. If improper acts go unpunished, the people will question the very essence of authority. Once this begins, it is a small step to lawlessness."

"You paint a dire picture," said Amora. "One that is unlikely to ever happen in Merculon."

"Unlikely, perhaps, but still possible. The goal of security is not to prepare for likelihoods, but to protect against the chance of catastrophe. Tell me," Krelmar again changed the subject, sensing he was getting close, but also aware that these leaders were unlikely to admit their own authority was being questioned. "What would you do if offworlders came here and tried to take your city by force? Not everyone is as peaceful as the Lemians." The lie rolled easily off his tongue.

"As we have said, we have little that offworlders would want," said Methurgem. "Why would they do that?"

"Why does anyone do what they do?" asked Krelmar, laying the groundwork for his next gambit. "Perhaps they are deranged. Perhaps it is just for the sake of power. You have a rule of law. It is religious law, I understand, but it is a law nonetheless. Many peaceful societies have been ruined by those who do not accept such rules of law— those who reject the notion of laws, and work outside of them. I applaud all that you have accomplished, for this seems to be a peaceful planet. But your laws are best suited for those who accept them without question, who fear the consequences of actions against the law. I can tell you from experience that trouble often comes from where you least expect it. Especially from those in your own backyard who reject the basis of the very laws which keep the peace."

"This security of which you speak," said Cemb. "How would it work?"

This time Methurgem did not look at the younger priest, and now Krelmar was certain that this entire conversation was an elaborate ploy. Methurgem was using Cemb as a tool to elicit Krelmar's reactions. Krelmar smiled inwardly, for he didn't care. It was actually making his job easier.

"We can discuss that," said Krelmar. "Our goal would be to help you in a way that is complementary to your existing security. And of course we would help protect you from offworld threats, rare as they may be. Your temple guards would be no match for the weapons that evil offworlders may wield." He gestured toward Neel. "Commander Neel directs a very capable force." He said this to not only make his point about the offworld threat, but to remind the Pertise about his own position of power, and what he could do if they refused.

"What would you expect in exchange for this security?" asked Cemb.

Now we are getting to it, thought Krelmar. "Only that you accept the protection of the Lemian Empire," he said. "Nothing more."

"I do not understand," said Cemb. "Why would this be of value to you?"

Krelmar smiled. "Just as you have your ways which are understood by you—and you value things that others do not—so too do the Lemians have their own sense of what is important. Though this may be hard for you to believe, it is important to the Lemians that others accept their protection. It is—it is a way for them to discourage threats from unfriendly forces."

Cemb appeared skeptical, a look that did not seem rehearsed. But Krelmar could see a gleam of understanding in Methurgem's eye.

"By protecting more planets, you appear to have a greater strength yourself, which discourages others from threatening you," said the older priest.

"Yes," said Krelmar, "you understand perfectly." Methurgem was referring to the Lemians, but Krelmar could sense a new communication being established with the elder priest. Methurgem was hearing Krelmar's subtle message: that the Lemians could also protect the Pertise from local threats.

"We could not pay for such help," said Amora. "We have nothing of value."

Krelmar waved his hand in dismissal. "As I have said, these things have a value to the Lemians beyond what coin can bring."

"Still, this is a major decision for us, one that we cannot make so easily," said Methurgem. "We would have to consult with our brethren."

Krelmar almost laughed, for he suspected that Methurgem was used to getting his way. But he would play the priest's game. "Certainly. And in the meantime, might I suggest something that will make it easier for you to decide?"

"What do you propose?" asked Amora.

"Before you agree to full protection from the Lemians, let us prove to you how we can be helpful," said Krelmar. "When you are faced with some kind of security—problem—simply bring it to my attention. We will deal with it—and then you will see how beneficial our presence can be."

There was a silence, the priests appearing to be deciding. Finally Methurgem spoke. "That path we can accept," he said. "But I warn you it may take some time for such a situation to present itself. We have no problems at present."

Krelmar willed himself not to look at Neel. "Of course. As long as it takes."

Cemb appeared ready to speak, but Methurgem put his hand on the younger man's arm and stood up. "We must return to the temple," he said, ushering Cemb and Amora out of the room without another word.

"That was odd," said Neel. "I thought Cemb was about to ask for something."

"He was," said Krelmar. He was elated that he had been able to move the conversation all the way to discussions of Lemian control—*protection,* he corrected himself—at the first meeting, and he had to keep himself from being disappointed that the agreement had not been completed. But it was a great start. Obviously he would not wait a long time, no matter what he had said. But a little time would be fine, since it was now clear to him that Neel had been right, these people *did* want something from him. Cemb had almost blurted it out at the end, before Methurgem had stopped him.

"I don't understand," said Neel. "Why didn't they just come right out and say it?"

"Deniability," said Krelmar. "They want to be able to later deny they asked for our help. Asking for help with security is an admission they do not have enough control, which is a great danger to their authority. It means they want us to help them with something within their religion, or at least connected to it—something they have been unable to deal with themselves. You were right in that regard."

"But who would know? There were just the three of them. Did they think we would tell anyone?"

"No one would believe us," said Krelmar. "As for the priests, Methurgem would be able to make this arrangement with us and not feel that any authority was being compromised—for he *is* the authority. Perhaps too for Amora. But the younger priest would always wonder. Methurgem could not make a deal in front of him. They thought they were being smart, making Cemb ask all the questions. But they made a mistake bringing him."

"What do we do now?" asked Neel.

"We wait," said Krelmar. "They'll be back."

* * *

In the temple, Methurgem and Amora huddled after sending Cemb off to prayers. "That Lemian heathen is a fool," said Amora. "He obviously wants more than what he is asking, yet he thinks we cannot see it."

"Of course," said Methurgem. "But his arrogance will work in our favor. The Lemians all think we are stupid peasants. They live in a world of technology, and therefore see us as primitive beings who cannot think. Krelmar is nothing more than a glorified trader. He will be no threat to us, because he does not feel we are a threat to him."

"What of his offer?"

"We have little need of their help," said Methurgem. "But that does not mean we will not find use for it. We may have found a way of dealing with the radical."

"Ahh," said Amora. "I understand. He can be the test for the Lemians."

"Exactly," said Methurgem. "This is something the Lemians can understand, for they will view the radical as an insurgent, someone their military way of life cannot abide."

"But the radical has not really threatened the peace," said Amora. "In fact he has not even directly threatened the Way."

"Not yet," said Methurgem. "But he will. When he does, it will be a challenge to the Temple and its authority. And though he has not endangered the peace, the Lemians certainly don't know that. It will not take much to convince them he is a threat—to all of us."

BOOK II

Chapter 17

The path to Paradise is lined with the sacrifices of love, not of fear.
    —The Teachings: 2:2

"What's going on?" Prentiss asked. "I thought this is where Symes said Jesus was going to be speaking."

"They seem to be making a lot of noise for an audience," agreed Win, as he led them up the back side of the temple. They had spent much of the day searching for Garrick, to no avail. As the day wore on the locals began moving toward the arena, leaving the crew vulnerable in the deserted streets. The frantic Symes kept looking over his shoulder until I'Char told him to leave and go ahead separately. But it was only after Prentiss explained to the old man that it was for his own safety had he obeyed.

At the edge of the clearing around the temple they had immediately entered into a throng of people who all seemed intent on something in the opposite direction from the grand temple portico. The noise of the crowd was loud and incomprehensible.

Prentiss, her hood pulled tight, forced her way through the crowd, not waiting for Win and I'Char. Win tried to keep her in sight; he could sense I'Char right behind him, intent on any possible threat. But it appeared to be just an excited group of K'Turians; there wasn't a Lemian in sight.

Yet Win's *gheris* sense threatened to overwhelm him. He staggered, recognizing it as the same sensation he had felt when they had first landed. That feeling had never really left him, but he had muted it. Now it was back, even stronger than before; it could not be muffled. Whatever it was, it surpassed even the emotion of the crowd.

Without warning Prentiss stopped and spun around, colliding with Win. She grabbed his arm. "My God, I saw him!"

"Where?" asked Win, as he was jostled by someone. They were in the midst of it now.

She did not answer but pushed forward, only stopping at the edge of the knoll, blocked by the mass of people filling every inch of the stone amphitheater.

"There!" She pointed down into the arena.

* * *

To Prentiss, the figure of Jesus was both simple and awe inspiring, even from a distance. She had not expected Jesus of K'Turia to look like this at all, and yet she could not imagine Jesus looking any other way. From him emerged a force that she could not describe, a power she knew must have some scientific explanation, as she had long argued. But right now she was unable to think of science and fact gathering but was only able to watch in wonder. Never before had the sight of any single person moved her so much. Her body reacted without her conscious control, trying to move closer.

All at once the yelling and pushing stopped. Prentiss pulled her eyes from Jesus to see what had happened. Four richly dressed men stood at the top steps of the amphitheater. A small space had cleared around them, the people averting their gazes.

Prentiss heard whispers: "Priests!"

One of the priests, his voice haughty with command, yelled out, "Why have you come here?" and his voice echoed through the amphitheater. "Beware those who would confuse you, and distract you from the Way. Go back to your homes!"

No one moved, and the crowd began to mutter. Across the amphitheater, far away from the priests, someone called out, "We only want to listen!"

"Listen to what?" demanded the priest, his voice filled with disdain. "You should listen only to the Pertise, and those who speak for the Temple. What does this Jesus know of the Way?"

Prentiss sensed the unease in the crowd as people turned back toward Jesus, awaiting his response.

But Jesus said nothing. He seemed neither disturbed nor rebuffed. His quiet strength encouraged the crowd. A few called out, "Leave us alone—we have done nothing wrong!"

Prentiss could see that the priests were taken aback, apparently not expecting such open resistance. Emboldened, the crowd grumbled, the noise increasing to a clamor. The people closest to the priests crowded in.

Jesus raised his hand, and the crowd quieted. He slowly walked across the arena and began climbing the steps of the amphitheater toward the priests. The people opened a way for him, some reaching out shyly to touch him. As he drew near, the priest who had spoken took a step back, drawing his robe about him. Jesus stared at the priest, who looked away.

"Would you like to join us?" Jesus asked. His voice was not threatening or angry, but calm and welcoming.

The priest laughed, but no one joined in; instead, another wave of muttering broke out. Jesus again held up his hand for silence. "The people would like to know why you have interrupted them."

The priest stepped forward and said sharply, "We don't have to explain anything to you. Do you know you could be banished for your words?"

"Banished?" Jesus seemed slightly amused. "Why? This is a place of public assembly, is it not? Have I broken a Temple Law?"

The priest turned from Jesus and addressed the crowd. "Do not listen to him! Those who do not keep the Way will be punished!"

Instead of cowering the crowd reacted with a tumultuous noise. People began to climb over the tiered seats toward Jesus and the priests, pressing against each other. "If this is wrong, why do the Pertise not come here and say so? Can we not listen to who we please?" In their whispered questions, Prentiss heard anger, frustration. Fear.

Jesus raised his voice, quieting the tumult. "I have come here in peace, to speak about love and of the Sacrifices of the Way. Do the Pertise say we should not speak of love and sacrifice? Or that we cannot speak of the Way?"

The priest stared at him, but said nothing.

"Come, come," said Jesus. His voice was soft, yet incredibly strong, carrying clearly to Prentiss across the large amphitheater. "Tell me what Law I will break, if I speak of peace, what tenet of the Way I will taint if I speak of love and Sacrifice in one breath?"

Still the priest said nothing.

"Love and peace are equal parts of the Way," said Jesus. "And so, if you wish to keep the Way, as these people do, stay here in peace with us, and listen."

"Who are you to tell us about the Way?" responded the priest, his voice full of scorn. "You should watch your tongue." His voice rose to a yell. "No one but the Pertise can translate the Way! No one!"

The priest turned and pushed his way through the crowd, the other priests following, the people quickly moving out of their way, shouts of anger following them as they climbed the temple steps and disappeared inside.

* * *

"Now that we are alone . . . ," said Jesus, as he made his way back down the steps. The crowd laughed. His tone became more serious, but a certain gaiety still lingered as he continued. "Let me tell you a story."

At this the crowd became animated again, the tension gone. They clapped and yelled, "Yes, a story!"

"One day, two farmers who lived near each other woke up very early in the morning, preparing to go to the fields. When they met in the street outside their homes, they looked up at the sky, which was dark and foreboding. One of the farmers said, 'I think we will have a very bad storm today. We should not go to the fields, for tonight is the eve of the worship day. If the storm becomes so bad that we are unable to return from the fields, we will not be able to make it to the temple for prayer.'

"The second farmer said, 'But it is harvest time. If we do not go to the fields the crops will die, and all our work will be in vain. Does not the Way teach us that such waste is wrong? Yes, we may be caught in the storm. But that is a small hardship, compared to the loss of what we have sown.' The first farmer replied: 'No, we cannot risk not being at the temple, for if we are not there others will notice and say we have not kept the Way. How will you explain it if other farmers make it to the temple, and we do not?' The second farmer shook his head, and said, 'If we cannot return we can still hold the worship day, and pray in the fields. We can face the temple, and in our hearts we will be there, not in the fields.' But the first farmer gathered his things and would not go to the fields. And so the other went by himself, and he was caught in the storm, and was unable to make it to the temple. Yet instead of being angered, or saying, 'I should have listened, for now I cannot be in temple with the others,' he simply stopped his work and began to pray, and in his heart he kept the worship day holy."

Win could sense the emotions of the others around him as they listened, mesmerized. What he had not expected was how much he himself would be affected by Jesus. Jesus spoke with an intimacy that made Win feel he was being spoken to personally, as if no one else was there. Even the movement of Jesus' hands, gesturing as he spoke, seemed to reach out to Win. His hands seemed to have an acute awareness of their own, as if they were a part of his communication, an added dimension of his speech.

Win made a deliberate effort to pull his eyes away.

He whispered to I'Char, "I have never felt anything like this before."

"This man is very powerful," said I'Char. "Even I can feel his energy."

Without fully entering the heightened state of *nore,* Win turned his focus inward, trying to separate his own emotions and reactions from that which his *gheris* was picking up from the crowd. He felt nothing wrong, but the entire sensation was totally new to him. It was more—powerful, more direct, than anything he had ever sensed. He tried to think of a scientific reason. "Is it possible he is doing something to us, manipulating us in some way? Crowd control, perhaps? Some kind of mass hypnosis? It is far more than just his voice, it's *him*." He touched I'Char's arm and indicated Prentiss, just ahead of them. She appeared to be awestruck.

"Look at these people, they're all enthralled." The K'Turians around them seemed unaware of their conversation.

The crowd waited for more, but Jesus had stopped speaking. Someone called out, "Jesus, what does this story mean?"

"Before I answer that," said Jesus, "let me ask you this. Why do you go to the temple to pray?"

There was a hesitation, as if no one wanted to be the first to speak. Then a young boy in the front row called out, "So that we may keep the Way!"

Jesus smiled at the boy. "It seems you have been well taught! But how does praying in the temple keep the Way?"

After a moment, a timid voice called out, "Because that is the Law, as explained to us by the Pertise."

"Ahh," said Jesus. "Let me see if I understand. The Law says that to find the Way, you must pray in the temple, and only by praying in the temple can you stay within the Law?"

Win sensed the confusion in the crowd. Someone said, "It is the Law, that is why we pray in the temple."

"And which is more important, obeying the Law, or finding the Way?" asked Jesus.

Some of the people called out, "The Law!" while others cried: "Finding the Way!"

"You see, the Law is supposed to be the clear guidance for you, and yet you cannot answer this simple question. You are confused, just like the farmer in the story, the one who will not go to the fields. He has confused the Law with the reason for the Law, which is to find the Way, the road to Paradise. He worries about not keeping the letter of the Law, but he does not understand its spirit. But the other farmer—he sees. He understands. He knows that as long as he keeps the Way in his heart, it will be right to pray in the fields, and he does not have to be in the temple."

There was a silence as the crowd digested this, a few heads nodding.

"Now you should understand that it is the Way which is important, and that the Laws are just rules that have been created."

From the top of the amphitheater, on the knoll, a tall man stood and called out, "The Pertise have long told us that the Law and the Way are one and the same, that we cannot find the Way without following the Law exactly. And the Law says that we must keep the Order, and make our Sacrifices, so that stability and harmony will be maintained. We have been taught that this is how we reach Paradise, and how we avoid suffering in this life, and in the next. Are you saying this is wrong?"

"You have heard," said Jesus, "but you have not yet understood. You have heard my story of the two farmers, but you have not understood that the Way is more important than the Law.

"Let me tell you another story. A rich builder is walking along a road. Behind him come the farmers who work his land, pulling a cart laden with food. Now a poor village woman happens to be walking on the same road, just behind the farmers, carrying a very small sack. Sitting along the side of the road are two invalids. The invalids call out to the rich builder, 'Please, share with us some food!' The builder stops and sees the farmers and the old woman watching him, and he puts on a great show of giving the invalids a large basket of food, and then he goes on his way. As the poor village woman passes the invalids, she stops and empties her sack at their feet, and two shriveled pieces of fruit tumble out. 'Here,' she says, 'you can have this fruit.' And she picks up her empty bag and walks away.

"Now I ask of you, who has made the greater Sacrifice? The rich builder, because he has given them a large basket of food, or the old village woman, who has given away her only two pieces of fruit?"

No one answered, and Jesus continued, "There is nothing wrong with Laws, but they cannot become more important than the Way.

And the Way is one of Sacrifice, not because the Laws demand it, but because love demands it. The Way is about love and compassion. Sacrifice is about helping others, as you are able, to the best of your abilities, no matter what your place in the Order."

Jesus pointed at the temple steps. "Those steps lead into the temple, where they continue on, up and up, to the altar. When you are there, the rich sit closest to the altar, and on the steps behind them and below them come those lower in the Order, all the way down to the traders, who have to strain their necks just to see the priests."

He pointed at the people in the front rows. "You here, you are builders. And you back there are craftspeople, and behind you, the caretakers, the farmers, the traders. You have sat according to the Order! Yet here in this amphitheater, the rich are down below, and the poorest are above. Who is to say which Order is right?

"Wake up! You have been willed to sleep by the rituals of the Laws. You live as sleepwalkers, blindly groping in the dark. Before you can see, you must awaken! The Laws have trapped you in a life of stagnation. You have so come to rely on those who tell you what to do that you no longer think of what you need to do yourselves!"

Someone called out, "But Jesus, if we do not follow the Order, how will we survive?"

"By not letting the Law become an empty ritual. If you do, you will live only out of habit or out of fear. If you live out of habit, you simply expect everything will fall into place for you. There is no sacrifice in this. You must do more than what the Law tells you to do. You must think of what you are responsible for, and what you need to do for others. And if you live out of fear, you will not be making true sacrifices. A sacrifice is not a payment of a debt or a tax, it is an act of love and compassion. Sacrificing because you want to help others is what will keep you alive! It is what will keep you in peace, and show you the Way to Paradise."

The crowd was silent. Finally the tall man spoke again, almost beseechingly. "But if we do not make the Sacrifice as we have been taught, how will there be anything ready for us in Paradise?"

Win's *gheris* surged as Jesus replied, "The sacrifices of the Way are not about *things!* Your life is about who you are and how you act, not what you own. Those who covet possessions, who keep what they do not need, who dress themselves in finery—none of these people will find the Way, for you will not need *things* in Paradise! Material things are a sign of greed, not sacrifice!"

There was a shocked silence. People shifted uneasily and cast wary glances toward the temple.

* * *

Prentiss turned to Win and I'Char and whispered, "No wonder they don't like him."

"Excuse me, my friend, I did not hear you." It was Jesus.

At first Prentiss thought he was speaking to the tall man, but Jesus seemed to be looking right at her. Or was she imagining it? He was in the arena far below; how could he have heard her comment?

"Yes, you, my sister," said Jesus.

Now Prentiss was sure Jesus was speaking to her. For a moment she remained silent, and then, almost as if the words were drawn from her, and she was speaking to no one else, she said, "I'm sorry. I was saying it is no wonder that the Pertise do not like you."

Someone grabbed her arm, and she knew it must be Win or I'Char, but she did not turn around, she was not sure if she could have taken her eyes off of Jesus. She felt the crowd around her move away.

But Jesus smiled, and said, "I noticed that you and your friends were speaking before. Is there something troubling you?"

How could he have noticed us speaking? They were but faces in a multitude. She heard Win whisper, "Careful," and squeeze her arm in warning, but she ignored him, and said, "Don't you ever worry that the Pertise might do something to you for preaching as you do?" Then she caught herself, becoming aware that everyone was staring at her, and she felt as if she were one of the crowd, watching herself, and knowing what they were all thinking.

Who was this woman?

"I will leave that up to the Pertise!" exclaimed Jesus, without a trace of anger in his voice. He laughed, and this seemed to calm the crowd. Then his voice turned very serious, more serious than he had been before. "I see your concern, and it is a generous thing. I say to you: you must have faith, and believe that all who hear my voice will come to see the Truth. For you, the truth of sacrifice is to help those who are lost, for only with your help can they find the way, and only thus can you yourself find the way. For while even one is lost, there can be no true peace in the universe."

Prentiss felt a jolt. It was as if Jesus had seen through them, and especially her, their purpose discovered. She looked around, suddenly realizing their risk, but the audience was already once again absorbed in Jesus, who was answering another question. Prentiss turned and stumbled away, as if in a daze, back through the crowd, trying to get free, free of the people and the bright light shining into her very soul.

Chapter 18

What do you seek? By that are you known.
—The Teachings 3:5

Prentiss opened her eyes. She was in a small alley, sitting against a cool wall. How did she get here?

An image flittered into her mind. The amphitheater, the crowds, Jesus.

Jesus.

She looked around. Win was leaning against the wall, looking the other way. Beyond him the street, much brighter than the alley, a few people passing by. She got up just as Win glanced toward her.

"Are you okay?" he asked.

"Yes, I'm fine. For a moment I thought I had been dreaming. But it was real, wasn't it?"

"Something was," said Win. "Come on, we should get moving. We might attract attention here; this alley leads back toward the temple."

"I'Char?" she asked.

"Off looking for Garrick. We'll meet up on the other side of the amphitheater, beyond the arena."

"How long have we been here?" She meant the alley.

"Not long. Are you sure you are all right?"

"Yes. It was just so overwhelming." She grabbed Win's arm. "Back there, did you feel something?" Her eyes were bright with excitement.

"I did. I'm not sure what. Perhaps the emotion of the crowd."

She shook her head. "No, it was more than that. These people felt a power emanating from that—" she hesitated, wondering what term to use—"man. Even we felt it. He could be the transformational catalyst that will allow this society to leap forward. It fits all of the patterns I have seen before and analyzed."

"I thought you said that the religious figure needs to be viewed as a deity? I didn't get the sense the audience thought of him that way. They seemed more afraid of being punished by their religious leaders."

She gave a little laugh. "You listen and remember well, Captain Win. If everyone on the Research Council listened as you did, I might not be here right now. But we might be seeing just the early stages of the transformation. I agree with you, the people do not appear to see him as a deity—at least not yet. If you recall the story of Jesus of Earth, you will know that he was not accepted as such for a long time."

Win looked back out toward the street. People continued to pass by, but no one appeared to be suspicious of them.

"I admit what you say seems to fit your theory, but there are still other possible explanations. This man could still be some kind of imposter, someone who knows the story of Jesus on Earth. Or someone who is very good at crowd manipulation."

Prentiss held his eye. "I don't believe that, and neither do you. Someone who had the power to affect so many people wouldn't need to take on the guise of another. As for manipulation, do you think you were being manipulated?"

Win hesitated. "I don't think so—but that is the point of manipulation. You can't feel it."

"Look, I understand your skepticism. If I hadn't seen this happen before on other planets I'd be skeptical too, as any good scientist would. But what we have here is a perfect—perhaps a once in a lifetime—opportunity to see whether my theory is true. We can document this step by step. Don't you see? We would be able to show once and for all how cultures develop, how they make the great leap beyond primitive technology." Her voice grew in excitement. "We can't pass this up!"

They heard voices from the street. Two men had stopped and were peering into the dark alley. Win nodded toward the street. "Follow my lead," he whispered.

He led her out of the alley, pausing just slightly as they passed the two K'Turians. "Just trying to cool down," he said to them. "Good day." Without waiting for a response they kept going, feeling the men's eyes on them. They headed off down the street, slowly, trying not to attract attention, and once they reached the market area lost themselves in the throng of people.

* * *

At sunset, Win and Prentiss were waiting for I'Char just outside the city, beyond the outer edge of the amphitheater. Here a low wall had been built, probably to keep dust from blowing into the arena. I'Char had seen the wall from the knoll atop the amphitheater, and had pointed it out to Win as a good meeting place. Now the area around the long wall was almost empty, just a few people here and there. Win chose a spot as far as possible from anyone, and where they could also have a clear view in every direction.

They had searched the city for Garrick, but had found no evidence of him. As Win and Prentiss had passed through the streets, they heard a few whispers of "pilgrims" and "Truthseekers," but no one seemed suspicious, just somewhat surprised, and though some people stared at them, they were left alone.

He and Prentiss had covered the city in sections, up one street, down the next, crossing over at the end of each quadrant. They had passed I'Char only once, the Illian ignoring them.

The search was both harder and easier than Win had expected. He had thought perhaps they would need to sneak around furtively. But many of the K'Turians wore their hoods as shields from the hot sun and the blowing sand, and so their disguises seemed to be working well. On the busy market street they even overheard a conversation about Jesus, one man excitedly telling a market seller who had obviously not been at the amphitheater about the drama of the priests. When the man noticed Win and Prentiss he nodded slightly, perhaps to convey some mutual experience. Win nodded back; Prentiss smiled at the man and touched her chest, as if indicating some kind of personal shared secret. The man smiled and watched them as they walked away.

But their robes and hoods had a drawback—everyone was dressed so alike, it would be hard to spot Garrick unless he walked right up to them. From the back, everyone looked the same.

They had barely covered the major streets when it was time to meet I'Char. Giving the temple a wide berth, they cut across the city beyond the market square and followed a small street to what looked like a staging area for grain. Beyond that, they could see the valley open up before them, and where the farmland began. Just past the staging area they turned to the left, so as to come upon the arena from the other side. Above them rose the amphitheater, empty now, and the temple, its bright stone shining in the setting sun.

As they waited, Win thought about what Prentiss had said in the alley.

Much of her argument appealed to him. Perhaps he was being affected by how passionately she believed in her theory. In many ways, Prentiss's ardor reminded him of Sooni, for she too had lived her life as her passion had guided her. He understood the concept of envy even though he did not think as a Treb he felt that emotion. Part of him wished he had as much ardor for something as Prentiss obviously had for her theory.

Or could there be another reason he was drawn to Prentiss's idea? The loss of Sooni had left him with a void, a void that could never be filled by another mate. Maybe he hoped some of this void could be filled by something else, something spiritual.

Was he intrigued by Prentiss's theory because he was a scientist, or because he wanted to believe in something—or someone?

His thoughts were interrupted by I'Char, who appeared as if from nowhere.

"You'll have to teach me how to do that," said Win. His *gheris* had told him nothing about I'Char's approach.

"Another time," said I'Char. "We should be safe here for a while, at least until dark. But let's move a little down the wall." He led them to another spot. "Harder to approach unseen here," explained I'Char. It seemed no different to Win, but this was the kind of thing I'Char was good at.

"Anything?" asked Win.

"No, not yet," said I'Char. "But there are still a lot of places to look."

"We went street by street," said Win.

"I know," said I'Char, "I saw you four times."

"We only saw you once," said Prentiss.

"I know that too," said I'Char. From anyone else it would have sounded like a boast. From I'Char, it was just a statement of fact. He went on, "I searched as I thought Garrick would, looking for places where the freighter could be hid."

"We tried all the wider avenues," said Win, "and we searched the market, but did not have time to get to the smaller streets, and those leading out of the city. No sign at all of Garrick. We also stayed clear of the Lemian base."

"I covered that," said I'Char. "And most of the side streets with larger buildings, although not the dead end alleys."

"What's the base like?"

"Not large, although it appears they plan on expanding it. A dozen buildings, prefabs, two large crew quarters, a command post, a communication building, and some storage. At least three buildings are large enough to hide the freighter. I would estimate there is one Lemian regiment here. They have a guard posted on each entrance, a roving sentry, and a mobile guard unit like the one we saw on the way in. The locals do not go near the camp on the far side, away from the city, so it will be hard to approach from that direction. But on the city side you can get fairly close."

"Any unusual activity?"

"None. If they found the freighter I doubt they brought it here. It's not out in the open. If they found it important enough to hide, they would have posted extra guards on the building. I didn't see any."

"Unless they didn't want to draw attention to the building."

"Perhaps. But the Lemians are very lightly armed. I doubt they fear much from the locals."

"Did you see Jesus?" asked Prentiss.

"No, but I know where he has been," said I'Char.

"You do? Where?"

"After leaving the arena he went to a small house on one of the side streets on the other side of the market."

"How did you learn that?" asked Prentiss.

I'Char ignored her question, but Win, always intrigued by I'Char's abilities, asked, "His residence in the city?"

"More likely the home of one of his secret supporters. Given the crowd that came to hear him, I would expect that his residence, if he had one here, would be mobbed with people waiting for him."

"We should go there," said Prentiss.

I'Char looked at her quizzically, and Win explained, "Specialist Prentiss wants to document this Jesus as evidence of her theory of cultural transformation."

"Dangerous," said I'Char.

"Why?" asked Prentiss. "He seems to have a great following. Who will notice a few more people who are interested in him? I think we are already perceived as pilgrims who have come to see Jesus."

"You forget the reason we are here," said I'Char. "The freighter."

"The damn freighter!" Prentiss snapped. "We don't even know why the freighter is so important. It can wait. It might not even be on this planet. We can certainly afford to spend some time studying what is going on here. I didn't get put on your ship to participate in military missions. You go look for the freighter if you want—let me do my work."

"Don't forget that Garrick obviously thinks the freighter is very important—important enough for him to risk trying to find it himself," said Win. "And we are bound to our duty—we've been ordered to find the freighter. I thought I made this clear."

"You're starting to sound like Garrick," said Prentiss. "You're thinking like a spy."

"I'm thinking like someone who doesn't want to attract attention," said Win.

"Where's the threat?" demanded Prentiss. "I didn't see a Lemian all day. All we need to do is stay out of their way and we'll be fine."

"You keep forgetting about Garrick," said I'Char. "He's looking for the freighter. He's going to be trying to get near the Lemian base. Unless he's very good—and even if he is—he is a danger to us all. The locals might not recognize him as an offworlder, but the Lemians will. They'll wonder why he is here, and suspect he is not alone."

"All the more reason for gathering what information we can about Jesus, as soon as possible," argued Prentiss. "Or we can go back to my other idea. Let's just tell the Lemians we are on a scientific mission."

"I'm afraid I have to agree with Garrick on that," said I'Char. "They wouldn't believe us."

"Not you perhaps, or Garrick, but they might believe me."

"We can't risk it," said Win. "I understand your desire to discover what is going on. Under any other circumstance we'd try to find a way—and I admit, I am intrigued. It's not like we aren't taking chances—we are taking a big risk in just being here. Garrick wasn't even willing to wait a few hours to start searching for the freighter. He might have information that something has changed, or that the freighter is definitely on K'Turia."

"Information he didn't share with us, you mean," said Prentiss.

Win was having a hard time arguing with her. Not only was he upset about Garrick, he too wanted to find out more about Jesus. *What's happening to me?* He felt—he could not describe it. *Different.* Sensing he was about to change in some way, but not knowing how. But at the same time he realized he felt more *alive*. More decisive.

It suddenly occurred to Win that he had made more difficult decisions in just the last few days than he had made in years.

"Look, we simply have to find Garrick," he said. "If the Lemians catch him sneaking around, they aren't likely to believe we are here on some kind of scientific mission. I'll make a deal with you. If we find Garrick, we'll see if there is some way to gather information about your cultural transformation theory while we are searching for the freighter. Acceptable?" He knew he could technically order her to obey, but he had the sense she would resist.

She searched his face. "Agreed. But let's find Garrick quickly. I suggest we split up to search. We could cover more ground that way." She turned to I'Char. "You tell us where to look."

"Safer together," said I'Char.

Win knew what he meant—that it would be safer for Win and Prentiss. He looked at the setting sun. "The city should still be crowded for a little while. Let's take advantage of this time to look for Garrick, separately." He looked sternly at Prentiss. "But if you have even the slightest suspicion that you are being watched or followed, get back to Symes's hut. Understood?"

* * *

As I'Char started to explain where he wanted them to go, Prentiss let her mind wander. She had agreed they should look for Garrick, but that didn't mean she couldn't also be looking for Jesus. I'Char would be better at finding Garrick anyway, and she didn't care at all about him, or the freighter. But Jesus was another story.

After hearing Jesus, she was more than ever convinced about her theory. Not only did Jesus fit her prediction of the transformation catalyst, but his words had galvanized her to action. Could what he said have been a coincidence? For he had told her to "have faith." This could only mean one thing—she had to have faith that she would find the proof of her theory, right here on K'Turia. And because faith would not convince the skeptics, she needed proof. The only faith she could afford was that her proof would come.

She wasn't going to let this chance get away. No matter how many risks she had to take, once and for all, she was going to prove to everyone she was right.

Chapter 19

Do not let others define what you can and cannot do. Instead, you must decide what you should do.
 —The Teachings 4:8

Garrick awoke in pain. He was strapped to a chair, his hands bound tightly behind his back. A bright light speared into his brain. He squeezed his eyes shut, dots flashing on his eyelids.

He tried to move, to ease the ache in his arms and legs, but then remembered where he was. He froze, too late.

"He's awake," came a voice.

Even with his eyes closed, he could sense the approach of the drug filled syringe.

* * *

"What have you learned from the prisoner, Commander Neel?" demanded Krelmar. Krelmar was not in a good mood. He had been awakened by Neel in the middle of the night with a report of the capture of an offworlder, spying on the Lemian base. Now, sitting in his office with Neel in the early morning, he was trying to figure out what it was all about.

"Very little, Sire. He is either telling the truth, or he is very well trained at resisting interrogation."

"Telling the truth? About being a religious pilgrim? That's nonsense. He is human stock."

"I am just informing Lord Krelmar of what he claims," said Neel, emotionless. "That he came to K'Turia long ago, lived on the other side of the planet, and has been searching for someone he heard about, some preacher. He followed the preacher to Valdar and is now looking for him in Merculon."

"In the middle of the night? On the base?" asked Krelmar incredulously.

"He wasn't actually on the base, Sire. Just near it."

"So you believe him?"

"I didn't say that. In fact, I doubt his story. We've seen no other human stock on the planet. But we do know part of his story is true—there is a religious preacher here with a lot of followers, many of them from Valdar."

"I thought Methurgem was their religious leader?"

"This preacher is not one of Pertise—in fact, we believe the Pertise don't like him. He's one of the subversives I mentioned to you, the one the priests seem especially concerned about. It's a bit confusing. It's hard to understand their religious situation; we don't have any locals who'll tell us."

"Hmm . . ." Krelmar was thinking about Tsaph. He'd ask the K'Turian about this later. "What of his story of coming to K'Turia?"

Neel's eyes looked away briefly. "We know the League has been here before."

Now that was news, thought Krelmar. *What else are they keeping from me?*

"The League? When?"

"Not recently, Sire. We don't know exactly when. But I was told before our arrival that the League had been to K'Turia in the past, and to be on the lookout for League contact. We've seen no evidence of them since we have been here."

"Except this offworlder right under your nose! How long has he been in Merculon?"

"We don't know."

"Why didn't you tell me before about the League having been here?" Krelmar demanded.

Neel hesitated. "I assumed you knew."

He's a terrible liar, thought Krelmar. "Anything *else* I should know?"

"Not to my knowledge, Lord Krelmar."

I wonder, thought Krelmar. Why would Tera-Seil not tell him about the League? How was he supposed to get control of the planet without such information?

Neel's apparent discomfort told Krelmar that something was being purposely hidden from him. He'd have to be careful about what he told Neel. But he also needed the Commander—without the Lemian troops, Krelmar was virtually powerless.

"How much pressure have you put on the prisoner?"

Neel's eyes flicked away again. "Very little. A little discomfort, and some chemicals. It should have been enough to break anyone down. We wanted to check with you before pushing harder."

Krelmar considered. "If the prisoner is telling the truth and the Pertise find out about our interrogation of a K'Turian, it will be hard to explain, and might threaten our deal—our *potential* deal. But we have to find out if this man is a spy. Work on him some more."

"As you wish, Sire." Neel hesitated. "Do you wish to send a communication to the Lemian Command?"

"Not yet," said Krelmar. "For all we know this is nothing." He looked sternly at Neel. The last thing he needed was for Neel to report that someone from the League was on the planet, someone who had appeared soon after Krelmar. Tera-Seil may already suspect him of working with the League—and would not believe this to be a coincidence. "Unless, of course, you wish to explain to your superiors that a possible League spy has been lurking around your base."

Neel eyed him narrowly. "If he is a spy, we'll have to tell the Lemian Command eventually."

"Of course. But wouldn't you first want to know how long he had been spying on you? I'm not a soldier, but I do not think it would reflect well on your security if it turns out the man has been here all the time. In the meantime, I'd start looking around. If he *is* a spy, it is unlikely that he is alone."

*   *   *

In the room just above Krelmar's office, Tsaph waited for the sound of the closing door, then he straightened up, taking his ear away from the ventilation grate. Krelmar and Neel had been speaking in Galactic, but Tsaph had followed the conversation easily. The grate had worked perfectly as a way of eavesdropping on the conversation from Krelmar's office. Of course, he expected it to—he had installed it himself, during the conversion of his relative's house into Krelmar's office.

He had just heard the tail end of Krelmar's conversation with Neel. Something about a spy. Who were they talking about?

He needed to find out more.

*   *   *

Krelmar heard a light tapping on his door. Thinking it was Neel again, he said, "Enter," speaking in Galactic.

No one responded. "Come in!" He said, this time in K'Turian. "Ahh, Tsaph. I thought it was Neel again. Come in. I need to ask you something."

Krelmar caught a glimpse of worry on Tsaph's face. "Yes, of course," said the trader.

"Commander Neel tells me the city is a destination for some religious pilgrims," said Krelmar. "Is that because of the temple?"

"No, Sire. Each city on the planet has its own temple. The pilgrims came here for a different reason, to hear a certain preacher."

"Came here? Don't they come any more? And who is this preacher?"

"His name is Jesus. He is from Valdar, or so they say. When he began to spend more time in Merculon, pilgrims from Valdar would come to hear him speak. Some call them Truthseekers. But they do not come any more, at least not many do."

"And why is that?"

Tsaph looked around, as if afraid others might be listening.

"Because the Pertise have punished those who have followed Jesus."

Krelmar could see that Tsaph was uncomfortable with the conversation. He prodded, "Why did they do that?"

"Because the Pertise believe Jesus is a troublemaker, a disturber of the peace."

Krelmar waited for Tsaph to continue, but the K'Turian fell silent. "Is he a criminal?" Krelmar asked. "What did he do?"

"Nothing really. But—but you have to understand, Lord Krelmar, the Pertise are the keepers of the Way. They translate the Way for us, in order for us to understand how we should live our lives. Jesus' teachings seem to—contradict the Way."

"Your religious beliefs are of no concern to me," said Krelmar.

"But Lord Krelmar, the Way is our path, our direction in life, our only way to reach Paradise," said Tsaph. "It guides us in everything we do. How we work, how we live, how we pray. We live by the Order, which the Pertise tell us is part of the Way. The Pertise say the Order is what keeps us at peace."

"And everyone is content with their lot in life, their position in the Order?" asked Krelmar, not hiding his sarcasm. "Your religious leaders, the Pertise. Are they the ones who make up all these rules?"

"The Pertise are the translators of the Way. They describe the Way for us in means we can understand—in the Laws."

"And what happens if someone disobeys these laws?"

"Very few do. They would be banished. And there are—other punishments."

So that's how the Pertise get their power. "Tell me, Tsaph, this preacher, Jesus, has he come right out and disobeyed the laws?"

"No," said Tsaph, "but—"

"But what? Go on."

"Some of his beliefs might be considered contrary to our Laws. At least, that is how some people think the Pertise feel. The pilgrims from Valdar have questioned the Laws, and for this reason the Pertise have made it clear they are not welcome in the city."

"So what's the problem?" asked Krelmar. "Are the pilgrims still here?"

Tsaph looked around again. "I don't know any of this for sure, Lord Krelmar. I'm just telling you what I have heard."

"And what is that?"

"That there are many followers of Jesus in Merculon, and not just from Valdar."

"Interesting," said Krelmar. He was thinking of the prisoner. Could he be telling the truth, about being a pilgrim? "Tsaph, these pilgrims, are any of them offworlders?"

"Offworlders?"

"Yes, like the Lemians, and myself."

"I understand, I was just surprised by the question, Lord Krelmar. I don't believe so. Jesus is still of our religion, though his preaching may be controversial. Why would anyone from offworld be interested in our Way? It is ours alone—you see, if you are not K'Turian, you cannot follow the Way. You would not fit in the Order. And of course you can never find Paradise."

Krelmar decided not to argue the point. But Tsaph had told him something extremely useful. If there really were no offworld pilgrims, then where was the prisoner from, and what was he doing here?

He was of human stock, so Krelmar doubted he could be spying for one of the Empires. So it had to be the League. Was this the best the League could do, send a man armed with nothing more than sandals and a robe?

The spy had carried no technology, no sensors. Surely if the League wanted to scout the Lemian base there were much easier ways to do it. They could just use probes or deep space scans.

It made no sense. Unless there were others with him, with technology and sensors.

Or maybe whatever they were looking for could not be found with technology. This Jesus. Could they be looking for him?

It seemed unlikely. Maybe the human spy was not looking for someone, but for *something*. But what?

No matter what the reason, Krelmar had to assume the worst, that League spies were on the planet, and that there was some important reason for them to be here.

Whatever they were looking for, if he could find it before they did, it would be something he could bring to Tera-Seil, another way to prove his worth. If the League wanted something badly, surely the Lemian Empire would as well.

But how to find it? Should he have Neel and his soldiers conduct a search? He didn't even know what to tell them to look for. If he made too much of it Neel would probably inform the Lemian Command, and Krelmar didn't want Tera-Seil to think he didn't have everything under control.

He had another idea. "Tsaph, I want you to help me with something."

* * *

Tsaph walked quickly down one of the small side streets of Merculon. He had left Krelmar's house on the pretext of doing what Krelmar had asked of him. And he would begin that later, but first he had another duty.

He had not been entirely truthful with Krelmar. He knew much more about the teachings of Jesus than he had let on.

But he was confused. All his life he had lived by the Way, and now Jesus seemed to be saying that—he wasn't sure just what Jesus meant sometimes—but Jesus seemed to be saying that the priests had not been telling the truth about the Way.

As a trader, Tsaph was at the lowest end of the Order. The traders even had to pay for their food. This he had never questioned—the acceptance of his position was, after all, part of the Way. It was what kept the peace, what kept everyone alive. And it was why he had worked with the Lemians. No one else in the Order would, only the traders. Only they were so low that even the offworld heathens could not taint them. Though they never said it, Tsaph often wondered if the Pertise even thought the traders could reach Paradise.

So of course he had helped the Lemians. What did he have to lose? He probably wasn't going to make it to Paradise anyway—and it wasn't as if there were people below him in the Order making

Sacrifices to him, giving him things like the Lemians did.

But what if the priests were wrong—or lying? What if he could be more than a trader? Did he dare even think about that?

The street narrowed, and at the next crossing he turned, taking him into a maze of small alleys. Here the market vendors kept many of their wares, in these shadowed, cooler buildings with their thick walls. Though there was little crime in Merculon, these were some of the only buildings in the city with sturdy, locked doors.

At this time of the day few people were about, since the vendors were already at the market. Tsaph took one last look around to make sure he was unseen, then unlocked one of the nondescript doors. It would not have mattered if he had been noticed; he was a trader, and no one would be suspicious of him being in this area.

Still, he was cautious. He entered the room and lit a small lantern, then walked past crates of goods to the back wall. Here there was another door, which looked like a back entrance. This too was locked, and when he opened the door it revealed not a street but another room. A room within a room, actually; its thick walls originally designed to keep the space extra cool for storing wine. But now it had another purpose.

In the center of the room was a large crate. Tsaph pried off one end, and inside, instead of wine, was a complex piece of electronics. Tsaph was no longer in awe of it, having used it many times, but he realized no one else on the planet would know what to make of it. For K'Turians knew nothing about electronics, and would never believe that from here he could communicate to worlds far away.

The communications unit turned on with a muted click. He was unconcerned anyone would hear the minute sounds it made, or would hear him speak, for the walls were incredibly thick.

Tsaph reviewed in his mind what he was going to say in his report. Tera-Seil would certainly want to know about the prisoner. And the fact that Krelmar suspected spies were on the planet.

Even more surprising to Tera-Seil, he surmised, would be that Krelmar had asked Tsaph to begin looking for something from offworld—instead of asking Neel.

He didn't know whether Neel would have already told Tera-Seil about the prisoner, or whether the Commander was going to follow Krelmar's advice and keep that information secret. But it made no difference to him, for unlike Neel and Krelmar, Tsaph would keep nothing from Tera-Seil. Nothing at all.

* * *

Tera-Seil read the report carefully. His agent on K'Turia, Tsaph, was smart enough not to try to guess what information Tera-Seil might want, and so the report was full of detail, much of it of little use.

But even the K'Turian must have realized the import of what this report contained. The information about the prisoner was only marginally interesting, although Neel should have included it in his own report. Tera-Seil would deal with that later, perhaps there was a good explanation. After all, Tera-Seil couldn't be bothered by every minor security action on every planet.

What *was* of great interest, however, was that Krelmar clearly thought the prisoner was from the League and a spy. Why would Krelmar keep such information to himself?

Could Krelmar perhaps have known about the spy all along? And this last item, about some kind of secret search Krelmar wanted Tsaph to undertake. What did the spy—and Krelmar—think was on the planet?

It could only be one thing. *The missing League freighter.*

Could it actually be on K'Turia? Surely the League would know. Had they sent someone there to destroy any evidence it was carrying weapons?

He'd have to speed up his plan. If the League found the freighter first, he would lose his chance to use it to destroy any League-Rhean alliance. And if the freighter did not have weapons and anyone else found it, he would not be able to plant weapons in it to frame the League.

If Tsaph found the freighter first, his plan might still work. But it would be hard to keep the discovery a secret for long. Tera-Seil couldn't take that chance.

It was time to send Tsaph some reinforcements. In fact, he might even have to go himself.

Chapter 20

The Way to Paradise is one of sacrifice, not selfishness; choice, but not fear.
—The Teachings 5:15

Prentiss hurried across the almost empty market square, praying that the growing shadows of the early evening would keep her from being recognized as an offworlder. She was already late for the rendezvous with Win and I'Char.

But she had something far more important on her mind.

Earlier in the day, when she had been searching the city with Win, she had noticed a few side streets that had appeared deserted, but which were rich with aroma. Places that served food, she had thought. This is where people would gather in the evening, before returning to their homes outside the city.

Though she would normally hesitate to do anything which might corrupt the societal development, it was clear to her now that the Lemians, just by being here, had already done that damage with their modern technology. Garrick, that clod, had been right about that.

So just after sunset she had returned to this area, now crowded with people. Lanterns were lit in the windows, and the smell of cooked food was everywhere.

She wasn't there to eat. Normally she would have been eager to try the local food, but she had no way to buy it or trade for it. She kept her hunger at bay by sneaking a few bites from the concentrated food bars she had hidden under her robe.

She wandered up and down the streets, just one more person trying to decide where to eat. But instead of looking for food, she was listening to the conversation, hoping to overhear something about Jesus.

She didn't have to eavesdrop. It was almost hard not to hear about Jesus; he was the topic of almost every conversation. As she walked she heard excited discussions recounting the scene at the amphitheater. No priests were here, and the talk was freer, more open.

She hurried past any streets where she saw few women. Near the end of the food neighborhood was a small square, gaily lit, but subdued. Most of the tables were filled with women, some with small children.

Prentiss paused to listen to one of the conversations. A middle aged woman was describing how the priests had challenged Jesus, recounting the dialogue and the story of the two farmers almost word for word. Her audience listened raptly, and when the storyteller was done someone asked: "Jura, did Jesus explain what this story meant?"

"Jesus said it does not matter where we pray, that if we cannot be in temple on the worship day we should not worry, we can still follow the Way in our hearts," said Jura.

"That is hard to understand. The Law says that we must pray in the temple on worship day. We have been taught to obey the Law to the letter!"

Jura shook her head. "Jesus said the Laws cannot be more important than the Way—that we should not follow the Laws out of fear. And he told another story about sacrifice, saying the true Way requires that we make sacrifices to help each other—no matter where we are in the Order."

"Were the Pertise there?" asked another. "I cannot believe they would let him speak like this!"

"There were no Pertise, just some Temple priests. I tell you though, the people were not afraid of the priests, and shouted at them."

"That's because the Pertise were not there," said another woman, lowering her voice. "Such talk is dangerous."

"It is more than dangerous, it is blasphemy," said another. "Maybe that is why Jesus waited for the priests to leave."

"Jesus is not afraid of the priests," said Jura. "I have heard him speak many times, he speaks as he will. He has said before: 'You should believe in the truth, and directly in the truth. Do not rely on rituals or rules, but rely on the Way.' Now I understand what he meant by this. He is saying we should be responsible for how we live the Way, that we should not just do what the priests tell us because we are afraid of being punished by them."

"I have heard these words too," said a woman who had been silent. "But I think it means more than this. I think Jesus means we cannot just go to temple and pray and pay the Sacrifices. He is saying we need to do more, even if it means helping those below us in the Order, even if it means making sacrifices for those below us instead of only those above us." She paused, and then less sure of herself, said, "I think Jesus is saying we do not have to settle for our place in the Order."

"Hush! Do not let anyone hear you speak like that!"

"Wait, she is right! There is more," said Jura. "After the priests left, Jesus said, 'The sacrifices of the Way are not about *things*. You will not need *things* in Paradise!'"

This led to a shaking of heads, and whispers of disbelief. "That cannot be!"

"That is what he said," insisted Jura. "I was there, I heard it."

"I cannot believe that," said another. "No one who believes in our Way would say such a thing. Mark my words, he will be banished soon enough."

"I tell you, it is what he said," Jura repeated.

"You must not be remembering this right," said someone, and all the women began to talk amongst themselves, shaking their heads. "Jesus would not have said that."

The storyteller looked around helplessly. Her eyes settled on Prentiss.

Prentiss, listening quietly at the back of the group, noticed the woman looking at her. Slowly she stepped into the light from one of the windows so Jura could see her more clearly.

"You, pilgrim! You were there!" said Jura. "Tell them!"

All eyes turned to Prentiss. "I was there," she said quietly. "This woman speaks the truth."

The conversations abruptly ended, everyone staring at her, and Prentiss quickly retreated into the shadows. When the dialogue began again it was in much more hushed tones, and a few of the women hunched over, not wanting to be overheard by the outsider. Prentiss sensed their discomfort and moved away.

But her gambit had worked. Before she had gone halfway back up the street she heard footsteps behind her.

"Excuse me, pilgrim."

Prentiss turned to face the storyteller, Jura. Up close, the K'Turian woman was not pretty, her skin pockmarked and rough. Dark hair peeked out from under her hood. But her eyes were bright.

"I wanted to thank you for your words," Jura said haltingly. "I was telling it as I heard it."

"I know," said Prentiss. "You have a gift for memory."

The woman laughed, but it was without much feeling. Her hands went to her face, touching the blemishes. "I have not much else except my mind," she said, and looked away, hiding her hands in her robe.

Prentiss reached out for the woman's arm. "Sister, I understand why you hearken to him."

Jura smiled, clasping Prentiss's hand. "You are a believer?"

When Prentiss hesitated, the woman went on, "Do not fear, I will tell no one."

"It's not that," said Prentiss. But she didn't know what to say. "Yes—I mean, no. I believe, I believe that . . ." What exactly did she believe?

"Don't worry," said the woman. "I understand. It is hard to talk about."

That wasn't it, thought Prentiss. I can't just tell this woman about my scientific views of religious figures. But she didn't want to appear out of place to Jura, who obviously thought Prentiss was a pilgrim, come to see Jesus.

"I have come to hear more, before I can . . . before I can make up my mind," she finally said. "I was hoping to hear Jesus speak again."

The K'Turian woman looked deep into Prentiss's eyes. Apparently pleased by what she sensed, Jura said, "You seek the truth. I can help you. I know where he will be tonight."

* * *

Later, Prentiss had wandered the streets, but had carefully covered her face, impatiently waiting for dark. Now she was following the directions Jura had given her. Once across the plaza, she headed toward the tor, away from the temple. Win would be furious, but she couldn't help herself.

The streets narrowed and became darker, the buildings shabbier. This was not the better part of town. She imagined people were watching her from their windows as she hurried by. But the few people in the streets did not seem interested in her.

Unlike the road from the valley, where the homes had gradually petered out, here the city abruptly ended. As she passed by the last house she could see why. The area in front of her steepened and grew rocky. To the right, a mass of boulders, and evidence of rockslides from the hill above. To the left were fewer rocks and an orchard, lines and lines of neatly planted trees.

She made for the trees. Away from the sounds of the city she could hear the slight rustle of wind in the branches. She climbed a hill. From the top she could see down into a small vale, between the hill and the tor. She walked along the ridge formed by the hillside, the city to her left, sensing more than seeing the trees in the vale, for they lay in the shadow of the mountain.

Ahead, a light flickered down in the vale, just as Jura had promised. At the end of the ridge there was a trail, and in the dim light she made her way carefully down the slope, toward the light, a beacon in the darkness. The trail widened into a lane through the trees. Using the light as a guide she followed it along until she came to a clear space, an open circle amidst the orchard.

There, in the clearing, sat about a dozen people, listening.

She had found Jesus.

Chapter 21

The Truth will overcome even those who deny they are in darkness.

—The Teachings 6:5

It was hard for the young Temple acolyte known as Sahme to hold her tongue as she listened to the crone Jura tell the story about Jesus. The acolyte had not been at the amphitheater, but Jura had to be lying. Sahme could not believe anyone would have stood by while that Jesus heretic had uttered such blasphemy. Especially hard to accept was Jura's claim that the audience had believed the preacher—and that the priests had done nothing except yell out a few challenges and then leave.

But the acolyte had been instructed by Amora to wait, listen, and learn, and that is what she was doing. And when the crone had dared to say that the people did not have to live by the Order, Sahme smiled under her hood as the crone was shouted down. Even the support from the stranger, the pilgrim woman, did not sway the others.

When the pilgrim left, the acolyte followed after her, careful to stay in the shadows. Suddenly she heard footsteps from behind, and her pulse quickened. But it was only Jura, rushing to catch the pilgrim. Sahme slipped into a doorway, out of sight. When Jura was safely past, the acolyte carefully followed. Rounding a corner she could see Jura and the pilgrim in animated discussion, but she was too far away to hear what they were saying.

It did not matter. Amora had told her to also be on the lookout for pilgrims. When the crone left, Sahme followed after the pilgrim.

* * *

"Where is she? Where is she?" muttered Symes, over and over. He kept pacing back and forth along the city wall, as if this would hasten the appearance of Prentiss.

Not far away, near a building against the wall, Win and I'Char also waited, appearing calmer but no less anxious for her presence. It was well past the time when Prentiss was supposed to meet them here, just inside the city gate.

Symes stopped in front of Win. "She is in trouble, they must have found out about her. We have to find her!"

Win again tried to calm the old man, but he was running out of excuses to offer Symes. Win was not only worried about Prentiss, but angry at her for not obeying him. First Garrick, and now Prentiss.

Anger. He hadn't felt this angry about anything since . . . he couldn't remember when. What was happening to him?

"Perhaps he is right," said I'Char.

"Yes, yes," said Symes. "We must go find her."

Win shook his head no. He didn't want Symes running around the city at night in his excited state. He would be sure to attract attention, and there was no telling what he might say. But in the gathering gloom there was less risk of he and I'Char being recognized.

"Symes, we will go and find her, but you must go back to your hut," said Win.

"No, I will help you look," said Symes.

Win tried again. "If she returns when we are gone, she will think something bad has happened to us—to you," said Win. "If we are not here when she returns, she'll go back to the hut. If you are not there she will worry about you."

Symes stopped his nervous movements. "Worry about me?"

"Yes, I'm sure of it," said Win. "So you see, the best way you can help her is to go back to your hut."

"What will you do?" asked Symes.

"We'll go find her," said Win. "And if we miss her we'll all meet back at your place."

Symes's eyes blinked, as if he were trying to find a hole in the argument. Finally he said, "Yes, I will go and wait. I cannot have her worry." He started walking back toward the archway. "I will wait there," he repeated, and then he practically ran out of the city.

"Why do you think he is so worried about Prentiss?" asked Win.

"Maybe no one has taken him so seriously before," replied I'Char.

Win remembered how gently Prentiss had treated the old man. "Or maybe no one has been as kind to him as she was. Any ideas on where she might be?"

"A lot of possibilities," said I'Char. "Not many of them good."

"Garrick missing, and now her. Too much of a coincidence," said Win.

"Maybe," said I'Char. "Don't forget her other interest."

"Jesus," said Win. "I know. But that might be hoping for too much. I'm more worried about the Lemians."

"As am I. If she doesn't show up by morning we will have to assume the worst. In the meantime, we can look for her."

"She could be anywhere," said Win. "But if she has been caught by the Lemians, or the priests, she'll be in a state of anxiety, as will they. That might help me find her."

"*Gheris?*" asked I'Char, using the Treb word.

"I didn't know you spoke Treb," said Win.

"I'm just full of surprises," said I'Char, which was exactly what Win was thinking. It would have been humorous if not for the situation. "Can you do it from here?" asked I'Char.

"No," said Win. "It would have to be a mass of emotion for me to sense it from a distance. If that had happened I would already have felt it."

"Like the amphitheater?"

"Yes, but that was different. I didn't need *gheris* to feel that." It *had* been different, almost as if he were sensing the emotion without the need for his *gheris*. "Let's walk around." He pointed toward the Lemian base. "Starting there."

* * *

The acolyte waited until the pilgrim had crossed the plaza. Sahme gave the temple a glance over her shoulder, knowing she should report back to the Pertise. But surely they would want to know what the pilgrim was doing, for she was acting very odd, her movements hurried and furtive. So the acolyte followed the pilgrim, but as the streets narrowed and became less crowded she had to stay farther back so as not to be noticed.

* * *

Win was trying to walk and reach out with his *gheris* at the same time. It was not easy. His ability to sense strong emotions had been sullied by working for so long with other races, many of them so excitable that he had learned to build some internal shields, otherwise he'd be overwhelmed. This was one reason why most Trebs kept to themselves.

Ever since landing on the planet, his senses had been so—heightened. He still didn't understand exactly why. But he was beginning to suspect a reason—a reason he was reluctant to accept.

Could Jesus have some power over him?

Right now he had to try to get control over his *gheris* in order to try to find Prentiss. It would have been easier if he could sit quietly and enter *nore*, but here, just outside the Lemian camp, that would be suspicious. So they passed by only once, under the watchful eye of the Lemian sentry.

For a brief instant he felt a jolt, someone in pain. Then the sensation was gone. He looked over at the camp, but it told him nothing.

They turned around and headed back into the city.

"This is no good," said Win. "I need some quiet space."

"This way," said I'Char. Once through the entrance arch they followed the wide lane which ran along the wall, heading toward the hills. Torches were alit along the wall, making it relatively easy to see.

The street was mostly deserted. On their right the buildings became progressively smaller, and then ended, as did the wall. Just past that point the ground sloped upward to a small ridge.

"Quiet here," said I'Char.

"Surprised the wall ends," said Win.

"Probably built to keep the sand out, not defense," said I'Char. "It's like this on the other side of the city as well."

Win wondered how I'Char had managed to make it all the way around the city; the Illian's skills never ceased to amaze him. "This is a good spot," he said.

"I'll have a look around," said I'Char. He disappeared into the shadows.

Win sat down on the ground, his back against the wall. He relaxed, preparing to enter *nore*. Soon he was in the delicate state of awareness, his senses acute. Sounds sharpened; he heard footsteps, muted conversations. Now for the tricky part, to ignore the heightened effects of his senses, especially sound, and focus on his *gheris*.

He opened himself up, and immediately was overwhelmed by a wave of emotion. He steadied himself, trying to probe for any perception of fear, or pain. But all he felt was—he gave up on trying to identify it, and instead just let the sensation engulf him.

Suddenly he realized what it was. *Passion*. So long missing from his life, he had not recognized the emotion even when it had surrounded him.

This was what he had felt in the amphitheater, and here it was again. At a level he had never believed possible.

He stood up abruptly, his *nore* shattered. Out of nowhere I'Char was at his side. Why hadn't Win sensed him coming?

"You okay?" asked I'Char.

"Yes, it's just . . ." Win struggled to put it into words. They were still speaking K'Turian, for fear of being overheard. But he couldn't think of a word to describe how he felt in any language he knew.

"I'm getting the same—sensation—as I did at the amphitheater. An emotion yes, but it is different from what I normally feel with *gheris*."

"Trouble?"

"I don't think so. It's—it's—the only way I can describe it is *passion*. Like a multitude of people, feeling strongly about something." *Or one person, with a power beyond comprehension.* "Could there be another large gathering nearby?"

"Nothing very close," said I'Char. "Nearest larger buildings and open space is back by the market."

"A smaller group then," said Win. "But it would have to be much closer." For some reason he couldn't bring himself to tell I'Char what else he was thinking. But that wasn't fair to I'Char—he needed to know.

Win looked back toward the well spaced small buildings they had passed. They were dark, and he had sensed nothing when he had walked past them before. He pointed off in the other direction, beyond where the wall ended, toward the tor. "Do you know what's that way?"

"A ridge, then an orchard of some kind. I didn't go through it," said I'Char.

"Let's check it out while we are here," said Win.

I'Char started off, but Win said, "Wait. I have to tell you something." He didn't know quite where to begin. "You've known me a long time. But you don't know much about me—about who I was before I joined the League."

"None of my business," said I'Char.

"It is now," said Win. "I should have told you all of this before, I don't know why I didn't." And then it all came out in a rush, the Treb search for *ana*, their higher purpose, his falling in love with Sooni, the *ana* within their grasp. Then the loss of Sooni, and his fall.

"I've been lost," he said, and was surprised by how sad he suddenly felt. He had been too numb to even feel sorry for himself. "It's like there is—a blackness, where the seeking used to be. It's why I've had so many problems making decisions, why I ended up as a scientist. I've been hiding in science, in facts and data. I stopped seeking—this is death to a Treb. Perhaps it is something you cannot understand."

Jesus of K'Turia

The Illian gave him an odd look. "We all have a purpose."

Win looked up. "What's yours?"

I'Char's facial features briefly shifted back to something closer to how he usually looked. "The same as it has been since I have known you: to help you. It may not be the higher purpose you seek, but it is enough for me."

Win was speechless. Is this what I'Char felt he was living for? To help Win? He looked at I'Char, seeing him in a new light. He hadn't felt this close to anyone since—

"Thank you," Win finally managed.

"No need," said I'Char. "It's my choice. But you're welcome."

Suddenly the words Jesus had spoken in the arena filled Win's head: "Sacrificing because you want to help others is what will keep you alive."

Win hoped no one would have to make such a sacrifice. Not for him.

* * *

The acolyte Sahme could just make out the pilgrim woman in the darkness ahead. The pilgrim was leaving the city, heading—toward the orchard? There was nothing there. Still, Sahme followed, careful to stay in the shadows. She watched the pilgrim climb a hill just beyond the edge of the city. When the pilgrim disappeared over the ridge, Sahme followed as quietly as she could. She wanted to find out where the pilgrim was going. Surely the Pertise would want to know.

* * *

I'Char led Win past the end of the wall. The lane they had been on kept going, as if leading right to the tor. The few lights from the city were now behind them, making it difficult to see.

Soon the ground to the right of them began to rise up. They were at the base of what looked like a small hill. They continued on, and after rounding the hill they came to a small ridge, the darker shadow of the tor ahead of them. Below them, at the base of the tor, lay the orchard.

I'Char had been surprised by what Win had told him. Not only by what had been said, but just the fact that Win had said anything. He had known Win for years, and this was the first time Win had shared anything so private.

His words to Win had been the truth—all Illians had a purpose. Those who did not know much about Illians—which was most of the galaxy—confused it with a function, as if Illians were machines. But the Illian purpose went far beyond function, beyond duty. I'Char had chosen a purpose; one that was more complex than the duty to the League—more complex even than the duty to Win. But right now, his purpose was best served by helping Win, just as it had been for years.

What had made Win suddenly reveal so much about himself? Ever since listening to Jesus, Win had seemed—different. More curious, more interested in what was going on around him.

That was good. But it also brought the risk of distraction. And distraction could get Win and Prentiss killed.

He wasn't worried about himself, although the risk was just as great for him. He could take care of himself, and he could face death. Win and Prentiss—they weren't ready. He'd have to protect them both.

Through the trees he saw a glimpse of light. Win continued forward but I'Char grabbed his arm and whispered, "Wait." He nudged Win around until he was looking up toward the ridge. There, silhouetted against the moonlit sky, stood a single figure on the far end of the ridge. The figure waited momentarily, then began to make its way down and was soon lost to sight.

"Probably going the other way around," whispered I'Char. "We can—" He stopped when another figure appeared on the ridge briefly, then disappeared quickly in the same direction as the first. They waited, but no one else appeared.

"Let's go the other way," said I'Char, just loud enough for Win to hear. They retraced their steps back to the lane, then followed it toward the tor. Soon they were amidst the trees of the orchard, the light still flickering to their right. They came to an intersection with another lane, barely visible in the dimness, heading off to the right. They went that way, the newer lane narrowing to a mere path. Quietly they approached the light, and when they got closer they could see a large campfire, set amidst a clearing in the orchard. Just before the clearing they stopped, still in the cover of the trees.

In the clearing, brightly lit by the fire, a dozen people sat in a circle. The sounds of laughter and the scraping of pots drifted over the night air. They edged closer to the last of the trees, but still within the shadows.

Suddenly the group quieted, and one of them began to speak.

* * *

Prentiss paused in indecision. She desperately wanted to hear what Jesus was saying, but she did not want to intrude upon the small gathering. Finally she began to make her way through the trees, trying to be as quiet as possible.

She got as close as she dared, and began to listen.

"Just as this fire keeps the dark at bay, so too can Light show you the path to Paradise. Without the Light you can stumble, or be led astray. The Light is the Truth, it will lead you along the right path, the true Way."

Jesus paused, and one of the disciples asked, "Where do we find this Light to guide us?"

Jesus turned to him. "Tthean, that is a good question. Let me tell you. The Light is within you! Each of you have this Light, but it has been obstructed and dimmed by the corruption of the Way. You have become so intent on maintaining the rules and rituals of the Law that you have not nurtured your internal Light. Blindly following the Laws have made you blind to the Light that is within you. You must rekindle this Light, just as you would light a lantern, or as you did this fire. This Light will guide you, so that you will know the Truth, and you will be able to shout it for all to hear. Such a Light is also a beacon, and it will attract anyone who seeks the Truth. And the Truth will overcome even those who deny they are in darkness."

Prentiss felt a rush. Once again it sounded as if Jesus were speaking to her. For this was what she was trying to do, bring truth to the disbelievers, those who rejected what she knew to be true. But she had been unable to open their eyes, for they refused to accept that their minds were closed.

"Jesus, do we all have this Light?" Prentiss put her hand to her mouth. Had she spoken? No, it had been one of the women around the fire, voicing the very thought in her mind.

"You do!" said Jesus. "But you must believe it is in you. Until that time I will help you, I will be your Light. And I will walk ahead of you on the path to Paradise; you have only to follow my footsteps. Yet you must do more than follow blindly along. I can show you the Way, but you must choose whether or not you will walk the path. And once upon it, *how* you will walk the path."

"Isn't that the same thing?" the woman asked.

"No! Think of it this way," explained Jesus. "You are walking on a road through the hills, and you reach a crossroads. You do not know which way to go. You see me there at the crossroads, and you ask of me: 'Which of these roads will lead me to Paradise?' And I say to you, 'As long as you stay on the road that I will show you, they all do!' Thus each of you will walk the path a little differently, for the path is one of sacrifice, and helping others. Each of you will make different sacrifices, each to your own gifts. This is why I say that you can be shown the paths, even though you are not blindly led."

"But the Pertise and priests tell us there are many rules we must follow to find the Way—and if we don't follow the Laws we will suffer. Are their teachings wrong? What of the Order?"

"You must discover the Truth, and then choose to follow the Way of your own volition, not out of fear. Remember my words: there can be no true peace while there is fear. If you choose the path out of fear and compulsion instead of belief, you will be lost. Many of the priests and the Pertise are good people, and those who are will find the Way. But many others have become lost to meaningless rituals which have crowded out the real reason that the Laws were created. They have become slaves, shallowly following a set of rules, thinking such a life will lead them easily to Paradise. What sacrifice is there in this? I say to you: the true Way is not one of harsh rules and punishment. Yes, you must make many sacrifices, but these sacrifices must be those you choose to make out of love, not those you are told to make. The Sacrifices of the Order are not the sacrifices of the Way. They are nothing more than taxes, material goods and other things from without. Surely there will be times when a sacrifice of a worldly good is worthy and right, such as when you help your neighbor by giving him food when he does not have enough to eat. But you must do *more*. You must give something of yourself, out of love.

"The suffering which the priests threaten you with is nothing more than a creation of the Pertise, a yoke to hold you in their power. If you act out of love, there will be no need for you to suffer."

"I still do not understand, Jesus," said another. "The path we have been taught by the Pertise is very clear. The Laws tell us exactly how to act, how to live. It is very real. Yet you tell us we must decide how we will walk the path, and which sacrifices we should make. How will we know which sacrifices are the right ones? How will we know which sacrifices will show us the Way? The path is invisible to me."

The fire had died down, and much of the clearing was now in shadows. Jesus said, "Look around you! See how everything grows dim in the darkness. It is as if the trees that you know are here are no longer real." He stood up and put a log on the fire, and the flames crackled, growing higher. He put on another and another, and the clearing grew as bright as day.

"Just as these logs are sustenance of the fire, faith is sustenance of the spirit. You must feed the light within you as I feed this fire. You worry that the path is not real because it is not laid before you out of strict rules, and thus you feel you cannot see it at all. But much that is invisible is real. Look around you now! See how this light makes the trees real again? If you have faith, then the light within you will show you all that you need to see, and it will bring forth wondrous things which were hidden. Once you know the Truth, your lives will be changed forever, and for you especially, you who hear my voice, you will have a special mission, to shout the Truth, so that you can change the lives of others. If you speak from your heart, your voice will be heard by even those who do not believe in me! The very power of your faith will cast aside their disbelief, and open their eyes to the Truth."

Jesus cast another log on the fire, and then looked across the clearing, directly at Prentiss. "Don't you agree, Sister?" And this time, without a doubt, she knew Jesus was speaking to her.

* * *

On the other side of the clearing, I'Char had pulled Win back deeper into the shadow of the trees even as Jesus had thrown the first log on the fire. There they had listened, Win knowing for sure now that the sensation he had been feeling, the passion, had come from this place, from these people, and from Jesus himself.

As the flames shot up, Jesus said, "Don't you agree, Sister?" and in the new light they saw Prentiss across the clearing. She hesitated, then stepped forward. The people around Jesus jumped to their feet.

"What are you doing back there, spying on us?" one huge man demanded. "Who are you?"

"I'm sorry," said Prentiss. "I did not mean to disturb you. I—I—saw the light."

"Yes, I believe you have," said Jesus. "At least you have seen the light of the fire. Tell me, pilgrim, what do you seek?"

"I seek the truth," she said confidently.

"So you say," said Jesus. "Many claim to be interested in what is called truth, and many offer what they say is truth. Which truth do you seek? And will you be willing to live by what you discover? As you seek the Truth, remember that proving what you already believe, and learning the Truth, might not be one in the same. Tell me, Sister, do you believe in one Truth?"

From his vantage point, Win swore, *Damn that woman!*

"There can only be one truth," said Prentiss.

The one called Tthean said, "Jesus, we must be cautious. She might be from the Pertise. After what happened today they may wish to punish you."

"What Tthean says is true," spoke up another. "This gathering place is supposed to be secret. How did she find us?"

"How little you understand!" said Jesus. "My Truth cannot be hidden, and thus will be easy to find for those who seek it with an open mind. Many others will find me, ere I leave you."

"Leave us? What do you mean?" Tthean cried, but at that instant there was a sound in the trees behind Prentiss, the snapping of a tree branch.

"Who is there?" called Tthean. "She has brought someone! It is a trap!"

Still hidden in the trees, I'Char whispered urgently, "We have to leave—now."

"You get Prentiss out of here. I'll buy us some time." Trusting I'Char to obey, Win sprinted through the trees, skirting the clearing, toward the sound they had heard. In his peripheral vision he could see that none of the disciples had yet ventured out of the clearing.

Win pushed through the trees, the branches slapping at him. He stopped, heard a thrashing in the woods. He ran toward the sound, in time to see a slight figure, moving away. The person heard him and turned, and Win caught a glimpse of a young woman's face. With the fire at his back he knew she could not see his features.

"Quick!" he called to the woman. "They are after you! Run!"

She didn't hesitate, but ran off through the trees. His gambit had worked.

Behind him, Win could hear voices calling out in worry. His *gheris* was tingling, mirroring the intense shift in emotion to fear. He waited until he was satisfied the woman was not coming back, and then retraced his steps toward the clearing. I'Char and Prentiss were gone. He stopped at the edge of the woods, peering into the clearing from the shadows. The group had reformed, all facing in his direction.

"You see," he heard Jesus say, a voice of calm amidst the tumult, "many others will find me."

Knowing he had been seen, Win took a step forward.

"I was right, Jesus! Another spy!"

"I am no spy—and neither was the woman," said Win. He meant Prentiss, hoping no one had seen the other woman.

"Then why are you here?" asked one of the disciples, suspiciously.

Before Win could respond, Jesus said, "He is looking for someone."

"They are looking for you, Jesus!"

"Perhaps," said Jesus, "but they do not know that yet, for we do not always know what we seek, isn't that true?"

Somehow, Win knew that Jesus' words were meant for him. Yet surely Win knew what he was looking for. Garrick. And the freighter.

As if reading his mind, Jesus said, "Often you will think you know what you are looking for, only to find that you should have had another mission, another goal. It is as I was telling you, if you follow the path that has been created by rules, you will not find the true Way."

Even across the clearing, Win could feel the power in the words, the presence of Jesus, like an aura, magnifying the light from the fire. He didn't know what to say. Part of him knew Jesus was making a point to his followers, but he sensed that Jesus was saying something else, something about Win.

Jesus' next words convinced him that he was right. "Your friend who was here, she must find her own true path," said Jesus. "As must you."

And then Jesus turned and walked out of the clearing, and as he did so the fire seemed to dim. The others followed, leaving Win in the growing shadows.

Chapter 22

Those with inner conflict will never find their way.
  —The Teachings 7:22

"What were you thinking?" demanded Win.

"Me? What was *I* thinking? How would you feel about being physically dragged away from a breakthrough scientific study?" Prentiss replied, heatedly.

Back in Symes's hut, in the middle of the night, Win, Prentiss, and I'Char stood in the old man's front room. Symes had been overjoyed when I'Char had brought Prentiss back, and only when he was convinced she was unharmed did he go to his sleeping room. As soon as he was gone Prentiss had exploded, berating I'Char for forcibly pulling her out of the orchard.

"You are *not* here to conduct a scientific study," said Win, "I thought I made that clear."

"We agreed I could gather data while looking for Garrick," said Prentiss. "And that is what I was doing."

Win wanted to believe her, it would have been much easier. But after the incident in the orchard, he knew she was only interested in Jesus.

He had to get her under control.

"That wasn't what we agreed at all," he said, as sternly as he could. "You hear only what you want to hear. Do you even realize the danger you put us all in? I cannot let you continue doing this."

"What will you do?" asked Prentiss. "Take me back to the ship?

You don't have time for that. Nor do I care if you report me to the Research Council. What are they going to do—demote me again? You'd be better off if you just let me be. You go find your freighter, and I'll do my work."

"Right now your work is to help find the freighter," said Win.

"To hell with the damned freighter! Look around you! Don't you see what is happening here? This society is at the tipping point, ready to be transformed. We will be able to see it happening!"

"And what exactly would you do with that information?" pursued Win. "Are you suggesting we should help societies along their path of technological development?"

Prentiss looked at Win as if he had uttered something profane. "Of course not. I would never let that happen."

"You wouldn't be able to stop it," said Win. "If your theory is true—and I'm not saying I believe it—then you would be identifying one of the keys to societal transformation. What would stop someone from injecting the catalyst into primitive societies to change them?"

Prentiss shook her head. "That is too simplistic. All the right factors would have to be in place, including the belief—and existence—of a deity figure. That can't be artificially created."

"Listen to yourself, Specialist Prentiss. You are starting to sound like the very people you criticize for not being open to new scientific thoughts. Are you saying your theory cannot be wrong because it is right? What if what we are seeing here is exactly what I have described—an artificially induced outside entity, one that fits your messiah leadership role?"

"You don't believe that any more than I do," said Prentiss. "You heard Jesus, you saw him. Was that some imposter, someone playing a part? Could an imposter engender such emotion?"

Win didn't think so, nor did he want to believe he had been manipulated. But this was not the time to bring up his own questions. "Consider this. You said you have seen these phenomena before. What if you have been actually seeing a series of imposters, put in place by someone from the outside?"

Prentiss looked at him, shocked. "What are you suggesting?"

"Just that perhaps someone thought your theory had merit—or at least could be used for their own purposes."

"Are you saying they believe my theory, and are testing it? That is too outlandish to even consider."

"Think about it," said Win. "You may have convinced more people than you realize. Someone could be using it to nudge certain societies along, societies that would be stronger and of more use to the League if they were more technologically advanced."

"The Research Council would never do such a thing," said Prentiss. "They'd have no reason to."

"They might not, but Central Command might," said Win. "Just because we often see a clear distinction between the two, that doesn't mean it exists, especially with something that is, in effect, a weapon."

"I don't believe it," said Prentiss, shaking her head. "What I see here, and what I saw on the other planets, was real. Not some charade."

"I don't really believe it either," admitted Win. "But you have to acknowledge—as a scientist—that it fits the facts, just as much as your theory does. My point is that you seem to be losing your objectivity."

Prentiss's eyes flamed. "Who are you to criticize my objectivity? Everything I have done has been flawlessly documented. Just because some people don't like the conclusions doesn't mean the science is flawed."

"That is not the point!" argued Win. "You have to understand what it looks like to someone else. And to me it looks like you are trying to fit the facts to the theory, rather than examining the facts and considering all the possibilities."

"I've done all that!" said Prentiss, exasperated. "Look, I understand your skepticism, it's not like I haven't heard it all before. And I admit that I might be so tired of the cynics that I don't take the time to connect all the dots. What's the use, if someone isn't going to be even willing to consider my conclusions? I thought you were different."

Win felt a pang of compassion for her. How would he react if he felt so strongly about something, and no one was willing to even listen?

He softened his tone. "Look, I understand your arguments, Specialist Prentiss. And I have every respect for your dedication to research. But that is not the issue. Right now, no matter what else is going on here, we have a duty to perform. And there *is* a lot at stake."

"I don't buy it," Prentiss persisted. "Are you going to tell me that uncovering fundamental secrets about the universe, secrets about the possible connections between religious beings across the galaxy, is less important than finding some missing cargo ship?"

Win sighed. His heart wasn't in this argument. "I told you before, if we find Garrick and the freighter, then—and only then—we'll see what we can do to help you gather your data. But right now we are in great danger. Every minute we are here we run the risk of being found out." He saw her about to protest and he held up his hand. "Yes, I know you believe you can just explain all of this to the Lemians. You'll just have to trust me that won't work. You are thinking like a scientist, and how a fellow scientist would react. But whatever scientists the Lemians have, you can be assured they are not here. This is a military installation. They would simply assume you are a spy—and in many ways, that is what we are. If the Lemians interrogated you, you would not be able to keep our mission from them."

"Don't you think you're being paranoid?" Prentiss asked.

Win turned to I'Char. "You tell her."

"You were followed to the orchard," said I'Char.

Prentiss looked at him in disbelief. "Followed? By whom?"

"It was a woman," said Win.

"Probably just someone wanting to hear Jesus," said Prentiss. "Like us. Besides, how do you know she was following me?"

"We saw you on the ridge," said I'Char. "She was behind you there, and then again in the woods."

"And she ran," said Win. "She clearly didn't want to be found out. She was spying on you—or Jesus."

"She was probably surprised," said Prentiss. "I'd run too if

Jesus of K'Turia

someone came rushing at me through the woods at night."

"You don't understand," said I'Char. "You've obviously attracted attention. It will only be a matter of time before the Lemians find out."

"But why would anyone be following me? I can't believe whomever you saw was a Lemian. From what you've said about them being so militaristic, they wouldn't run away."

"Probably not a Lemian, I agree," said I'Char. "But that doesn't mean the Lemians won't find out. You already spoke out at the arena. Have you done anything else to call attention to yourself?"

Prentiss paused. "I can't imagine what."

Win sensed her hesitation, his *gheris* prickling. He considered confronting her, knowing she was lying, but he realized she would probably not admit to anything. He tried another approach. "The reason we got you out of there was that the people with Jesus thought you were a spy, that you had brought someone to their hiding place," he said. "We were doing you a favor."

Prentiss eyed him narrowly. "Oh, really? Explain that."

"It's simple," said Win. "You say you want to document Jesus. How can you ever expect to do that if his followers think you are a spy from the Temple? They'd never let you near him. By us chasing off the other woman they can't be sure that someone else was there. Better for you if they believe it was just us, some pilgrims."

"I don't believe you did that for me."

"It doesn't matter what you believe, or why we did it," said Win. "Think the worst. But the result is the same. No one else saw her. At least for a while we can go on with our disguise."

"But not for long," said I'Char. "Everything right now is against us. We have to assume that woman was spying—for the Lemians, or the Pertise. It doesn't matter which, both are bad for us. If the Lemians or the Pertise are looking for pilgrims, we don't have much time. We have to get off the planet fast, and to do that we have to find Garrick."

"I thought you wanted to find the freighter?" asked Prentiss.

"I do," said Win quietly. "But I also want us to survive this mission." He watched Prentiss's reaction. She was visibly shaken. It wasn't his arguments that had affected her, but the fact that she had been followed.

"You have to see how this changes things," Win said. "If your theory is correct, it has to progress on its own, without outside influence. You argued quite convincingly on the ship that it is wrong to corrupt a society—something even the League has been guilty of. Certainly you can see how you might be contaminating the very thing you are trying to study. You cannot let yourself become part of this, or influence it."

"It is a risk every anthropological scientist deals with," argued Prentiss. "The need to get close, but at the same time stay separate. I know what I'm doing." But her voice lacked conviction.

Win knew he had struck a chord. "You cannot risk it. If you don't want to do what I tell you for my reasons, then do it for your own."

"But we don't have much time! You said so yourself. I can't just hide out here while all this is going on. I might miss something, something critical."

"Or you might cause it," said Win. "And as a scientist, that would seem to me a much greater risk. Not only would no one believe you, but you have to ask yourself, would you believe it? Or would you always have doubt, that it was you who caused the transformation?"

"No one person could do that," said Prentiss.

"Except Jesus," said Win. "Isn't that what you would have us believe?"

She held his eye. After a long time she said, "Very well. I'll help you look for Garrick, and I'll stay out of things. But I can't help but keep my eyes open to what is going on here. And once we find Garrick, the deal is off."

Win knew that this was the best he was going to get. "After we find Garrick, we'll talk about it," he said.

* * *

On watch in the darkness outside Symes's hut, Win kept thinking about what Jesus had said in the orchard: *'Often you will think you know what you are looking for, only to find that you should have had another mission, another goal.'*

Was this a reference to Win's mission to find the freighter, a mission he did not really understand or trust? Or to his forsaken quest for *ana*? How could Jesus possibly have known about that?

Or was he just taking Jesus' words and applying it to himself? No good scientist would make that mistake.

He wondered if that was the mistake Prentiss was making—not only trying to fit Jesus to her theory, but also reading something into what Jesus was teaching, something that had to do with her own beliefs.

The door behind him opened. I'Char coming to take over the watch.

"You okay?" asked I'Char.

"Yes, why?"

"I didn't want to say anything in front of Prentiss. But ever since we've been here, you seem—different."

"I am. I think—no, I *know* why. The things Jesus has said—he's making me think. Think about things I have not thought about in a long time."

"That's fine. Just don't end up like Prentiss. I don't trust her."

"I'm not sure I do either," said Win. "But she has a point. What are we going to do, bring her back to the ship? Tie her up? We have to hope that her obsession with proving her theory is strong enough to keep her from getting involved and tarnishing her data. She may see this as her last chance for redemption."

"All the more reason to be concerned," said I'Char. "She is desperate. She might do something stupid."

"I won't let it get that far," said Win. "If she gets in the way of us finding the freighter, I *will* take her back to the ship."

"It's not the freighter I'm worried about," said I'Char. "It's getting out alive."

Win was surprised. He could not recall I'Char ever being worried, about anything. "I was just saying that to scare Prentiss into reality.

I know we are at risk. But Prentiss was right about one thing. The Lemians don't seem to have much presence in the city. If we stay out of their way we should be safe."

"Don't forget about Garrick," said I'Char. "We should have been able to find him by now."

"Could you have stayed hidden for this long?"

"Perhaps. But the longer he—or any of us—searches for the freighter, the greater the risk. We've already looked in the obvious places. We either have to assume it is not in Merculon, or to be sure, we have to start looking deeper. That means going into buildings—and getting into the Lemian camp."

"Do you think Garrick would have tried to do that on his own?"

"You saw their security, it is not extensive. I could get in. And we know nothing of Garrick's ability to assess security risks."

"You're right. I still don't know if he is a military spy or a desk analyst."

"Probably both, which is the worst combination," said I'Char. "But he's only part of the problem. Prentiss might be right about the K'Turians being at some kind of crossroads."

"How does that affect us?"

"You saw the audience in the amphitheater. How would you characterize it?"

Win thought back, letting the emotions wash over him. "On edge. Questioning. Very passionate."

"Yet this is a very orderly, rule-based society. Think what must be happening for these people to be openly questioning authority. This didn't start today, it's been brewing for some time. It has all the ingredients for a revolt."

"I see your point. But that wouldn't happen overnight."

"I agree. But the first response of authority when it is challenged is self protection. Obviously the priests see something amiss. The powers here will try to stem the uprising before it begins. They'll be on the lookout for anything out of the ordinary—and *we* fit that description."

"That could explain why Prentiss was followed."

"Yes. But it's worse than that. The Lemians don't seem very involved now, but they want this planet. They don't like a troublesome population. This Jesus might be bringing down more on these people than he realizes."

* * *

In the hut, Prentiss lay awake. She had heard I'Char go outside, and when Win did not come in right away she assumed they were talking about her. *Let them.* They already don't trust me, it can't get any worse.

Much as she hated to admit it, Win had made some good points. He's probably a good scientist. Just too caught up in this military fearmongering. She wanted to believe that if she were in his place she'd be different, but maybe after a while it wore you down.

No matter. She had worked the better part of her professional life refining her theory of cultural development, and she was not going to lose this chance to collect the proof she needed to confirm it.

Though she had seen evidence supporting her theory on other worlds, she had never been this *close,* never actually in place when it was about to happen. Win was wrong about one thing. Whatever happened on K'Turia would happen whether she was here or not. How could she affect such a tidal change?

So she was clear in her mind about that. And she totally rejected the notion that Jesus of K'Turia was some kind of imposter, especially one put in motion by the League, of all things. Although wouldn't that be ironic, the very people who demoted her because of her theory trying to use it for their own aims.

No, everything was as she had predicted. The stagnant society. The appearance of a messiah figure, questioning the religious order and the laws, opening the minds of the people to other possibilities, other ways of living their lives. Showing them a better way, transforming them so they could break free of their ritualistic inertia.

Yet she was troubled. She had argued for so long that the scientific community had to remain open to the idea that the religion of a society could impact its technological development, in essence, that religion was a necessary component for advancement. She had always carefully skirted the concept of God in these arguments; *that* was a topic which even the most open-minded scientists often avoided for fear they would not be taken seriously. This part of her theory had always been cloaked in the rather broad concept of universal consciousness, or simply a cultural belief in a religious figure.

Her own thoughts on the topic were—in flux. As a scientist she had long ago rejected the notion of a deity. But even if she could not state it to others, her theory required her to at least hold open the possibility that the messiah figures were *real*—that they were in effect, godlike, or gods, or personifications of some super being. And as she continued to find evidence supporting her idea, it became harder to believe that it was all just a matter of randomness, that all it took were the right elements being present, to create such a historic transformation. It reeked too much of a chemistry experiment.

And the transformations were truly momentous. She had focused on the issue of technological development, for that was easiest to measure, and one she felt the scientific community could accept. But the cultures also transformed in other ways. They became more open, more creative, in short, more *advanced.*

Could it really be nothing more than a big, anthropological chemistry equation? Mix so many parts religion, a certain level of development, a particular person, and just like that, an entire world was changed forever?

Part of her wanted to believe such a transformation could evolve in such a cold, clinical way. It meant she could avoid having to ascribe some superhuman powers to the religious figures in her model. After all, what good was a theory—what good was scientific thought—if some higher power was the cause of everything?

But while her theory neatly described what happened to a society, it didn't seem to explain the effect on the people themselves, on the individuals. What made them such believers? What made them feel so passionately about their religion—and their messiah?

She had seen it today, in the amphitheater. She was more shaken by the event than she had let Win know. Perhaps it was because she had been born on Earth; she was far more familiar with the story of Jesus Christ than the others. But knowing the story and seeing it happen before your eyes were two different things.

And later, in the orchard. Jesus had spoken of the truth, about how many could feel that they alone knew the truth. Just as the truth she believed in was different from what the rest of the scientific community believed.

But who could deny the truth of Jesus? He was here, now, affecting the people, the society.

Affecting her.

She had to be careful. She could not let her personal feelings get in the way of her science. If she did, others would no doubt sense it, and she'd never prove her case. She'd be doomed to spend the rest of her life on some tiny research ship. She was too young for that.

She had told Win the truth when she said that this was an opportunity of a lifetime. It might also be the turning point in her life. She was tired of being ridiculed, tired of being ostracized by her peers. She was not going to let this chance pass by. She would collect the proof she needed, right here. This was more important than any duty to the League, no matter what Win said.

Jesus was right. She had a mission, to find the truth, and to convince others.

Whether or not Jesus was some kind of god didn't really matter. Whether what was happening on K'Turia was the result of divine intervention or simply a matter of chemistry, the outcome would be the same. But it could take some time, and time was something she didn't have. She could not contaminate what was happening here any more than it already was. And if it were divine intervention, then whatever she did was destined anyway. Wasn't that a paradox.

They might only have a few days. If she had to help the process along, so be it.

Chapter 23

I bring you spiritual salvation, not worldly salvation. Change your lot in life so that you may help others, not because you expect more for yourselves.
—The Teachings 8:3

Krelmar couldn't sleep. Though it had been a long day, he was wound up after setting in motion the sequence of events that could get him back home to Colltaire. The scheme would have to be carefully orchestrated, and so he had spent the better part of the evening perfecting his plan.

Tsaph had left for the day, the servants were in bed, the house quiet. So Krelmar was surprised to hear someone knocking on the outer door. *Who would be calling at this hour?*

Warily, he approached the door. "Who is there?"

"It is I, Methurgem."

What could he want? Krelmar cracked the door open. There, in the shadows on the transom, wearing an unadorned grey cloak, stood the K'Turian high priest.

"I wish to speak to you—alone," said Methurgem, his face partially hidden by his hood, pulled tightly over his head.

Hiding his surprise, Krelmar said, "Come in."

"No," said Methurgem. "It would not be wise to be seen here."

"Why?" asked Krelmar.

"You will understand later. I do not have much time. Will you come with me? I will take you to a private place—it is not far."

Jesus of K'Turia

Krelmar shrugged. "Very well." He took a cloak from near the door and went outside. Methurgem immediately set off, forcing Krelmar to hurry to keep up. *Was this some kind of trap?* The city was quiet and empty. Ahead, torchlight flickered in the square, but Methurgem turned down a narrow side street.

"Where are we going?" asked Krelmar.

"Just down here," said Methurgem, over his shoulder. Partway along the street the priest stopped in front of a plain door, unlocking it hastily with a key he drew from under his robe.

"Hurry," said Methurgem, beckoning Krelmar into the room. When Krelmar hesitated, Methurgem said, "It is safe." The priest opened the door wide and stepped aside, indicating a small room, totally empty except for a small table and a lamp that was already lit. When Krelmar did not move, Methurgem went in first. Only then did Krelmar follow, watching as Methurgem latched the door.

"You are a cautious man, Krelmar," said Methurgem.

"Perhaps I have need to be, Methurgem," said Krelmar. "I did not know locks were needed in Merculon."

"Just because there is little crime does not mean there is no need for privacy," said Methurgem. The priest pulled back his hood and raised the lamp. Long shadows from the two men loomed on the walls.

Krelmar's annoyance with being dragged away from his house was overcome by his curiosity. Though he had predicted such a meeting, this is hardly what he had expected. "How can I help you, Methurgem?"

"I have been thinking about our conversation," said Methurgem.

"Yes? About how you may benefit from Lemian support?" Krelmar bit his lip, realizing he may have said too much. Methurgem was not someone he should push.

"No, not yet," said Methurgem. "But of course that may be a matter for a future discussion. But we are willing to consider your offer of a test of some kind. To see how the Lemians might prove their worth to us."

Krelmar smiled inwardly. *You arrogant fool!* While he himself was not particularly fond of the Lemians, they certainly did not have to prove their worth to anyone. Methurgem would shiver if he realized what the Lemians would do to K'Turia if the balance of power in the galaxy was not so tenuous.

Even given that, if the Lemians became impatient they might decide to take K'Turia by force anyway. And that would mean Krelmar had failed. Like it or not, his fate was tied to that of Methurgem's.

At some point he might have to explain all this to Methurgem. But now all Krelmar said was, "Yes, the test."

"I offer this up only as a means of exploring cooperation," said Methurgem, "since it looks like you are here to stay. We really do not need any help."

"Of course," said Krelmar, not believing a word Methurgem said. If they didn't need any help, what was Methurgem doing here, hiding in the night?

"While our religious laws are quite specific, they are most appropriate in dealing with people who stray from our Way, our religious path. Do you understand?" The priest's voice was condescending, as if he were lecturing a schoolboy.

Krelmar tried not to smile. This priest thought he was an idiot, that he could not understand their primitive religion. He played along. "Yes, I believe I do, Methurgem. Your religion is very important to you, and thus guides your entire way of life."

"Yes. And it has served us well for thousands of years. But every so often there arises a—situation—that is not easily dealt with by the Laws."

"Something outside of your religion," said Krelmar.

"*Nothing* is outside our religion," said Methurgem. "I cannot expect you to understand, but we have no distinction between our religion and our lives. To us it is one and the same."

Here for help, but still haughty, thought Krelmar. "Something the Laws were not designed to deal with then?" he suggested smoothly.

"Yes, you could say that. It is—how did you say it before?—a security threat."

"From offworld?" asked Krelmar. His mind leapt to the possible spy in custody. Was that what this was about?

Methurgem paused, as if he had just thought of something. "Perhaps. We don't really know where this—*threat*—came from. It may very well be from offworld. But it is a threat to the peace, and it is in all of our best interests to contain it."

That isn't what he meant to say, thought Krelmar. "Certainly, peace is something we understand."

"I thought you would," said Methurgem.

Krelmar could not tell if the priest was mocking him, so he said nothing.

"There has appeared in Merculon someone who has supposedly come from Valdar," continued Methurgem. "He purports to be a teacher. We have long ignored him, for his teachings were of little interest to us or to the people. But others—pilgrims—have followed him here, and have been a disruptive influence. And now it seems this man has developed something of a local following."

"I don't understand," said Krelmar, but he was remembering what Tsaph had told him about the preacher. Could it be the same person? "Who is this man? And what is he teaching?"

"His name is Jesus. As for his teaching, he is telling the people it is acceptable to reject our Way. Such words breed discontent, and disturb the peace."

So it was the same man. "If this man's message is so disturbing, then why does anyone listen to him?" asked Krelmar.

"He is clever," said Methurgem. "He cloaks his ideas within our Way, so that they appear to be one and the same. We have wondered where he acquired this skill."

"So you feel he is a serious threat? Why?" asked Krelmar.

"Because he has begun to openly confront the Way, and is now urging others to do so. He is questioning the Order—you are familiar with the Order? It is what maintains stability amongst our people. It keeps the peace. Everyone is born into a place within the Order. They accept this. No one covets anything held by another. But Jesus has started to attack the Order, telling people they need not be content with their place. That they need not obey the Laws. One person straying from the Laws is a small matter. But many doing so is dangerous."

"Why not deal with him as you do any other transgressor?" asked Krelmar.

"Our Laws rely on the threat of banishment or separation from the Temple. Such threats mean little to someone who does not accept the Way and who feels emboldened by an ever-growing following."

Krelmar thought about the insurgents back on Colltaire. "He isn't afraid of the punishment."

"Yes," said Methurgem. "You understand."

"I would like to help you," said Krelmar, "but this seems to be a religious matter. I thought you said we must stay out of that."

"It is a religious matter only until the peace is threatened. Should that occur, it will be a different problem, wouldn't you agree? If the people reject our Law, there will be anarchy."

Anarchy, thought Krelmar. That was something he could not afford to let happen.

"And there is something else," said Methurgem. "This Jesus, he might be an offworlder."

"I thought you said he was from Valdar?" asked Krelmar. Yet the possibility of Jesus being from offworld made him think again of the captured pilgrim, and it gave him an idea. Since Methurgem obviously did not like the pilgrims, Krelmar could be much more aggressive in questioning the one they had captured.

"We don't know for sure," said Methurgem. "But we know little of this Jesus. He supposedly came from Valdar, but even those we have questioned from there do not know much of his past. We are told that he and his mother simply appeared one day. She married a Valderian, a craftsman, who adopted the boy. No one has ever seen his real father. Few recall much about his youth. Such is odd for our people who often trace their and their neighbor's ancestors back for generations by heart. I ask of you—could this not be an offworlder? That would be even more of a security threat."

Krelmar's mind was racing. First the captured pilgrim, perhaps a spy. And now another possible offworlder. Tsaph's story about a religious preacher. Neel's perception that the priests would try to use the Lemians for their own needs.

Krelmar had to be very careful. This *could* be what he was looking for, something he could do for the priests in exchange for their agreeing to Lemian control. But if this Jesus had a following, then it might just as easily turn the populace against him, poisoning his chances for support. Priests or no priests, he could not afford a repeat of Colltaire.

"Any threat to the peace is something to be taken seriously," Krelmar said carefully, "no matter where it comes from. If this is really a religious matter, then perhaps it might not be the best test of our help. However, if this Jesus is an offworlder, or is causing trouble outside of your religious Law, that is another thing entirely."

"Yes, and if he is from offworld, who is to say others may not follow him here?"

Now Krelmar sensed Methurgem's anxiety. Whether or not the priest was really worried about a threat to the religion, or just afraid of losing his position atop the Order, Methurgem was clearly afraid of Jesus.

And the priest wanted Krelmar to do his dirty work.

Could he turn this to his advantage? "I would like to meet with this Jesus," said Krelmar. "I can perhaps assess whether he is an offworlder, and will also be able to help determine if he is truly a threat."

"That may be difficult. He is rarely alone, and when he is not teaching he stays in hiding."

"And so you are telling me you have no idea where Jesus is? You do not keep track of someone you tell me is a threat to the peace?"

Methurgem hesitated. "We know of some places he frequents. Still, it may not be easy for you to draw him out."

"Leave that to me," said Krelmar. "I will find a way to persuade him to speak to me. With your permission, of course."

"We'll consider your request," said Methurgem. "If we agree, it will have to be done quietly."

"Of course. After all, what we are trying to do is keep the peace, not disturb it ourselves."

Methurgem eyed him, a new understanding in his eye. "You are more than you appear, Lemian representative Krelmar."

"As are you, Methurgem," said Krelmar, now knowing for sure that the priest was trying to set him up. "As are you."

Chapter 24

The new beginning that I teach is one of action, of good deeds, of doing what you can do, not praying for things out of your control not to happen.
—The Teachings 9:23

Just after sunrise, Win, I'Char, and Prentiss split up at the city's entrance arch. They had left Symes at the hut. More confident in their pilgrim disguises, Win had decided to search the city one more day. Repeating his admonition to Prentiss about concentrating on Garrick and the freighter, he had sent her to the market area to listen for gossip about anything that might suggest the freighter had been found, or that Garrick had been seen or captured. I'Char was to search a maze-like area of the city filled with storage buildings. Win decided if they could find nothing by the end of the day, I'Char would sneak in to the Lemian camp under cover of darkness in a last attempt to find something—anything.

Win walked through the city, extending his *gheris* sense for any strong emotions. By midday he was tired. Though his *gheris* was as much one of his senses as his sight, he was not used to focusing on it for such a long time. After a while he began to doubt he would learn anything at all. It was like straining to hear a sound for hours, and then finally hearing something and wondering if it was real.

He was also hungry. The food bars had almost run out, and soon they would have to figure out how to get some local food, or go back to the shuttle.

He angled over to the food courts. Here a few stalls were set out, offering fruits and vegetables and even some cooked foods. Only a few elderly people were about. Now and then a young boy would come running, be handed a sack of food, and run off again, probably collecting the midday meal for one of the craftspeople.

Win watched as a man bought some food, carefully counting out coins from his purse. Win edged closer, trying to see the local currency, while pretending to be looking at the vegetables.

When the man left, Win began to walk away, but the vendor, an old woman, said, "We have some nice vegetables, pilgrim."

Realizing it would look suspicious if he ignored her, Win replied, "Yes, they look very fresh."

"Won't you try some?"

"I'm afraid—I have no money," said Win.

The woman did not seem surprised. "We have not seen many pilgrims in Merculon for a quite a while," she said. "Did you come a long way?"

"Why yes, I have," said Win. "A very long way."

"You must be tired." She lowered her voice. "Have you come to see Jesus?"

Win sensed no suspicion in the woman, only a warm interest and friendliness. "You might say I have come—seeking." He chose his words carefully, knowing even those without his extraordinary senses could often recognize deceit.

The woman laughed. "Aren't we all!" She picked up some of the vegetables and put them in a small brown sack. "Here, pilgrim. As you seek to nourish your spirit, may these nourish your stomach." She held out the bag.

Win hesitated. "I do not know if I can repay you."

"The presence of pilgrims in the city once again makes me happy," she said. "This is payment enough." She lowered her voice. "And Jesus says we must help each other as we can. Take these, please."

Win took the bag. "I really am quite hungry. Thank you." He turned to go.

"Pilgrim?"

Win turned back to the woman. "Yes?"

"The places you have been, is Jesus respected there? Do the people follow him?"

He thought a moment, then answered truthfully. "Oh yes," he said. "People have followed him for a very long time."

* * *

In a large room in the basement of the temple, Methurgem eyed the group of acolytes that he had carefully chosen. Not normally this close to the high priest, they stood tall and stiff, clearly nervous.

Methurgem wasn't concerned about their nervousness, in fact it would serve him well. They were unlikely to talk about what he was about to ask them to do, a secret mission he had not even shared with Amora.

Methurgem knew more about Jesus than he had told Krelmar. And what he knew worried him.

In the beginning, Jesus had seemed harmless enough. His interpretations of the Way were simply misguided. But now Jesus was questioning not only the Laws, but the very Order.

The entire society was built upon the Order. Without it, there would be no acceptance of the Sacrifices. People would no longer fulfill their obligations, payments which kept the entire economy functioning. How would everyone live?

The younger farmers were already beginning to wonder why they should keep farming, their crops withering in this long drought, one of the worst in Methurgem's lifetime. And now Jesus was telling them they should help each other. It would only be one small step from that to saying they did not need to pay the Sacrifice.

From there, it was only one more step to anarchy and ruin.

Many of the Pertise would not agree with what he was about to do. But he had no choice.

"I have a special assignment for you, a mission of protection for the Temple and our Way," he said. "The heretic, Jesus, will be speaking today. You are to dress as commoners and listen quietly. You will hear someone in the crowd ask him about the offworlders, the Lemians, questioning why they are here. Others will ask if Jesus approves of the Lemian presence, and if the Laws should apply to offworlders. Follow their lead, and repeat the questions to those around you. When the crowd disperses, convince as many as you can to go to the Lemian camp. Once there, listen for others who begin to call out for the Lemians to leave, and take up this cry." He had already met with another group, some younger priests, who would be asking the questions to enflame the crowd. No matter what Jesus actually did say, the disguised priests would twist it to make it sound as if Jesus had turned the people against the Lemians. The more devout K'Turians would also be angry if Jesus claimed the offworlders could find the Way. "Do you have any questions?"

As he expected, he got no response. The high priest was sure the acolytes had questions, but were just too afraid to ask. Still, he knew they would do as they were told.

The plan was dangerous. The Lemians had to be made to feel Jesus was enough of a threat that they would deal with him in order to help the Pertise. On the other hand, he did not want the Lemians to feel so threatened that they would crack down on the entire city. He was walking a tightrope, but it was a chance he had to take.

This had to be stopped now. He could not let Jesus become so powerful that the people would turn away from the Order, away from the Laws.

"Now, change out of your Temple garments—wear your oldest robes. Leave every mark and symbol of the Temple here. You must appear to be ordinary people. If you spot anyone in the crowd who might recognize you, avoid them. Now go."

* * *

Tthean picked at his food. He couldn't eat. There was nothing wrong with the breakfast meal; he had prepared it himself for Jesus and the other disciples. But he was worried. First the priests had appeared at the amphitheater, challenging Jesus. And last night, their camp had been discovered. Jesus didn't seem concerned, but then, he never did.

Tthean was the one who had to worry for all of them.

"What troubles you, Tthean?"

Tthean looked up into Jesus' eyes. As always, they gave him strength. "I am afraid, Jesus," he said. "We have been discovered."

Jesus smiled. "Isn't that what we want?"

"Yes—I mean, no. I know you want everyone to hear what you say, but the priests—." He looked around at the other disciples, all listening intently. He knew most of them were afraid. They often waited for him to speak first.

"Let me tell you a story," said Jesus. "Long ago, before the drought, there was a time of a great rain. It began just before the sowing season, and lasted for one hundred days. Now, the rain was so heavy that the farmers could not plant, because their seeds would have been washed away. The ground was not ready, and so they waited. Finally it stopped raining, and little by little the ground began to dry out, becoming fertile again. But the weather would change soon. Unless the farmers sowed their seeds, they would miss the chance for a harvest.

"When they could wait no longer, they began to sow in earnest. They had little time, and so decided to sow not only during the day, but at night as well. During the day they were able to sow the seeds easily, but at night, in the darkness, it was much more difficult. Some of these seeds fell onto good soil. But others fell onto pathways, where they were eaten by birds, or on rocks, where they dried out, or in thorns, where they sprouted but were choked."

"Jesus, tell us, what does this story mean?" asked Tthean.

"This you should know by now," said Jesus. "But I will tell you. The seeds in the story are the seeds of Truth. But the people, like the infertile land, have not been ready for the Truth. The rules of the Pertise have willed the people into a sleep, just as you might be lulled to sleep by a long rain. Now is the time for them to awaken. And so the seeds of Truth must be sown, even though the world is in darkness. Now, some will hear the Truth, as you have. These are the seeds that fell on fertile ground. But there are those who hear and do not understand, like the seeds that fell on the hard path. And others hear the message, but it does not sprout, but withers and dies, like the seeds that fell on rock. And others are too worried about this life, and what they have in it; their thoughts are choked out by worry, like the seeds that fell in the thorns.

"And so we must keep sowing, in darkness and in light, until all hear the seed of Truth, and understand it, and accept it."

"Jesus, what is the darkness you speak of? What has brought it upon us?"

"The darkness is always there. It is the darkness of temptation, of laziness, of envy, of scorn. You have all felt it, and have fought this darkness, even before hearing my voice. The very Way was created to battle this darkness, this evil. But see what has happened! The Way has become nothing more than ritual. It is without body, without strength. People go through the motions, thinking it will guarantee them a better life. But the darkness feeds on these empty actions, and thus grows stronger. In this strengthening darkness, many no longer live by the true Way, but have fully succumbed."

"Do you mean the priests? The Pertise?"

"Everyone who has lost sight of the true Way is touched by the darkness; everyone who is jealous of what others have, everyone who lives only for themselves, everyone who covets what their neighbor has. No one is immune from the threat of darkness! The priests are like everyone else—no more, no less. Like others, some are merely misguided. Yet some no longer even pretend to follow the true Way. They have created rules that do more harm than good; they envelope, instead of open; they keep the Truth from the heart.

"Now, we are like the farmers in the story that I have told you. The sowing season is upon us, but time grows short. We must quickly sow our seeds, by day and by night. Some will find fertile ground, hearts and minds open to the Truth. Others will fall on hard and rocky soil, or in thorns. And thus we must keep sowing, and even then our work is not done, for like the farmer, we must see that the seeds take hold, and then the young plants must be carefully tended, and nourished.

"This will be your responsibility. For no matter what you are now, traders, craftspeople, builders, you will have to be as farmers, helping to sow the seeds, helping to nourish, helping to grow."

The disciples were silent, absorbing Jesus' words. Tthean had come to know them well, and he could see that some were still afraid. Once again he would have to speak for them.

"Jesus, I understand what you say. You know I believe in you with all my heart. I believe that your Way offers us a new beginning. A new freedom. But I fear we do not have enough followers to overcome all who would deny your message. Many will fear the punishment of the Pertise, or fear . . ." Tthean stopped, ashamed, his eyes filling with tears.

Jesus looked at him, full of compassion. "You fear both that which is known, and that which is unknown. The fear of the Pertise is real, because of the Laws, and the punishments they have meted out. Yet Laws built on fear cannot be righteous. How could the beauty of Paradise be built upon fear?

"And you fear the unknown. You do not know what is going to happen, and so you are afraid. But this is the natural course of things, to not know what is going to happen. You might be tending your crop, and a storm could wash it away. You might succumb to a terrible illness. These are the uncertainties of life. Because of these fears, you have let the Way and the Laws become a crutch. The Pertise tell you that if you follow the rules they have created, then you will not suffer, and the acts of this life will be safer, more secure. But this is a false promise, a false security. Nothing you do can guarantee what will happen in this life, the life you face. But you can prepare for Paradise, for your next life, the life not of this world.

"I can tell you to not be afraid, but still you will fear. You worry about being overcome by the Pertise. I ask you: why do you worry about things you cannot control? You should instead look to what you *can* control. The new beginning that I teach is one of action, of good deeds, of doing what you *can* do, not praying for things out of your control not to happen. Remember my story of the seeds, and how we must sow. Every tree begins as a single sprout, and is subject to all the circumstance of this world. Does the seed worry? Is the sprout concerned about the circumstance of the world? It cannot control them. Instead it prepares for its new life, when it becomes a tree."

"But the Pertise will come after us! Should we not defend ourselves?"

"How do you want to defend yourself? Would you fight them? What would that accomplish?" asked Jesus.

"But we cannot just sit around talking about a new beginning, while the Pertise and the Lemians plow us down! We must take some kind of action!"

Jesus replied, "Yes, you must. But the actions should be the actions of sacrifice, not fighting. You will not find the Truth of a new Way by fighting, or going against the flow of circumstance, nor will you convince others of the Truth by forcing it upon them. You must set an example, even if it is dangerous, even if you are afraid. Afraid of punishment, or afraid of the darkness of not knowing how to live, of having no rules to rely on, no crutch to live by, no external thing to blame if this life does not turn out the way you want.

"Remember what I have told you: I will be your Light, and I will force the darkness away, so that you may see the true path. You have only to act as I have shown you, and keep me in your heart, and the darkness will have no power over you. And thus you will have the strength of true Sacrifice, to not only carry my message but to live it."

And as Tthean looked into Jesus' eyes he saw a light within them, glowing, so bright that it warmed his very heart, and in that minute all his doubts were washed away, and he was no longer afraid.

Chapter 25

I bring a sword, to cleave you from your old beliefs.
—The Teachings 10:17

Prentiss did do what Win had ordered. At least, she went to the marketplace. And she did keep her ears open for any talk of Garrick or the freighter. But all the talk she heard was of Jesus. At first she thought she was being overly sensitive, listening for his name, but then she realized *everyone* was talking about Jesus. Whenever she was recognized as a stranger she was either welcomed warmly or shunned, the conversation around her quieting. It appeared there was a passionate divide within the city, those who supported Jesus and those who did not, or were afraid of retribution from the Pertise.

Every so often she would leave the market square and go down one of the quieter streets. She needed the time to compose herself, to try to commit to memory exactly what she was seeing and hearing. If only she had a recorder! She was foolish to have insisted they not bring any technology. Without a record, even a written one, it would be difficult to convince the Research Council of what was happening. Would Win back her up? Even if he did, it would be an uphill fight.

Should she go back to the shuttle to get a recorder? It would take the better part of a day, and Win would be frantic.

Once more through the market. Then I'll decide.

But when she got back to the square, something had changed. The crowd was noisier, anxious. People kept glancing around, not focused on their transactions.

A ripple ran through the crowd, like a stone cast upon water. At the other end of the square, a separation, a space which opened but then closed again around a figure.

Jesus.

Almost as one the crowd rushed forward, pulling Prentiss along. Halfway across the square she realized Jesus was coming in her direction, so she stopped and waited. Part of her wanted to watch the reaction of the crowd to document in her mind the response of the people. But she found it hard to take her eyes off Jesus.

As Jesus drew near she felt herself straining forward, edging closer, just as she had at the amphitheater. She had to almost will herself not to move toward him.

What was happening to her? Her senses and her body had broken from her reason. Did she so want to believe that here was the vindication of all she had wished for, the final proof of her theory, that she was losing her ability to think like a scientist?

As Jesus passed by he looked her way, and though his eye lingered on hers for just an instant it was as if they were connected, her innermost secrets revealed, but at the same time she was almost overcome by a feeling of exhilaration.

"Follow me," she heard him say.

Oblivious now to her surroundings, she began to follow him.

* * *

Win met no one as he walked along the lane which paralleled the city wall. Where was everyone? At the end of the wall, he again climbed the ridge, but instead of passing over it and down into the orchard he turned left, back toward the valley.

Not far beyond the wall stood the Lemian camp. It appeared quiet. The sentries on the city side looked bored, and gave him nothing but a passing glance when they saw that he was alone on the ridge. From this vantage point Win could see about half the buildings. Nothing seemed out of the ordinary. No freighter, no obvious extra guards. A few soldiers moved lazily about.

Two Lemian shuttles sat parked at the edge of the camp. If the Lemians knew about the freighter, the shuttles would have been out searching for it. So that meant they had either found it already, or didn't think it was on K'Turia.

Or didn't know about it.

Too many unknowns. He'd stick with the plan. I'Char would search the Lemian camp that night, and if he found nothing they'd leave K'Turia.

Time was running out for Garrick.

It struck him then how much all he seemed to be doing now was *searching*—searching for Garrick, searching for the freighter. After so many years of *not* searching, here he was with no other mission.

He had believed that looking for a thing or a person was different than seeking a goal, a higher purpose.

But was it?

Win had told the woman in the market that he was *seeking*. In the orchard, Jesus had said, *'We do not always know what we seek.'* Like *ana*, a seeking for something that could not be easily defined, especially along the way.

And Jesus had said, *'If you follow the path that has been created by rules, you may not find the true Way.'* What did Jesus mean by "the rules?" To the K'Turians, they were the Laws. But to Win, it could mean his duty, his mission.

Would seeking the freighter keep him from seeking his own higher purpose?

It didn't matter. He had given up his search for *ana* long ago. He had drifted so far from *ana* it was overwhelming to even consider starting anew.

And he *had* to find the freighter, and Garrick. So much was at stake—their lives, and perhaps the entire League.

Yet the words Jesus had spoken had moved him. He was hearing the siren song of *ana* again, calling him back to the spiritual path of his Treb heritage.

But even if he wanted to resume his path toward *ana*, it would be selfish to put his own needs first.

And he felt no desire to. The numbness had its benefit—it dulled the pain from the loss of Sooni.

Too much to risk, too far to go.

He'd stick with the mission. But in the meantime, like Prentiss, he'd be looking for Jesus.

* * *

When she reached the temple, Prentiss could see that she and the others from the marketplace were not the only ones who had followed Jesus. Before the temple were hundreds of people, and more were arriving from every direction. Soon the entire plaza was jammed, people jostling to get closer.

Jesus sat partway up the temple steps, surrounded by his disciples. The steps below him were filled with people, but those above him, leading up to the temple entrance, were empty.

Prentiss did her best to work her way through the crowd, but she could not get any closer. She couldn't believe that Jesus had come to sit on the very steps of the foundation he was attempting to cast aside. Around her, faces were lined with expectation.

She tried to separate herself from the sensations in order to objectively collect information. Nothing here, she cautioned herself, would support her case. This was just a crowd, waiting for a speaker. To people who spent the better part of their lives just eking out a living, any speech might be a major event.

No, that wasn't quite right. This was a technologically primitive culture, perhaps poised for a transformation. The state of their development was obvious from how they lived. The temple which loomed over her was a reminder of the power that religion held over their lives, a power that defined—and limited—their aspirations, their skills, their development. It channeled all their energies into blindly following a set of rules, rules which left little room for questioning and for creativity.

It all just depended on how you looked at it.

'Follow me,' Jesus had said. Those simple words captured the

struggle in Prentiss's mind—and in her heart. Would following Jesus lead her to the truth? And would it be a truth she wanted to know?

Her theory said that a civilization could be shocked out of its constraints, and that such a shock had to be inherently religious in nature. Any other challenge would only solidify the existing religious shackles, as people turned to the comfort of what they knew for protection. Only if the underlying tenets of their religious beliefs were disputed and defied would the people begin to question them, which would then undermine the very stability upon which the religion was based. This in turn would allow the civilization to finally progress as people began to free their thinking, as they began to focus their energies toward creating change instead of maintaining the status quo.

Would Jesus be the one to unleash this creativity by challenging the religious ways? This was the linchpin of her theory, that a messiah figure would engender a huge following, and would be revered enough to entice people to question, and ultimately reject, generations of rules and ways of living.

She knew her theory still begged the question of whether a single individual could actually do this. While history was full of individuals who had motivated large groups of people, such changes were typically short lived, and tended to simply hone existing cultural characteristics or tendencies, not change them.

Thus she had always left room for one final solution, an idea she dared not share with anyone. The only explanation of how such an individual, the catalyst, could shatter the very essence of how people lived.

The catalyst would actually have to be a god.

It had taken a long time for her to accept this implication. At first she resisted it, even though the theory almost seemed to demand it. So she had built complex arguments which allowed for her theory to be true without any need for a divine power.

But what if only a god could so transform a civilization? Who would believe her then?

Would she believe it herself?

The crowd stilled, as Jesus began to speak.

"Look upon this building. It is beautiful, is it not? See how the stones all fit together to create intricate patterns. See how it reflects the sun, like a beacon. It is a marvel of K'Turian architecture. Do you know what stood here before this temple was constructed? It was a farmer's store. Much less imposing than a temple, but important to the farmers of ages past, just as the market is today. But as important as the farmer's store was then, the very passage of time itself brought the store to an end. And in its wake, a new structure came to rise, in this case, a beautiful temple.

"Yet we must not confuse the beauty of this new building with its purpose, just as we must not confuse what one sees on the outside with what is within. Think of some plants, how they may have beautiful flowers, but their roots are poisonous, or some fruits and nuts, whose exteriors may be hard and crusty, but where there is nothing but goodness within. So I say to you, look not at the exterior, but at what is within.

"People are like buildings, like this temple. What you see on the outside may be very different from what is inside. You must look beyond the superficial, even if it is ugly, to see the truth beneath, for you may find great beauty there. But you must also not be overwhelmed by beauty, for there may be ugliness and deceit just below the surface."

There was a stirring in the crowd, and Prentiss heard someone whisper, "What is he saying? That all who are in the temple are bad? He has never spoken like this before."

"As I have told you," said Jesus, "do not confuse why you pray with where you pray. Just as the temple rose to replace the farmer's store, so too must the old rules be replaced. The Truth I bring you is that the ways of this life, how you act, should be determined by you, not told to you by others. This does not mean there is no right or wrong, or that you should act out of greed or selfishness. The very steps of your path to Paradise will be formed by what is right, and it will be lit for you by the beacons of Truth, which will cast aside the darkness of evil.

"This path is not easy, it is one of great sacrifice. Yet the sacrifices of this path must be those you make from the heart, not those defined by the Laws. Rules and rituals alone will not show you the Way, instead, they will lull you into a false sense of security, into a blind sleep.

"I say to you: Wake up! Your sleep is deadly! You must act, you must do something positive. Paying the Sacrifice is not a positive act, it is negative, done out of fear. It is not a choice you make. You must *choose* your sacrifices! I do not speak of the sacrifices you make to the priests, which leaves them full and you empty. The path I speak of calls upon even the priests and Pertise to make sacrifices, for the benefit of everyone.

"And you must make these sacrifices out of love, and because they will help others, and not because you want to be seen making them. One true small sacrifice in private is worth a hundred showy falsehoods!"

There was more nervous whispering, and someone called out, "What do you mean? Are you saying we should not follow the Law? That we should not listen to what the priests tell us to do?"

"Do not confuse the Law with the Way!" cried Jesus. "The Way is a promise, a path to a better place. A Law is a rule on how to act. Those who blindly follow the Laws will never find the Way, for they will forever be looking down to see if they are stepping on a stone or in a hole. You will not see Paradise unless you look up!"

From the back of the crowd came an angry shout, "Who are you to tell us that the Law will not show us the Way?"

"Do you build your house on rock and solid ground, or on shifting sand?" said Jesus. "Just as your house must have a foundation, so too there must be a base beneath your beliefs. But just as a house must have some flexibility, else it will be torn asunder by the wind and movements of the land, so too must your beliefs have freedom, they must have the ability to mold, to grow, to absorb what is around you. You must be free to see this Truth!"

This is it, thought Prentiss. He is talking about breaking from the laws, about creativity and freedom. *I'm witnessing it!*

But the crowd around her had begun to mutter. "What you say makes no sense!" someone yelled. "We cannot question the Laws, for they show us the Way!" And another voice, harsh, "You are not one of us, what gives you the right to tell us what to believe?"

No! Prentiss thought. *They don't understand . . .* He's not telling them what to believe, he's only trying to free them, so they can decide for themselves!

But all around her she could hear whispered questions, and she could feel the confusion and anxiety. It was too much for them to absorb. Many eyes kept glancing up at the temple, as if expecting the priests to appear.

"How dare you speak this way on the very steps of the temple! This is blasphemy!"

"Tell me," replied Jesus, calmly, "What Law have I broken?"

There was a sudden silence. "You cannot think of a Law that I have broken," said Jesus. "So how do you know what I say is blasphemy?"

A voice called out. "It is because you reject the Order!"

"Spoken cleverly, almost like a Pertise!" said Jesus. "Yet your answer only proves what I say. Blasphemy is a term created by the Pertise to define what is outside the Laws they create. It says nothing about the Way. So too, living blindly by the Order will not save you. The Order is nothing but a set of rules, another ritual. And it has become shallow, without significance. It's original purpose of helping others has been lost, replaced by nothing more than meaningless custom. You are all called upon to make Sacrifices, and because you are told what to sacrifice, you grumble and fret. What love is there in this?"

"But we must make the Sacrifices to keep the peace, and so that we may be prepared for Paradise!"

"Who tells you this?" replied Jesus, incredulous. "The priests? I ask of you, what sacrifices do *they* make? Do as they say, but not as they do! We will have peace by helping each other, not by having things taken from us! Those of you who are traders, and farmers, you give up so much for those above you—as the others above you give.

Yet those above heap scorn on those below. What peace is there in this? Are you at peace with yourselves? With your neighbor? You will find Paradise not because of where you were born in the Order, but by what you choose to do, how you act.

"We are all here, alive in this world, to do good deeds, to help each other. We must sacrifice for each other now, in order to reach Paradise, where sacrifice will seem as effortless as breathing. We must be free to help everyone, not be enslaved to help the few."

"This is crazy! Do not listen to him!"

But a few voices called out, "Let him speak! If this be blasphemy, certainly the Pertise would come out and answer him!"

"Yes," said Jesus. "And you should be more wary of those who throw stones from behind walls than those who challenge you on the open road."

There was some nodding of heads. Prentiss sensed the crowd was at a tipping point, those who wanted to listen, and those who could not shake their old beliefs. *If Jesus could only convince a few more . . .*

A new voice called out, "You talk about being enslaved by the Pertise. What about the Lemians? Are they not more of a threat than our own kind?"

An expectant hush fell over the crowd.

"Why are you concerned about them?" asked Jesus. "Is it because they are different? Remember what I have said, it is not what is outside that is important, but what is inside."

"But they are not of our people . . . they do not follow our Laws!"

"All peoples can find the road to Paradise!" said Jesus. "Let them choose, just as you must!"

"What are you saying? They can never find the Way—it is ours alone!"

Jesus replied, "The offworlders are like the forces of nature, forces over which we have no control. Think of the Lemians as you would the rains, or the drought. Do you stop praying or working because the weather has changed?

"I say to you: Everyone can find Paradise, no matter what they have done, no matter how misguided they have been, no matter where they are in the Order. Even the offworlders can find the Way, for it is for everyone."

Angry voices shouted out. "The Way is ours! Only ours!"

"Who are we to say that?" asked Jesus. "Just as you respect the rights of your neighbors to keep their own grain, or livestock, so must you allow others to choose their own beliefs!"

"But these people carry arms! What if they threaten our Way?"

"I too bring a sword!" said Jesus. "But this sword is not to divide you from each other, or even from the priests or offworlders, but to cleave you from your old beliefs!"

"We don't believe you! This is why the Pertise do not want you here! You are trying to keep us from the rightful Way! Get out!"

Others picked up the cry. "Get out! Let us cleanse ourselves of outsiders! They must leave!"

Prentiss was shocked. *What was happening?* How had it turned so quickly? Jesus needed to convince them, to get control of the situation. He needed to use whatever power he possessed before he lost their support.

But Jesus said nothing, and the tumult mounted. The disciples drew tightly around him, but he did not appear afraid.

Prentiss didn't know what to do. Part of her wanted to scream out: "Listen to him! Don't you see how he is helping you!" Yet another part of her wanted to rush to him, to protect him from the mob.

Someone grabbed her arm and spun her around. "You! Where are you from? Have you come to cause trouble too?" She was surrounded by angry people, all glaring at her. "Go away! Leave us alone!"

Shaking in fear, she broke free and ran off, weeping uncontrollably, fighting her way through the crowd.

* * *

Win felt a sudden pang, a lurch in his *gheris*. Something was happening. Something massive. But the Lemian camp below him looked the same; nothing hinted at anything out of the ordinary.

Past the camp, nothing but sand and the glimmering haze of heat. To his right, the city appeared quiet.

He began to walk along the ridge toward the orchard, where he had seen Jesus and his followers, to find out if they knew of anything that had been found outside the city.

But in his heart he knew he was just making an excuse. What he really wanted was to see Jesus again.

* * *

Tsaph ran toward the temple. He was hoping to hear Jesus, but he had been delayed because he had to organize a series of search parties to go and look for—he still wasn't sure. Something that looked like it came from offworld, according to Krelmar. The only thing he knew of for certain that was from offworld was the hidden communication device he possessed, and he certainly could not tell Krelmar about *that*.

The plaza was full of people, and Jesus was already speaking.

"Those of you who are traders, and farmers, you give up so much for those above you—as the others above you give. Yet those above heap scorn on those below. What peace is there in this? Are you at peace with yourselves? With your neighbor? You will find Paradise not because of where you were born in the Order, but by what you choose to do, how you act."

Tsaph was stunned. He had heard followers of Jesus say similar things, claiming Jesus taught that where one was born in the Order did not matter. But he had not believed them. Yet here was Jesus, questioning the Order, on the very steps of the temple!

Could it be true? Could it mean that Tsaph was not destined to live his life at the bottom? That he had the same chance to reach Paradise as anyone?

Could he be forgiven for helping the Lemians?

He smiled at the very thought of not being shunned by everyone else above him in the Order.

But the crowd did not seem happy. People were asking questions, and they were not friendly. Tsaph was puzzled; he had never heard such harshness before.

Many of the questioners were at the back of the crowd. Tsaph was close to one of them, the speaker's face hidden under a heavy hood. Something about the voice sounded familiar.

Tsaph moved closer, and when the cloaked figure turned Tsaph caught a glimpse of his face. *He knew the man!* He was one of the priests.

Tsaph was confused. Why was a priest dressed as a commoner?

More yelling, and soon the crowd had become a mob. Tsaph watched in dismay as a group of farmers began to push and hit a trader. Tsaph ran at them yelling, "Stop it! Stop it! This is not what we are about!" He tried to pull the attackers away, but one of them spun around and hit him squarely in the face. Tsaph fell back, struggling to his feet as the mob surged out of the plaza, toward the Lemian camp, yelling epithets against the Lemians, and against Jesus.

Were there other priests in the crowd, inciting the people?

Tsaph ran the other way, toward the temple. But Jesus was gone.

He ran up and down the streets, but Jesus was nowhere to be found. He didn't have much time, because Krelmar would be expecting him. But first he had to find Jesus, and the other disciples.

He had to warn them of the treachery of the priests.

* * *

Prentiss staggered out of the plaza, winded and frightened. Never in her life had she been caught up in a mob. But when she looked back, no one was following her, the crowd massing off in a different direction.

Willing herself not to run, she headed the other way, around to the side of the temple. The streets were deserted. Pulling her hood even tighter, she tried to appear calm as she walked along the outer temple wall. She wasn't sure where she should go. All she could think of was getting away from the mob.

Jesus of K'Turia

At the corner she looked back over her shoulder again to make sure she wasn't being followed. She tripped, and suddenly felt someone there beside her. Holding out her arm in defense, she heard a calm voice. "Let me help you, Sister." And she looked up into the eyes of Jesus.

Stunned, she froze on the ground, her arm outstretched toward him. Jesus reached out to her and she allowed herself to be lifted up.

"Did you not just hear me say you must look upward to see your path?" His voice was light and playful.

Prentiss was shocked. *How could he have known I was in the crowd?* But then her scientific mind whispered: *Maybe he just assumed I was.*

"Where are you off to in such a hurry?" asked Jesus.

"I was trying to escape," she replied. "The crowd—they seemed—dangerous."

"They are good people," said Jesus. "Most of them. They are just confused."

Prentiss was trying to collect her wits. First the riot, and now, face to face with Jesus. Out of the corner of her eye she saw the disciples, their faces filled with anxiety. But she did not look at them, she could not take her eyes off of Jesus.

"We must go now!" she heard someone say.

Jesus held her eye. "Come with me."

She trembled, clenching his hand even tighter. "I cannot," she whispered. Finally she looked away, her eyes downcast, ashamed.

"You cannot be committed to two paths," said Jesus softly. "The moment is coming when everyone will have to decide what they must do. The day of Great Sacrifice is upon us."

"Aren't you afraid?" she asked, meeting his eyes again.

"Why should I be?" said Jesus. "What will happen will happen. I do not want to change that."

"But isn't that what you are trying to do? Aren't you trying to change the way these people think?" She bit her tongue at her slip, referring to the K'Turians as 'these people.'

"Yes, but changing how they think is not trying to change what will happen."

She wanted to scream: *No! Changing what they think will free them forever!* But all she could manage was, "You must have patience with them. I—think they will listen to you, but it will take time. They have thought this way for generations. It cannot be rushed."

Jesus looked at her, full of compassion. "I know," he said. "But I do not have much time, and neither do you. For you must make your own decision. You too must decide what it is you believe in." Then he kissed her lightly on the forehead and walked away, his disciples surrounding him, leaving Prentiss standing in the middle of the empty crossroad.

Chapter 26

The Rhean Ceme reached out for Prome in sympathy.

Even if Prome had wanted to, the sense of disappointment could not be hidden. Yet no Rhean would want to conceal such a feeling, even one of such disenchantment, for this very sharing was what made them unique.

"The test is not going well," admitted Prome.

"The League does not yet even see the true test," sensed Ceme. "We must give the ones on K'Turia more time."

"They do not have that luxury," responded Prome. "Neither they nor we can control these events. If he is not saved, they will have failed."

"Yes, but much still may come of this. You were right, they have great potential. We see that now. They have already begun to change, to transform. For us, this would mean little, but for them, it is a great advancement."

"But will it be enough?" asked Prome. "Do they have the capability to achieve a higher level?"

"This is not for us to decide."

Still sad, Prome sensed, "The path is clear, the perfect example manifesting before their eyes. Even we could not have created anyone so ideal. If they cannot recognize him for who he is, they will not be worthy."

"Perhaps the League is not yet ready. But some within it may make the leap to Illumination, as others have. The Illian is special, like many of his race. And the other two on K'Turia—the human and the Treb. Both are on the verge of understanding."

Prome brightened. "Yes. Though that would be just the first step, it would be wonderful. And from there—who knows what might happen?"

Chapter 27

Many will fear the Truth, because they will no longer be able to hide behind false rituals.
—The Teachings 11:10

When Win reached the clearing in the orchard no one was there. Not even the light of day could remove the sense of emptiness surrounding the bare fire pit and the hard packed ground.

Across the clearing another lane headed through the orchard, toward the mountain. Win followed this path, the branches of the trees rustling slightly. A peaceful place, cut off from the city, feeling more like woods than a farm.

The lane ended at the base of the tor, opening into a second clearing. Another fire pit, and behind some large rocks, a small camp made up of a few rough shelters. A lone tree, solid and tall, stood sentry over the deserted camp.

Win slumped against the tree. He couldn't seem to find anything or anyone—the freighter, Garrick, Jesus.

Why was he even searching for Jesus?

He could understand why Prentiss felt the way she did. She was driven by her demotion, and saw in Jesus her vindication. Yet there was more. She had a passion, an emotion that went beyond trying to get proof for revenge.

Maybe she did believe in what she dared not admit, that the cultural transformation required the existence—and appearance—of a true deity. Of God.

Yet now, after being so long in his mental coma, he was awash in emotions. His disappointment over not finding Jesus was a startling revelation. His sensations were coming alive.

Was something within him telling him to change? Or was he yearning for someone to help him wake from his stupor?

Was he searching for his own God?

The thought made him catch his breath. Could he be—

He heard a sound behind him. He jumped up, and there on the lane were two men, dressed in fine robes.

Priests!

The sound of a door opening, and another priest emerged from one of the shelters. Then another, and another.

He was surrounded.

* * *

The Lemian soldier knocked on Commander Neel's door. He would not have bothered the commander if he could help it, but Neel had told him specifically to report anything out of the ordinary. This certainly seemed to qualify.

"Yes?"

The soldier opened the door. Neel, behind his spotless desk, waited expectantly, but the soldier did not know exactly how to phrase his report. "Sir, I think you should come see this," he finally said. "There's a mob outside the camp."

* * *

Tsaph couldn't find Jesus anywhere. *Tthean!* he thought. Tthean was a trader like himself. And one of the disciples, those closest to Jesus. Tthean would know how to reach Jesus.

Tsaph ran to the market, but Tthean was not there. Nor was he at his hut. Tsaph finally found the trader at one of the storage buildings, carrying a large sack.

"Tthean," said Tsaph, breathless. He didn't know how to begin.

"I think that Jesus is in great danger!" he blurted.

Tthean dropped his sack. "What do you mean?"

Quickly Tsaph told him about the disguised priests. "I think they are trying to turn the people—and the Lemians—against Jesus!"

Tthean was silent. "I will tell Jesus." He indicated the sack. "I am on my way to bring him and the others some food."

"You must hurry!" said Tsaph, his voice trembling. "I don't know what they plan, but I think it will happen soon."

"Jesus will know what to do," said Tthean. He picked up the sack and started to go.

Tsaph reached out and grabbed Tthean's arm. "Is it true what Jesus says?" whispered Tsaph. "That it doesn't matter where in the Order we were born?"

"I believe him," said Tthean.

"But what does it mean? Does it mean we don't have to be traders? That we don't have to stay at the bottom of the Order?"

"It means that the Order does not matter—that you will find Paradise because of the sacrifices you choose to make, not because of the ones that the Order forces upon you."

"How do I do that?" asked Tsaph.

"Be like Jesus, as much as you can," said Tthean. "No one can ever be exactly like him, but we should try. Listen to him, and watch him. See how he helps others. Be like him."

"But what of the priests, and the Way?" asked Tsaph. "If we listen to Jesus, we'll be punished, or banished!"

"We must be wary of everything the priests tell us," said Tthean. "You have seen yourself their deceit. I'm not saying they are all bad—and neither does Jesus. But he has opened my eyes to many things."

"But how do I know what to believe? We traders have so little chance of reaching Paradise. If I do anything outside the Law I will be lost forever!"

"You must have faith," said Tthean gently. "As I do. Jesus has much to teach us. Open your heart to him, and give him the chance to guide you."

* * *

Win knew there was no sense fleeing. The two priests in the lane approached, warily stopping a few paces away. They studied him carefully.

Win tried to stay calm. Almost instinctively he hunched over, dropping his gaze, letting his hood fall over his face. He had seen others in the city often wearing their hoods to protect them from the sun and blowing sand. But if the priests asked him to remove it, his alien features would certainly be recognized.

"What are you doing here?" demanded one of the priests.

Was the priest asking why he was in Merculon? He decided to answer the simpler question of why he was in the orchard. "Nothing. I am new to the city, and was merely walking along this path."

"Don't lie to us, pilgrim," said the priest. "We know you are here to see Jesus."

Once again Win tried to avoid the question. "I have been listening to him, as have many others."

"Don't try to be clever. We know this is Jesus' camp. Where is he?" demanded the priest.

"I don't know," said Win.

"I don't believe you," said the priest.

"I tell you, I don't know!" said Win. "What do you want with him?"

"That is no concern of yours. If you know where he is, it would be better for you if you tell us."

When Win did not reply, the other priest asked, "Where are you from? Why are you here?" His voice was quieter, less suspicious.

Win pointed back in the general direction of the shuttle, and Valdar. "I come from far off. I mean you no harm. I am only here to listen, and seek the truth, for myself. I do not wish to cause any trouble."

The first priest said harshly, "You cause trouble just by being here, you and all the other pilgrims. Don't you know you are not welcome?"

"I did not know," said Win.

"How many others are there?"

Win answered carefully. "There are many who seek the truth."

"Tell them to stay away," said the first priest. "None of you are wanted here."

Win sensed his anger, and also some fear. He knew he should simply acquiesce; it would be of no help if they probed into his background or his answers. But he was weary of being told what to do. First by Central Command, and then Garrick, and now these priests.

Even if he had known where Jesus was he would have told them nothing. Win had to fight the urge to look the priest in the eye. "Why? Why are we not wanted?"

The priest glared. "Because Jesus is a heretic. He preaches poison, he brings a stain to our Way. You pilgrims, and all who listen to him, encourage him."

"What has he said that is so bad?" asked Win, trying to keep his voice neutral.

"We don't have to explain ourselves to you!"

But the quieter priest said, "You are an outsider, perhaps you would not understand." His voice was calm, as if he were trying to reason with Win. "You see, our ways are different here in Merculon. We have lived in harmony for many years. All my life I have believed in the Way taught by our Temple. It is my—our—very heart and soul. What Jesus teaches tears at me, for it threatens all that I believe in. It threatens the very Order, which brings peace. It threatens our very existence."

Win sensed that this priest believed in what he said, his words heartfelt. And suddenly it occurred to Win why this priest was afraid. He was not afraid of pilgrims, or even of Jesus, rather, he feared that if Jesus was right, it would mean everything the priest had been taught was a lie. His honest belief in his own ways made it hard for him to accept anything else. Even if it was the truth.

But the other priest, the suspicious one, he was afraid for a different reason. He was afraid of what Jesus stood for. He was afraid of the power he would lose. That one would not try to reason with Win—or with Jesus.

"Please," said one of the priests who had not spoken, his voice almost entreating, as if Win were a lost, misguided soul, "though you are not from Merculon, we can help you find the true Way."

Win breathed a sigh of relief. They were not going to harm him today.

"I will consider it," he said. "For surely I want to know the truth."

* * *

"How did this happen?" Krelmar was screaming at the Lemian commander, Neel. Neel merely sat impassively, waiting for Krelmar's tirade to subside. Realizing he was shouting, Krelmar took a deep breath. He didn't often lose his temper, but Neel's news had stunned him, an image flashing in his mind of all his carefully made plans falling apart.

Quiet now, but still raging inside, he said, "Tell me again exactly what happened."

"Everything was calm, as usual, and then a large crowd appeared at the camp," replied Neel. "They were shouting for us to leave, that we were offworlders, and did not belong here. That we threatened the Way."

"Did your soldiers do anything to provoke them? Enter the temples, argue with the priests, *anything*?"

"No, nothing. We have had no soldiers in the city in days. There is only one roving sentry unit, and it is outside the valley. All standard procedure. The rest of the garrison is within the camp."

Krelmar was at a loss. "But what happened?"

"I don't know," said Neel. "I was hoping you could tell me."

But Krelmar could not think of any reason. His last contact with a local had been with Methurgem. Had he done anything to upset the priest? He could not imagine. Besides, if Krelmar had caused a problem, the mob would have been surrounding his home, not the Lemian camp.

Then it struck him. *Offworlders.* Methurgem had hinted there was a possibility that the preacher, Jesus, was an offworlder.

Had Jesus done something to inflame the people against the Lemians?

"Tell me exactly what you heard them say about the Way," he demanded.

Neel considered. "Something to the effect that 'all who threatened the Way must leave.'"

"I think I know what caused this," said Krelmar. Briefly he told Neel about his meeting with Methurgem. "The priests see this preacher as more of a threat than they let on. Or at least Methurgem does. And now it appears Jesus has done something to incite the people against us. He's not only a threat to Methurgem and the Temple, but to us."

To me, he thought.

"If this goes too far, even the priests may not be able to keep control, and that will jeopardize our plans," said Krelmar. "We must stop this *now.*"

"How can we do that without turning the people against us even more? Remember, we don't have enough troops here to deal with a revolt."

"We must remove the source of the discontent—we must find a way to neutralize Jesus. That will quell the disturbances, and at the same time show the priests how helpful we can be."

Neel looked skeptical. "This preacher has many followers. We will alienate them."

"Perhaps. Obviously Methurgem is not being honest about how popular this Jesus really is. The Pertise are clearly afraid of him. And there's something else. Methurgem did not come right out and say this, but he thinks Jesus might be an offworlder."

"An offworlder? From where?"

"Who knows? But I keep thinking about the pilgrim you captured. He said he is from Valdar. Methurgem told me Jesus is also from Valdar. An interesting coincidence."

"We sent a sentry detail there a while ago. A much smaller city, but similar to this one. Religious. Locals were just as disinterested in us."

"Still," said Krelmar, "it makes me wonder. What if the pilgrims are offworlders? They could be another problem. We need to learn more. I want you to get whatever information this pilgrim has about any contacts he may have had with offworlders. And anything he knows about Jesus."

"He still claims to know nothing."

"Then push him harder. Use—whatever means are necessary."

"I understand," said Neel. "And I will double the sentry patrols. If the pilgrims are from offworld, there may be others sneaking around. I will also order a new sweep for . . ." Neel stopped, his eyes searching the room.

"What is it?" asked Krelmar.

Neel shook his head, then slowly got up and began looking around Krelmar's office. "As I was saying, we'll do another sweep of the city." He turned to Krelmar and put a finger to his lips.

Krelmar nodded his understanding. Neel was checking the room for bugs. Conversationally, he changed the subject, in order to give Neel time. "Anything to report regarding our supply situation?"

"Everything is as planned, Lord Krelmar." Neel stood in the middle of the room, his eyes darting everywhere, finally settling on a ventilation grate in the ceiling. Neel whispered in Krelmar's ear, "Keep talking," and then he quietly left the room.

To the empty office, Krelmar said, "I want you to prepare a report on the following." He conjured up a long list of requests. He was interrupted by a commotion from the room above. In a few moments Neel returned, shoving Tsaph before him. The K'Turian was cowering.

"I found him eavesdropping on us, through that grate," explained Neel. "We had swept for bugs, but you should have told me his room was directly over your office."

Krelmar was about to say, "Security is your job," but thought better of it. No sense alienating Neel now. He had a bigger problem on his hands.

Jesus of K'Turia

"What is the meaning of this?" Krelmar demanded.

"I swear, my Lord, I was just cleaning," stammered Tsaph. "I didn't do anything wrong."

"He's lying," said Neel. "I noticed the grate because it doesn't lead outside to fresh air. And it appears to have been recently installed." He prodded Tsaph. "Talk."

Tsaph lowered his eyes, but said nothing.

"Talk!" Neel ordered again.

Krelmar eyed the trader carefully. Tsaph was clearly frightened. *He must be hiding something.* "I will give you one chance to speak. If you do not, I will have you incarcerated for the rest of your life as a spy against the Lemian Empire."

Tsaph looked up, his eyes pleading. "I was only—you aren't going to harm Jesus, are you, Lord Krelmar? He is not to blame for what happened at the camp."

"So you heard us speak of that, did you?" asked Krelmar. *Who was Tsaph spying for?* The pilgrim? Jesus? "How do you know Jesus wasn't responsible for the mob?"

"Because it was the priests! I was at the temple when Jesus spoke. There were priests in the crowd, but they were dressed as commoners. They turned the crowd against you!"

Could that be true? thought Krelmar. Why would the priests do that? If they had, surely Methurgem was behind it.

And why was Tsaph so willing to protect Jesus? He thought back to his earlier conversation with the trader, and how Tsaph had spoken about Jesus. *Ahh, Tsaph's one of his followers.*

"Tsaph, I know you are a follower of Jesus!" he said sharply. "If you don't tell me who you are spying for, I will bring you before Methurgem!" Tsaph cringed, and Krelmar knew he had guessed correctly.

"No! He will banish me!" said Tsaph.

"Then tell me what I need to know. Who you idolize doesn't concern me. Who you are spying for does. Is it the League? Are you working with the pilgrim?"

"Who? What pilgrim?" Tsaph appeared genuinely confused.

"Offworlders." said Neel. "Are you spying for offworlders?" He grabbed Tsaph's arm and twisted it.

Tsaph stood mute, though the pain showed on his face.

"If you don't tell me what I want to know, I'll not only bring you before Methurgem, but we'll have Jesus punished—and imprisoned!" said Krelmar.

Tsaph's eyes widened. "You cannot! You must not!"

"I will, and you know the priests would not stop me," said Krelmar. "Now tell me, who are you spying for?" He nodded at Neel, who twisted Tsaph's arm even harder.

The K'Turian yelled out in pain. "I'm only doing what I was told by the Lemians!"

Krelmar's head snapped up to look at Neel, but the Lemian commander looked just as surprised as he was. "What?"

"I report to the Lemians—to someone named Tera-Seil!"

Krelmar was stunned. "Tera-Seil?"

"Yes! Please don't tell him, he'll kill me!"

Krelmar was momentarily at a loss for words. He turned a sharp eye on Neel. "What do you know of this?"

Neel released Tsaph and stepped back. "Nothing, Lord Krelmar. I swear!"

Krelmar believed him. If Neel had known he would not have brought Tsaph's spying to Krelmar's attention.

So Tera-Seil was spying on him. Krelmar certainly expected that Neel would be reporting to the Lemian Command as part of his duties. But why would Tera-Seil need another source of information?

Krelmar watched Neel closely, and saw the realization dawn on the Lemian that the presence of a spy meant Tera-Seil did not trust him either.

"It appears we are in a similar situation, Commander," said Krelmar. "We'll discuss that later. But first—." He turned a withering gaze on Tsaph. "How long has this been going on? And what makes you think Tera-Seil would have you killed?"

"They told me he would!"

"Who? Who told you?"

"The Lemians!" Tsaph was panic stricken.

Krelmar forced himself to calm his voice. "What Lemians?"

"The ones who came before and left—before you arrived. They told me I'd been chosen to be your aide—and to report back."

"He must mean the advance team," explained Neel. "They were with us when we first landed. They made the initial contacts with the locals, and once the camp was established, they left."

"They report to Tera-Seil?"

"I don't know, Lord Krelmar. But such an advance team is standard procedure."

Krelmar breathed a sigh of relief. He had been worried that Tsaph would have passed along information about the pilgrim and about the search for something from offworld, neither of which Krelmar had reported to the Lemian Command.

Krelmar caught Neel's eye. "It appears there is nothing to worry about." To Tsaph he said, "If the advance team is gone, I guess you have no one to report to. Perhaps I will turn you over to Methurgem anyway. I'm sure he will know how to deal with a follower of Jesus."

Once again Tsaph seemed confused. "But—but I've already reported."

"What? How?!"

"I—I have a device."

Krelmar was shocked. Tsaph had some way of communicating with Tera-Seil! *What else could go wrong?*

"What have you told him?" demanded Krelmar.

Tsaph looked away. "Everything. Everything I hear."

"Did you tell him about the pilgrim?" asked Neel.

"Yes—everything!" said Tsaph. "And about the search."

"The search?" asked Neel.

"I'll explain later," said Krelmar. So Tera-Seil knew there was a possible offworlder spy on the planet! Tera-Seil would wonder why Krelmar had not reported this.

If the pilgrim *was* a spy, and Tera-Seil found out, he would assume that Krelmar was working for the League. Krelmar would be doomed.

"Commander Neel, we'll have to—update our report to Tera-Seil," he said. *Time for damage control.* "We need to let the Lemian Command know of the pilgrim, and that we hope to have additional information about him—in a few days."

"Very well, Lord Krelmar," said Neel.

They would have to carefully craft the report, downplaying the pilgrim. "Tsaph, I'm very disappointed in you," said Krelmar. He tried to sound stern, but he understood why Tsaph had spied—out of fear. Now Krelmar had to try to minimize the damage. "We are going to tell you what to report to Tera-Seil from now on. Unless you do as I tell you, I will turn you over to Methurgem—and tell him you are not only following the preacher, but you have been spying on your own people for offworlders."

"But it's too late!" cried Tsaph. "Tera-Seil—he's on his way here right now!"

Krelmar fell back in his chair. Tera-Seil coming to K'Turia! It could only mean one thing. *They were coming for him.*

Only a miracle could save him now. It was time for drastic action.

"Commander Neel, follow my orders regarding the pilgrim. *Immediately.* We must know if he is a spy. And take this—liar—with you and lock him up. I'll decide what to do with him later."

* * *

Prentiss walked aimlessly, her head still spinning from the altercation at the temple and the words Jesus had spoken to her. Almost unconsciously she found herself in the same alley where she and Win had hidden before.

Slumped in a doorway, she tried to sort out what to do.

She had come to K'Turia so disinterested in this mission. Stripped of her power and assistants, and banished to a solitary research vessel, she had been marking time, trying to figure out how to get back her position and recover the respect of her peers. And then as if a miracle, the very means of doing just that appeared before her, but so frustratingly out of her grasp.

And Jesus. He was everything she had theorized about a messiah figure. But he was much more. Though her theory called for the messiah to certainly be someone out of the ordinary, even she hadn't expected anything like this. His strength, his influence over the people.

Over *her*.

But instead of resisting, as she would with any other attempt to influence her, she found herself wanting more. She needed to hear more of his message, feel more of his presence.

Whether it was because of her desire to prove her theory, or her need to believe in something more than science, in that instant, she only knew one thing for sure: she had to find him, to be with him.

She pulled her hood tightly over her head and ran to find Jesus.

* * *

"We have a problem," said Neel. "The pilgrim. He *is* a spy. For the League."

Krelmar groaned, his worst fears realized. "Tell me everything," he ordered.

They were in the Lemian base. Neel had assured him the new scan had turned up no bugs in his office, but Krelmar wasn't taking any chances.

"We haven't—finished the interrogation," said Neel. "And I doubt we'll get much more out of him. He is obviously with the military—he's well trained in resisting interrogation."

"What *do* you know?" asked Krelmar.

"You must realize, Lord Krelmar, that we had to put him under a lot of pressure. At that level of pain, we only get bits and pieces, with a lot of denial. All I can tell you is that he is from the League. He admitted it, but still claims he is no spy. We don't even know how long he has been on K'Turia, whether he is here because of us, or if he was in place before we arrived."

Krelmar thought that unlikely. Why would the League waste a valuable asset on this planet? The spy was either here to keep an eye on the Lemians, or, as Krelmar had earlier guessed, he was looking for something.

What could it be?

He'd worry about that later. His biggest problem was Tera-Seil.

"You realize the position we are in," said Krelmar. "When Tera-Seil finds out about the spy—and now we have to tell him everything we know—he's going to think we have been keeping something from him."

"I know," said Neel. "Still, we don't report everyone who is suspicious."

"You forget that something is making Tera-Seil come here," said Krelmar. He didn't mention to Neel it was probably because Tera-Seil thought Krelmar was also working for the League. "So he doesn't think this is routine. He'll think we are inept—or hiding something. We must be ready."

"What can we do?"

"We have to win back his trust. We have to find out why the spy is here—I will question him myself." He considered. Perhaps it was time to tell Neel about his suspicions. Krelmar had nothing to lose now. "I believe the spy may be here looking for something. I don't know exactly what—but it is something the League would risk being here for. This is what I had Tsaph trying to uncover. If I'm right, we need to find out what it is—*before* Tera-Seil gets here. Organize your men—I want *everyone* looking for anything out of the ordinary. And the spy is probably not alone. Start with the pilgrims. Find them—and lock them up."

Chapter 28

Once the light of Truth is lit within you, it cannot be extinguished.
—The Teachings 12:33

The bored Lemian guard snapped to attention as Krelmar approached.

"Unlock the door," ordered Krelmar. When he entered the room he had to blink and shield his eyes. The light was blinding. *Sleep deprivation techniques.* This wouldn't do. He turned to the guard. "Turn off those lights—and wait outside."

The guard hesitated, just enough to make it clear he didn't like getting his orders from a civilian—and a non-Lemian at that. A moment after the guard left the room the lights dimmed.

When the door closed behind him, Krelmar looked around the windowless room, bare except for two small tables and a chair. One of the tables held an array of electronic equipment and what looked like medical devices. On the other were the remnants of a cloak, cut into pieces. In the chair sat a haggard man, totally naked, his arms and legs strapped down. His dark skin hinted at years in the sun, but according to Neel the tan had been artificially induced.

"I know you are awake," said Krelmar. Without waiting for an answer he went to the table and picked up the largest piece of the robe. He draped it over the prisoner, covering him as best he could. Still the man had not moved.

"You can pretend you are asleep, or we can get on with this," said

Krelmar. "If you won't talk to me, I'll send the Lemians back in here. I can assure you, talking with me will be less—unpleasant."

The man lifted his head slightly. His eyes, swollen and bloody, cracked open. Krelmar had to fight the urge to look away.

"Who are you?" The voice was flat.

"I am Lord Krelmar. And who are you?"

"You are not from K'Turia."

"Neither are you," said Krelmar. "You've already admitted that much. You are in no position to be asking questions. But so you fully realize the terrible position you are in, let me explain. I represent the Lemian Empire on this planet, and as such have full authority."

"You have no authority over me." Even in his pain the man was still defiant.

"Your tone, even more than your words, prove to me you don't belong on K'Turia," said Krelmar. "We know you are from the League. Why continue this charade? Just tell me why you are here, and I can end your discomfort."

The man did not respond.

"Who else is with you?" Krelmar asked.

"No one."

"Lying will not help you. We already know of your accomplices." Krelmar watched the prisoner's eyes for any indication his bluff had worked, but the man's blank stare revealed nothing.

Krelmar decided to try something else. "I am not a Lemian, as you are undoubtedly aware. As a non-Lemian, but someone with authority, I am in a rather unique position. I can—understand you—and also help you."

"If you have such great authority, and if you want to help me, then why don't you let me go?"

"Perhaps I will—once I determine how much of a threat you are. If, for instance, you have been on K'Turia for a long time, perhaps trying to get the planet to join the League, then I might be persuaded you are not a threat at all. But for me to believe that, you would have to be able to prove you have not just arrived. Can you do that?"

The prisoner blinked. Krelmar could not tell if he was in pain or considering the offer. He left the man to his own thoughts, because he needed time to think himself.

When Krelmar had been ordered to come to K'Turia, he thought he had escaped Tera-Seil's ultimate punishment. But the prisoner shackled before him, surely a spy, was evidence of how much Krelmar still had to lose. And the discovery of the mole Tsaph, and the news that Tera-Seil was coming, could only mean that Krelmar's life was in imminent danger.

Obviously Tera-Seil did not trust him, and had perhaps sent him here as part of some elaborate trap to find out if he was helping the League. The presence of a League spy would certainly lead Tera-Seil to believe Krelmar was a traitor. It was too late to have the prisoner killed—both Neel and Tera-Seil would be suspicious.

Krelmar was trapped.

He didn't believe the prisoner was on K'Turia alone. He needed to find the other spies. And even then, he might need an escape plan.

It was time for desperate measures.

* * *

Win sat alone in the deserted camp long after the priests had left. The kind priest had thought Win a lost soul. And he was. Not for the reason the priest thought, but because of how his life was being wasted.

Yet here on K'Turia, he had felt a stirring, a light from within, reminding him of what he had almost reached. It was agonizingly painful; as if looking into the sun after years of blindness.

That image grew before him, turning into a reality. The heat seared into his brain, becoming a vibrant and intense light. He closed his eyes, but the energy forced its way through his eyelids. He tried shielding his face with his hands, but it did nothing to block the light.

Win could think of nothing else, nothing but the light. It pushed away even his despair.

He forced his eyes open, into the radiance. The pain disappeared.

A figure stood before him, an apparition, the light flowing from it, the energy engulfing Win. Instead of feeling smothered, he could now breathe again.

"Do not be afraid," came a voice. "I am the light which has called out to awaken you from your slumber, your spiritual purgatory. Come forth, and see this new light."

The apparition faded, transforming into the image of Jesus.

"What is happening?" Win heard himself saying.

The voice surrounded him, its timbre caressing his very bones. "It is time to fulfill your purpose."

"I cannot," said Win, nearly sobbing. "Without Sooni, how can I? It is too much to bear."

"You must try," said the voice. "I will help you."

"I dare not," said Win. "Sooni was my *ana*. Without her I cannot even be myself, I cannot be whole."

"Why do you speak so of her? It is not she who has deserted you, it is you who have deserted her."

The light dimmed ever so slightly, and now Win saw an image of Sooni, silhouetted in the light. She was smiling at him, her countenance one of peace. Then her expression changed, to one he had never seen on her, ever. She was frowning at him. Then she was gone, and the light intensified anew, the face of Jesus once again before him.

No! Sooni, come back! Why are you angry at me? Now he was crying convulsively, as if all the years of pent up emotions were being freed.

"The priest was wrong," said the voice, but this time it sounded just as much like Sooni as it did Jesus. "You can no longer remain a lost soul, you can no longer hide in darkness."

Win shook his head. "What if I fail? Then even the numbness cannot save me."

"Numbness is not survival. For you, it is death. You know this. You have always known this."

Win looked away. "I am not ready."

The apparition spoke, the voice of Jesus again, so powerful it pulled Win's eyes back up. "How will you know unless you take the first step? You must leave your darkness for the light. The Truth of this has always been with you. My words have merely opened your eyes to this Truth."

"We were so close," said Win, the devastating sadness overwhelming him.

"And what have you allowed yourself to do? You have hidden behind her loss, using it as an excuse to avoid your purpose. Remember what you have heard me say: *You must think of what you are responsible for.* Now I say to you: you must think of what you need to do for yourself."

The words were like a slap in the face. In that moment Win realized what had happened to him—what he had allowed to happen. He had given up on *ana*, not by making a choice, but by drifting into a morass of uncertainty and darkness.

"It hurts." He choked out the words. "It hurts so much. Please, this can't be better. I want to go back."

"It is too late," said the apparition, the voice of Jesus. "Once you have seen the light of Truth, you can no longer hide in darkness." The apparition came closer, bringing with it the warm and comforting light.

"I will help you," said the voice, and Win felt the light engulf him, smothering the pain of remembered sadness, a blanket of security more potent than any comfort he had achieved from trying to repress the memories of his beloved Sooni, and his search for *ana*.

* * *

In Neel's office, Krelmar said, "I think you are right, he is a League spy."

"He *told* you that?"

"No." Krelmar sat wearily on the hard seat by Neel's desk. "In fact, he told me nothing. I gave him the chance to prove me wrong. All he had to do was produce some evidence of history on K'Turia, someone who knows him. An innocent man would have jumped at that chance."

"So what do we do?"

"We still must learn why he is here and if he is alone. Have your men found any others?"

"None," replied Neel. "But if they are here we will find them."

"We don't have much time. By now, anyone who came with him will know he is missing. They are probably in hiding. If we do not find them and discover what they are up to before Tera-Seil arrives—I'm sure you can imagine what his reaction will be."

"Perhaps we should just wait for him," suggested Neel.

"You forget, we aren't supposed to know he is coming. Besides, do you want to have to tell him you did nothing after you found out a League spy was here?"

"If we try to force any more information out of the prisoner, he may die. That is also something Tera-Seil would be very unhappy to learn."

"I agree," said Krelmar. "That is why I have decided to let the prisoner go."

"Let him go? You can't be serious!"

"Yes. We won't get any more information out of him. Let him think he's fooled us. Once he is released, have him followed. He is in no condition to get very far away, and will certainly try to rejoin whomever he is with. If he is alone, we will be in no worse a position than we are now, and can pick him up again. But should he lead us to others, we will get all of them—and be in much better shape to deal with Tera-Seil."

"I cannot take responsibility for this," said Neel. "It is highly unusual."

"I will take responsibility," said Krelmar. "Don't worry, in his present condition I am certain he will try to get help. We'll know soon enough."

* * *

Long after Krelmar had left his office, Commander Neel still had not moved. He did not like the position he was in.

He was already faced with the daunting task of explaining to his superiors—to Tera-Seil, no less!—why he had delayed in informing them about the League spy. Neel couldn't lie to Tera-Seil— too many people already knew about the prisoner. Now Krelmar wanted to let the spy go free. While Neel understood the logic of the scheme, too much could go wrong with the plan.

Krelmar was right about one thing. Finding out why the spy was here would help assuage Tera-Seil. And though they might uncover the same information if they were to capture other League spies, who knew how long that could take? Any others would be in hiding, and Neel already had *this* spy in custody.

He would follow Krelmar's orders, but first he would interrogate the spy one last time. His plan was dangerous, it might kill the prisoner. But Neel feared Tera-Seil far more than he feared Krelmar.

After all, Krelmar wasn't even a Lemian.

Chapter 29

Belief is not a fate or a destiny, but a choice.
—The Teachings 13:20

The sun had moved behind the hills, casting the camp in shadows. Still Win had not moved. He had tried—and for the first time in his life had failed—to enter *nore*. He could not calm his beating heart, he could not still his thoughts.

He opened his eyes. The Jesus apparition was gone. Had someone even been there?

His skin still tingled from the light which had enveloped him. And he felt—*transformed*, as if the light had not only warmed his body but had also awakened his spirit.

No longer protected by his self imposed numbness, the sadness engulfed him, a giant wave, pushing him to his knees. Just as the weight of his anguish and desolation began to crush him, he heard a voice. *I will help you.* It sounded like Sooni. Or was it Jesus?

Could it be possible? Could he escape his despair?

The voice gave him strength. He lifted his eyes. The tree towered over him, a guardian against the infinity of the sky, holding up the enormity of the universe. Its sturdy trunk reassured him, and he leaned on it as he pulled himself to his feet.

With each step he grew stronger, and as he left the camp and entered the orchard, the path, which should have been hidden in darkness, was miraculously easy to see.

***

Prentiss had failed to find Jesus anywhere in the city. Three times she had cautiously returned to the temple and arena. But the arena was deserted, and only a few people were at the temple. The city was eerily calm after the day's chaos.

At first she had avoided the market, fearful after being challenged by the mob. As the day wore on and she still had found no sign of Jesus, she forced herself to make her way toward the market, staying on the outskirts, turning away quickly when anyone noticed her.

But no one accosted her, and she risked a brief, fast walk through the central market plaza. She overheard plenty of talk about Jesus, whispered discussions about what he had said at the temple, and tense retellings of the near riot at the Lemian base.

The smells in the market reminded her how hungry she was, and without thinking she stopped and stared at the food. When she tore her eyes away she was taken aback by a young man who was watching her intently from only an arm's length away. He held a small sack in his hand. She tensed, ready to protect herself or run.

The man nodded at her and said, "Can you tell me where to find Jesus?"

Not expecting the question, she stood dumb.

When she did not respond he said, "I'm sorry. I thought you were a pilgrim. I want to hear Jesus again, and I was hoping you could tell me where he will speak next."

Was this a trap?

"I don't know," she responded cautiously. "I was actually trying to find out the same thing myself."

"No one seems to know," said the man, and he sounded genuinely disappointed. "I hope he has not left the city after what happened today."

"You were there?" asked Prentiss, still cautious.

"Yes," he said. "I was very confused. Some said it was Jesus' fault for what happened. I've never heard such anger, and I don't understand who was causing all the trouble."

"I don't know either," said Prentiss.

The man shook his head. "Jesus is teaching us about a new way of living, bringing us a new hope. I cannot understand why he was treated so."

Prentiss thought immediately of the priests. "Perhaps those who do not like his message."

"Perhaps," said the man. "Some high in the Order worry that if the farmers listen to Jesus, they will no longer pay the Sacrifices, and we will have no food. I am a builder, and because of my place in the Order I have more than I need, while the farmers struggle. Until I heard Jesus speak, I never gave a thought to this unfairness. Most of the other builders are happy with the way things are. And sometimes—sometimes I feel that way too. That we should leave everything as it is. Yet I am troubled."

Prentiss lowered her head, not sure how to respond. The man's dilemma had struck a chord, for she too anguished over an inner conflict, the message of Jesus tearing at her, pulling her from the safety of her scientific life.

Half to herself, she said, "Many are afraid of change."

"When I listen to Jesus, I do not feel afraid. Yet I do not know if I have the strength to follow the way of Jesus."

She raised her eyes to his. "You sound like a good man," she said gently.

The K'Turian's face broke out into a broad grin. "The priests would not think so, if they heard me speak this way!" Then he grew serious again. "We all know the Pertise do not like Jesus. But if they are so upset, why do they not intervene, or banish him?" He glanced in the direction of the temple. "We are all very confused."

"As I have been," said Prentiss, honestly.

"How should I decide what to do?" asked the man.

Prentiss considered. The man's simple question had suddenly clarified her thinking, shining a light on the decisions she had to make. "Follow your heart," she said.

* * *

Win was the first one to reach the rendezvous point behind the arena. Since returning from the orchard he had fruitlessly searched for Garrick and the freighter. If I'Char and Prentiss had also found nothing, he would face a difficult decision.

Should they leave Merculon, and search elsewhere on the planet? Garrick's disappearance complicated everything.

With each passing moment there was less and less chance of finding Garrick alive.

But as long as there was hope, one of them would have to stay behind. It would have to be I'Char. Prentiss would want to be the one to stay, but she could not be trusted to focus on Garrick; she'd be too interested in Jesus.

He could not allow himself to stay, for the same reason. But he knew it would be hard for him to leave.

K'Turia had changed him. *Jesus* had changed him.

It was getting dark. Where were the others?

* * *

Prentiss could think of only one other place to look for Jesus. The orchard. In the growing darkness she hurried there, knowing each step took her farther away from the arena and the rendezvous point.

But she had to go. Suddenly everything was clear in her mind. The simple question she had been asked by the confused K'Turian in the market had galvanized her thinking.

Now she understood what Jesus had meant when he had said: *'For you must make your own decision. You too must decide what it is you believe in.'*

What exactly had she chosen to believe in? She had put all her belief into a theory of her own making. Driven by science, she had been searching for a means to describe in unemotional, utterly detached terms how entire masses of people could be transformed by a single figure.

But she had not made the choice she thought she had made. She had it all backwards. *She wasn't searching for the science, she was searching for the messiah.* For *her* messiah, to bring about her own transformation.

She was searching for her own god.

It had taken this long for her to realize it because she had always felt that if God existed, He would be found internally, within one's own consciousness, an internal spiritual power. Yes, her theory called for a messiah. She understood that such a messiah might be imbued with some essence, some power that could be ascribed to a deity, to validate the faith of the followers.

But all that was so—theoretical, so *mechanical.*

She had missed the truth because she had never truly allowed herself to believe the obvious: that the power of the messiah could *transcend* the realm of science.

That the messiah could be the intervention of God.

And that her messiah would be someone she could see, and hear, and touch. Someone she could believe in.

Like Jesus.

As she finally admitted it to herself she began to run.

* * *

Hidden within the crowd at the marketplace, the acolyte Sahme kept a sharp watch on the pilgrim woman from beneath her hood. Sahme did not want to make the same mistake she had made before, when she had been run off in the orchard. She had been so ashamed of that failure she had said nothing of it in her report to the Temple.

This time, Sahme would not be deterred, even if the heretic Jesus himself chased her. She would have something of value to report, and she was sure it would please the Pertise. Though she wondered why they wanted some of the acolytes to merely spy on the pilgrims instead of openly denouncing and banishing them, she did not question her orders. After all, it gave her a chance to prove herself. She hoped she would one day rise to a high position in the Temple, and if the will of the Pertise was that she was to help in this way, who was she to question it?

When the pilgrim woman had left the market, Sahme followed discreetly behind. Sahme continued to stalk the pilgrim as she wandered aimlessly through the city.

Later, as night fell, Sahme started to think the pilgrim was lost, for she had been going around in circles. But suddenly the pilgrim began to run. Did she know she was being followed? But the cloaked figure never looked back, and now seemed to have a purpose in mind, a destination.

Sahme followed carefully. There were few people in this part of the city so late in the evening. If the pilgrim turned around she would certainly notice someone chasing her.

The acolyte kept up as best she could, but in spite of her efforts the pilgrim was soon lost to view. Sahme stopped, suddenly realizing where she was. A smile crossed her lips. She knew where the pilgrim was headed.

* * *

I'Char watched as the Lemian sentry passed by, a scant dozen steps away. Unlike the day before, the sentry was alert and focused, no longer unconsciously repeating a set routine. Something had changed.

Yet I'Char wasn't concerned about this particular guard seeing him. The sentry was looking outward, away from the camp.

And I'Char was already inside the camp, behind the sentry.

The Illian waited until the sentry was well past before moving. The Lemians had doubled the sentries, and had also added a roving guard inside the camp.

Keeping in the shadows, I'Char circled around the main building. Soon he was in the very core of the camp. He had already discovered that the ground shuttles were missing.

More perimeter guards, plus more roving searches. That could only mean the Lemians were looking for something outside the camp, and protecting something *inside* the camp.

They had either found the freighter, or Garrick, or both. Garrick might already have been forced to tell the Lemians about not only the shuttle, but about the crew.

I'Char didn't have much time.

He made his way to the other side of the camp, farthest from the city. Hiding behind a wall of containers, he watched as a few soldiers came and went into the buildings, moving supplies. While they did so the doors remained open.

Not a place to keep a prisoner. To his right there was a solitary building with no windows. The structure was guarded by a sentry unit on the two sides he could see, plus two guards at the door. A lot of security for one small building.

He settled in to watch.

He didn't have to wait long. The door of the windowless building opened, and two soldiers emerged, supporting another man, whose head hung limp. Behind them came another soldier, and the guards at the door snapped to attention.

As they passed under the bright light over the door, I'Char saw the features of the man being pulled along.

Garrick.

The soldiers half dragged Garrick across the camp. At the corner of the main building the group split up, the lone soldier entering the building while the two guards with Garrick continued on, heading toward the city.

After waiting to be sure no one else was coming out, I'Char hurried after them, staying close to the wall. He was barely in time to see Garrick and the guards disappear among the outbuildings across from the barracks.

He was just about to sprint across the open space when the door of the barracks slapped open and six soldiers trooped out, carrying bundles. They stood outside the doorway, talking, the light from the door spilling over them. I'Char watched as they donned robes over their uniforms. After a few moments they paired up and headed off, all in the general direction of the city.

I'Char raced across the compound, flattening himself against the wall of one of the smaller buildings. Quickly he made his way through the cluster of structures. At the far side he had to wait; the perimeter sentry would pass by again soon.

From his vantage point he was able to see Garrick. He wasn't being put into any of the buildings, instead, the guards were taking him out of the camp, toward the city. The soldiers passed by the perimeter guards and were soon lost to sight in the darkness.

I'Char counted in his head. Precisely when he expected, the second sentry passed in front of him. I'Char was forced to wait until the sentry crossed the compound and disappeared out of sight.

This was his only chance. I'Char sprinted across the unprotected expanse, not stopping until he reached the city entrance arch.

Crouched in the shadow of the arch, he heard someone coming from the direction of the city. The two guards who had been carrying Garrick were returning to the camp. I'Char passed under the arch and immediately began walking calmly in plain sight, in the middle of the road, just a local going in to town. But his eyes were everywhere.

Within a few steps he saw two robed figures in the shadows, watching him. Then ahead, a movement in a doorway. As he passed by he felt their stares. He glanced to the left, down the road which paralleled the city wall. A huddled mass lay in a doorway well down the road, barely visible in the weak glow from the torches on the wall.

I'Char continued on, and once past a few buildings turned right, and then right again at the next street. There he waited, peering around the corner to see if he was being followed. But the street was completely empty.

Had they released Garrick? Perhaps he had convinced the Lemians that he was no threat.

But then why all the extra security?

The huddled figure he had seen in the street could have been Garrick. He could just retrace his steps to find out. Garrick had appeared unconscious and hurt, and he would need help.

All too easy.

The robed figures he had seen would be watching Garrick's every move.

It was a trap.

Chapter 30

Who are they who would say that the truth of faith is any less than the truth of evidence?
—The Teachings 14:10

Prentiss didn't slow until she reached the top of the ridge. In the dark she was afraid she would trip and fall, and now that she finally knew what she wanted she didn't want to take any chances. She hurried as fast as she could, as the sight below brought joy to her heart. For she could see a light through the trees.

At the clearing she hesitated only briefly. There was Jesus, sitting against a tree, somewhat apart from three of his followers. Everything was quiet.

Gathering her courage, she entered the clearing.

At first, she didn't think anyone noticed her. Then she realized the disciples were sleeping, and Jesus appeared deep in thought. She paused, embarrassed, not wanting to disturb them.

She heard Jesus say, "You must not blame yourself for what will happen."

Prentiss was confused. Who was Jesus talking to?

His voice seemed to arouse the others from their slumber, for they rolled over and rubbed their eyes. One of the disciples caught sight of Prentiss and jumped up, moving protectively in front of Jesus. "You again! What do you want?" he challenged.

"I'm sorry," she said. "I—I only wanted to see Jesus."

Jesus nodded. "Come, Sister," he said. "Join us."

Jesus of K'Turia

Prentiss approached the fire. The disciples moved aside, guarded and still watching with suspicion. But Jesus beckoned for her to sit by him.

"So you have found me, at last," he said. "I am glad."

She wanted to yell out, "Yes! I have not only found you here, but also in my heart!" But now, before him, she was dumbstruck. She sunk to her knees, her head bowed.

When she finally found the courage to look up into the eyes of Jesus she was comforted by the compassion she felt there, cradling her. She had never been in the presence of someone so powerful, so complete. Jesus' calmness radiated into her, bringing peace to her inner conflict. Whatever doubts she had before were swept away.

Jesus asked her: "Tell me, Sister, what do you believe?"

"I believe in you," she said, and she meant it, like she had never meant anything before. Now she could truly see the difference between having a theory about something and knowing the truth.

"Yet still you are troubled," said Jesus.

"Yes," she said haltingly. What right did she have to burden him with her worries? Yet she felt compelled to speak. "I am troubled because I do not know *why* I believe. My whole life has been a search for . . . truth. And now I feel—I *know*—that I have found it. But the truth I long sought for was one that could be proven, a truth of evidence, one that could be demonstrated to others, so they too could believe." She hesitated; how could she go on? Her theory seemed so unimportant now, so insignificant.

"And now you have found a different kind of truth?"

"Yes! That is it. I believe—but I don't know why."

Jesus smiled at her. "What you have discovered is the truth of faith. Answer me this: Have you ever known a thing, but could not prove it?"

"Why yes," she said. "My parents, the love they had for me. I never doubted it. But I could not prove it." And then she smiled, understanding.

"Now you see," said Jesus. "Who are they who would say that the truth of faith is any less than the truth of evidence? Any who believe this are mistaken, for they have one faith, in the reality of evidence, but deny another faith, that in and of itself. I tell you, faith is stronger than any logic, more powerful than any evidence."

"I see that now," she said. "If only everyone could see this truth!"

"Many have, and more will," said Jesus. "Each will find the path to the Truth in their own way."

"I must tell you something," she said. "The message you bring—I have it many times before. As have others. I did not hearken to it, and may never have, if I had not met you. Many others will also not accept this truth."

"And does that mean I should be silent, simply because some may not listen?"

"No. But I fear—I fear for you. You know that I am—not of this place."

"That is not of my concern," said Jesus. "The Truth I bring, it is for everyone."

"I understand. But from where I am from, and have been, terrible things have happened to those who have tried to speak this truth." How was she to say this? That the Jesus of Earth had been crucified? That for every one of the other messiahs she had learned about who had succeeded, three had been violently turned upon by their own people?

"So what would you have me do?" asked Jesus. "Would you have me struck dumb, or hide in the mountains? One does not light a lamp, only to hide it under a bushel. You certainly know this. The truth you sought, the one of evidence. Did you hide it away, or shout it aloud? Such is the power of belief."

"But what if the people are not ready to believe? I worry they will hurt you."

"Do not concern yourself with me," said Jesus. "Instead, look to yourself. We each have our part. Now that you have found your truth, do not think that your road is over. In many ways it is just beginning, and the path ahead will be filled with hardships. Belief is only the first step. From there, you must embrace the Truth, so it becomes part of you, and transforms you. You will be challenged with temptation, and thus you must have faith, faith that the Truth will guide you and support you. You must use this faith to hold onto, to keep you steady." He reached out for her hand. "I have seen the torment in you. You have crossed over the threshold of belief, and in that way your time is now. But my time, it has not yet come, though it is soon. Then I will proclaim anew, and even those who doubt will hear my voice."

"And will they believe?" asked Prentiss.

"Belief is not a fate or a destiny, but a choice. Belief cannot be forced on people, it must be embraced by them. I come not to remake people, but to enable to remake themselves."

Jesus stood up. "Arise. There is much to do and little time left. Where are your companions?"

"They are waiting for me, in the city."

"Go to them. They will be worried."

She had a million questions, not about science, but about him, about what it all meant. About what she needed to do now. About how to have faith.

"I want to stay here, with you."

Jesus guided her to the edge of the clearing. "So soon you forget the power of belief! Always remember: no matter where you are, no matter what difficulties lie before you, I will always be with you. You have only to listen to your heart's call, and for the sound of my voice."

He gently let go her hand, and she immediately felt as if she had lost something. But when she looked back he was there, watching her, and the sense of loss was replaced by a warmth, deeper than the fire which blazed behind him. Twice again she turned back, and he was still there. Finally she reached the ridge and was forced to watch the steep path, but when she turned back she could still see the light.

For many moments she stared down into the orchard, thinking about how her life had changed so quickly. After all this time, the years of research, the painful arguments, the battles to convince her peers, she finally had the evidence she needed to prove her theory. Yet her theory now seemed meaningless and empty. She had reached the top of her mountain, only to find that there was another whole world before her.

From farther along the ridge ahead came the sound of voices. The moonlight silhouetted a group of people climbing the hill from the city side. For some reason she felt suddenly afraid, and scrambled out of sight. The group passed her, a voice calling out, "This way! This is where the heretic hides!"

A chill ran through her. *They were talking about Jesus!*

She waited until they were past, then scrambled down the dark slope, trying not to make any noise. The sounds of conversation drifted away, the group was taking another route down to the orchard. Seeing her chance, she went back up the ridge and ran along the path she knew, down the hill and through the trees. But when she got to the clearing no one was there, and the fire was out.

Voices behind her made her whirl around, and suddenly the clearing was filled with dozens of people, all staring at her, blocking her escape.

A woman called out, her voice harsh in the emptiness: "Where is Jesus?"

Cautiously Prentiss replied, "He is not here."

"Lying pilgrim!" snarled the woman. "Tell us where he is!"

"I do not know," said Prentiss, her voice rising in anger. "What do you want with him? He has done nothing wrong."

"That is not for you to judge," said the woman. "Search this place!"

A few of the group split off and raced through the clearing. When they returned one of them said, "There is no one else here, and the fire is cold."

The woman who had spoken stepped forward. "We know you have been with him. You will tell us where Jesus is hiding."

"I would not, even if I knew," said Prentiss.

"Then you will come with us," said the woman. "The Pertise will know how to make you talk. Take her!"

Two of the men roughly grabbed her arms, and Prentiss fought the urge to cry out to warn Jesus, knowing it would only confirm he had been there. The only thing she could do to help him now was to get these people away, so she let herself be led out of the clearing, praying in her heart that Jesus had escaped.

Chapter 31

Wherever you find the Truth, pursue it with all your heart. It will give you strength greater than you had ever dreamed possible.
—The Teachings 15:11

I'Char crouched in the darkness. He suspected the Lemians wanted Garrick to lead them somewhere. But they might not be expecting someone to approach Garrick. It might give I'Char a slim chance.

Garrick could be desperate. No telling what he might do.

I'Char quickly made his way back toward the city wall. His earlier searches, combined with his memory for detail, served him well; he knew his way around the city. At the end of the street the wall loomed overhead. Without a sound he moved to the right, stopping when he came within sight of the city arch. Here, in the shadow of a doorway, he stood motionless, watching, keeping his eyes away from the torches.

Within moments he had marked the location of all the robed Lemian watchers. He counted three sets of two men. Plus the team he had passed on the entrance road.

Stealthily he retraced his steps back to the main street and crossed over, putting him on a road parallel to where Garrick lay. This late at night few people were about. He continued on until he was opposite where he estimated Garrick to be on the next street.

Three of the buildings he passed were lit inside. *No good.* The next one was dark. Satisfied, he sprinted across the road, and using his momentum vaulted onto the windowsill of the dark building, leaping up to catch the edge of the roof. He pulled himself up and froze. Still no sounds from below.

I'Char was confident the roof would hold. He had already been on the roof of Symes's hut, testing it for just such a need. If Symes's old hut could support him, so would this building. Quietly he made his way across the rooftops until he was on the other block and could see the wall across the street. Silently he made his way back toward the arch, then crept to the edge of the rooftop.

He had judged the distance well; Garrick lay slumped against the wall directly below him.

Slowly I'Char craned his neck to peer down the roadway. He could see no one. Garrick had only two ways to go, along the road either toward the arch or toward the orchard. I'Char was gambling that the Lemians would be guarding the entrance and exit to the road, but would stay at a distance away from Garrick so as not to spook him.

This would be I'Char's only chance.

He cupped his hands and whispered, "Don't move. I'm right above you. They are watching you." He spoke in K'Turian.

The figure stiffened. Then came a raspy voice: "Who are you?"

"No names. I was—with you as you came to the city."

"I understand." A bit stronger, but still in a whisper.

Good, thought I'Char. He still has his wits about him.

"I was taken by the Lemians," said Garrick. "Tortured."

"How badly are you hurt?" asked I'Char.

There was a slight delay, then a hacking cough. "Don't think I'll be making it back."

I'Char accepted the statement. He'd try to save Garrick if he could, but for now he had to assume the man was able to assess his own health. "They let you go so they could follow you."

" I wouldn't let them do that," came back the reply. "That's why I haven't moved."

"I believe you," said I'Char.

"Not sure I could get very far even if I wanted to." There was an effort at levity in the voice, then it turned serious. "Listen—it's a little hard to remember everything, but I don't think I told them much. But they do know I'm from the League—and they suspect others are here with me. You must be careful."

"How long can you hold out? I can go for the others, and we'll create a diversion to get you away." But I'Char knew the odds were against them. By the time he got to Win and Prentiss and returned, it might be too late.

"Thanks, but I don't think I . . . have much time," said Garrick. "There is something you must know." He lowered his voice until I'Char could barely hear him. "The freighter—it contained weapons en-route to Colltaire. For the insurgents. Anyone finding it would be able to figure it out." Garrick coughed again, a long hacking sound. His breathing was so labored I'Char could hear it from the roof.

Finally, Garrick continued, "There's more. The Rhean alliance . . . there are secret terms. They prohibit us from interfering, from being aggressive. Do you understand?"

It was painfully clear to I'Char. If the Rheans found out about the weapons and the League aid to the insurgents, it would destroy any chance for the alliance, the last ray of hope for the League. "Yes. Do the Lemians know about the freighter? And about the terms of the alliance?"

"We have to assume the worst," said Garrick, and now his voice was very weak. "You must find it—and destroy it."

"Are you sure it is here, on the planet?"

"No. But in this system, somewhere. Everything depends on us finding it first. Everything."

"I understand," said I'Char.

Now came the hardest decision. He could not help Garrick here. He felt confident he could take out one, or perhaps two, of the watcher teams, but he would never avoid notice of the others. If the Lemians captured him they would know for certain that others were on the planet, and it would not be long before Win and Prentiss were discovered.

I'Char could not let that happen.

He knew he had to go, but still he hesitated. It was not like him to leave someone behind. If he were in Garrick's position, he knew what he would do, but he was—different.

Or not so different. He heard Garrick say, "You have to leave, now. And I know what that means. Which way do you have to go?"

"Back into the city center."

"I'll head off . . . in the other direction . . . to give you a chance to get away. Then I'll lead the Lemians around in circles."

Wouldn't Prentiss be surprised, thought I'Char. Garrick was giving his life so the others might escape.

He didn't try to argue with Garrick; he had gained a greater respect for the man. All he said was, "If you make it to morning, get back to the entrance arch. There is a lot of coming and going then. That would be the best chance for a distraction." He didn't say it to give Garrick false hope, it was the truth.

But Garrick said, "No. Too risky. Get away, find the freighter. I won't let them take me alive. That should buy you some more time. Now go."

Garrick staggered to his feet, using the wall for support. He took a step, fell, and slowly got up again. Then another step, and another, and, with every move evident of great pain, he made his way down the road until he was lost from sight.

* * *

At the rendezvous behind the arena, Win waited in the gloom for the others. Even though he was straining to hear if anyone was approaching, I'Char was magically there at his side, materializing out of the dark.

"Prentiss?" asked I'Char.

"She never arrived," said Win.

"Not good," said I'Char. "Garrick was captured by the Lemians. We don't have much time." He told Win what had happened.

Win listened to the report without interruption. In characteristic I'Char style, it was concise and complete. Win only had one question.

"Do you believe Garrick? Will the Lemians be able to take him again, and find out more?"

"I believe him," said I'Char. "Though he was captured, he's more than he appeared to be."

"Now I understand why we were given this mission, why the League did not send a bigger ship, a military ship," mused Win. "It would have drawn too much attention. There must be other teams like ours, out looking on the other planets in the system. The situation is worse than we thought. But right now all I'm worried about is Prentiss." He told I'Char about the priests who had accosted him. "The priests are out looking for pilgrims. She might not know to avoid the priests—I fear she is in great danger."

"Once the Lemians realize Garrick isn't going to lead them anywhere, we will be too."

Win nodded. "There's something else. The priests—they are becoming more afraid of Jesus. I sense they are getting desperate." He paused. "I fear for him too."

"Careful," said I'Char. "We shouldn't get involved in that."

"I know," said Win. "At least, I know we shouldn't. But—this change that is happening to me. It has something to do with Jesus."

"You must make your own choices," said I'Char. "I don't have to remind you why we are here. But none of it will matter if we can't get off the planet alive."

"I realize that," said Win. "One thing may help us. There seems to be some disagreement amongst the priests about how much of a threat the pilgrims are. I think that is why they let me go. But if they find Prentiss she might not be so lucky. And the Lemians—could they have captured her already?"

"I don't think she was in the camp when I was there; the only building with extra guards was where they had Garrick. They would not have kept both prisoners in the same place for interrogation."

"We'd better go find her," said Win.

"She's probably looking for Jesus," said I'Char. "We can start at the house where he goes in the city." He pulled a small pouch out from under his robe and handed it to Win. "You can eat on the way.

The Lemians are much better at guarding prisoners than they are at keeping watch over their food supplies."

* * *

Prentiss stared at the ceiling from the uncomfortable bunk. She was being held in some kind of storeroom, deep under the temple. The priests had questioned her for what seemed like an eternity; there was no window, and she had lost track of time. At first she was afraid, for they had been fierce in their interrogation. But after a while she realized they were probably not going to harm her.

Seeing that their threats of banishment were having no affect, they brought another priest into the room and left her alone with him.

This priest had terrified her. He threatened her with death, and she believed him.

Chapter 32

Acceptance and faith may come easily for a few, but many will need to give up much of what they have believed.
    —The Teachings 16:4

Krelmar slammed his hand on the table. "He's *dead?!*" Neel sat impassively, as always, which got Krelmar even angrier. "How can he lead us to anyone if he's dead? He was fine when I left him!"

"Let me remind you, Lord Krelmar, it was not my idea to let the prisoner go."

Krelmar glared at him. "What are you saying? That this is *my* fault?"

"No, only that the plan had certain risks. The interrogation may have harmed the spy more than we realized. Or maybe he knew he was being followed and he didn't want to lead us to his accomplices. We found him dead."

"Where?"

"Near the temple. He may have fallen, or jumped. Or been pushed."

"The temple? Why would he have gone to the temple? Could the Pertise have had something to do with this?"

"Perhaps you should ask them."

Krelmar couldn't tell if Neel was being sarcastic. "Perhaps I will. They are on their way here right now."

* * *

Win made his way carefully through the maze of alleys. Every time he heard a footstep his pulse quickened.

The entire mission was spiraling out of control. He was being pulled along by events, making him even angrier. He never wanted to come to K'Turia in the first place.

It was time to take charge, not get forced into a corner. But the morass Win had been living in had dulled his decisiveness. I'Char was right, he was changing, but would he have the strength to make the vital decisions? Like who should stay behind in the city. Whether to leave Prentiss.

Who should live and who should die.

It made him starkly aware of how long it had been since he had been truly responsible for others.

Or for himself.

* * *

Once again the Pertise Methurgem and Amora sat across from Krelmar. This time they had not brought the young priest along.

As before, Methurgem dispensed with any pleasantries. "We have decided to accept your offer of helping us with a—problem."

"Excellent!" replied Krelmar. Perhaps he'd have some good news today after all. He still didn't know how he was going to explain the death of the spy to Tera-Seil, and he was desperate for anything that would deflect the Lemian's anger.

"As you know, we are a peaceful people," said Methurgem. "But our peace is being threatened by the heretics. They are a danger to all of us. So we have taken one of the troublemakers into custody."

"Jesus? You've taken *Jesus*?"

"No," said Methurgem. "One of his followers. A pilgrim woman. We believe she may be an offworlder, come to incite the people against us."

Krelmar was stunned. Had the priests succeeded in capturing another League spy? Could luck finally be turning his way?

Cautiously, he asked, "What have you learned from this pilgrim?"

"Very little," said Amora. "But she has been seen with Jesus, and probably knows where he is hiding. There have been disturbances every time he speaks. Unrest is spreading through the city. This situation is becoming dangerous."

Krelmar was thinking about the mob at the Lemian camp. "I see." What exactly did the Pertise want?

"As we have said," said Methurgem, "there is little more we can do about these pilgrims. They do not fear banishment. We have but one other punishment, that of death. It has not been carried out in generations. We fear such punishment would arouse the supporters of Jesus even more. We would have a mob to control."

"Still, this seems to be a religious matter," said Krelmar, trying not to sound too interested. He did not want Methurgem to know how sorely he wanted to question the pilgrim woman.

Methurgem stared at him. "We will be the judge of that. Do you want to establish relations with a peaceful city, or one in the midst of upheaval? You said you wanted to prove your worth to us, to show us how helpful you can be. This is your chance."

"And I appreciate your offer," said Krelmar smoothly. "But won't the people be just as angry if we get involved?"

"We will say that the woman is an offworlder, sent here to disrupt the peace, and thus she should be dealt with by other offworlders—by you. The people will accept this."

"What would you have me do?" asked Krelmar.

"Make an example of her. Take her offworld, or put her to death, as you see fit," said Methurgem.

The words hung in the air. Krelmar was shocked at what the priests were asking him to do. *They must truly be afraid.*

"I cannot believe this one pilgrim is such a threat to you—to the peace," said Krelmar.

"Perhaps not her alone, but what she represents, and who she is hiding. If she is punished severely, the other pilgrims will flee. And it shall serve as a reminder to everyone what the consequences will be if they stray from our Way."

Krelmar doubted the woman had anything to do with the

preacher Jesus. She was more likely a League spy, and was only disguised as a pilgrim, as the dead man had been.

"Your problem is not the pilgrim, it is Jesus," said Krelmar. "He's the one you need to arrest."

"We cannot justify that, at least not yet. He has not broken a Law worthy of a serious punishment. Without such a crime, his arrest by the Temple would confuse and anger the people," said Amora.

"Then how did you arrest the woman?"

Amora looked away briefly. "We haven't. We have merely—detained her. She is a stranger here. No one is likely to complain. But Jesus would be another matter. *We* cannot arrest him."

"So now you want *us* to take Jesus," said Krelmar.

"As you yourself have said," said Methurgem, "*Jesus* is the threat—to all of us."

Chapter 33

Paradise is open to anyone who sees the Truth and follows the right path.
—The Teachings 17:6

Back at the Lemian camp, Krelmar paused just outside the door to the interrogation room to get his thoughts in order.

The meeting with the priests had given him hope that he could squirm out of his predicament. The Pertise had finally admitted they wanted the Lemians to take care of their problem with Jesus. Krelmar would help them, but only if it would get him what he wanted—control of the planet. But how long would it take to capture Jesus? Krelmar needed a backup plan.

Krelmar had tried to get Methurgem to accept Lemian protection. But the crafty priest had made no promises. So Krelmar had also held back, insisting on first questioning the pilgrim woman before deciding her fate. The priests were not pleased, but had finally agreed.

Jesus was the key to getting the priests under his power.

Finding Jesus was the real reason Krelmar wanted to question the pilgrim. If the priests could not find Jesus, he doubted the Lemian soldiers would be able to do so. But he was just as certain the Lemian interrogation techniques were more effective than those of the priests.

If the captured pilgrim woman did not know where Jesus was, Krelmar would set another plan in motion.

He entered the room. Tsaph cowered in a chair under the watchful eye of Commander Neel.

Krelmar loomed over the trembling K'Turian. "Tsaph, Tera-Seil will be very unhappy you have not reported to him," he said.

"But you've been keeping me here! I could not!"

"How unfortunate. And of course if and when you communicate with him, you should not tell him you admitted to us you were spying for him. I can tell you, he would not be pleased to hear that, not at all. He is—," Krelmar looked over at Neel, "—rather prone to anger, wouldn't you say, Commander?"

"Yes, Lord Krelmar, I think Tera-Seil would punish *any* failure."

"You see?" said Krelmar, smoothly. "Now . . . ," he paused, letting the implications sink in, ". . . perhaps I can help you out of your dilemma."

"Why would you do that?" asked Tsaph, suspiciously.

"Let's just say it is in everyone's best interest to keep Tera-Seil happy. Here is what you must do. You must go to your friend Jesus, and bring him a message for me."

"A message? What message?"

"Simply this: one of the pilgrims has been detained. It appears she has been inciting the people against the priests. This woman, she is also a friend of Jesus. She is in great danger. The Pertise are going to put her to death. They have already killed another pilgrim."

"I don't understand. What does this have to do with Jesus?"

"He can save her. If he comes forward and convinces me she is no threat, then she will be freed."

"That's all? You just want Jesus to say she is not a threat?"

"And that he will be responsible for making sure she doesn't disturb the peace," said Krelmar. "That's all."

"I don't know," said Tsaph, sounding unconvinced. "The priests don't like Jesus. Why would he take such a chance?"

"I understand," said Krelmar. "That is why Jesus should come to me, instead of the priests. I am not concerned with him, only the pilgrim. We are trying to establish a friendly relationship with your people, but we cannot do this in an environment of discontent. I'm sure Jesus doesn't want the pilgrims causing problems for all of you."

"So you will keep Jesus from the priests?" asked Tsaph.

"Oh yes," said Krelmar. "You can be certain of that."

* * *

Win was as close to panic as he had ever been in his life. He and I'Char had scoured the city for Prentiss, but she was nowhere to be found. During the night they had split up to search, Win going back to the old man's hut, I'Char back into the Lemian camp. There was no sign of her.

Now, midmorning, they huddled behind the wall at the back of the arena.

"Something is going on," said I'Char. "There are Lemians in the city, a lot of them. And more priests in the streets than we have seen."

"Looking for us?"

"Probably. And if the priests are helping the Lemians, it will be difficult for us to move about the city. Prentiss may have already been captured."

Win thought about what Prentiss had said, about trying to explain to the Lemians her scientific mission. Even if they believed her, which he doubted, they'd want to know who she was with, and how she got there.

"The shuttle," said Win.

"Yes. If they find it first we'll be trapped here. But getting to it will be risky. The Lemians will be watching the roads."

Win looked out over the city, hoping it would give him some guidance. But there were no answers there. "We can't just leave Prentiss."

"No need for both of us to go. I can stay here and try to find her."

"But if they are on the lookout for pilgrims—"

"Better me than you," said I'Char.

* * *

Tsaph didn't know what to do. He doubted he could send a

message to Tera-Seil. Neel had forced him to divulge where the communication device was hidden, and certainly he would not be allowed near it now.

Though Krelmar had let him go, Tsaph felt trapped. Everyone was mad at him, or would be, if they knew what he had done. Tera-Seil. Krelmar. The priests.

If the priests were willing to put the pilgrim woman to death, what would they do to Tsaph? And to Jesus?

Could he trust Krelmar to protect Jesus? He was so confused.

Jesus. Jesus would know what to do, if Tsaph could only find him.

He could think of only one place to look: Tthean's house.

He raced through the streets, taking a circular route toward Tthean's house and avoiding any place he thought there would be priests. Twice he passed through the market, trying to lose himself in the crowd in case he was being followed.

An arm reached out and grabbed him. Tsaph spun around in fear, expecting it to be one of the priests or a Lemian. But instead he recognized one of the men he had sent out searching for the offworld object.

Tsaph breathed a sigh of relief. "I am in a hurry. What do you want?"

"We found something!" whispered the man. "Something from offworld!"

Tsaph was anxious to go, but the man's excitement was contagious. "What is it?"

"I don't know. I've never seen anything like it. It is as big as a small house, but there is no way to get in."

"You mean like one of the Lemian buildings?"

"No, it's not a building. It—it's a—I don't know. And I don't know how it got to where it is. There are no tracks. Like it just dropped out of the sky."

"Maybe it's one of the Lemian flying crafts," said Tsaph. "Like the ones they have at the camp."

"No, I have seen those. This is much bigger."

"Was anyone around it? Where is it?"

"No one. I have drawn you a map." He handed it to Tsaph.

That was odd, thought Tsaph. *If it were a Lemian ship, then where were the Lemians?* "Tell no one about this," he warned. "No one!"

He left the man bewildered, knowing that this discovery could not be kept secret for long. Could it be the mysterious object that Krelmar had him searching for?

Slowing his steps so as not to attract attention, Tsaph made his way to Tthean's house. On the threshold he knocked, glancing over his shoulder and praying that Tthean was at home.

When Tthean cracked open the door, Tsaph almost fell over with relief.

"I have an urgent message for Jesus," said Tsaph. "Please. It is very important."

"Jesus is here," said Tthean, opening the door and leading Tsaph into a room where Jesus sat with the other disciples.

"Jesus, I am sorry to disturb you. My name is Tsaph. I am a trader."

"Come," said Jesus. "Join us."

Tsaph was nervous. Though he had listened to Jesus many times, he had never addressed him directly. And now he was surrounded, everyone staring at him.

"Do not be afraid," said Jesus. "You are among friends."

"Jesus, I have done a terrible thing!" Tsaph blurted out. It was not what he had meant to say, for some reason it seemed terribly important to confess.

"Tell me what it is you have done that you think is so terrible," said Jesus.

"I—I have been helping one of the offworlders, a Lemian named Tera-Seil," said Tsaph. "He is—far away. He ordered me to spy on another one of the offworlders here on K'Turia, the one called Krelmar."

"Why have you done this?" asked Jesus.

"Because I was afraid of Tera-Seil!" said Tsaph. "And—the Lemians have given me things from offworld. I wish they had never come here. I'm so sorry! I have been selfish, thinking only of myself. Krelmar found out I was spying on him, and he is going to turn me over to the priests!" Tsaph rung his hands. "And Krelmar knows that—that I have listened to you, and that I—I believe in you!" Saying it aloud, he felt relieved.

Jesus smiled. "And you are afraid of what the priests will do to you?"

"Yes, I—was. But now here with you, I am afraid no longer." Tsaph had expected Jesus to judge him, to criticize his helping of the offworlders. But Jesus' words had been soft and welcoming. Tsaph stood up taller. "Let them do with me as they wish."

"Stay here with us. You will be safe with me." Jesus turned to his disciples. "This man has spent little time with me. Yet look at the strength his faith has given him.

"Let this be a lesson: it does not matter what you have done, or whether you have been misguided or led astray, or even whether you acted selfishly of your own accord. As long as you repent of these acts, and change, you will be saved. Paradise is open to anyone who sees the Truth and follows the right path."

"But Jesus," said one of the disciples, "is this fair? Are you saying that one who has been bad his whole life, but who repents, is equal to someone who has always been good?"

"This is not a question of fairness, this is not a contest to be won!" replied Jesus. "There is room enough for *everyone* in Paradise, as long as they accept responsibility for their actions, and show their love for each other, not just with words, but with deeds. It is not enough to repent, one must act as well."

"Jesus!" said Tsaph. "There is more! I have a message for you, from Krelmar. He said the Pertise have detained a pilgrim woman. I don't know her name, but she is someone you know. The Pertise are going to put her to death! Krelmar said you can save her."

Jesus whispered, "It has begun."

Jesus slowly stood, and one by one he looked at each of the disciples. "As I have told you, our time grows short." He turned to Tsaph. "I will help this woman. What does Krelmar want?"

"He wants your assurance that the woman will not be a threat, that she will not disturb the peace. Who is she? What has she done?"

"She has done nothing wrong, and neither have you," said Jesus. "Listen to me! No matter what happens, you must believe that you have done nothing wrong."

"Jesus," said Tthean, "I don't understand. Why must you help this woman? It will be very dangerous. We don't even know who she is."

Jesus looked at Tthean and said gently, "It does not matter who she is, or where she is from. She has risked much for her beliefs, in her own way. I tell you, we must embrace both friend and foe, neighbor and stranger. I could no more abandon her than I could abandon any of you."

"But how can you teach us, and bring others your message, if the priests banish you, or—" Tthean's voice trailed off.

Jesus smiled at him. "Do not fear to say it. Put me to death? Do you think the message I bring will end if I die? Remember what I have told you. I am the light of the true Way, the light to awaken those who are asleep. Once they have taken the light into their own hearts, as you have done, it is there forever. I need not be seen in the flesh to be known, I need not be felt with your hands to be real, I need not be before you to be with you. *You* can show the light I bring to others, and they will show it unto others, until the entire world is ablaze!"

"But what of the Pertise?"

"Wait!" said Tsaph. "Krelmar said he will protect you from the Pertise, that you need not go to the temple, but to him."

"How can we trust this Krelmar?" asked Tthean. "The people are angry. The Lemians may think we have turned the people against them. Why would Krelmar help us?"

"You're right," said Tsaph, sheepishly. "I don't know if I believe Krelmar, either. I explained to him that it was the priests who had turned the people against the Lemians, not Jesus. But I don't know what Krelmar really thinks. The Lemians are very suspicious, and have been seeking out strangers and pilgrims ever since they captured someone spying in their camp. An offworlder, I believe. They tortured him."

"Jesus," said Tthean, "if the pilgrim woman is an offworlder, the Lemians will think she is a spy too."

"And so she will need our help," said Jesus.

"Jesus, I am afraid," said Tsaph. "Not for myself, but for you. Something bad will happen if you help this woman."

"What happens to me will happen because of who I am and the message I bring, not because I help the woman," said Jesus. He turned to the disciples. "But her fate is not cast in stone. She has given up much. How would it be if we turn our backs on the very people who have harkened to our word? What message will that send?

"There are many kinds of dangers, some spiritual, some physical. I have spoken to you of the spiritual dangers of this life, but this does not mean I do not think of the worldly dangers that must be faced. No one should have to be put under the yoke of another, or fear them. Just as you would come to the aid of your neighbor if someone were trying to take them into servitude, so too we must help those who would be held against their will because of their devotion to me.

"The priests and the Lemians use the lives of people as bargaining tools. You must go and find the other pilgrims before they do, and bring them to me. Hurry, for there is not much time."

Chapter 34

All choices have consequences.
　　　　　　—The Teachings 18:19

The priest led Krelmar through a maze of catacombs, deep beneath the temple. Either the religious law about not allowing him into the temple didn't apply underground, or the Pertise were now so afraid they were willing to bend the rules. Krelmar had been silently ushered into a nondescript side entrance to the temple, the door quickly closing shut behind him.

Neel had wanted to be present for the interrogation of the pilgrim woman, but Krelmar insisted on going alone. He told Neel the woman would be afraid of Lemians.

The real reason he was going in secret was that he could not afford having a witness as he initiated his backup plan, the way out he would desperately need if he could not deliver K'Turia to Tera-Seil.

The priest stopped in front of a plain door, watched over by two temple guards armed with short swords. The priest unlocked the door and handed Krelmar a lamp. "You will need this. We'll be right here if the woman causes any trouble."

The door closed behind Krelmar with a dull thud. *Good*, he thought. *We won't be overheard.*

The room was larger than he had expected, lined with stone. On a bunk against the far wall sat a woman, blinking in the harsh light from his lantern.

Cautiously, Krelmar examined the room. The walls appeared solid. It did not look like it had been made as a jail, more likely a storeroom. Nothing hinted of a place where someone could listen in. He'd have to chance it, anyway.

He put the lamp down and went to stand in front of the woman. Though her hair was set in the local way, and her skin had the telltale K'Turian hue, she had features he recognized as human.

"I am Krelmar," he said, "from the planet Colltaire."

Krelmar watched her carefully, seeing the recognition in her eye. "I know you are from offworld," he continued. "Don't try to deny it. I have already spoken to one of your companions, from the League." He was surprised when she did not reply. *Not even trying to pretend she was a pilgrim?* His guess had been correct. She was associated with the spy, the one who was now dead. "Perhaps he spoke to you of our conversation?"

"I don't know what you are talking about," said the woman.

"Now what do you mean by that?" asked Krelmar, in his friendliest tone. "That you didn't speak to him, or that you don't know him?"

When the woman didn't respond he continued, "You are going to have to talk if you want me to help you. The priests are growing impatient."

"Why would I need help? I have done nothing wrong."

"Ahh, but you are mistaken. Why do you think you are being held as a prisoner? You need help more than you can imagine. And I can give it to you."

The woman scoffed. "Why would you want to help me? You must be with the Lemians."

"I have my reasons," said Krelmar. "But the Pertise are another matter. They think you are a troublemaker, here to cause an uprising. I actually know this is not your intent. You are really on K'Turia to spy for the League."

"I am no *spy*," said the woman, her voice full of disdain. "And I'm not here to cause any trouble."

"You will have a hard time convincing the Pertise," said Krelmar.

"They've seen you with Jesus, and they think he is a threat to the peace. I can see their point. Jesus is turning the people against the priests. There are mobs in the streets!"

"Jesus didn't cause that," said the woman with some emotion. "Maybe the priests don't like the Lemians, but Jesus is not to blame."

Interesting, thought Krelmar. *She's defending Jesus.*

"How do you know that?" he asked.

The woman, perhaps sensing his trap, did not respond.

"Do you not see the difficult position you are in?" asked Krelmar. "The priests are convinced Jesus is the reason for the upheaval that is going on. And they believe you are with Jesus. If you want to protect Jesus from the priests, you will have to convince them he is not a threat. Given the current situation, you are going to have a very hard time doing that. And no matter what they think, the priests will know you are a—believer. They don't like believers, as I'm sure you know. Now that the people are riled up, the priests are going to deal harshly with any of you who follow Jesus."

"I fear nothing from them," said the woman, but her voice trembled.

"You would fear banishment—at least, you would, if you were a K'Turian," he said. "But we both know you are not. And you certainly should fear death, a punishment the priests are quite willing to carry out." He changed his tone, once again friendly. "But come, come, we need not speak of anything so dire! As I said, I can help you. There is no reason we can't have a civilized conversation here—and to make it easy for you, I will tell you what I think, and you don't have to say a word if you don't want to."

After a moment the woman said: "I'm listening."

"Good. To demonstrate my good faith let me tell you what I know. I know you and your companions were sent here by the League to spy on the Lemians. I don't know why you are spying, not yet, but I will discover that eventually. Perhaps it is just to learn of the Lemain plans for K'Turia. No matter. But the fact is, you are in great danger. The Lemian Command knows you are on K'Turia, and they don't take kindly to spies. They are sending someone here who will force me to use very—*persuasive* measures to uncover the truth. Do you understand?"

"I am *not* a spy," the woman repeated.

"Well, perhaps not, but what of your companions? Ahh, I see the indecision in your eye." She hadn't corrected him when he referred to her companions, so there *were* others. *You may think you can keep things from me by being silent, but I have outwitted people far more clever than you.* "Now that I have told you what I know, why not tell me some things?"

"You said I didn't have to say a word," she snapped. "Why would I tell you anything?"

"Though I am not a Lemian, I am in a position of great authority here," Krelmar replied. "And so I am in a unique position to be of help to you. That is, if you help me."

"I can do nothing to help you," she said. "I don't know anything."

"The priests and the Lemians will not believe that. But for me, I'm less concerned with what you know than with who you are. That is why I am not going to ask you why you are here. Instead, I will help you, help all of you, in exchange for passing along a simple message for me."

"What message?"

Still not admitting anything, but not denying anything either. Totally unlike the other one, at least until they tortured him. Very odd. "You are obviously not a trained spy," said Krelmar. "Your responses are all wrong. So if you are not spying for the League, just who are you?"

Somewhat defiantly, the woman responded, "I am a scientist."

A scientist? Krelmar was momentarily at a loss. She certainly did not act like a spy. *Could she be telling the truth?* "That's an interesting admission. There are no scientists here. So you admit you are from offworld?"

The woman ran a hand through her hair and shook her head, suddenly looking very weary. "I'm just tired of all these—politics, and fighting. I'm a scientist, not a soldier—or a spy."

"Then what are you doing here?"

"I'm here to study Jesus."

"That's ridiculous," said Krelmar. "How did you even know he was on K'Turia?"

"Tell me, if our positions were reversed, and you were found on a League planet, would you tell them why you were there?"

"If I had nothing to hide, perhaps I would. Especially if I was on a scientific mission. How did you get here?"

"I gained passage aboard a merchant ship," said the woman. "Now, I have told you something. It is your turn. What is this message, and how can you help me?"

Krelmar leaned close to her and whispered, "I seek political asylum with the League."

She pulled away from him, studying his face. "You're kidding," she finally said.

"Believe me, I'm deadly serious."

"Is this some kind of trick, to get me to admit something?"

"It's no trick. That is why I let your companion go, as a sign of good faith. And if I am willing to believe your story about being a scientist, shouldn't you be willing to accept what I say? I want asylum. Surely you see the conditions here? I am not a Lemian, I am being used by them. If you are truly a scientist—and not a military spy—you should be more than willing to at least pass along my request."

The woman indicated the locked door. "I'm in no position to communicate anything on your behalf—to anyone."

"I can fix that," he said.

"Really? The priests will follow your orders?"

"The Pertise are willing to bargain. These priests are far more pragmatic than they would have you believe."

The woman closed her eyes. Finally she sighed, and said, "I don't believe you. I am a specialist in primitive religious cultures. This is a very religious society. They do not accept the rule of outsiders. The religious leaders would not do anything for you."

"Unless their religious way of life is threatened," Krelmar argued. "The Pertise are more afraid than they let on. They have been watching you, did you know that? How do you think they captured you? The Pertise think you are here as part of a movement to turn the people against the Laws—against *them*. They know you do not fear banishment. And so they have asked for my help to deal with you."

"If all that is true, they will not let me go," she said.

"Perhaps not, but they will turn you over to me, and then I can do as I please. They know you are an offworlder—and they would prefer that you be dealt with by an offworlder. It would relieve them of any responsibility for you. They would be happy if I were to remove you from K'Turia."

The woman shook her head. "They cannot be that afraid of me."

"The Pertise want to make an example of you. And you must know there is someone they do fear—Jesus. They want him dealt with as well."

"What are you saying? That you would take Jesus offworld?"

"Would you like that?" Krelmar asked. "It could be arranged. It would protect him from the priests."

The woman flared. "You must not take him away! He belongs here! There is something happening on this planet, something far more important than your petty wars and stupid politics. The very future of the K'Turians is at stake. They just need to be left alone—by everyone! Jesus must be allowed to finish his work."

"Perhaps, but here he is in great danger. If the priests feel threatened enough, they will put Jesus to death, whether he breaks a law or not. They'll find an excuse. The Lemians are also beginning to see Jesus as a threat to their plans, and they will have no reluctance to— eliminate such a problem. They will do this whether *I* am here or not."

The woman jumped up, her weariness gone. "If you are in such a position of power, you cannot let Jesus be harmed!"

"Your concern for Jesus is touching," said Krelmar, smoothly. "And do I detect a bit of anger at the League? You must see, however, that there are forces at work here which will soon prevent either one of us from getting what we want. The priests are looking for Jesus right now. Who knows what they will do once they find him? There are mobs in the streets, there is violence. The Lemians have little patience for such behavior. Soon the matter will be out of my hands, and even I will not be able to save you—or Jesus."

"Why do you want asylum with the League?"

"That is my concern. Let's just say that I don't think the Lemians trust me as they once did. But you need not take my word for it. If you tell your superiors that I, Krelmar, have important information for them about Colltaire, I assure you they will want to hear what I have to say. But we must act quickly—*very* quickly—if you want to save yourself. And Jesus."

The woman paced the room, then came to stand before him, defiant. "I will do as you ask, but on two conditions. First, you must convince the priests to leave Jesus alone. Second, you must let me meet with Jesus and put the choice before him on whether he wants to leave K'Turia."

"I will do my best with the priests," said Krelmar, "but once I let you go I will have little leverage with them. They will no longer trust me." *As if they already did . . .* He pretended to consider her offer. "I will have to tell them you are going to turn Jesus over to me, in exchange for the lives of your companions."

"Tell them whatever you want," said the woman. "As long as you keep them from harming him."

"That will be more up to them than to me," Krelmar said. "You are the one who must convince Jesus to leave with us. That is the only way to assure his safety."

Krelmar turned to leave, hiding his smile. She had no idea that she had just been manipulated. Even if she were a spy, she would pass along his plea for asylum—the League would not miss a chance to learn more about Colltaire. So he would have his escape plan. But if she delivered Jesus to him, he might not even need it.

Krelmar turned back to her. "You must remain here while I make arrangements for your release. Remember, once you are away, you must hurry to convey my request for asylum, and immediately return to me with the answer."

The woman appeared ready to interrupt, but Krelmar cut her off.

"No more arguments. I will require safe conduct off the planet. If I have not heard from you by morning, our agreement is off."

Krelmar once again leaned in close to the woman, forcing her to look up at him. "The Lemians want control over this planet. They can take it by force, if they so desire. But they would prefer to have the support of the people, which means the Pertise. If I cannot get asylum with the League, I will have to protect myself from the Lemians. I will make a trade with the Pertise—their support of the Lemian presence in exchange for my helping them with their problem. And their problem is Jesus. His fate is in *your* hands."

Chapter 35

I pray not only for those who listen to me now, but for all those who may come to believe in me.
—The Teachings 19:6

Outside the cell door, the same priest who had led Krelmar through the catacombs was waiting.

"Take me to Methurgem," Krelmar ordered.

"I cannot. He is in Temple," said the priest.

Krelmar sighed. "Very well. Just get me out of here. Then tell Methurgem I wish to see him, immediately."

As he followed the priest through the dark passageways, Krelmar thought about how much he had learned from the League woman who claimed to be a scientist. He was now certain there were others from the League on the loose in Merculon. And she didn't know that the other spy was dead.

The spy's death was still something of a mystery. Neel was hiding something.

What would he tell Tera-Seil?

Tera-Seil. Krelmar had to have K'Turia under control before Tera-Seil arrived. Or be safely off the planet.

The Pertise would not be happy about Krelmar's decision to let the woman go. But once they saw the beauty of his plan to capture Jesus, they would be more agreeable.

He'd have the woman followed, and this time would make sure it was done properly. He couldn't count on the Lemian soldiers to do the job; after all, they had failed with the other spy. But the priests could do it. They had apparently been following the woman for quite some time.

Having the priests track her would be a compromise they could live with—they could always capture her again. And she would lead them to Jesus. So if the woman betrayed Krelmar, he'd have Jesus either way.

Jesus was the key. Capture Jesus, and he would both remove the source of discontent and have the priests beholden to him.

It would have to be done quietly, away from the crowds.

* * *

Prentiss lay on the bunk in the dark cell, thinking about Krelmar. He had appeared sincere, but he seemed—too polished, too smooth.

Yet if he could get her released, what would be the harm in passing along his message of requesting asylum?

Krelmar had confirmed her worse fears—the Pertise were after Jesus. If she accepted Krelmar's deal, once she was released she could try to help Jesus.

But could she trust Krelmar to protect Jesus from the Pertise?

She had no doubt the Pertise would kill Jesus. It was happening, all over again, just as it happened on Earth, so long ago.

Would she be the one to betray Jesus, in order to save him? The very thought turned her cold.

She couldn't let him die—again.

* * *

Win had decided to risk one more search for Prentiss before attempting to escape the city.

"Three possibilities," said I'Char. "Captured by the Lemians, captured by the priests, or with Jesus."

"We can't do anything right now about the first two," said Win. "Let's try the orchard again."

Win had barely taken a step when he felt a gentle tug from his *gheris*, calling to him in a whisper. The same sensation he had felt upon landing, but more subdued. He pushed it away, just as he had muted it before. He didn't have time for distractions.

Win followed I'Char along the arena wall, heading away from the central part of the city. Once again he felt his *gheris* rise up, not reaching out, but something reaching *in*. With each step the pull grew stronger. His feet dragged, and he couldn't keep up with I'Char.

"I'Char!" he gasped, and fell backward, his body spinning toward the city.

Win felt I'Char beside him, helping him up. "What is it?" asked the Illian.

"I—I don't know. Something . . ." But the pressure was gone, only a hint of it in his gut. "I'm okay now. Let's go." Yet no sooner had he turned his *gheris* rocked him again, pulling him back.

"We need to go into the city," said Win.

"Trouble?"

"Maybe. I can't explain it." Win looked up at the temple. "Something that way, I think."

They crossed into the open space behind the arena. As they made their way up the amphitheater steps, Win's *gheris* shifted; now he felt a tension, as oppressive as the heat. He forced himself to reach out with his senses, trying to push through the nervous energy.

At the top of the amphitheater they elbowed their way through a throng of people going to and from the temple. The tenseness was so great Win doubted he needed *gheris* to feel it. The other sensation, the whispered calling, was still there, but calmer now, as if in waiting.

"Anything?" asked I'Char.

Win shrugged. "Lots of nervous energy here. Let's try the market."

"Be ready to move fast if the Lemians spot us," I'Char warned.

They had scarcely entered the market when I'Char said, "We are being followed."

Without looking back, Win asked, "Lemians or priests?"

"Neither. One local. Could be a priest in disguise though."

"Just one?"

I'Char paused as if to examine some food, and as he turned back to Win he scanned the crowd. "Just one. Let's see what he does. Wait, he's coming this way."

The K'Turian stopped at the same table. "I am Tthean," he whispered. "I am a friend of Jesus. He has sent me to find you."

Win turned to I'Char as he was deciding how to respond, but the Illian had disappeared. He looked back at the K'Turian but did not reply. Had Jesus reached out to Win through his *gheris*?

The man said, "I mean you no harm. I have a message from Jesus."

Still unsure if it might be a trap, Win asked, "Are you alone?"

"Yes, I—"

Suddenly I'Char was there at his side, materializing out of the crowd. "No one else with him that I can see."

"Sorry," said Win. "We have to be careful."

"I understand," said Tthean. "That is why I am here, to warn you. The offworlders—the Lemians—are looking for you." He stopped when the merchant approached them, but when the seller saw who it was he left them alone.

"Though we have friends everywhere," said Tthean, indicating the merchant, "we should not talk here. Jesus would like to see you."

"Where is he?" asked Win.

"I can take you there."

Win considered. It could still be a trap, but it seemed too elegant for the Lemians. The priests, perhaps?

"Forgive us if we hesitate," said Win. "I'Char?"

The Illian studied the crowd again, then said to Tthean, "Is Jesus at the house over that way," he indicated with a nod, "two streets down, about halfway up the block, with the white door?"

"Yes," said the K'Turian, surprised. "How did you know?"

"The secret is safe with us," said I'Char. To Win he said, "Let me go first, just to be sure. I'll meet you out front." Once again he disappeared.

"Where did he go?" asked Tthean.

"I never can tell," said Win. "Come. Let's walk through the market to give him some time. I apologize for all the suspicion."

"It is understandable. Our times have become most difficult."

They made their way through the market, now and again people giving them knowing looks, or pressing food into their hands. *Jesus has a lot of support,* thought Win. *I wonder if the priests truly realize how much.*

When he felt that I'Char had had enough time, he said, "We can go now."

He followed Tthean out of the market. Within a block, I'Char stepped out of a doorway to join them.

"It's clear," he said.

At the house, Tthean rapped on the door twice, paused, then knocked again. It was opened immediately and Tthean led the way in.

At the orchard it had been dark, but now, in these much more intimate surroundings, Win got his first up-close look at Jesus. Though Jesus had the look of a K'Turian, there was something familiar about him, as if Win had seen him, or someone like him, before. His features were timeless; his age impossible to guess.

Jesus welcomed them. "Once again you have found me," he said to Win. Jesus turned to I'Char. "You, I have not met. But I do know you . . . and why you are with him."

I'Char nodded, and Win sensed a connection between the Illian and Jesus, hinting at a link, or a common purpose.

I'Char pointed at Tsaph. "I have seen this man coming and going from the building of the Lemian leader in the city."

"As you have," said Jesus. "But Tsaph is with us now. Will you accept this?"

"For now," said I'Char.

Jesus smiled. "Having both doubt and suspicion is a heavy burden."

"But sometimes a necessary one," said I'Char.

"Excuse our suspicions," said Win. "But one of our friends is missing, perhaps taken by the Lemians."

"You are right to be cautious," said Jesus. "But it is the priests who have your friend, not the offworlders. This man, Tsaph, has told us this."

"The priests have her? Is she safe?"

Jesus nodded to Tsaph. "Tell them."

"I have not seen her with my own eyes," said Tsaph. "I only know what Krelmar told me to tell Jesus: that a pilgrim woman had been detained by the priests—"

Win cut him off. "Do you know where she is?"

"No, but the Pertise are going to put her to death! They have already killed another one of the pilgrims."

"Why would they do that? And who is Krelmar?" asked Win. *The other pilgrim had to be Garrick.*

"Krelmar is the leader of the Lemians, the man I was—assisting. But he is not a Lemian, he is from a place called Colltaire."

Win exchanged looks with I'Char. "Colltaire? Are you sure?"

"Yes," said Tsaph. "At least that is what he claims. As for your friend, they think she has helped inflame the people against the Temple."

What was someone from Colltaire doing here? Win wondered. "We need to help our friend. Why did Krelmar want Jesus to know the priests have her?"

"So that Jesus would appear before them, to promise she will no longer cause problems. If he does that, Krelmar says he will protect Jesus from the priests."

"Her name is Prentiss," Win offered. "I am called Win. This is I'Char. We are from—"

"Where you are from does not concern us," said Jesus.

"But Jesus," said Tthean, "They are offworlders!"

Jesus looked at him. "And so they are. Why should that matter? Because they are different? How much have you listened to me, and how little you have heard. I am here for everyone, my message is for everyone. If you say that my message is only for certain people, you prolong the corruption of the Law the Pertise have created. If you say only K'Turians are capable of hearing my message, then you are as selfish as many of the priests. There is no virtue in being righteous. The welfare of these offworlders is as important to me as your welfare. Who can say that only people who look a certain way can be our brothers and sisters? We are all the same, no matter what we look like, or where we are from."

Jesus turned to Win. "I know you are not here to cause harm."

"No," said Win. "We—came to look for something, something from offworld. A vessel. I fear that what we seek could bring danger to your people, for it is of great import to the Lemians. They will stop at nothing to possess it—and if they do, many others will suffer. If we find it first we can take it away, or destroy it."

"I know of this thing!" blurted Tsaph. "Please—take it away! We have already had enough trouble from offworlders!" He stopped, then mumbled, "I'm sorry."

Win smiled at him. "Don't be. You are right, offworlders often do more harm than good. It is why we have come here disguised. But please tell me, what is this offworld object you speak of?"

Tsaph looked at Jesus, who said, "Leave the offworld things to the offworlders."

Tsaph said, "Krelmar wanted me to search for an offworld object. I have been told something has been found, something large."

"Can you tell us where it is?" asked I'Char.

"I have a map," said Tsaph. He dug it out of a pocket and handed it to I'Char.

"Thank you," said Win. "We will do what we can to remove this danger to you. But first we must help Prentiss." Win looked at Jesus. "I don't know what it will take to free her, but I must try. She is no threat to anyone."

"Threats are in the eye of the beholder," said Jesus. "Many are threatened by what they do not know."

"I understand," said Win. "That is why the priests fear you as well. And so will the Lemians, but for different reasons."

"They will not fear me," said Jesus, "but what I represent. For I represent the power of choice, and the power the priests believe they possess is the denial of choice. Your friend Prentiss, she is facing her own choice. It is not one she should have to make, for it is being forced upon her. If she is to give up everything she has lived for, she should make such a decision free from duress."

"What do you mean?" asked Win. But he knew. He had sensed Prentiss slipping away, away from the League, away from science. "She will be lost," he whispered.

"Only if you see it as her losing something, instead of seeking something new and embracing it," said Jesus. "You should understand this, her seeking. You too were a seeker, yet you have become cloaked in darkness. I ask of you, where instead is your cloak of acceptance, your embracing of belief? Such is it with Prentiss."

Win was stunned. How did Jesus know this about him? For Jesus spoke the truth. Prentiss's emotion, her passion, which he had seen as a weakness, was what had allowed her to free herself, to transcend science. But Win couldn't rely on passion, for his had been lost.

"You too must make a decision," said Jesus, gently. "Will you free yourself from the past, so you may seek once again? That is one choice Prentiss has already made, and thus we cannot let her suffer for it."

"She is in danger?" asked Win.

"You still think of the scientific, of the body!" said Jesus. "She is in a different danger. For if she begins to think her new acceptance has come at the price of harming others, she will never forgive herself."

"I do not understand," said Win. "Who will she harm?"

"You will see," said Jesus. "And soon enough. It will be better for you to witness these things than to hear them. And now I must go, so that she will not have to make this fateful decision."

"How can I help her?" Win pleaded.

"It is me they want," said Jesus. "I must be the one."

"No!" shouted the disciples. "It is a trap!"

"There must be another way," said Win. "If you go to the Lemians they will take you into custody."

"And so they would," said Jesus.

"It will accomplish nothing," said Win. "Once they have you, they will have no reason to let Prentiss go. You cannot trust the Lemians."

"You must leave this to me," said Jesus. "I know where I am going. Do you?"

Win was at a loss. Jesus had summed up all his indecision, all that had happened in his life since the loss of Sooni, in those few words. *Where am I going?* He didn't know, and he had not known for a very long time. All these years he had just been marking time. For what?

Could it have been for this—for Jesus? Is that what Prentiss had learned?

As if once again reading his thoughts, Jesus said, "She is in a different place in her heart. You must first awaken, and then commit yourself to your search. If you have inner conflict, you will never find your own self, and will never be able to take the first step on *your* path. Do not be afraid. You can free yourself from the past without fear of hurting those you have lost. Their spirits will live on within you, even as you find a new way."

And then, so quietly that Win wondered if Jesus had spoken, he heard the words, *Let her go.*

The image of Sooni filled his mind, and though he had never remembered her ever being unhappy, he realized that if she could see him now, she would be sad, sad for what he had become, sad for how lost he was.

Win could picture it: freedom from his guilt, an end to his wandering, the abandonment of his wasted years. A return to his search for *ana*.

Jesus had shown it all so clearly, and all Win had to do was reach out and grasp it.

But he was overwhelmed by the enormity of what he would have to do. He didn't have Prentiss's desire, her inner energy. He didn't have Sooni to help him. It was too big a leap for him. Too much to do alone.

Jesus said, "You see a chasm before you, so you will have to build a bridge. From the other side I see you, and I too will build a bridge toward you. Yet though these bridges will grow ever close, they can never fully meet. Someday you will see that all it takes is to leap over the last step, and the belief you will reach the other side. This is the power of faith. Do not fear, I know you will make it. You have only to think of me. Do not be distressed if today is not the day. You have come far, and soon, very soon, you too will find your path. And even if I be not there in body I will always be with you, as will others who understand my message. You will not have to walk this path alone." Jesus looked at I'Char, who nodded.

Once again Win sensed something pass between them.

"Now it is time," said Jesus.

Win looked into Jesus' eyes, and Win felt the power behind them, beckoning.

Jesus touched Win's shoulder and turned to his disciples. "My mission has been to seek the lost, and show them the way. When the one who is most lost has seen the path, my message has been understood. This does not mean that no one else is lost, instead, it means the light of Truth now shines brightly enough so that all may see it. You must go on, each of you, and spread the light, so that there will be no place left in darkness."

Jesus turned back to Win. "Come, let us go together to save your friend."

Chapter 36

No deed is well done that is followed by regret.
    —The Teachings 20:9

Krelmar felt the building shake, immediately followed by the unmistakable rumble of a landing ship. A big one.

Tera-Seil! He was already here!

Krelmar hadn't even had time to meet with Methurgem to put his plan in motion. The League woman was still being held by the priests. Now he would have no way to gain asylum with the League.

Only one chance to save himself. He had to take control of the planet, *immediately.*

Any way he could.

* * *

Win and I'Char followed Jesus and the disciples out of the house. The street was filled with people, who cried out as Jesus appeared.

Without speaking, Jesus made his way into the crowd, which opened up for him, people gingerly reaching out to touch his robe.

"They look friendly enough," said Win. "Wonder how they knew to be here?"

"Yet another mystery," said I'Char, thinking of how much Jesus seemed to know about Win —and about I'Char as well. In that brief moment when Jesus had said *'I do know you,'* I'Char had felt the power of awareness behind the words.

As Win started toward the crowd, I'Char grabbed Win's arm. "Not a good idea," he cautioned.

Win turned to face him, his eyes full of intensity. "I don't trust the Lemians. We have to get Prentiss."

"They could get all of us—and the freighter," said I'Char.

"I realize that. You go find the freighter. I'll get Prentiss."

I'Char thought about arguing, but knew it would not do any good. "I'll get back as fast as I can."

"No. Take care of the freighter, then go to the shuttle. If you don't see us by morning, assume we won't be coming. If you've managed to destroy the freighter, get off the planet." Win clasped I'Char's arm, holding his eye. "Good luck. And thanks—for everything."

Win pushed his way into the crowd, following Jesus.

I'Char watched him go. It made more sense for Win to go and find the freighter. But I'Char knew Win had other reasons for going with Jesus. In all his time of working with Win, he had never seen Win so conflicted—yet at the same time, so alive, so absorbed. It was Jesus. Jesus had changed Win.

He'd go find the freighter, but he wouldn't leave Win behind.

* * *

The crowd followed Jesus through the streets, growing ever larger. It passed through the deserted marketplace, as if some silent message had been sent, and all who heard it had come to follow Jesus.

Jesus led them to the temple. At the wide steps he paused, and Win watched him as he cast his gaze over the huge crowd. Jesus' face was hard to read. He seemed gladdened by the crowd, but at the same time his face was stern, hiding an inner anger or burden.

When his eye reached Win, Jesus said, "Here I must leave you. Had we more time there is much you would have discovered on your own. What I tell you now you would have come to realize: The light of Truth you have now seen with your own eyes has always been with you. For how else could you have been shown that she was the one?"

Jesus spread his arms wide, and Win staggered, the sensations of the Great Meet engulfing him, the memory of the spark of light that had led him to Sooni vividly flashing into his mind. Win felt rather than saw it was the same light Win had experienced in the orchard, the same light he was seeing now, before him.

Jesus smiled, as if pleased by Win's understanding. Then Jesus walked up the first few steps and turned, addressing the hushed crowd. "Many times you have come to listen to me. I have always spoken to you from here, near the base of the temple steps, for I did not wish to stand between you and the temple, between you and the priests. Why did I do this? Because I did not come to tell you that all you have been taught is false, that you have done anything wrong in how you have lived your lives. Verily, much of what you have learned will help you find your way to Paradise.

"Yet I tell you today: a disease has crept into the temple, creating a darkness which will keep you from the Truth. This darkness has corrupted the true Way. Some of the Pertise have become so lost in the darkness that they have created Laws not for you, but for themselves, Laws which protect their own selfish desires. These Laws have been forced upon you, making you fear punishment if you disobey.

"But the true Way must be one of choice. You must choose to act, and you must believe in your choice with all your heart and soul. You must never be forced onto a path of rules. Such is an abomination of the truth of choice.

"This is the Truth I bring: the Way to Paradise is one of sacrifice, not selfishness; choice, but not fear. Though the road of sacrifice is hard, you need not rely on Laws for support. For those who might falter, you have only to look to the light I carry, the light I will always hold aloft for you to follow, whenever you think of me, even if I be not here. If you believe in that light, if you believe in my example, in my sacrifices, you will find the Way.

"And so I have always spoken to you from here, to show you that my message is like the base of these steps, leading to something much more. These steps lead to the temple, a holy place, and one that should be a place of refuge, of safety for all. But now a cancer is upon it; it has within it some who would no longer guide and support, but threaten.

"And so today is a new day, a day to shout our message from the temple itself, so all of you may clearly see the difference between my message and the one that has a shadow upon it. Together we will bring this shadow into the light so you will see it for what it is, and it can be dispelled!"

Jesus climbed the temple steps to the very top. The crowd waited in the plaza below, quiet, but full of expectation.

Below the huge lintel stone, Jesus called out, "You who call yourselves the translators of the law, come out! For your judgment is at hand!"

Nothing happened, and the crowd, far below, began to mutter. "What are they afraid of? Why won't the Pertise come out?" The muttering increased to a clamor, and then a din, calling for the Pertise.

Finally the temple doors opened, and a priest emerged, stately and dignified in his elegant robes. The crowd grew silent.

Win heard Tsaph whisper, "It is Methurgem, the high priest of the Pertise!"

Methurgem looked out over the crowd. "Why have you come here?" he demanded.

Jesus responded, "So that you may stand before the Light, and everyone may see the truth!"

Methurgem looked scornfully at Jesus. "And who are you to judge me, and judge our Ways?"

"Our Ways? You mean *your* ways! Many of your Laws no longer lead to anything but resentment and envy, and yet you enforce them with fear. You say the Pertise hold the key to Paradise, yet you have created Laws that lock the door, rather than open it! The people feel this in their hearts, else they would not be here."

"How dare you!" said Methurgem, angrily. "You have broken our Laws, and your misguided teachings have confused the people."

"Listen to yourself!" said Jesus. "My message has been for each to help each other, and yet you say those who would do so are misguided. Hypocrite! How can a message of sacrifice be misguided? You only want the people to sacrifice when it suits you, when it keeps you in finery, when it keeps you in power, atop the Order, a false hierarchy you have created!"

Methurgem raised his voice to the crowd. "Some of you may have been misled by this man. We have lived by our Laws for generations, through times of prosperity and times of suffering. The Laws have made our lives bearable in this difficult world. The Pertise have faithfully translated the Law for you, your families, and those who came before you. Suddenly we are told—by this single person—that we should abandon all we have lived by. What is this need now for change? Will you risk trying to find another path, and lose your way, and your chance at Paradise? You need not! For we know the true Way, and have always known it, and will forever know it! You do not need this temptation, this confusion. Go back to your homes, and leave this matter to us."

But the crowd did not move. Methurgem said to Jesus, "You think you are powerful, because you feel you have all these people following you like livestock, watching your every move, waiting on every word. But it takes more than a following to lead people, to guide them."

"They will be guided by the Truth," said Jesus. "And I have come to show it to them."

Methurgem laughed. "And only you know the Truth? I tell you, any belief they have in you is newly born, while the belief in us and the true Way has been nurtured for years, for generations. Your will cannot overcome this."

Jesus turned to the crowd. "Methurgem says you are misguided, that what you believe today will blow away tomorrow, that your beliefs are like the wind, shifting to and fro. He says you must live in fear, trapped in the Order, forced to act the way the priests tell you to act. I say instead, the Order is an abomination! The truth that will free you is this: all of you are equal on the path to Paradise! You must sacrifice, but should not pay Sacrifices!"

The crowd let out a roar, a deep resonant sound, as if releasing a pent up frustration, finally spoken aloud.

At the sound, dozens of guards streamed out of the temple, surrounding Methurgem, their hands on their swords. The crowd stilled, but then shouted anew, angry. Tsaph and the disciples ran up the temple steps to protect Jesus, and Win rushed to join them.

Methurgem warily eyed the crowd. In a low voice, he said to Jesus, "You think you have won something, but you have not. I pity you, you misguided fool. You have no idea of the threats we face, and right now, when we can least afford to be divided as a people, you risk creating anarchy."

"Hypocrite!" said Jesus. "It is not I who have corrupted the Ways to play a game of power with the offworlders. For I know you have detained a woman, and mean to use her as a pawn, to bargain with. What have you become, that you would use an innocent life as a tool for your own desires?"

Methurgem's eyes flared. "What I do, I do to protect our people!"

"Do you?" said Jesus. "See what you have done! The people distrust not only you, but now a shadow has been put on all the Pertise and priests, whether they deserve it or not."

Methurgem stared at him. The crowd began to chant Jesus' name.

Methurgem seemed to deflate, nothing but an old man in an ill-fitting costume. "What do you want?" asked the priest, wearily.

"Let the pilgrim woman go," said Jesus quietly. "Her part in this is ended."

"You don't understand," said Methurgem. To Win, he sounded more frustrated than angry, almost pleading. "The Lemians, they want to take over our planet. It will change our way of life. If we cannot keep the peace, they will use it as an excuse to take control." His voice turned harsh again. "And it is you who have brought them down upon us!"

"Then it is me you want, not the woman," said Jesus. "Let her go, and take me in her stead."

Win almost shouted, *No!* for now he understood Jesus' plan. Jesus wasn't going to accept the Lemian offer of protection. He was going to sacrifice himself, give himself up in exchange for Prentiss. Win tried to push through the disciples, but Tsaph blocked his way.

"They will recognize you as an offworlder," whispered Tsaph, pulling Win's hood tighter over his face. "It will only make things worse!"

"You're going to lose him," said Win, thinking of what had happened on Earth, long ago. He had been so selfish, thinking only of how Jesus' message had affected him. Jesus wasn't here just for him, but for all the people on the planet. "You don't understand!"

"I do," said Tsaph. "Finally, I do. Now I know what a true sacrifice is."

Jesus turned to the crowd. "Many of you have wondered, why do the Pertise not question me, and find a Law I have broken? It is because they too have become confused, for they have come to believe their own version of the truth. And many of you have wondered, why did I not challenge the Pertise? I say to you, this could not come to pass until all heard my voice, no matter how hard they tried to deny the truth of my words, no matter how much they had cloaked themselves in darkness and despair."

Jesus looked at Win. "Now I know my message has been heard not only by the believers and doubters, but by those who did not even think they could believe in anything."

Jesus raised his voice to the crowd. "Today is the day the message of Truth is shouted from on high! No longer will we hide the light, but cast it anew! From this day forth, you shall live in equality, not in fear!" A giant roar rose up from the crowd.

Jesus turned to Methurgem. "There are many kinds of power. Yours is insignificant compared to the power you see before you, the power of belief. Come, release the woman. Then you may judge me as you wish."

Methurgem gestured, and a guard came out of the temple, pushing a woman before him. Prentiss. She shook free and ran to Jesus, falling to her knees.

"I heard everything," she said. "You cannot do this! Not for me. I don't deserve it!"

Jesus gently lifted her up. "You deserve much more, but I do not do this just for you." He stepped aside, and she saw Win on the steps below. Jesus said: "He too does not feel worthy, and like you, feels responsible. I tell you, what happens here was meant to be, whether you be here or not. No deed is well done that is followed by regret. Now go, and doubt no more."

"Wait!" she said. "You must tell the people—who you really are. And why you are here."

"Who do you think I am?" Jesus asked her, his voice gentle.

"You are the Messiah," she said, her eyes filling with tears.

Jesus smiled, his face radiant. "It is for you to tell them this."

And they watched, helpless, as the guards surrounded Jesus, and led him into the darkness of the temple, the sound of the doors slamming shut like the closing of a tomb over their hearts.

Chapter 37

Never settle for what you are, but resolve for what you might become.
—The Teachings 21:15

As soon as the temple doors closed, the crowd grew restless, shouting. "Where are they taking Jesus?" Soon the steps were full of people, pounding on the entrance.

"Let Jesus go! Release him!" But no one answered their pleas.

The crowd grew louder, angrier. Win pushed his way to Prentiss. He had to shout over the noise. "Are you all right?"

"Yes! But we must do something. The priests will kill him!" She was frantic.

"Maybe not," said Win. "Look at the crowd. Jesus has too much support." But he was not sure he believed it himself. Every day that went by would make it harder for the Pertise to act. Now that they had captured Jesus, they were unlikely to let him go.

Tsaph grabbed Win's arm and pointed. "Look! Lemians!"

A host of armed soldiers had appeared, storming through the crowd.

"Let's get out of here!" yelled Tsaph. "This way!" When neither Win nor Prentiss moved, he yanked Win's arm. "Hurry! They will take you!"

Reluctantly Win followed, pulling Prentiss along. Tsaph led them and the disciples around the back of the temple. They raced down a smaller stairway to the street.

As they ran, they heard the sound of weapons fire, and screams.

* * *

When he heard the first weapons blast, Krelmar ducked into the alcove of a building. Stunned, he gingerly peered around the corner, toward the temple.

What had moments before been a relatively peaceful audience listening to Jesus and Methurgem had turned into a panicked melee. K'Turians ran from Lemian soldiers, who methodically moved through the throng, firing.

"No!" screamed Krelmar. He had ordered Neel to get the people under control. *But not like this!*

Tera-Seil would be furious.

Too busy running for their lives, the K'Turians were no longer paying attention to the group at the top of the temple steps.

But Krelmar was.

* * *

In the safe house, the mood was somber. The disciples spoke amongst themselves in quiet whispers, leaving Win and Prentiss alone in a corner.

"What happened to you?" asked Win.

"I was taken to the temple. The priests kept trying to get me to tell them why I was on K'Turia, and who I was with. They wanted to know where Jesus was hiding. They finally gave up. Then another man came. He said his name was Krelmar, and that he was from Colltaire. He accused me of being a League spy, and said they had captured another one of us." She stopped. "Was it Garrick?"

Win nodded. "Garrick is dead. I'll tell you about it later."

She shook her head in disbelief. "And I'Char?"

"He's looking for the freighter. Go on," Win urged.

"Krelmar seemed sure that we were spies, or at least that Garrick was. I guess I didn't do a very good job of keeping our secret, especially after he asked for asylum with the League."

"He what?"

"That was my reaction. But that is exactly what Krelmar claimed to want. He said he has valuable information about Colltaire, information the League will want, and he will trade it for asylum. Krelmar promised he would get the priests to release me into his custody, and then he would let me go, so I could pass on his message to the League." Her voice grew distant. "And he wanted me to convince Jesus to turn himself in."

"They let Garrick go too, but only so they could follow him," said Win. "The plan didn't work—Garrick turned out to be tougher than we had thought. We might all have been captured if it weren't for him. Krelmar was probably going to try the same thing with you—let you go hoping you would lead them to us."

"I don't know," said Prentiss. "Krelmar said we could check out his story first." She grabbed Win's arm. "This means Jesus gave himself up for nothing! They were going to release me anyway!"

"We don't know that," said Win gently. "The priests might not have turned you over to the Lemians, and Krelmar knew his plan didn't work the last time."

But Prentiss was distraught. "It's my fault!"

"No, it's not," said Win. *It's not her fault, it's mine.* Jesus said that his work was done when the one who was most lost had heard his message. Who could have been more lost than Win?

But how had Jesus known Win would be on K'Turia? Was Win just an example of a lost soul, or had Jesus known all along that Win would come, and would be the one to determine Jesus' fate?

"We have to do something to stop this," said Prentiss, tears welling up in her eyes. "You know what is going to happen."

"I don't understand," said Win. "I thought this is what you wanted. Your theory—you were right. The messiah has come to these people, and has shown them how to be free of their religious bonds. This society will evolve."

"I don't care about that anymore," said Prentiss. "Don't you see? I was wrong. I kept thinking only about the culture, about technology, and that the messiah was just a catalyst, like in a chemical reaction. I had it *backwards*. It's not the culture that is important, but the people, and their beliefs. It's about the messiah, and what the messiah gets them to believe. It's about *Jesus*."

"What are you saying?" asked Win.

Prentiss tried to compose herself. "Listen. I kept looking for patterns, finding events that would fit the theory, knowing that in all the worlds it would appear somewhere, like some probability distribution. Enough worlds, enough societies, enough religions, and just by mere numbers the right combination would present itself. But it is the other way around. The people don't create the messiah, nor is it just random; he comes to the people at the right time. It happened on Earth, and I've seen it over and over, but I kept looking at it backwards, as if the right ingredients would inevitably create a messiah figure. But it is the messiah who is the reality, where it all begins. I was just too ingrained as a scientist to admit it."

"Or be willing to admit it to others," said Win. "Because no one would have believed you. You had to create a convoluted set of arguments to explain your theory in order to avoid including any kind of deity. You were having a difficult time getting anyone to listen to you. Any supernatural element would have doomed your ideas. No one would believe this has nothing to do with science."

Prentiss gave him an odd look. "You sound as if you believe me," she said.

Win wanted to say, "I do!" He thought again of Jesus, about making the leap to acceptance. He *wanted* to believe.

One more step and he could be on the path —*his* path, his search for *ana*, his purpose. Jesus had awoken him, and showed Win it was possible.

But though Win accepted the truth of its possibility, it was still just out of reach. Was it because he was a Treb? No, he was sure that wasn't it. It was because he had locked everything out of his life; with the death of Sooni, he had lost his ability to accept and fully believe in anyone, in anything, as he had in her and in what they had shared.

In a flash of clarity he realized Prentiss had tried to use science to find her way, to resolve her complex ideas about religion—and perhaps, without even realizing it, to prove the existence of God.

But Win had hidden behind science, because science required proof, not belief and faith.

"I'm—I'm not sure what I believe right now," said Win. "But I understand what you are saying. Jesus—Jesus affected me too. I'm not sure I can explain it."

"We can still do something!" pleaded Prentiss. "Find out if Krelmar's story is true. We'll tell him the price for asylum is that he has to get Jesus away from the priests."

"And then what?" asked Win. "What would you do? Take Jesus off the planet?"

"If that's what it takes to save him!"

Win shook his head. "You know Jesus wouldn't allow it. Don't you see? This is all part of his plan. This is *his* sacrifice."

"You sound like you've given up on him!"

Win held her eye. "No, that's not true. But would you try to force him to leave? If he is who you believe he is, then you know his work cannot be finished unless he is here."

An insistent knocking at the door startled them. The disciples looked at each other, alarmed.

Tthean rushed over to Win and Prentiss. "It's the right code, but no one else but those here should know it. Something is wrong! I can lead you out another way."

The knock came again. Tsaph cautiously lifted a curtain and peered out the window. It had grown dark. "It is just one." He pointed to Win. "Your friend, I think!"

"Let him in!" said Win. "Quickly!"

Tsaph opened the door then immediately slammed it shut behind I'Char, whose robe was ripped and dirty, spattered with blood.

"You're hurt," said Win.

"Nothing that won't heal. Good news and bad news. I found the freighter. It—" I'Char looked around at the disciples, all staring at him. "It's taken care of, although there was nothing aboard. It may have been emptied."

"Is that the bad news?" asked Win.

"No. There are mobs everywhere. The Lemians are all over the city, and they are taking prisoners. A large transport ship has landed at the camp, and I saw another one coming in just now. The Lemians are setting up a wide perimeter, with large armaments. They are getting ready for something, maybe a full assault. If we are going to get off this planet, it has to be *now*."

"What about Krelmar?" asked Prentiss. "We can still save Jesus!"

"Too late," said Win, and in that moment the full realization of it fell on him, a crushing blow. Now he knew what else Jesus had been telling him, what it meant when Jesus had said: *'If you have inner conflict, you will never find your own self, and you will never be able to take the first step on your path.'* Jesus was telling Win that no matter how long Win had been adrift, no matter how many years had gone by since he had truly believed in something, there was always hope, but he would have to make a decision, he would have to take some positive step, because life was finite. It was never too late to begin, but every day that went by meant the end might come before he had a chance to start anew.

Back on Treb, Win had believed the most important thing in life was achieving *ana*. With the death of Sooni, he realized how selfish he had been; surely her loss was more important than even *ana*. Once with the League, Win discovered that the galaxy thought nothing of his search for *ana*, nor was it affected by his loss and despair. There were more important things to worry about. The war. The end of entire civilizations.

Yet here on K'Turia, Win had learned that there was something more important than the war, more important than the ebb and flow of entire planets. For Jesus had opened his eyes to the truth that it was individuals who made up the universe. The search for inner purpose, for meaning, for harmony, was much more important than anything else. The trials of the galaxies had to be overcome one person at a time.

For Win, Jesus' message meant taking back his life, resuming his quest. It meant rejoicing in what he had learned from Sooni, not wallowing in her loss.

He pulled himself together, more sure of himself, the commander once again. Ready to take the first small step in his renewed life. "We don't have time to check out Krelmar's story, and we probably can't get to him anyway. It's time for us to go."

* * *

Krelmar had recognized the League woman on the temple steps. So the Pertise had let her go.

When the shooting died down, Krelmar had followed the woman and her companions. He was certain some of them must be the others from the League.

Krelmar was just in time to see them enter a small house on an obscure side street. He waited in the shadows of a doorway, the nearby streets now deserted.

As darkness settled, Krelmar noticed three of them leave: the woman, and two men. They made their way quickly out of the city, joining a host of others who appeared silently out of darkened buildings.

Krelmar followed from a distance, watching them as they broke off from the exodus of refuges to enter a small hut, well outside the city. He ducked behind a stone wall as he heard a Lemian scout craft speed down the road.

Moments later, the woman and the two men stole furtively out of the hut and turned the corner of the building, toward the back.

One last chance to initiate his escape plan.

Just as Krelmar was about to leave his hiding place, another Lemian ship appeared in the sky. *Tera-Seil*. He was sure of it.

His course of action was now clear, bolstering his confidence. He was Krelmar, Lord of Colltaire, and he had an offer he was sure the League would accept.

* * *

Crouched behind Symes's hut, they watched a large Lemian ship descend to a landing near the city.

"A command ship," said I'Char. "Somebody important. That explains all the extra security. We—" He was interrupted by the sound of a Lemian patrol craft screeching to a halt. I'Char motioned for Win and Prentiss to remain still, and he disappeared around the corner of the hut.

A voice shattered the stillness. "I'm telling you, I saw them come this way!"

"That's Krelmar!" whispered Prentiss.

Another voice, a Lemian. "You are ordered to come with us."

"Do you know who I am? I am Lord Krelmar, the Lemian appointed authority on this planet, and you will treat me accordingly."

"We have been instructed by order of High Councilor Tera-Seil to take you to him. Immediately."

"And I am telling you, there are League spies here, and if you don't go after them now they will escape!"

"Come with us. Now. Or we will take you by force."

"You fools! I will not!"

"Take him!"

A door slammed shut, drowning out Krelmar's curses. The Lemian craft sped off back toward the city.

I'Char reappeared from out of the darkness. "If he convinces them we are here and have a ship, it will be even harder for us to escape," he said.

"I have faith you'll get us out," said Win. He smiled in the darkness, for it suddenly occurred to him that he had always had faith in I'Char. Another lesson for him. "Everyone ready?"

Prentiss stood up. "I'm not going."

"What?"

"I'm not leaving with you. There's nothing for me," she pointed up, "up there—anywhere. I'm staying here."

"You can't," said I'Char. "If the priests don't capture you again, the Lemians will, eventually."

"Eventually," said Prentiss. "But in the meantime, I have . . . something I must do. Look, you were right, I know that now. I can't stop what is happening here. But I can do *something*. Something for Jesus. The story of what is happening on this planet, it has to be told. So someone needs to document it, to see that it is remembered—for future generations here, for people elsewhere. That is the only thing I was right about. Maybe it is why I am here after all, to record the message of Jesus of K'Turia, so that others may hear of it, and learn from it, without having to suffer as these people have suffered, and as Jesus will suffer. Don't you see? Maybe that was part of the plan all along."

Win did see, sensing again how much more Prentiss was capable of with her belief, feeling the enormity of how far she had gone, how far he still had to go. *This is what true faith could do.* Faith in someone else, and in yourself. A faith so strong that you would risk everything, and still not be afraid.

For the first time in his life, he understood what envy felt like.

Prentiss saw the understanding in his eyes and smiled. It was the only time Win had seen her look truly happy.

She turned and walked away, back toward the city.

I'Char started after her, but Win held his arm.

"Let her go," he said. "Let her go."

Epilogue

The Rhean neural net hummed, the tendrils reaching out, out, until the network spanned thousands of galaxies. Such connections brought great joy, and they luxuriated in the sensation.

Much knowledge was passed, each absorbing what all the rest knew, making them stronger, more sentient, and even more connected. All that was known by any one of them was now known to all.

Still, they maintained the process of what lesser beings would think of as conversation. It was a tribute to their past, to the ages before when they had been lesser beings.

The Rhean once called Prome sensed, "They are so unlike us. See how individually they can progress faster than their entire race, than all their races."

"Yes," projected Ceme. "So it has ever been with them. The advancement of these two is truly joyous. One is on the very doorway of Illumination, and the other—we will see. But I have faith in him. He has sensed what true Enlightenment can be. This knowledge will never leave him. And one walks beside him to help him on his path."

"Yet altogether, the League has failed the test. As a whole, they are not ready."

"Perhaps we expect too much of these beings," sensed Ceme. "They did not even recognize the nature of the test."

"Yes. They think it is about the weapons."

Ceme could feel Prome's disappointment, as could they all. "There will be others who will face this test. In this we are mere observers; we cannot determine who will be given the opportunity.

That is for another to decide. And no matter how long it takes, no matter how far away, we will search for and find all who take this test. Those who pass will have attained true Enlightenment, and even we will learn from them."

"So many have tried already," sensed Prome. "Such a simple thing, to save one single being, to recognize the Truth. Are we asking too much?"

"Perhaps," responded Ceme. "Or perhaps it is we who are being tested."

The network vibrated, as it absorbed the impact of what that implied.

Printed in the United States
152619LV00004B/1/P